THE WIND CAVE BOOK II
THE
AFTERMATH

MICHELA
MONTGOMERY

A POST HILL PRESS BOOK

ISBN (trade paperback): 978-1-61868-915-3
ISBN (eBook): 978-1-61868-916-0

THE AFTERMATH
The Wind Cave Book 2
© 2015 by Michela Montgomery
All Rights Reserved

Cover Design by Martin Kintanar
Author Photograph by Pasadena Photography

Post Hill Press
275 Madison Avenue, 14th Floor
New York, NY 10016
http://posthillpress.com

This book is dedicated to every woman who has been told that they have too much passion, too much energy, too much...something, to succeed. And to every woman who didn't listen and went on to achieve great things. And finally to our daughters, who will see our efforts and model our tenacity of spirit.

CHAPTER ONE

Deep within Iran, 46 miles East of Ãbãdãn, the entrance to the war room was planted deep within a cliff. Hidden from all aerial views, it was guarded by heat and motion sensors scattered throughout the hillsides three miles in each direction. There were no roads or trails that could be detected by satellite. The only way in was a GPS guided car that used the exact latitude and longitude of the location to make its way across the barren desert.

Twenty-six men gathered within the bowels of the underground fortress, nine of whom were wanted by the U.N. as terrorists and war criminals. No two nationalities were the same, though each was joined by a common thread: hatred. The tenor in the room was thick despite the recent victory in the United States three weeks past. As Abu Al-Fadl entered the room, a hush settled over his guests.

"Welcome." Many of the men near him inclined their heads and he nodded in response. "There is much to discuss, and the time to release our final plan is upon us. We have nine submarines now, all well equipped for their journey. We await more submarines to join our cause. The Americans will not find our fleet. Our allies from Russia have succeeded in obtaining the new fluid and metamaterial cloaks that will make us invisible to both sonar and radar."

Commander Urzhumov raised his glass to those surrounding him. "To the first of many victories using that technology."

"Once our fleet has moved into position, the battle will begin at the designated entrances," Al-Fadl continued. "We have been promised North Korea's support with General Zhen's army, and Abu Ahbadi has promised us forces from Syria."

There was no expression on Abu Ahbadi's face. He had come to hear a plan to destroy America. If he did not believe in the strength of the effort, he would withdraw his offer of support and leave.

General Zhen bowed slightly and handed the case to the man on his right. Ten million dollars bought forgiveness after Abu Al-Fadl's victory. Each of the men in the room either passed their cases or their wire codes to the soldiers filing into the room. They collected and removed each of the numbered cases from the room. Each would be quickly verified and cataloged. Deceit of either the amount or the code would be unwise.

"And now," Abu Al-Fadl smiled and raised his glass, "we drink. To death."

* * *

Light. Blinding light from all around and with it, oppressive, smothering air. The kind of air that hurts as you take it into your lungs.

"Just keep moving."

The sun burned as it beat down on my head and shoulders, my skin so tender from weeks underground that I could feel it turning me beet red with each step. Reflexively, my eyes squeezed shut, watering as they tried to acclimate themselves to the extreme sunlight.

Percy wasn't going to give us time to look around or unhook our harnesses from each other when we left the mouth of the cave. Like a chain gang, we walked single file behind him. Head down, Percy was following his compass and leading us south. I was able to make out the visitor's center. It looked as if it had been abandoned right along with us. The vegetation that had surrounded us when we'd arrived was gone. Only bare, scorched earth remained.

Hot wind rolled over us, and with it, dust. I coughed and shaded my eyes. There had been a road when we drove in. Surely it was still here. It was as if someone had taken their hand and wiped it across the landscape. Fine red soot covered everything. The sun became hotter with each step and I strained against my lead. Pressing onward behind Percy, I could feel the incline in my legs.

No one spoke. I could feel Ano's pain from fifteen feet behind me, and it tore at my heart. What good would it have done to tell her weeks ago? The knowledge had been difficult for *me* to bear. I could only imagine what it would have done to her. No, I had made the right decision in keeping it from her. We still didn't know how badly Los Angeles had been hit, or any other cities for that matter. She would understand why I'd done it. Ano would forgive me, in time.

"Matt," Jazz called out, "switch." He handed Matt the bag of water we'd brought with us from the streamlet and Matt gently took it from his hands.

I looked down, easier than looking ahead to where Percy urged us forward. My boots were covered in the chalky red dust that blew around us and caked around our noses and mouths. My eyes burned with the dust and overexposure to sunlight. My throat felt as though I was trying to breathe in a sandstorm, and my mouth was filled with grit.

After two miles, Percy allowed us to stop. We all rinsed our mouths and drank thirstily from the bag of water. Percy pulled the Geiger counter from his pack and held it up. I looked over his arm to see the screen, but couldn't read it. Even Percy had to shade it from the extreme brightness in order to read the levels.

"Well?" Jazz asked.

"We need to keep moving." Percy wiped away the sweat from his forehead, accomplishing nothing but making a red smear.

Matt resealed the bag and lifted it up into his arms, slightly lighter than a few moments ago. My ears strained for the sounds of a car, a truck, an animal; anything. The sound of the wind in my ears was all the answer I was given.

"Let's go. We can't stop." Percy slung his pack back onto his shoulders.

"Do we hook up?"

"No, for a while we can walk independently. Let's go."

All around me were rocks, hills and dust. The heat pressed down and slowed my gait, as if I were walking knee-deep through sand. I looked down at my arms and hands.

"It's okay," Matt said beside me. "No blisters. Besides, I've got the water bag. We're okay."

We kept walking, the pace making the muscles in my legs strain once again. All of us felt like targets in a shooting gallery. In the cave we were shielded, protected. Now, we were in the open, raw. Exposed to the elements and susceptible to whatever had changed our world.

"Four o'clock," Matt called out to the group.

Another two miles and we could see the edge of what *used to be* the road to the Wind Cave. We trudged along on our current course, and I heard the grating sound of an engine.

"Wait!" Percy said, and we all stopped.

"I hear something," Jazz said.

We stood silently, the hot wind blowing against us. With a billow of dust coming from behind it, a truck barreled down the dirt road that intersected our path about a quarter of a mile up ahead. Matt let out a whoop. Needing no encouragement, we ran.

Close to the truck I got a stitch in my side, but kept running until it hurt to breathe. We stopped fifty feet before the intersection. The truck slowed when the driver saw us, and Percy raised his arms over his head for him to stop. It was an old 1950's work truck, rusted along one entire side. Gray bondo covered the rear bedside panel, and it had patches of mint green paint along the hood and door. I exhaled with relief when the truck slowed and pulled alongside Percy.

The windows were both rolled down and the flatbed of the truck had boards along the top. The tires were worn and the dust that it had kicked up billowed around us as we stood together on the side of the road. Percy approached the driver, who appeared to be either Hispanic or American Indian. His hair was black and shoulder length. He leaned on his elbow and watched Percy approach the truck. His skin was dark brown and dry; almost the color of the earth around us. I realized how insane we must look; all of us filthy with tattered clothing. With his black eye and split lip, Percy looked like he'd caught the worse end of a bar fight.

"Hola. Um...me llamo Percy."

The driver tilted his hat back on his head. "I speak English. Whaddya want."

Percy sighed gratefully. "Is there any way we can...um, hitch a ride in the back of your truck to Hot Springs?"

He grunted and looked at all of us through the narrow slits of eyes. "Whaddya wanna go there for. Ain't nothin' there."

Percy swore under his breath. "Oh. Right. Um. Could you tell us where the nearest city is?"

"Nearest city. To what?" He looked at Percy carefully, and then at all of us. "Where ya tryin' to get?"

"Denver."

He nodded and sat silently for a moment. "You on the run?"

"No, sir."

He thought for a minute, looking all of us over, then swore under his breath. "Name's Charlie. We're burnin' up fuel just sitting here. Get in the back. I'll take ya as far as Fall River."

We rode in the back of Charlie's truck to Fall River, our legs and backs grateful for the rest. Next to me, Carlie closed her eyes and fell asleep on my shoulder despite the bouncing over the rolling hills. Ano and Jazz leaned against each other and closed their eyes against the dust that still came into the bed of the truck kicked up from the tires. Percy sat on my side, looking out behind us, his head leaned back against Charlie's rear window.

"Percy," I said, trying to be heard over the sound of Charlie's engine, "do you know where Fall River is? Are we traveling east, or—"

"We're traveling away from the Cave, Kate," he said tersely. "The further the better right now."

I nodded, my cheeks burning.

Across from me, Matt stared out between the boards above the bedside. His hair, longer than when we'd entered the cave, blew in the breeze. Sensing my gaze, he opened his eyes and his expression softened. He smiled at me, then turned back to stare out beyond the truck.

Less than an hour later, the truck slowed as we approached Fall River, an actual road underneath the tires. I nudged Carlie, who awoke with a start and looked around.

"Hey," I said, rubbing my shoulder where she'd been sleeping. "We're here, I think."

She yawned and looked around the town. Although as we passed the buildings with peeling paint and boarded up windows, I wondered if the place we were driving through could be considered an actual town. Charlie was taking us through what probably used to be the main drag, and was now nothing more than a lot of abandoned storefronts and empty homes. Cars sat on the side of the streets, forgotten. It was like driving onto the back lot of a Hollywood western movie; the kind where the entire town is abandoned, and a shootout happens in the stables at the end. Charlie pulled in front of a store with a whitewashed front that had a hand painted sign that read 'Peterson's Market'.

Jazz hopped over the back of the truck, then reached for Ano. I stepped down and moved aside for Carlie, Percy, and Matt. We all stood at the rear of the truck.

Charlie got out and stood staring at us. He pointed to the store. "Ya got Peterson's for some groceries, then there's still Mill House down the way if you want a hot meal."

"Do you have...could we find a phone?" I asked him. "We need to use a phone."

"All we got is local here, same as most places. 'Bout the furthest you'll be able to call is fifty miles." He shook his head in disbelief. "You come from somewhere that still has long distance?"

I exhaled hard. "No, we...we didn't. I was just wondering."

"I brought the charger for my cell," Carlie said. "Battery's dead right now, but I bet if we found somewhere with—"

Charlie looked incredulously at us. "What the hell're you talkin' about? Ain't no cell phone that'll work anymore. Not least out here. Once you're in Denver you'll get some access, but..." he took a step backwards. "Where the hell've you been? Don't you know what's goin' on?"

Percy ran a hand through his hair. He looked at Charlie and sighed. "We were down in the Wind Cave for the last month." Charlie's expression changed and he looked at all of us quietly. "We felt something like an earthquake about a month ago, and just came up to the surface today. We're from Stanford...and...we need to get to Denver."

"Stanford, huh?" There was something that flickered across his face, and then it was gone. I'm sure that, looking at Percy and the rest of us, it was near to impossible to imagine that any of us had ever *gone* to Stanford – let alone set foot on any college campus. Charlie narrowed his eyes again and leaned against the truck. "Bet ol' Pete Windmere was still there. Teaching... economics."

Percy's brows knit together. "Professor Windmere teaches geology."

A slow smile spread across Charlie's face and he nodded at the truck. "Get in. I'll take you back to my place. You can get a hot shower and a meal."

We stood next to his truck, gauging whether he meant what he'd said, and he laughed out loud. "I gotta go into Petersons and get some flour and meat. I'll be back in a minute. Stay here...*Stanford*."

"Name's Percy," Percy said and reached out to shake Charlie's hand. Percy pointed to us each in turn and introduced us.

"All right, well stay here. I gotta go into the store."

Matt stepped forward and dug through his pack for his wallet. "I can pay, and if they take ATM I can—"

"Nobody takes ATM, son. Nobody. You don't got cash, you don't got money. Stay here." Charlie disappeared into Peterson's, still chuckling.

We all looked at each other in shock. "You think it's safe to go with him?" Carlie asked Percy quietly.

Percy looked around at us. "We're together and he drove us here, and he didn't have to."

"How far are we from Wind Cave?"

"About thirty miles."

"I think we should go with him and find out as much as we can about what happened. Maybe he'll be able to take us further, or get us somewhere we can catch a ride."

"Do they still have buses?" Ano asked. "If they have Amtrak...or—"

"If they don't take ATM, though, how are we gonna ride? I think I have around ten dollars cash to my name."

We all looked at Matt, who was counting his cash.

"Okay," he said looking at us all. "I have a hundred and thirteen. We'll count up what everyone has tonight and if...*if* there's a bus, we can ask Charlie where it picks up at and get there. I don't know how much a bus ticket is, but it can't be much."

I pointed to the signs in the windows of Petersons. "Look at that, you guys." The sign read, '**We have fresh milk! $10/gal**'.

"Ten dollars *a gallon!*" Ano said loudly. "Are you kidding me?"

"It's a small town. They're probably lucky to get anything. And the farming industry might have changed because of...because of everything."

"Okay," Percy said in a low voice. "There's likely no internet if there's no long distance."

"If there's no cell, does that mean the satellites are...what, knocked out or something?"

Percy sighed. "Or disabled. I...don't know."

"Maybe Charlie will know," suggested Jazz.

"If there's no internet...then the banks likely shut down too. But if there *is* internet then..." he massaged his temples. "How can everything be gone in thirty days?"

"If the banks backed up each night then likely that data is stored and can be retrieved manually. Not by internet but other ways. It really depends on what the Federal Reserve and the President..." I stopped when I realized that we might not have a President anymore, either. "Well, what the *government* decided to do."

Charlie returned with a bag of groceries in each arm. "Well, whadd'ya waitin' for? Climb back in."

CHAPTER TWO

Charlie's house was about seven miles from town, down a dirt road, in the middle of several large crop fields. He stopped the truck and pulled the bag of groceries from the cab. "C'mon, Stanford. Inside."

His ranch style house was long and had once painted the same mint green as his truck. The trim was once white but was now a dingy gray and the front porch dipped down at the front and side, giving it a sad appearance. The fact that there was a hot shower inside added to the house's value considerably.

"I'm home, Mother!"

A thin, wiry woman in her early sixties came in, her brown hair in two thick braids on either side of her head, her skin tanned and leathery.

"'Bout time you came home! I was wonderin' if..." she stopped when she came into the kitchen and saw us all standing there, as if right off the pages of *National Geographic*. "Oh, my."

Charlie hung up his hat on the rack behind us. He pointed to Percy. "Stanford students. Lost their way." He paused when she didn't say anything and added, "Down in Wind Cave when the blast hit."

She nodded and patted Charlie on the shoulder. "I see."

Matt extended his hand to her. "Matt Skylar. It's a pleasure to meet you."

I smiled at the fact that he could conjure impeccable manners looking like, well, like he panhandled on the side of Palo Alto Boulevard.

"Carlie Mannis." Carlie smiled and shook the woman's hand.

"Percy Warner."

"Jazz Taylor." Jazz motioned to Ano. "And Anobelle Johnson."

I tried to smile, though I think it came out looking pained. "Kate Moore. Nice to meet you Mrs....uh..."

She smiled back at me. Her expression was kind, her voice soft. "Caroline Blackhawk. Everyone calls me Carrie."

"'Cept me."

She smiled and squeezed his arm. "Yes, except you. And shame on you bringing me home strays and not even calling me from town! I could've had biscuits ready!"

The mention of biscuits, or anything not freeze-dried, had my mouth watering.

"Business at Murphy's took too long."

"You get the seed?"

"He agreed to the trade."

She clapped her hands together and Charlie shook his head. "Doesn't take much to make you happy."

"No, it doesn't." She turned to us. "Well, now that that's settled, come in. Come in."

There was a banana on the table with an apple beside it and I looked at it hungrily. Beside me, I could tell that Carlie was thinking the same thing. "I saw it first," I whispered.

"Told 'em they could clean up a bit. Looks like the fellahs here could stand the use of my razor."

She laughed and nodded at the men, and then to Charlie. "Take the boys to Ralph and Mark's room to clean up. I'm sure we have something from the boys still in there that will fit them. I'll take these three in with me and get them cleaned up."

Carrie reached for me, but I pulled my hand away quickly.

"It's okay, honey," she said. "I was just gonna show you to the spare room. My mother-in-law lived there for a while. It's out back. More private than in here with the men." She extended her hand to me and this time I took it. Her hand was callused, cool to the touch. "C'mon. We can get you all cleaned up."

We followed her out back where a small, whitewashed cottage stood all alone next to a field. She pulled open the screen and stepped inside. It was hot, humid and smelled like old quilts and cedar.

She stepped inside and opened each of the four windows in a futile attempt to bring in fresh air. "Come on in. It's clean, and there's a bathroom in back."

Each of us peeked around the corner as she said it. I thought I would die of happiness. Carlie, Ano and I walked into the bathroom, all standing side by side in the doorway, holding hands - just staring. It was small, with a shower and a commode next to it.

"Did you ever see anything more beautiful in all your life?" Carlie whispered and Ano and I regarded it in reverent silence. Carlie, next to me, was nearly crying.

"Why girls," Carrie asked, "what's wrong?"

Carlie wiped her eyes with the back of her hand. "You have a shower," she said, nearly jumping up and down. "A *real* one."

"And...a toilet. That *flushes* and everything," Ano added.

Carrie reached into the small wooden cupboard next to the bed and pulled out a stack of brightly-colored mismatched towels down and set them on the bed. "One at a time in the shower, though. Don't all of you try and pile in there at once." She winked and reached to the small table in front of us. "Soap in here," she pointed to the drawer. "Wash cloths there." She clasped her hands and turned to go. "I'll go try and find you each somethin' to wear. Get your clothes together and we'll wash them when you're done."

We thanked her several times. We were all still thanking her when she left, the screen door slamming shut behind her. A communal victory yell was heard from that little cottage, loud enough to be heard back at Wind Cave.

Regardless of the heat, all three of us took as hot a shower as their poor water heater would allow. The last one to shower, I stood under the stream of water with my eyes closed, just letting it wash over me. It was the first shower I'd taken without two people pouring water over me in a month. For the second time in thirty days, I felt like crying.

The amount of dirt that washed down that shower drain was enough to clog it several times over. I washed my hair twice with the sweet smelling shampoo that Carrie had left us, shaved nearly every part of my body and scrubbed all my skin until it was bright red.

I emerged thirty minutes later, cleaner than I had been in a month. Carlie and Ano were both lying on the bed in t-shirts, fast asleep. Their hair, still wet, spread across the pillows like feathers. I smiled and slipped into the clothes that Carrie had left me on the chair. They were larger than I would normally wear, but clean, and I held the shirt up to my nose and smelled it. Cedar. I exhaled and my stomach growled. I had to get food. Looking at Carlie and Ano, I tiptoed out the door, careful not to let it slam on my way out. A pair of large sandals lay on the ground and I slipped my bare feet into them, grateful that my caving shoes were off my feet.

Carrie's kitchen smelled wonderful. And there, sitting at the table, were three of the handsomest, most clean shaven men on the planet.

"Wow," I said, trying not to gawk as I admired their clean-shaven faces. Matt's face tipped up to look at me, and he smiled.

"Thought we were gonna need a chainsaw for Matt's beard," Jazz said. I could actually see the dimples in Matt's cheeks. Normal. We all looked completely normal again. Across the table, Percy glowered.

"Water in the cottage hot enough for you?" Carrie asked from behind me. I turned to see her kneading a lump of dough at the counter.

"Yes. It was wonderful, thank you."

"And I was right! There was a pretty girl under all that dirt!" Carrie winked at me and pulled a can of lard from inside the cupboard.

I thanked her and turned to face the table of men I'd shared the last thirty days with. "You guys found the soap I see."

"Don't think I've ever enjoyed a shower so much in my life!" Jazz admitted.

Matt stood and pulled out a chair next to him. "C'mon, Blue Eyes. Sit with us."

I pursed my lips at his pathetic attempt at yet another pet name but let it pass.

"That's right," Carrie said, "C'mon in and sit down. Got biscuits that just came out of the oven and fried chicken comin'."

"Can I help with anything?" I asked out of politeness, my stomach growling so loudly I was sure she would wonder if they had a dog.

She turned and smiled at me. I liked the way the crow's feet showed in the corners of her eyes and her braids bobbed when she moved her head. "Nope, now go on there and sit."

"Ano still in the shower?" Jazz asked.

"No, she and Carlie crashed out on the bed while I took mine. They'll be in here as soon as they smell the food."

Matt helped me sit and pushed in my chair. Percy's expression didn't change, but he didn't look at me, either. All three of them had empty plates in front of them, and half empty glasses of either milk or juice.

"Here," Matt said, sliding his glass over in front of me. "Drink. It's so good."

I accepted his glass, draining the remaining juice from the cup. I'd died and gone to heaven. I just sat there, the taste of the orange juice on my tongue. "Oh my gosh."

He grinned. "I know."

A plate appeared in front of me, filled with two buttermilk biscuits and three sausage links. I looked at Matt, Jazz and Percy. "Aren't you going to eat?"

"We already did," Jazz assured me. "While you all were taking your time? We got the first set of biscuits."

I eyed the plate for about three seconds before picking up the hot biscuit and taking a huge bite.

"Careful, it's still hot, you'll..." Carrie saw me fairly devour the biscuit in three bites. "I'll have more out of the oven in a few minutes."

The sausage links disappeared equally fast.

"Don't eat too much, too quickly," Percy warned me. "You'll be sick."

My smile faded and I swallowed the last bite of biscuit over the lump in my throat. "Okay, Percy."

"It's not like she hasn't eaten at all," Matt reminded him. "Just let her enjoy it, would you?"

"I'm trying to make sure she doesn't get—"

"Boys," Carrie admonished, and set a plate of fried chicken down in the middle of the table. "G'on now and help yourselves."

All three helped themselves to a piece of fried chicken and began to devour it in the same ravenous fashion that I was. Before my plate could get empty, Carrie walked over and set a piece of chicken on my plate and rubbed my back gently with the other hand. "Look like you could use fattening up."

I tried to catch Percy's gaze several times, but he never looked directly at me. Matt, however, touched me throughout our entire meal. His hand grazed my arm, his knee rested against mine under the table. It was odd to touch someone this much.

"Mrs. Blackhawk, this is delicious."

All three of us echoed Matt's sentiments, but Carrie hushed us. "No more of that *Mrs. Blackhawk*. Call me Carrie."

"Well, Carrie, thank you for the meal. And the hospitality." Matt was pouring on the charm and I rolled my eyes in mock disgust.

Percy looked up to Carrie. "Where's Charlie?"

"Out at the barn. He'll be in for supper in 'bout a half hour, I suspect."

"Jazz, Matt, you're on dish duty," he said. For a brief moment he looked at me. "If you're done eating, you could go tell Ano and Carlie there's food in here." As soon as he finished his sentence, he stood and walked over to Carrie.

I'm sure my face fell, despite my best effort to conceal it. "Percy, I thought we should check the—"

"Kate," he said, without turning, "go and do as I asked, please."

I stood up, plate in hand. I wasn't used to being ordered around, and certainly not by him. Both Matt and Jazz sat silently, watching for my reaction. I lifted my chin and, even though his back was to me, I gave an exaggerated salute.

"Yes, *sir.*"

Carrie took my plate while the three men moved in to do dishes. Her face was soft and she smiled at me kindly. "Here, honey. I've got that."

Percy didn't react to my irritation. "I'll be in the barn. I need to talk to Charlie."

CHAPTER THREE

Born and raised in Manhattan, Percy had never seen the inside of a barn. He wasn't a 'country boy' by any means. However, walking into Charlie's barn, he was fairly certain that this wasn't how a barn was supposed to look. Machinery was parked inches from each other, tractors, ploughs, shovels and hay bales were stacked up on top of each other along one entire wall. Three makeshift chicken coops were lined side by side against the far barn door.

Wearing the clothes of Charlie and Carrie's son, Percy thought he looked as out of place as everything else. He swung open the large barn door cautiously and stepped inside. "Charlie?"

From the loft above, Charlie called out, "Just a minute, Stanford. On my way down." He descended the ladder quickly, having much more agility than a man who looked every day of his sixty-five years. "Carrie sent you in to call me to supper, I s'pect."

"About thirty minutes, she said."

"Good 'nuff."

They stood in silence for a few minutes. Percy asked Charlie, his tone low, "Charlie, what happened?"

A darkness fell across Charlie's face. He walked over to one of the hay bales and leaned against it. "When'd you go down? Into Wind Cave, I mean."

"June twentieth."

Charlie nodded, but didn't say anything.

"It was *supposed* to be a four day expedition," Percy explained. "Before my PhD."

A slight smile caught the edge of Charlie's mouth. "D'you know that Pete Windmere grew up out here?" Charlie motioned towards the fields outside of the barn door. "His old man used to have a farm few miles from here. Back then," he said and sighed, "he went by the name Peter Wind Hawk. Family name."

"I didn't know that."

"Course, he moved out west, changed his name to something so people wouldn't know his heritage." He paused. "What a waste."

"Charlie," Percy insisted.

Charlie's sigh was heavy. "On June twenty-second, a nuclear bomb was detonated in the subway in New York, 'bout three miles from where they hit us on 9/11."

Percy closed his eyes.

"Thirty seconds later, a second nuke hit less than a quarter mile from the White House." His face lost all expression and turned gray as the sun had begun to fade from the sky. "By then it was all over the news. Air raid warnings, emergency signals went off." He shook his head in disgust. "Too goddamned late."

He turned to Percy and saw the pallor of his face change. "Two more went off a half-hour later. One in Kennedy Space Center, one in Houston." He pulled a long piece of hay from the bale underneath them. "West Coast got hit worse. Three nukes went off...oh, 'bout ten minutes later."

Percy's voice was barely audible. "Where?"

"LA, San Francisco, and Seattle. We knew, hearing all this on the news, we'd be next. Been telling the folks in Washington for years to get those nukes outta the Dakotas."

He'd been right. Percy closed his eyes and listened to what had actually happened. The story that, up until now, he'd only been able to speculate about. It was worse, hearing the truth of it confirmed, and he felt nauseated.

"By then, we were all scramblin'. Getting the livestock in, tryin' to get enough food into the cellar so we could survive if we were next." He looked at Percy. "Safest place, you know. Underground."

Percy nodded.

"Last bombs hit North Dakota at 4:35 on June twenty-second. Blew everything skyhigh." He took a breath and looked at Percy. "'Bout a hundred and fifty miles from where you were."

Percy's stomach lurched. He needed air. He stood up, but swayed. Charlie stood up next to him, held him by the arm, and led him out into the South Dakota twilight.

"C'mon, let's go for a walk."

He slid an arm around Percy's shoulder; no small feat considering Charlie wasn't an inch over 5'9, stocky and muscular. They walked down a path that had been well worn with machinery but was now overgrown. They got to the end of the trail and looked out over the horizon where the sun threatened to leave them in the dark. Percy took a shuddering breath, fell to his knees, and was sick.

Charlie knelt with him and said nothing, then helped him up and kept him from falling again as Percy stumbled backwards. "Take it easy, Stanford. Jus' take it easy."

Percy couldn't stand. He sank down to the ground, the reality of what had occurred in their absence too staggering to contemplate. His entire family. His brothers. His parents. Everyone he knew. He asked the only question on his mind. Oddly enough, it was the same question that everyone in America had asked for the last thirty days.

"Why?"

Charlie actually laughed. A bitter, harsh sounding laugh. "That's the question, right?"

The sun finally disappeared, leaving them in darkness. Crickets began to sound in the distance and Percy struggled to stand. Charlie reached down for him and helped him up, dusted him off.

"Do we know who..."

"Nope. Some say North Korea, some say it was the same bastards that hit us on 9/11 but nobody knows for sure." He paused and a sad smile touched his lips. "And the President's not talkin'." He chuckled at his own sick attempt at humor.

"Jesus Christ."

"Yup."

"And the rest of the county? Any other states hit?"

"By the time the last of the bombs went off, everything stopped. Planes were all going down, airwaves were jammed. It wasn't *just* the bombs. Satellites, cell towers, computer mainframes. It was like they knew just how to hit us so that we were blind mice. Damage everywhere. Hundreds of planes crashed that day. *Hundreds*. Looting, killing. It was like...it was like the entire country just..." Charlie shook his head, not finding the word he needed.

"Went insane."

"Yeah, I guess."

"And now?"

Charlie let out a breath in a whistle. "Well, Stanford, *now* isn't much better. Carrie and me, we stay here in Fall River because, well, it's safe enough. We've got one cow left, and some chickens. We know the folks that stayed, and we all help out each other. That, and I've got enough guns in my cellar to blow anyone who aims to do us harm to Kingdom Come."

Percy smiled and they were quiet for a minute. "You don't have a way of contacting anyone, though? What about satellites, or—"

Charlie laughed out loud. "You think we got a satellite receiver out here, Stanford?"

"No, sir."

"We've got a short wave radio and a long wave radio in what used to be the post office. It's enough that we pick up transmissions from time to time. Some make sense, some don't."

"What about the President? I mean, who's running the country?"

"Don't know."

They were both quiet for a moment, listening to the chirping of the crickets around them. "Don't know who the next in line was, don't know what they're doin' to help the country back on its feet."

"What about foreign aid? What about all the countries that we helped when they were—"

"Yeah, well, I guess they all got real short memories, cause we haven't seen or heard of anyone comin' to the U.S. wantin' to pay back for our good deeds. Like they say, I guess. No good deed goes unpunished."

"Is everything gone? Internet, phone reception?"

"We got short distance with phone lines, maybe about fifty miles. Some folks say they can call as far as Nebraska, but that's about it." Don't know if it's the planes goin' down that knocked out the lines, but..." his voice trailed off for a moment. "We've tried calling our boys in Ohio and the calls just won't go through. Nobody knows what was hit and what wasn't, though nothing seems to be workin'. It's like they've got us..."

"Isolated," Percy finished for him, and looked around them at the desolate fields.

"That's about it."

Percy swallowed, caught somewhere between rage and grief. He hung his head.

Charlie motioned towards the house. "They know?"

"No."

Charlie let out a breath in a whistle. "Well, shit."

"I...I have to tell them."

"You all made it this far, Stanford. Thirty days, you said? Down in Wind Cave?"

Percy nodded. "Yes, sir."

Charlie laid a weathered, calloused hand on Percy's back. "You'll make it the rest of the way."

Percy's head hurt. He needed more answers, but for now, he'd absorbed all the information he could take. They turned and headed back towards the house, Charlie's arm around Percy's shoulders, leading him back inside to tell the others.

CHAPTER FOUR

After Charlie shared the news of what had happened, none of us spoke. Ano had been crying for the better part of an hour when Jazz finally got her to take some aspirin and lie down with him in Charlie and Carrie's son's room. Carlie, fed but exhausted, gratefully accepted the couch and some blankets. She abandoned the rest of us in the kitchen for the comfort of sleep. The strain of it all finally claimed Percy who, after listening to Charlie tell everyone the news, fell asleep in Charlie's recliner, stretched out in the chair. He snored softly from across the room. Carrie emerged with a quilt and draped it over Percy's lanky body.

Matt sat in the kitchen, looking at his folded hands in front of him. Carrie touched his shoulder. "You should get some sleep. Cottage is all made up. You an' Kate can stay out there."

Carrie motioned for me to follow her into her bedroom. "I've got more blankets in the cupboard, but it's a warm night and you 'probly won't be needing them," she said and peeked back at Matt. "You stay with him. He needs someone to comfort him."

"Oh, I'm not very good at that. He'll be better on his own."

She waited, and an expression crossed her face that I didn't recognize. "He won't be. He's suffering. He needs someone to help him."

"I know he does, but..." I held my hands in front of me helplessly. I couldn't begin to explain to her how I lacked the skills to do any of the things Matt needed right now.

She laid a hand on my shoulder. "I know it's hard, honey. You've all lost everything."

"No, it's...it's watching my *friends* lose everything that's so hard," I admitted. The sight of Ano's face when she heard the news made me want to run down the hall into the room where she was. I should be the one with her, *not Jazz.*

"You...seem..." she paused. "It's all right to cry, you know."

"Oh. I don't have...I'm not like the others." I took a breath and then exhaled. "I'm...alone. On my own. It's just me."

Carrie tipped her head slightly to the side, her hand absently reached out and tucked a strand of my blonde hair behind my ear. Amazingly, I didn't flinch. "Your parents have passed?"

I nodded.

"And you got no family? No other..." she searched my face, hoping I could provide some shred of family tree and I shrugged.

"No, it's just me." I hurried to add, "Except Ano. She's like family."

Unlike everyone else who wore an expression of pity after I told them, Carrie's expression was unreadable. She patted my cheek and linked elbows with me as we walked back into the kitchen. "Just take care of him, then," she whispered into my hair. "He just lost everything. Let him grieve."

I knelt down by Matt's side and hesitantly touched his arm. I reached for his hand. "Come on," I urged. "Come on. I'm..." I stole a glance at Carrie and she nodded at me. "I'm going to take care of you. Let's go."

He allowed me to lead him out of the house towards the cottage. The air was still humid and warm and the crickets chirped all around us. The screen door creaked loudly when we entered, and I fumbled around for the lamp next to the bed.

The sound of his voice startled me. "Leave it. Please, turn it off."

I turned off the light and stood in darkness. He found his way to the bed and sat on the edge. Pulling the fluffy chintz pillows off, I scattered them on the chair and turned down the bed on both sides. Walking over to Matt, I knelt in front of him and pulled the boots his boots off. His face was immobile; stoic. Unlike in the cave where the oppressive darkness afforded us a modicum of privacy, there was enough light in the cottage – even in the evening darkness – to see the outline of his face.

"C'mon," I urged him, "you need sleep."

"Why?" he asked, his voice dead. "What the hell is sleep going to accomplish?"

I had listened to Ano enough to know there were four or five stages of grief. Although I couldn't remember most of them, I knew that anger was one of them. I also knew that arguing with him wouldn't do any good.

"Okay. We won't sleep," I conceded. "Would you just lie down?" He didn't say anything, which I took to be assent. He also didn't move from his perch on the edge of the bed.

I studied him for a few seconds. He seemed drained, like he was so overwhelmed that he was unable to single out one emotion at a time and so, instead, he shut down. Remembering what Carrie had said, I reached forward and began unbuttoning his shirt. I slipped it from him and hesitated before trying to get him out of his pants. They were really big on him, nearly falling off his hips, secured by a thick belt.

"Matt," I said, trying to keep my voice soft, "I need you to step out of your pants for me."

He stood and, with one swift movement, the pants were on the floor. Thankful that the process was going easier than I thought, I manipulated him, now clad only in his boxers, to the right side of the bed where he laid down. Exhausted myself, I pulled off my clothes and walked around to the left side of the bed and crawled under the covers to lie next to Matt. I turned onto my side to face him.

"There," I said. "Much better, right?"

He didn't respond. With my head against the soft down pillow, my eyes began to close. My limbs were heavy. Sleep was just seconds away. From next to me, I heard the muffled sounds of...

I opened my eyes. Matt's back was to me, but his whole body was shaking and his face was buried in the pillow. I exhaled, hoping his crying would stop. It didn't. His rounded shoulders shook and he pressed his face further into the pillow as he cried.

How many times, had I assumed that exact position when I was younger? Hundreds? It had felt like thousands.

I touched his shoulder lightly. He shook his head vehemently against my touch, but for once, I knew exactly what he needed. I reached out again and this time slid closer in bed towards him and wrapped my arm around his waist.

Instead of rejecting me, his arm was like a vise, pulling my arm around him tighter. His face came out of the pillow and I could feel his sobs. I lay against him and held him as tightly as my arms would allow.

"They can't be. It can't be." He whispered it over and over, until the words began to all sound the same.

Fighting off sleep so badly that I was nearly shaking my head in an effort to keep from drifting off, I reached my other hand up to Matt's back. Slowly, delicately, I began to trace circles on his back with the tip of my index finger. Around and around I went, until my arm ached and my eyes closed from sheer necessity. His sobs faded and I could feel him take shuddering breaths until even those came infrequently. Finally, he turned over to face me and I rubbed my thumb across his cheek, as if to clear the tears that he'd shed.

"I'm...I'm so sorry, Matt."

He pulled me against him tightly, wrapping both arms around me; both of us finally allowing blessed sleep to claim us.

For the first time in a month, I woke up and didn't feel pain. Through the thin curtains, I could see the faint early morning light. Matt's arms were still around me and I looked up into his face at the trace of stubble on his chin and cheeks. I marveled at how perfect his features were. His eyes fluttered open a few seconds later and he caught me staring at him.

I blushed. "G'morning."

Reality came back to him before he had the chance to greet me and a shadow passed over his face. He leaned his head down and rested it against my neck. I wrapped my arms around him, grateful that he hadn't started crying again.

He lifted his head and looked at me, his eyes red and tired looking. "Hey."

Everything that came to mind was trite, so I said nothing. I ran a hand through his hair and stroked his cheek with my index finger. I traced the lines of his chest and the angle of his neck. With each touch, his face relaxed a little more. When I stopped for a moment, he opened his eyes and stared into mine.

"Hey, Kate?"

"Yeah, Matt?"

His hand reached over and stroked my arm under the covers. He scooted closer until his legs were touching mine and I began to retreat.

"No, don't. Please?"

The pain returned to his eyes, so I stayed where I was. Scooting closer to him, I felt his body relax and I smoothed the hair back from his forehead. "There," I said, managing a slight smile. "Better?"

"Better," he agreed, and tilted his head towards mine. His fingers traced up my arm to my neck and then down again, his hand resting on the curve of my hip. His body edged closer to mine and he pressed a kiss to my temple.

I began to panic slightly, but it wasn't for the obvious reason that I was in a bed with a gorgeous, half-naked man. It had suddenly dawned on me what Matt was trying to mask his grief with, and that I was going to be faced with a choice in the next few minutes that I wasn't ready to make.

"Matt," I began, "we shouldn't…"

"Kate," he said, his voice low between us, "I *need* you." His voice had a desperate tone to it, but I knew he was pleading with me to respond with words I didn't possess. "I would do *anything* for you." He looked into my eyes. I saw the unasked question there, behind his pain.

He kissed my shoulder; waiting for me to pull away. When I didn't, he moved to my collarbone and then the base of my neck. Again he waited. When I retreated, his eyes pleaded with me not to. My mind was waging an internal battle that he couldn't hear. Pros and cons flew through my mind as his hands slid around to cup my behind and pull me against him.

The pain and emptiness that I'd seen last night had linked me to him in a way I never thought I would share with anyone. If he was now an orphan too, that made us similar. Percy had seemed so close to me those last few nights in the cave. Was that real though? Was his offer to go to Virginia an offer of convenience for him that offered me little in return, or was he really offering me a chance to be together? He was so distant now, and I was tired of being pushed away for reasons I didn't understand. I heard Ano's voice in my head, telling me that it was time to make a choice. I had played both sides of the field and it was time to choose a team.

His voice pulled me from my internal conversation. "You are everything to me, Kate. I will *never hurt you.*"

Painfully slowly, I tilted my head up towards his face and kissed his jawline, the small cut that was healing from where Percy had hit him, the edge of the black eye that threatened to turn green in an effort to heal. He tipped his face toward me to allow me better access and I slid my hands up along his chest, his skin warm and hard against my fingertips.

I paused at his lips, knowing that once I kissed him, there was no turning back.

"Kate," he said, his voice low, "please?"

My mouth found his and I pressed him back against the pillows, my hands on his shoulders. He lifted me as he rolled onto his back, his hands like solid iron, crushing me to him. His hands slid underneath my shirt and slipped it from me in seconds while his tongue explored my mouth and his teeth tugged at my lower lip.

I straddled him and he sat up, burying his face against my chest. One of his hands twisted in my hair, the other slid down to cup my behind. I tipped my face down to his and cradled his face in my hands. I knew this face; knew what it looked like in the morning, after a hard hike, and after weeks of living underground. I touched his bottom lip with my thumb before taking it into my mouth and sucking on it gently.

While I didn't know everything there was to know about Matt, I knew at that moment what he needed; to feel something besides the pain that was tearing him apart. And for once, I wasn't afraid of my ability to comfort someone. I had been where he was and I knew the pain that was ripping through him. I wanted to comfort Matt with all my heart.

He rolled on top of me and I accepted his weight. Instinctively, I wrapped my legs around him. His kisses were greedy; his hands everywhere. I pressed against him until we began to move together as if in sync. I couldn't tell where one kiss ended and another began.

Deftly, one hand slipped his boxers off and then moved to remove my thin cotton bikinis. And, for the first time, we were against each other – nothing between us, nothing stopping us. He lay against me, still on top of me, and we locked eyes. Both our chests were heaving, and he pulled himself closer so I could feel his breath on my cheek as he spoke.

"We don't have to...if...you don't want to."
"I know." I touched his cheek. "I...I want to."
"You sure?"
"Yes."
He kissed my face. "Then tell me. Please, Kate."
I shifted my hips, heat pulsing through me as I did so, mixed with a little fear of the unknown. I answered his kiss and whispered back, "I want *you*, Matt."
His entire body reacted to my words. He covered my mouth with his own and pressed against me. I knew from Ano that there would likely be some pain associated with my first time, so I closed my eyes and braced myself. Matt's voice made me open my eyes.
"Not yet, sweetheart."
His mouth left mine and trailed down the front of my body, lower and lower, kicking the covers from us until they fell completely off the bed in a heap. When his mouth touched me for the first time, I cried out a little with surprise and shock. It was nothing like that morning with Percy in the cave and yet the same feeling was building inside me, closer and closer with each moment. I opened my mouth but no sound came out. My hands clutched the pillow above my head as I felt his tongue and mouth moving against me, in time with the pulsing I thought only I could feel, a climax he was bringing with him every second he continued.
When the beat within me became frantic I pressed against him, my hand tangled in his hair. The explosions inside me came so intensely I cried out and arched my back. His hands held me to him until I felt the spasms inside me recede and I relaxed against the damp sheets, my breaths coming in ragged gasps. He slid up to me and I could feel him hard against my leg. Barely able to open my eyes, I shook my head in amazement. "That was... incredible." He leaned in and kissed me, and I could taste myself on his lips.
Matt rolled on top of me, and this time I didn't tense. He paused for a moment, and our eyes locked. In silent assent of what was coming, I nodded and felt him guide himself inside me, the contractions from moments before still pulsing. His breathing was labored and the muscles in his jaw hard. "Kate." He withdrew and then drove inside me, sharp pain replacing where pleasure had been just seconds ago.
I cried out and his mouth covered mine, rolling on top of me and waiting until the first pain subsided before withdrawing again. His kiss ended and I gasped. It still hurt, but not as badly. Cautiously, I moved my hips against his, the length of him inside me. He leaned his head against me, cursing under his breath, moving slowly in an effort to cause as little pain as possible. Heat began to fill me and I moved against him, harder this time.
His eyes were closed and his jaw clenched, and I kissed the line of his neck.

"Kiss me," I commanded him. Matt devoured my mouth and moved inside me with more force. His breathing became labored and we moved in time together. I arched my back and dug my fingers into his back.

"Say my name." He kissed me over and over, breathing hard against my neck.

Wrapping my legs around him, I felt his control slipping. His breathing was coming in short gasps and I called out his name.

Chapter Five

We showered together, sated with the feeling of tepid water and the blush of sex. His hands never left my body as he kissed me over and over, unintelligible endearments whispered into my hair. Being naked and against someone was like pulling away the curtains of yourself for all the world to see. I wasn't ready to do this yet. This was a level of intimacy that would take some getting used to.

"What's wrong?" he asked.

"Nothing, why?"

He sighed, his arms still around me. "Your nose is doing that scrunching thing that you do when you're deep in thought." He kissed my cheek and the nape of my neck. "What're you thinking about, sweetheart?"

I don't scrunch my nose up!

"Nothing, I'm just not used to this."

He smiled. "I know." His hand slid down my body and came to rest on my behind and I fought the urge to tense. He laughed out loud. "I felt that!"

I turned around so that my back was to him. "Sorry. Not used to anyone touching my body in a shower but me."

"Well, then, I'll have to get to know it better." He chuckled and cupped my breast. I pushed him away but he caught me by the waist and wrapped his arms around me securely. "We'll start with something more benign," he teased. His hand slid down my right arm to my elbow. "What's this?"

"I cut my arm on the top of the fence that used to surround my elementary school. I got over the top of it but my sweater got caught and I scraped my elbow on the way down."

"How old were you?"

I shrugged. "I dunno. Nine, I guess?"

"How many stitches was this?"

"None."

Pulling my arm up, he inspected it more closely. "None? This had to be pretty deep. It's a wicked scar."

"I guess so, but my dad was gone on a job that night. So by the time I got home, the bleeding had basically stopped. I poured some stuff on it, wrapped it with an Ace bandage and he noticed it a few days later. By then it was too late to stitch."

He was quiet for a moment, and let my arm fall to my side.

We dried and dressed quietly, the sun now glaring through the curtains in the cottage. I was anxious to get inside and see how Ano was, and reached for the door. Matt caught me by the hand and pulled me into his arms.

"I need you...so much," he said, holding me tightly to him.

His words took me by surprise. I didn't have a good response, so I kissed him back. I could still feel the pain in his embrace, and see it in his face.

"Kate, I want you to come with me. To Stanford." I wrapped my arms around his neck and sighed. He pulled away and looked at me. "You just gave me the most precious gift you had to give. That doesn't count for something?"

I smiled. "It does. It does count for something."

He hugged me tightly and kissed my neck. "I love you, Kate."

The words came out fast, and I was sure he didn't mean them. I was sure he'd said them to a hundred girls before me. I was equally sure that I didn't have the capacity to say them back. I'd never told a living soul I loved them; not even Ano. I'm not sure if I'd even told my own father I loved him before he died.

He pulled away and looked at me closely. "So, yes?" he searched my eyes. "You'll come back? To Stanford with me?"

At that moment, I wanted to give him the assurance he needed. I'd actually given myself to a man and not only did he want me but he had told me he loved me. I didn't feel about him the same way I felt about Percy, and that thought bothered me greatly. But I looked into his eyes, his arms tight around me and felt...safe.

"Give me some time," I said, and played with a button on his shirt collar. "I just...I'm not ready to make that decision."

His face darkened. "All right. A *little* time."

We walked into Carrie's kitchen, where it seemed everyone was already gathered for breakfast around the table.

"G'morning, you two." Carrie smiled at us as we entered and we greeted her in kind. "There's eggs coming and biscuits and sausage on the table."

"Carrie," I said, looking at the delicious food and shaking my head, "we'd really be okay with just cereal or fruit. You don't have to go through all this."

She came over and set a plate in front of me with two hot, fried eggs. "Nonsense. Been a while since I've had so many grateful mouths to feed and the chickens get cranky if their eggs go to waste. Now, eat."

I thanked her and looked over to Carlie, who'd worked her way through breakfast and was finishing a glass of juice.

"I forgot," she said, turning the glass, "how good orange juice tasted."

I stabbed a huge forkful of eggs in my mouth and reached for a biscuit. I looked at Jazz, who was finishing his breakfast, and saw the empty space next to him. "Where's Ano?" I asked.

"Shower."

Across from me Percy ate silently, looking only at his plate or Carrie.

"She doing better this morning?" I asked Jazz.

"She's not cryin' anymore, which is good. She just...you know, needs to get down there...see what's goin' on."

"Carrie," I asked, "if there's no long distance and no internet, how do people communicate?" And then a thought struck me. "Is the postal system still working?"

"Folks still mail letters for sure," Carrie said, turning around to face us, spatula in her hand. "But without planes and with a lotta roads still out, takes a lot longer to get through. Plus, a lot of people are..." she looked around the room. "...well, a lotta folks have moved on."

I turned to Jazz. "Maybe she'd feel better if she...you know, wrote a letter."

Jazz's face actually lit up, just slightly. "That's a good idea, Kate. I'll..." his face fell a little. "Maybe you could talk to her this morning. I think it'd sound better coming from you."

"Okay," I said, and hurried to finish my breakfast.

Next to me, Matt was eating his breakfast. I looked up at Carlie, who looked to Matt, then to me and raised an eyebrow. I scowled at her and gave my head a slight shake. She nodded and finished her juice.

"Carrie, I'm going to help you do dishes," Carlie said, "and then I'm going outside and I'll need some of those tools you promised me. Your side garden looks neglected."

Carrie wiped her hands on her apron and her whole face lit up. "Well, we haven't tended to it much since...well, that'd be real nice." She looked at me. "Kate, want to come with us?"

I laughed a little. "I've no idea how to make a garden grow. I'm more of a lab person."

Carrie walked over to squeeze my shoulder. "Well then, I'll teach you. C'mon outside after you've talked with Ano. Carlie and me, we'll be on the side of the house." Carrie's voice softened. "Charlie's out in the barn, messin' with the tools and such," she said to Percy. "He'd probly welcome a spare set of hands as well, if you're willing."

Percy nodded. "Of course."

"If he can handle both of us, I'll go to," Jazz said. "It's the least we can do after everything you've done for us."

Carrie smiled. "I'm sure he'd love the help. Been a while since we've had strong boys around to help us. All our help left on...well, they left 'bout a month ago." She left it at that and turned back around to the sink where Carlie was doing breakfast dishes. I popped the last part of a sausage link in my mouth and took my plate to Carlie, who accepted it with soapy hands. Down the hall was Carrie's sons' room and I approached it, listening for sounds of Ano in either the bathroom or bedroom. I leaned against the closed bedroom door, listening for a moment, and then, hearing nothing, entered.

Ano was lying on the bed on her side, hair still wrapped in a towel from her shower. I could see the creamy ebony of her bare shoulders above one of Carrie's quilts that was wrapped around her. She didn't roll over when I entered, but her voice sounded dead. "I told you, jus' leave me alone."

"That's gonna be kind of hard, seeing as how you're all the family I've got." I moved to the side of the bed and she rolled over, her face showing a mixture of relief and pleasure at my presence.

She reached for me and nearly threw herself into my arms. She rested her head in my lap and clutched at my arms; not crying, but so silent I knew her pain was deep.

"I'm so scared, Katie."

"I know."

She sniffled. "What if...they're both dead? What if I can't ever talk to my mom again? Or be with my family? Or..." She sniffed and I could tell she was at that point where something was necessary to break her out of the cycle she was in.

"Okay," I said and took a deep breath. "What if?"

She looked up at me, her eyes swollen as if she'd been in the same fight as Percy and Matt without the bruising. "Whaddyou mean?"

Ano was the only one who knew nearly everything about my past; the good, the bad...everything. It was finally my turn to pass on what little life experience I had to her.

"Okay," I said, keeping my voice soft. "Your mom and grandma are gone. Now what?" I used a line that Percy had used on me in the lab. "Go that next step."

She shook her head, her expression blank. "Then...I have no one." She sniffed again, her nose stuffy sounding, and I handed her a Kleenex from the nightstand. "I'm alone."

"No, you're not." I took her hand in mine and stroked it, her long fingers looking graceful against my own short ones. "Your cousin Christee from North Carolina?"

She made an exasperated sound. "The one who smoked pot at Thanksgiving last year?"

"That's the one. And your uncle in New Orleans, what's his name?"

Her response was quiet. "Robert."

"Right, Robert. His wife and their ten kids."

She snickered begrudgingly. "Four."

"Right," I said with a slight smile. "Four, whatever." I stroked her hand. "That's your *mom's brother*," I said, and waited for that to sink in before going on. "You've lost your mom. And that's a huge thing. But you're not alone. You've got family."

She nodded silently, and I could tell she was processing what I'd said, coming out of her grief slightly. "And you've got me. And Jazz. Although we're not blood rel—"

"Don't you ever say that to me again Katie Moore," Ano cut in.

I pressed my lips together. "I was talking to Carrie and she said sometimes the mail is slow, but it gets through."

Ano didn't say anything, just played with the edge of the quilt.

"Maybe you could write Grandma a letter. Telling her *everything*. And, even if it never makes it to her..." I let the silent meaning fall on her ears and she nodded, "...you've said your piece."

She looked down at her hands in her lap and the tears that I thought had all been spent began to fall again from her eyes.

"Tell her that you love her," I said, surprised to feel myself tear up as well. "Tell Grandma Vesper about Jazz. That you finally met your 'preacher man.'"

Ano snorted and half laughed through her tears. "She'd like that."

"Tell her that she was right."

"Ooooh!" she said, rolling her eyes. "She'd *really* like to hear that!" and we both laughed a little.

I leaned in and bumped her with my shoulder. "Tell her...that you'll be all right. That you're with someone who's going to take care of you. And that you'll wear flowers in your hair at your wedding."

The tears fell freely down Ano's cheeks and she clung to my arm. "Get it all out," I said. "Tell them I'll miss them both." I was quiet for a moment, knowing Ano would write the words to her mother and grandmother that I'd never had the courage to say out loud.

"I will."

"Tell her you'll be home soon. But right now, you're on this...amazing adventure."

I handed her another Kleenex and she blew her nose. "*What* amazing adventure?"

I smoothed the hair back over her shoulder. "The one you're on right now. The rest of your life. They live on...*in you*." It was something I'd once read in a story, or heard in a movie. Right now it didn't matter where I'd heard it; it was true. As the truth of the words struck her and she nodded, I knew I'd reached her on a level that needed to be reached for her to start healing.

"Okay," Ano said, and sat up in bed. "I'll write it."

"I'm gonna go outside and help Carlie and Carrie with the garden. If you want to come out and help us that's cool. "If you wanna get started on the letter," I said, "that's good too."

Ano nodded, knowing I was telling her to start moving forward. "Okay. I will."

I leaned in and kissed her cheek; completely uncharacteristic for me, but she closed her eyes and accepted the endearment. She swung her legs over the edge of the bed and reached for her t-shirt that Carrie had washed for us last night.

I turned to go but Ano's voice halted me at the door. "Katie?"

"Yeah?"

"Thank you."

I smiled at her. "S'okay."

And then, for the second time that day, someone said the words to me I'd heard so infrequently in my life. "Love you."

I nodded at her. "I know."

CHAPTER SIX

For the first time in ten days, all six of us gathered together for a meeting, sitting on hay bales in Charlie and Carrie's barn. Outside the barn door, the crickets sang. Percy spoke first.

"All right, I went into town with Charlie today and we got the information from John at Peterson's about a bus."

All faces turned to him to hear what he had discovered. "There's a bus that leaves from Fort Robinson that goes into Denver."

"How far is Fort Robinson?"

"About seventy miles from here."

"Do you think Charlie'd drive us?" I asked.

Percy nodded. "He said he would. The cost of the bus is going to be a problem though."

Matt looked directly at Percy. "How much is it?"

"Guy at the store said about seventy-five each."

"One way?"

"Yes," Percy said. "How much did we say we had?"

"With everyone's money we only had about three hundred. Maybe a little more."

Jazz sighed. "We're a little over a hundred short."

"Didn't Charlie say that there was a bank in Lusk that is taking certain credit cards?" I asked. "Or ATM cards again?"

Percy's voice was terse, and I wasn't used to him using that tone. "It's a *rumor*, Kate. And it's a three hour trip one way to Lusk. For something we don't know is true."

"All right," Carlie said. "Two of us will have to stay here until I get to my uncle's house. I'll borrow money from him, get a ticket back, and come pick up the two people and we'll all meet up in Denver."

"Would your uncle do that?" I asked.

"He's got no kids of his own, and he's my godfather. He'll do anything he can for me. Maybe the situation with banks is different in Colorado."

Nods from all around and then the silent question hanging in the air.

"Who's it gonna be? Who's staying and who's going?" Jazz spoke the words everyone was thinking.

"Carlie obviously has to go to Denver," I pointed out.

Percy snorted. *"Thank you, Kate."*

I narrowed my eyes, but he'd turned away.

"The only fair thing to do is draw straws."

"Straws?" Ano said. "For real?"

Percy looked around at the group. "If we can all agree to abide by it, then yes." Everyone nodded and Percy pulled five straws from a hay bale and put them behind his hand, so only he could see their lengths.

"Two shortest straws stay." He held out his hand to me first. "Draw."

Shit. I was bad at gambling, worse at cards. I reached up and pulled the very end straw of hay. It was about an inch long. *Crap.* I exhaled. *Great.* I held it up for the group to see. "I think this speaks for itself."

"Then I'll stay with her," Matt said from where he sat next to me and I smiled gratefully.

"We all agree to draw straws," Percy said, and held his hand out to Jazz.

"If the man wants to stay, I say it's settled," Jazz said. "We'll wait for them in Denver. It's only another couple of days, right?"

Knowing the group had made a decision, Percy tossed the straws of hay on the ground. "All right, Matt and Kate will stay. We all go to Denver and wait for them."

I turned to Matt and whispered, "Thanks." He nodded and winked at me.

Carlie hopped down off her hay bale. "Katie, c'mere. Walk with me a minute? I need to talk to you."

Ano and Jazz got up to go. "We're gonna turn in," she said, hugging me.

"Okay," I said and returned the hug. Jazz fist bumped me on his way out. "Way to go, shortie."

"Nice. Thanks for the support."

"I'll wait for you..." Matt pointed in the direction of the cottage and I nodded, following Carlie out into the night air.

I had to jog a few steps to catch up with her. "Hey! What's up?"

She kept walking and I fell into step beside her. We walked into the darkness, the crop field beside us, and she slowed, looking back to make sure no one was following.

"Kate," she said in a low voice, "I think maybe you were right. When you said Percy liked you."

"Oh, I think he knows I'm with Matt."

"Are you? With Matt, I mean."

"Yeah. I think so."

"I think Percy knows it too," she said. "I'm just not sure he's going to accept it."

"What'd you mean?"

"I was sitting a little behind Percy when he picked up the straws. Katie, they were all the same size."

"No, mine was short."

"Yes, I *know* that," she said as if stating the obvious. "I saw him dig a fingernail into the end of yours when you pulled it from his hand."

"To make it shorter."

"Yeah."

I waited for what she'd said to sink in. "Are you sure about that?"

"Yes, I'm sure."

"So, you think he was going to let everyone draw straws and then take the last straw, which he would break in half or something."

"I think he's jealous."

I snorted. "Then you don't know him. Percy doesn't get jealous. He isn't like most men. You should know that. And the way he's been to me since we left the cave? You're wrong."

We walked along in quiet camaraderie for a moment longer. "I know that Percy has a lot of feelings that he holds deep inside," Carlie said. "That he doesn't tell anyone about."

When I didn't respond, she said, "You're not speaking."

"I'm thinking."

"Okay, so you have to tell me what you're thinking, I can't read your mind."

I had told Carlie a few things in the cave and she'd proved that she could keep them to herself. I wondered if I could trust her with something as personal as my feelings for Percy.

"I...I'm wondering if he told you things. Opened up to you, I mean." I shook my head. "I sound like I'm five."

"No," she said and laughed a little, "you sound like someone who's having trouble realizing their crush is human."

I laughed out loud because of the ridiculousness of her statement really was funny. "I know Percy's human, believe me."

"I'm not sure about that."

"Why?"

She put her hand out and touched the edges of the crops that had died and needed to be ploughed under. "Because you treat him like he...he knows everything. Like he's more than just a guy."

"Percy *is* more than just a 'guy'."

She made an exasperated sound. "Kate, he's not."

"You don't know him like I do." Instinctively, I found the truth of that statement to be a comfort. "A normal guy wouldn't have been able to get us through the last thirty days. A guy would have caved under the pressure. A *guy* would have saved himself and let the rest of us die." She didn't say anything, so I went on. "Carlie, a 'guy' has room in his life for petty emotions and jealousy over some stupid girl."

"You think you're just 'some stupid girl'? To him, I mean?"

"No, I...that's not what I meant. You're confusing what I'm saying." We turned around and headed back towards the barn, the lights from the cottage showing us the way. "I meant that Percy has a plan in his life. He's not about to let, you know, petty emotions, get in the way of that."

She made a small sound that sounded like an 'mmmmhmmm', but stayed silent until we had almost made it back to the barn. "Are you privy to that plan? Percy's, I mean."

"I am."

She smiled, and even in the dark I could see it. "Does it include you?"

For a minute, I didn't say anything. Carlie was so perceptive, sometimes it was like I was transparent and everything was right there on my face for her to read. I wasn't comfortable with her ability to do that with me quite yet.

"What if I told you that it *could*? What would you say?"

"I'd say that *could* sounds an awful lot like you've already made up your mind."

I shrugged. "I guess I have. Maybe. I'm not sure."

She bumped me with her hip. "If you haven't, I'd say you have a really tough choice ahead of you."

"Thanks. Don't go becoming like, a guidance counselor or anything, would'ya? You'd starve."

Her crisp laughter echoed back at us from the hills. "I may starve anyway, but if I decide to ditch med school for counseling, I'll let you know."

"Thanks."

"I'd say you're really lucky either way."

"You saw it, right? How great he is?"

In a true moment of irony, she cocked her head to the side and asked, "Which one?"

I made an exasperated sound. "I didn't mean it like that!" Carlie laughed. "Both of them are great. Everyone is so hard on Percy. He has...passion. He just doesn't show it to most people."

"Including those closest to him."

"So, he didn't? You know, share any thoughts or..."

"No, Perce and I weren't really, you know...together long enough to have the 'feelings talk'. Bet that would have been a short discussion, though."

We both began to laugh at that.

Carlie sighed. "He's a good guy, I'm not saying he's not."

"You're the *only* one who's not."

"Ah, they're just being hard on him 'cause Percy has had to make hard decisions."

I was glad that she understood something about Percy. "He is an amazing leader. He's going to be a brilliant scientist."

"He will."

A few hundred feet from the barn I stopped and turned to her. "Do you ever wish..." I almost didn't ask, but needed to hear her answer, if nothing more than to clear the air once and for all on the subject. "That you and Percy...?"

"Would have worked out?"

I nodded and we started walking again.

"We're different temperaments, Kate."

"I know."

"I liked Percy. But I want someone who really gets me." Carlie shook her head and her long brown hair, which had a natural wave to it when it was clean, bobbed back and forth. "That person *isn't* Percy. But I'll know him when I see him."

I smiled at this, mainly because I loved Carlie's optimism. Secondarily because she was releasing me from any guilt I had over what had happened in the cave with Percy. And lastly, because I wanted to believe – as she did – that there was someone out there who would make her as happy as she deserved to be. We'd arrived at the barn.

"Whatever you choose, just do it for *you*, all right?"

My eyebrows knit together. "Of course."

"When we make decisions based on other people's happiness, we end up selling our own dreams to pay for them. Think about that."

"I will."

She turned toward the house. "Night, Katie. See you tomorrow."

"Night." I stood in the velvet darkness of the South Dakota air, thinking about what she'd said. I turned and walked around the barn towards the cottage.

"Nice night for a walk."

I almost cried out with fright at Percy, who stood leaning against the barn door.

"Jesus Christ!" I put my hand to my heart. "You almost gave me a heart attack!"

He laughed. "Sorry, Kate."

I waited for him to say something, but he didn't. We both stood silently for a moment, then I said, "You've been kind of short with me lately." I paused. "Why?"

"I'm not short with you. You said something self-evident in the meeting and I called you on it. That's not being short. It's making an observation."

"Justifiable rudeness."

"You see," he said calmly, "you bring emotion into it now. Whereas before, you would have understood that I wasn't being rude."

"Before." I looked at him quizzically. "Before what?"

"Why is your tone so defensive?"

"It isn't. I'm trying to ask you why you're acting differently towards me."

He crossed his arms over his chest. "Give me an example."

"Uh, okay, ignoring me yesterday in the garden when I asked you if you wanted some water?"

"I didn't hear you."

"Really?"

"Really."

I took a step towards him. "And today when I brought sandwiches out to the three of you in the field?" He regarded me in silence. "I must have held that stupid sandwich out to you for a full minute before you took it."

"Had my hands full."

"Your hands were empty at the time."

He took a step towards me. "How do you remember all this?"

"There are so many instances to choose from," I said, "it's not hard."

"Perhaps if I had a photographic memory, I'd be able to recall the exact reason it took me 1.2 minutes to accept a sandwich from your hand."

"No, if you had a photographic memory, you'd have remembered your Goddamned manners and taken the sandwich."

He closed the last two feet between us. "If I had manners," he repeated.

"Y...yes." The harshness of what I'd said to him hit me and I suddenly wished I hadn't been so blunt in my delivery. "I just...you don't even talk to me anymore."

He moved closer to me and his voice softened. "What would you like to discuss?"

"I don't know. Nothing's coming to mind right now."

"Well, we have forty-eight hours to discuss anything you'd like."

The thought of him leaving me behind while he went onto Denver made me break out in a cold sweat.

"What would you like to talk about?"

He closed the last gap between us. "We could discuss what happened between us before we left the cave," he said and I could feel the heat rising in my cheeks. "That would be a topic meritorious of our time, I think."

"Your mood swings are giving me whiplash."

"What does that mean?" he asked, a small smile touching the corner of his mouth.

"What do you think that means?"

"Yes, if I've been remiss in—"

"Remiss?" My tone was rising, and I wasn't going to back down. "I've tried to talk to you alone since the first day we left the cave!"

"To discuss what, exactly?"

His professor voice was on now, and it was fueling my irritation. Unfortunately, on the rare occasion I became angry, I didn't think before I spoke. This was no exception. "You're ignoring me, all the time! We're never alone! Before we left the cave you seemed almost..." I realized too late what I was about to say and pressed my lips together tightly.

"Well, we're alone now. Go on."

I felt unable to move. I lifted my chin up just slightly, and narrowed my eyes. "Forget it. I'm not in a position to talk about the...I'm..."

He chuckled and looked down into my eyes. "Kate." He reached out and touched my face tenderly. I closed my eyes and felt the warmth of his fingers touch my skin. "I want to tell you something. Before we go to Denver."

I didn't move. The shirt he wore, so different from anything he wore back home, was unbuttoned at the neck and I could see his collarbone and the base of his throat. And the scattering of hair across his...

"Kate, you're staring."

"No, I wasn't!" I took a step back and tripped, my arms flinging out to catch my fall. Percy reached forward and grabbed me, nearly falling himself. One arm wrapped around my waist, his face inches from mine. I pressed a hand against his chest and slid another behind his neck. "Thanks," I said, my mouth dry from either the shock of falling or the fact that I was so close to him.

"You're welcome." He didn't release me, and his arm tightened around my waist. Our faces were inches apart and I could feel his breath on my cheek, see the light stubble on his jaw, a spot below a sideburn where he'd missed shaving this morning. He chuckled again and whispered in my ear, "You're staring again."

I pushed gently against his firm grip. "I can't help it." I swallowed hard.

"You can't help staring at me?"

Mutely, I nodded and his face softened. "It's just when I'm around you, I can't..." I couldn't continue. My heart skipped a beat and I reached a finger up and touched the stubble along his jawline.

Percy closed his eyes as I traced the line of his face with my finger. "When you're around me," he repeated, waiting for me to finish.

Awakening from my trance, I shook my head. "Sorry, I...let me go."

His brows knit together in confusion. "Sorry, I can't hear you," he teased, tilting his face toward mine.

"She said 'let me go.'" Matt's voice was feet from us, and we both turned in the direction of it.

Percy set me gently on my feet and I looked at Matt for about a half second, debating whether to try and explain what we'd been doing or not.

"I got worried," Matt said, his voice soft, "when you didn't come back from your walk with Carlie."

"I bumped into Percy," I said, and watched the amusement on Percy's face as I talked. "We just got to talking and—"

"Saw it from there," Matt said. "Brought you some tea."

"Thank you."

He nodded his head in the direction of the cottage. "Why don't you go in and I'll be in in a minute."

I looked to Matt, then to Percy, whose expression was so bland it could almost be bored. "Why don't you come with me?"

"I will," he assured me. "I just need to have a word with Percy in private."

"The last *words* you had with him are still trying to heal," I reminded him. "It's no big deal. I tripped and Percy leaned down to help me up." I reached out for Matt's hand. "C'mon. Nobody needs to have a word with anyone tonight."

Still leaning up against the barn door, Percy smiled as Matt allowed me to pull him towards the cottage. "We'll have a word another day," Percy assured him. "I'll speak slowly and find ones with less than two syllables."

I glared at him and tugged Matt towards the door of the cottage. I didn't see the hand gesture Matt delivered, or the one Percy responded with before we disappeared into the cottage with the screen door slamming behind us.

CHAPTER SEVEN

"Two days," Carlie said, handing Matt the information to her uncle's house. "Three max."

Ano and Jazz shrugged into their packs, and suddenly I wasn't as brave as I had been back at the house. "So, why are you giving us the address and number if you're going to be back?"

She rested her hand on my shoulder. "Because," she assured me, "if something happens, I want you to have it. To know where we are."

I reached out for Ano, who clutched at me tightly. "See you soon," she said, and fear gripped my heart at the thought of being without our group, even if it was for a few days. Jazz gave me a reassuring smile.

"See you soon, Kate," he said.

All four of them hugged Charlie and thanked him for everything, then lifted their packs once again onto their shoulders. Percy handed his pack to Jazz. "I'll be a minute," he said. "Could you load this on for me?"

"Sure thing."

I hugged Carlie and Ano once again and Matt and Charlie did the same. They waved and headed towards the bus.

"I need to talk to you," Percy said in a low voice.

Matt walked over and stood by my side. Looking briefly at him and then back to me, Percy added, "Alone."

"Matt, give me a second," I said. "We'll be right back."

I followed Percy behind the wall of the depot. Out of his pocket, he pulled a sheet of paper with a name, address, and phone number written on it.

"What is this?" I asked.

"My uncle's information in Virginia."

My eyes snapped up to meet his. "No."

"Kate, I—"

I pushed the piece of paper towards him. "No! I'll see you in Denver!"

As always, he was calm. He was Percy. He closed my hand over the piece of paper. "I can't stay in Denver. There's nothing for me there. The others there are all waiting to see where they should go."

"That's right. As a group. As a—"

"We're *not* a family. We're just six people who got stuck in a bad situation for a month. That's all."

"I see."

He tipped my face up by my chin. "Except you and me."

You and me. I heard the words, but they barely registered.

"We started this whole journey *together*, Kate. In the pursuit of knowledge. Remember?" He took a deep breath. "Kate, they're waiting to see what they should do. I *know* where I have to go. I *know* what I have to do. If I've been...preoccupied the last few days, it hasn't been out of spite. I've been going over scenarios in my mind, trying to—"

"Why didn't you talk them through *with* me?" I asked him.

A smile tugged at the corner of his mouth. "Because you've been... *occupied* as well."

I allowed what he was saying to sink in. Percy wouldn't be in Denver when I got there. The thought of losing him, of not seeing him again was too much. I'd seen him nearly every day for three years. I couldn't *not* see him. "Wait! No! Please," I said, hating the begging tone my voice had taken on. "Don't go."

"It seems like you've made your choice," he said, without a trace of anger in it. "Waiting in Denver would do nothing but prolong the inevitable."

I wanted to tell him that I hadn't made up my mind. That I hadn't given Matt a decision. But Percy had seen my decision the other night at the barn. I *had* made my choice. Now I had the bitter reality to swallow.

"I feel like I'll never see you again."

"That's up to you." He waited for a moment, as if debating whether to say something to me. "When you decide you've had enough of...*playing house*," he said, "you'll remember who you *really* are." I could swear the look on his face was one of caring. "You'll come back to me then, and we'll be the team I've always known we could be."

From around the corner, the bus horn sounded twice and Percy turned quickly and walked to the waiting Greyhound at the curb. I stopped in front of the bus and watched him hop up into it, two steps at a time, without a backwards glance. The doors of the bus closed behind him. I stood in shock for a few seconds, then headed back to where Charlie and Matt stood waiting for me.

As I walked towards them, Percy grabbed me from behind and spun me around. "Couldn't do it," he said, out of breath. His eyes locked on mine. "I couldn't leave without saying goodbye."

I slid my arms around his neck and opened my mouth against his. One of his hands lifted my behind, and I wrapped my legs around his waist. He deepened the kiss and slid a hand into my hair. "Say goodbye to me, Kate," he whispered, his mouth hard against my own. "Say goodbye and tell me you'll see me in Virginia."

My hands wound through his hair tightly as he kissed me over and over. "Stay in Denver," I pleaded against his mouth. "Wait for me."

The bus driver honked again, urging Percy to get on the bus. Percy laughed and set me on the ground. "Say it!" he commanded, and kissed me hard one more time before pulling away and walking backwards towards the bus.

My chest hurt and my mouth burned from kissing him. He stepped up onto the first step and the doors closed, just as I called out, "Goodbye."

I stared out the window of Charlie's truck the entire way back, sitting in the middle between Charlie and Matt. I knew I should say something to Matt to try and take the sting out of what I'd done. However, putting my feelings into words was hard, and nothing really came to mind. We pulled up to Charlie's house an hour later.

"Could use some help with the tractor, getting' it outta the barn," Charlie said

Matt hopped down from the truck and waited for me to do the same. "All right."

He closed the door behind me, and I was walking up the path towards the front porch when I heard Carrie's voice behind me.

She was wearing old cut off jeans and one of Charlie's shirts tied at the waist and covered in dirt. Her work gloves on, she carried a basket of weeds and walked up to me, a smile on her face. "Kate, you all right?"

I nodded, shading my eyes from the hot mid-day sun.

"Everything go okay at the bus depot?"

I shrugged. Ano had surely seen my kiss with Percy, as had Carlie. I can only imagine what they were thinking at this minute. I needed to process what I was going to say to Matt, and go over the plan of what to do once we reached Denver. For about the thousandth time that hour, I wished that I was with Ano. Without realizing it, I had been silent for several minutes. Carrie stood in front of me, patiently waiting.

"Sorry, Carrie," I said, and held my arms out to her for the basket. "Want me to carry that?"

"No. You can come out to the garden and keep me company though. Charlie's got your young man in the barn getting the tractor running."

I followed her around the side of the house to the large fenced in garden. I shut the rickety gate behind me, walked down the main path through the unkempt portion until we got to the last five rows, which now appeared meticulously maintained and straight, and I could tell she'd planted seeds already on most of the rows.

"Wow," I said, careful not to disturb her hard work. I knew that Carlie had been out here helping a lot the last two days. She handed me a package of seeds. "It looks amazing!"

"It's gettin' there. Now, here. In the middle of each of those mounds you put your thumb here, like this." She depressed her thumb in the middle and made a hole. "Now, drop three of these big seeds in and fill in that hole with dirt, like this." She gently covered the hole she'd made. "Think you can do that?"

I nodded and something by the barn caught her eye. "You start on that. Charlie needs me out by the barn, I'll just be a stitch." She removed her straw work hat and placed it on my head. "Wear this, or you'll get a burn on that milky skin."

I looked up for a second and saw Charlie step away from the tractor to talk to her. Carrie glanced back at me and I turned my face down towards the ground but tried to watch them from the corner of my eye. When I looked up again, she was halfway back to me.

"All finished," I called and the smile reappeared on her face.

She grabbed the hoe and hand tiller and handed one to me. "All right, let's get started on the next row."

We worked side by side in the garden until three more entire rows were freshly tilled and seeded. I liked working with Carrie. The conversation was easy, she told me interesting stories about their farm, and kept me laughing with things she and Charlie had done to pass the time for two weeks while they were in their cellar after the blast. At four o'clock she stood, using the gatepost for support, and stretched her back.

"I've got lemons still good on that tree over there, Kate." She handed me the basket and nodded towards the house. "Go gather up about nine or so of them and we'll make fresh lemonade and you can take a couple of glasses out to Charlie and Matt."

I slipped my hands out of the work gloves she'd given me and walked to the lemon tree that grew near the kitchen window. We'd picked off a lot of the rotten vegetation, but the tree was enormous and a lot of the lemons were getting large. I picked off ten of the ripest and went inside the kitchen with my basket, heavy with fresh lemons. Carrie got down a large pitcher and the canister of sugar from the cupboard.

"How long have you and Matt been dating?" she asked, cracking the ice trays into the pitcher.

"A few…no. I mean, just a…I'm not sure, Carrie."

"Not a final exam," she teased. "Just a pop quiz."

I laughed easily at that, and cut open the first lemon to juice it. "I didn't know him at all really, until we went down into the cave."

"I see."

I reached for the other half of the lemon, turning my face so I wouldn't get juice in my eyes, "I got to know him while we were down there."

"So, not long."

"Not long," I confirmed.

She was quiet for a minute and cut open a new lemon as I finished juicing the last. "Men are so funny," she said.

"How long have you and Charlie been married?"

She grinned. "Thirty-one years next April."

"That's a long time."

"Yes, it is. Goes fast, lemme tell you." She paused for a minute. "Was nearly thirty when we got married."

"You were?"

She nodded. "That was old back then. I'm sure my mom thought I was never gonna get married." She shrugged. "But you meet the right one and... you just know."

I had nothing to say to that. This was one of those 'mom' conversations that clearly I'd missed out on, the kind where she tells you about her dress and the flowers and the daughter is supposed to roll her eyes and say how she's heard this all a hundred times before. But Carrie wasn't my mother, and I hadn't heard it before. Ever, in fact...from anyone.

"You and Matt, you have a lot in common?"

"No. Nothing, actually."

She kept cutting lemons and as the small bowl began filling with juice, I emptied it into the large pitcher.

"Carlie says you're in the science program?"

"Yeah. The Master's program. I mean, I was...before."

"Life has a funny way of changing your plans."

I smiled at that, and squeezed another lemon over the juicer. "Yeah, I suppose so. If you'd have told me a month ago I'd be with Matt Skylar, I'd have had you arrested for delusional behavior."

Carrie scooped small spoonfuls of sugar into the pitcher. "Why? You had someone else, then? A fellah before Matt?"

"Oh," I said. "No, um, not...really. Nothing like this." I thought about how I'd felt about Percy before we'd gone down into the cave and how things had changed.

She spooned sugar over the lemon juice and said nothing for a few seconds then, "Nothing like what?"

"Like, well, I had *someone*. Someone that I was in...that I cared for. He didn't know I cared for him though."

"Mmmmhmmm."

I watched her spoon small teaspoons of sugar into the pitcher until I wondered if Charlie would go into diabetic shock after drinking the lemonade.

"After we went down into the cave, I was going to tell him. Then the blast happened and everything got so crazy. I found out that he'd come down with Carlie," the story came pouring out of me, without meaning for it to, "and that he really liked her. After a few weeks they found out they weren't, you know, suited for each other. If you know what I mean."

"I think I can guess."

"Then I had this panic attack," I said, touching the base of my neck. "Have you ever had one?"

"Can't say as I have."

"Well, Percy told me what it was, I didn't know, exactly."

"Uh-huh."

"When we were in the cave he realized that we were..." My face turned red as I realized I'd chattered on about things that I hadn't shared with anyone except Ano. "Never mind."

Carrie pulled more ice cube trays from her freezer and cracked them on the counter. "Now, were we talking about Matt or Percy?" I didn't answer, and Carrie began to stir the lemonade with a long spoon. She didn't look at me for a minute then turned and tucked a strand of hair behind my ear. "It's not a crime to like two different boys, 'specially at your age."

I looked away, embarrassed.

"What are you, nineteen? Twenty?"

"Twenty-two in September."

"Twenty-two. So young."

I reached in the cupboard for two glasses and set them on the counter. Carrie kept stirring, with no indication of stopping.

"Must be hard, liking two different fellas at once."

There was nothing for me to say. I'd clearly already said more than I should have. I didn't even nod, just kept looking at the pitcher. I'm not sure what I expected. A lecture for possibly leading one boy on while the other still liked me...or something about how I should just 'know' which one was right and which one wasn't. Since I didn't believe in love at first sight, that talk would be a short one.

"What do you like about Percy?" She reached into the cupboard and pulled two more glasses out.

I closed my eyes and sighed. "He's everything I admire in a man." Carrie poured a small amount into the first glass and tasted it. Making a sour face, she reached over and began spooning sugar into the pitcher again.

"Well, what's that mean? What'd you admire?"

I could list Percy's attributes all day long, so it was no effort at all to describe him to her. "He's so smart. If he doesn't know the answer, he'll find it. I mean it's staggering, really."

She cracked another tray of ice into the pitcher. "Smart. That's a good one."

"And," I went on, "he's a leader. A survivor. You should have seen him in the cave. There's no one that could have gotten us through anything like that except him. He's brilliant."

"Brave, resourceful. All very good things."

Carrie was smiling and it was easy for me to go on. "He always has a plan. He pays attention to the smallest of details." I paused for a moment and a small smile touched my lips. It was insignificant to most people, but it had meant so much to me at the time. "In one of our labs last year, he noticed that I only wear my blue coat on test days. And the white for class."

Her head nodded and the spoon was hardly getting any sugar into the pitcher. "A good planner, pays attention to detail. Also very, very important." She began to stir once more. "What about Matt? Tell me, what you like about him."

"Matt is...he's not like what I thought in the beginning."

"What did you think of him in the beginning?"

"Spoiled, rich law student. Um, his family name's like being a movie star on campus."

She turned to me, her brow furrowed. "How so?"

"'Cause his family's contributed so much money to the school. They've got an entire wing in the library named after his grandfather."

"But what is it about *him* that you like?"

"About Matt?" I thought for a few seconds. Anything I would say would sound horribly sappy and ridiculous.

"Nothing comin' to mind?"

"No, it's not that." I sighed. "He's...kind." My voice came out small and I looked up at Carrie to see if she was laughing at my answer. She had poured another bit into the first glass and tasted it and again, made a face. The miniscule spooning of sugar began again. "He always asks me how I'm doing, which I kind of like."

Carrie nodded and I noticed miniscule amounts of sugar going into the pitcher on the spoon. "Asking about your feelings. That's a good thing to do."

And then, without thinking, I said something in a quiet voice, almost to myself. "I can't choose."

"Who says you have to, right now?"

"They do! Everyone!" I threw my arms up in frustration. "They're just... it's making me crazy!" Without meaning to, I sounded like I was in high school, complaining to my mom. "It's like if I choose one, I can't have the other! I like both of them for different reasons!"

I saw only kindness in Carrie's face. Her hazel eyes were soft and she had laugh lines around her mouth. She smoothed the hair from my eyes and I had the insane impulse to hug her.

"These boys. These...*men*," she said, "they're just asserting themselves." Her eyes narrowed in jest and she laughed gently. "Marking their territory, as it were."

"Well," I groused, "I don't want to be *marked*."

Her sweet laughter filled the kitchen. She smoothed my hair down with her hand. "I raised two boys. Believe me, there's no changing them."

"So, I don't choose?"

Carrie smiled gently at me. "Katie, if you're here, you've already chosen." I nodded sadly. "I know."

"If that choice doesn't make you happy, then it's up to you to take that other path. If it's still open to you."

Here was the advice I hadn't gotten. The advice I was dying to receive. The absence of a mother had left me sorely lacking in the 'what do I do?' talks from about junior high school until now. Only I'd never really needed that advice as badly as I needed it this minute.

"If I...make that other choice," I reasoned carefully, "then I lose Matt. Either way I turn I lose one of them."

"There is another choice, you know."

My head snapped up, and I was anxious to hear what she had to say. "What other choice?"

She shrugged. "Go your own way. What do you want to do? It's your life, Kate. Go where your heart takes you. You don't have to choose either of them. What do you want to do? Have you thought about that?"

Her words stopped me flat. I hadn't.

"I'm not saying you shouldn't follow one of them," she said. "I'm saying you don't have to. You're young, beautiful, smart. Any fellah'd be lucky to have you."

I blushed.

She leaned in and hugged me, patted my back, and then released me to pour the lemonade. "If one of them is the right one, they'll find you, wherever you are. Even if that choice takes you somewhere that option one and option two didn't."

CHAPTER EIGHT

We'd barely said more than four words to each other in the last three days. Both of us were too tired at night to do anything but fall into bed at the cottage. Matt was busy all day working the fields with Charlie and I was busy getting the farm back into shape with Carrie. I don't think I saw him for more than a few minutes at a time. But tonight after dinner, Carrie and Charlie turned in early, leaving us nothing to do but go to the cottage together.

"Want to take a walk?" Matt asked me as I hopped off the last step from the back porch.

"Sure."

We set off, walking next to each other. "I'm gonna miss this," he said, motioning to the fields around us. "Not seeing this come in."

"It'll be beautiful."

"Charlie says that farmers are getting mostly whatever price they ask for their crops now. With the big corporations gone from the business, it's going back to where actual people owned and worked the land."

"S'how it should be."

He was quiet for a minute and then pulled a piece of wheat from alongside us while we walked. "You wish you would have gone with him," Matt stated.

I knew this was coming, and had prepared a good answer. "No. I was sad to see him go. I didn't like how it felt to lose such a good friend." Silently, I congratulated myself for the seamless delivery.

"A *friend*."

"Yes."

"Kate, I have a lot of friends." He stopped walking and looked at me. "I don't kiss any of them like that."

I had no response, and we started walking again.

"Am I more than a *friend*?"

"Of course." I sensed a fatal flaw in my logic that this would be a simple talk and wondered if we could turn around and go back into the house with Carrie and Charlie.

He reached for my hand. His hand was warm and had calluses on it. I'd never held hands with Matt, which was odd considering we'd slept together.

"I love it here," he said simply, inhaling the sweet summer air around us. He looked up at the sky. "You never see this in the city. All the stars? Everything just feels so right here."

I looked at him. "You're not thinking of staying, are you?"

He laughed. "Would that be so unthinkable?"

"I doubt a wheat farmer is going to have a need out here for an environmental lawyer."

"Not as a lawyer! As a..." he realized I was joking just in time to swat my behind and I yelped lightly and giggled. "With prices increasing this way, a man could buy a piece of land and actually work it."

"Jazz would say, 'the way God intended.'"

"Yes, he would."

I remembered what Carrie had said to me about following my heart. "Is that what's in your heart?"

"I'll tell you what's in my heart. When I saw you kiss Percy," his jaw tightened, "anger was in my heart. I wanted to kill him."

"Him?" I said incredulously. "How about *me*? I'm the one who kissed him!"

"You won't ever let him get his due, will you?"

"Be mad at *me*. I did that. I..." I swallowed hard, "kissed him."

"Yeah. You did. Why?"

I had no good answer for him. I kissed Percy because I had to. Because I wanted to. Because to not have kissed him would have killed me. I couldn't speak. I just shook my head.

Matt swore under his breath. "Let me ask *you*, Kate. What's in *your* heart? Am I?"

I looked around and saw nothing but peace; in the gentle sway of what was left of the wheat in the field, the sound of crickets, and the smell of rain coming in the wind. I closed my eyes and tipped my head back, wanting to lock this memory away forever. Opening my eyes, I saw only Matt. And for no reason at all, I smiled. "Happiness. In my heart, right now, I'm happy."

He raised an eyebrow at me. "Really?"

"Yes."

He took me in his arms. His warmth radiated through me and I inhaled his smell. Matt's skin had an intoxicating scent. I thought about what Carrie had told me, about being happy. There was no rule that said I couldn't take moments of happiness as they came to me. Right now, as I stood here with him, Matt made me happy.

"Hey," I said.

He leaned his face down to mine. "Hmm?"

I sighed deeply. "I want you to take me...home. Back, I mean. To Stanford."

His eyes lit up. He smiled and pulled me into his arms, squeezing me too tightly. "You mean it?"

"Ugh....can't...breathe..." I said, until he set me back down and we laughed a little. "Yeah, I mean it."

I suddenly knew what women meant when they said they felt worshipped.

"You make me so happy," he said, and lifted me off my feet to spin me around.

I kissed his neck and wrapped my arms around him, holding him tightly next to me. He might not be mine when we got back to Stanford, and we might be 'playing house', but for now, I was going to pretend that it wasn't going to end. Right now, I would pretend that everything would be okay. When his lips found mine, I had very nearly convinced myself it would.

Carrie folded the piece of paper and unfolded it for the third time in ten minutes. Charlie finally took it from her hands and slid it back into the envelope. "Ya gonna wear it out before she leaves."

Carlie hadn't specified if it would take three days or four to come back to get us, so we'd gone yesterday to get her and came home empty handed. Today, we were fairly certain she'd come. Half of me feared she would, the other half feared the bus being empty once again.

It was worse for Carrie. Last night had been a quiet dinner even though she and I had cooked most of the day to make it special. Matt had gone into town with Charlie and spent the last of our thirteen dollars buying an inexpensive bottle of wine for the four of us. Carrie had loved the gesture and Charlie had broken out two cigars he had from his son. He and Matt had smoked them on the back porch while Carrie taught me how to knit.

I hadn't slept at all, despite Matt's reassurances that everything would be all right. I tossed and turned and finally gave up around three a.m. and went in to make coffee for Charlie when he woke up at four. Carrie made Matt and I a full breakfast and even though Charlie resisted, Matt helped him in the field until noon when he had to come in and get cleaned up for the trip to the depot. I'd packed our backpacks and helped Carrie in the garden, but she'd been quiet most of the morning. I didn't know if she was sad to see us go or ready to have her house back. Standing at the depot waiting for the three o'clock bus, I was pretty sure it was the former.

"Now, remember, it might take a letter a while to get through so don't fuss if it takes me a while to write back."

"I won't."

She smoothed her hand down the back of the shirt she'd given me this morning as a going away present. All of the clothes she had loaned me were much larger than the size I wore, so she'd gone into town and bought me a t-shirt in watermelon tie dye and jeans shorts in extra small. She fussed with the edge of the shirt and tucked my hair behind my ear until Charlie clucked at her to stop messing with me.

"As soon as you get to Denver, send me a letter telling me you got in all right."

Matt nodded. "We will."

Charlie put his arm around her waist and she handed me the small basket of food she'd prepared. "There's enough fried chicken and biscuits in there for the three of you," she said, looking at me and Matt, "and I wrapped up some of the apple pie you liked so well, Matt."

"Thank you, Carrie."

The bus approached and we all turned to watch it stop in front of us at the curb. Passengers began to emerge, but I didn't see Carlie's face until almost everyone had gotten off. Finally, I saw her mane of brown hair come down from the bus. I waved like a fool and ran to her as if it had been three weeks and not three days since we'd seen her last.

We embraced hard and then she hugged Matt, greeted both Charlie and Carrie then handed Matt two hundred dollar bills. "Hurry. Get the tickets now."

Matt and Charlie went to buy us tickets to Denver. The bus would only stay for twenty minutes, long enough to refuel and for passengers to load luggage.

"Carrie!" Carlie embraced her tightly. "I'm so glad to see you!"

Carrie asked her about the ride from Denver and Carlie filled her in with the three minute version that everything was fine. Her uncle was incredibly happy to see her and took everyone in. I saw something flicker over her face as she said it, and in that instant, I knew Percy had already gone. I would ask her about it later, when Matt wasn't around. Carlie left to find a restroom after the five hour bus ride from Denver and I turned to Carrie for what would be my last chance to say goodbye properly.

"I will miss you," I said, and meant it with all my heart. My voice cracked on the last word, and I worried that I might actually cry. Leaving Carrie was proving to be much more painful than I thought. "Thank you," I said, and swallowed the lump rising in my throat, "for everything. You…"

She waved the rest of my thank you off. Her lower lip quivered a little and she held me firmly by the shoulders. "You be a good girl, and take good care of yourself. Don't forget to eat. You do that when you're worried 'bout something."

"I won't forget."

"Say hello to Jazz and Ano for us. Tell them to write."

"I will."

Her eyes held the wisdom of a mother and she looked at me like she would a daughter. "And say hello to Percy...when you find him." Carrie knew he was gone, just as she knew that eventually, I would have to find him.

I didn't say anything, only nodded as tears burned behind my eyes. She pulled me into a hug, and held onto me, swaying back and forth. She patted my back as you would a child.

I squeezed my eyes shut. "I'll see you soon."

She nodded and we were quiet until the first call was made by the bus driver. Matt and Charlie returned seconds later, followed by Carlie.

"This is for you," Carlie said, handing Charlie a folded envelope.

"What's this?" he asked, turning it over in his hand.

Carlie closed his hand over it. "A thank you from my uncle for taking care of us for almost two weeks."

Knowing Carlie, I could guess that there was a great deal of cash in the envelope. "It was our pleasure," Charlie said.

Matt and Carlie hugged Carrie and thanked her for the food, and Matt shook Charlie's hand at least three times until Charlie had enough and simply hugged him hard and sniffed equally as hard after they'd embraced.

"Go on," he said, pointing to the bus. "It's gonna leave without you."

Matt picked up both of our backpacks and handed them to the bus driver. Sensing I needed a few seconds more to say goodbye to Carrie, Carlie followed Matt to the bus and we heard the driver give a second call.

"You take care of him, Missy," Charlie scolded, and I assured him that I would. He pulled me into a hug that only Charlie could give, and set me back down next to Carrie.

She was crying shamelessly now, tears streaming down her lovely tan cheeks. We both laughed a little as she pulled me in once again for a hug. Before she released me she said, "Come back and see us now and again."

I nodded and, when the final boarding call was given, I pulled away from her embrace and Charlie slid an arm around her shoulders. Sprinting for the bus, I turned as I reached the first step and waved. Carrie mouthed the words, 'be happy' to me one last time. I smiled in acknowledgement and boarded the bus bound for Denver.

CHAPTER NINE

We turned onto SR18 around seven o'clock at night. Carlie nudged me with her leg and I sat up in the bus seat, yawned, and looked around.

"Are we there yet?"

She shook her head, looking over to where Matt was sleeping soundly next to me. She leaned back in her seat and began to talk quietly, so as not to wake Matt. "Thought it would be easier to talk, you know, like this."

She had a cup of coffee in her hand that she'd gotten at the last stop, and sipped it. Her hair was clean and styled similarly to the first time I'd met her; naturally wavy, pinned back from her lovely face.

"He left the day after we got here."

I'd expected it, but the words still stung just slightly. "Did he say anything?"

"Nope."

We were both quiet for a few minutes, the only sound the humming of the bus tires on the road. I was pretty sure she wanted to say something else, so I stayed silent, waiting for her to continue.

"I know this seems weird," she said and looked out the window. "I just need to know if anything happened between you two that made him...when we were down in the cave and he started to back off me..." I opened my mouth to speak but she held up her hand to silence me. "Just give me a one word answer to this question," she said. "Did you *sleep* with Percy down in Wind Cave?"

"No."

She took a few breaths through her nose. "Okay, that makes it easy. I don't have to hate you now."

I tried not to laugh, but she chuckled and hit me on the shoulder.

She leaned her head back. "Something *did* happen, though, right?"

I didn't have to say anything. Like always, Carlie knew. What was she, part psychic or something? Still, she waited for my answer - the answer she already knew.

"Yeah, something happened."

"I knew it!" Looking at Matt she lowered her voice and whispered, "I knew it. It was that day I was doing pushups with Ano, right?"

I furiously whispered back, "How the hell do you know this stuff? Do they, like, teach this in med school?"

"You would be shark bait as a poker player," she said, and sipped her coffee. "He came back and looked weird, then you came back and looked something between elated and freaked. *Obviously*, something happened."

"Something happened."

She didn't ask and I didn't offer up details. I hadn't told anyone but Ano about the kiss and I didn't really think Carlie wanted to know.

"After that, things started to go really bad between us," she said.

"I'm...I'm sorry."

She shrugged. "At least I know you didn't sleep with him. I don't think I could have taken that. But you *did* sleep with him, right?"

I shook my head.

"What? You didn't!"

"Ssshhhhh!" I looked at Matt, who stirred, and then back at her. "A little louder, I don't think *the next bus* heard you!"

"All right," she conceded, "all right." Another sip of coffee. "So, not even at the farm?" I shook my head and she blew out a breath between her teeth. "Wow."

"I did. I mean, with Matt, that is. In the cottage." I really sucked at girl talk. I would be much better discussing the chemical composition of Trictochloride.

She leaned back in her chair. "I knew it."

"Shut up, you did not!"

She giggled and made a face at me. "Oh, please! That morning after Charlie told us? Oh my God! You looked like, you know, all lit up inside. No pun intended."

I sighed. "It was my first time."

She choked on her sip of coffee and began coughing. She leaned forward and I hit her back lightly until she held her hand up and cleared her throat about five times. We both turned to look at Matt, who seemingly could not be woken up. She turned her full attention to me. "You were a *virgin*?"

"Yeah."

"Well, no wonder! Sadly, I feel much better now."

"Wait, what does that mean?"

She shrugged. "Percy wouldn't have touched you if he knew you were a virgin." She turned to me quickly. "He *did* know, didn't he?"

I nodded. "Yeah, he knew." *Oh, boy did he know.* "But why wouldn't he have...?"

"Too much emotion tied to it." She held her hands up as if on a billboard, "Losing your virginity." She shrugged. "He'd never do it. It's not Percy."

I didn't say anything, but mentally reviewed everything that happened in the week we were together before we left Rebel River. Had Percy been avoiding having sex with me? Or had it been for the reason he gave me? It would take me a long time before I understood that Carlie lacked that part of the brain that prohibited her from saying something – no matter how badly it needed to be said – that might be potentially hurtful to another human being. I reasoned it was the small scientist in her.

"Better wake Sleeping Beauty there, we're close."

I nudged Matt's shoulder and he opened his eyes. "Hey." His dimples showed, even when he wasn't smiling.

"Hey," I said back. "Carlie says we're in city limits."

She was looking out the window as we entered into the Denver perimeter. I saw lights and began to sense normalcy. "Carlie, you said the transition has been hard. How hard?"

"We all had to go get identified yesterday. Took all freaking day."

"Identified?"

Carlie opened her bag and pulled out a hard plastic card about the size of a passport and handed it to me to look at. It had her picture on it, an image of a thumbprint, an ID number, and about three 'key codes' of various lengths. I handed it to Matt. "So it's like a driver's license?"

"No. It's like an 'everything'. Driver's license, bank ID, passport. You can't come or go without these things now."

"Where'd you go to get it done?"

"It's so weird. You actually go to the old DMV to get it done. It's also like a 'check in' for people so they know who's identified as 'missing' and who's accounted for."

"So you can look people up?"

She nodded, then closed her eyes in irritation. "It's a freaking disaster. They have these computers lining the walls and people have been standing for hours or days trying to get on the computers to look up their families. Ano was still waiting when I left this morning."

Ano would wait in line no matter what it took. And with Jazz with her, they would be able to see if her mother or grandmother had checked in. "So once you get...identified...what's the story? Do the banks work?"

"Um, sort of. Some of the banks do and some don't. When this happened, most banks shut down completely. Closed their doors, right? All accounts went on lockdown. Now when you get identified, if your bank was one that didn't shut down, your account gets opened again. They advise you if your money is at an available bank or not, and what you have to do to get it."

"So still no ATM cards."

"No. Guys, I'll warn you, there's a lot of poverty. It's a cash based system now. No credit cards because there are no credit card companies anymore to enforce the bills. Without availability to their jobs, most people, if they didn't have access to cash…"

"Are starving."

"It's not good."

"So what are people doing for money, panhandling?"

She laughed. "Uh, no. If you were lucky enough to have access to a truck, people are trucking in stuff from farms close enough to get produce and milk to the city quickly, before it spoils."

"What if you don't have a truck?"

She shrugged. "I don't know. My uncle says now there are these independent contractors, they're calling themselves 'locators'. They, like, go and try to find people for money."

"Oh my God."

She nodded. "Precisely. There's a lot of crime, too. A lot of looting was done when the attack happened, so anything of value is gone. It's not good."

"How did Denver fare?"

"Much better than a lot of places. The buildings are all still standing and everything. But a lot of the companies in Denver were based from major cities like L.A. and New York, so those employees have no jobs. Some companies are still functioning, and some aren't. It's complete chaos."

My head had begun to hurt. Still, I had to ask. "Stanford?"

The edges of her mouth turned down. "Part of it is still standing. I heard a lady behind me in line at DMV say that the bell tower still even chimes the hour."

"But as far as…"

"Kate, most of the Bay Area was destroyed. I guess the Golden Gate and Bay bridges are just…gone."

"Carlie, I'm so sorry."

She turned to stare out the window.

I heard Matt take a deep breath in and I reached for his hand.

"I'm…I'm sorry, Matt."

He pressed his lips together. "I know."

Carlie hesitated before continuing. "It's like information overload for the first day or so. You get used to it."

"So they have internet, cell phones?"

"Most internet is still coming up as 'unavailable' or it's like bad TV late at night and is just one single image over and over. Sometimes you can get something, but it's not reliable like before."

"And cells? Long distance?"

"Cell reception is horrible, and you can hear like fifty conversations at once. It's not worth it. Land lines are better. We get long distance in Denver, but it's only to certain places. You guys, lines are still down all over the country and there's no one to fix a lot of them, so we have to make do. Most of the lines for the Midwestern states function, but lines to the West and East coasts don't."

I thought about Percy's family. "New York?"

Carlie didn't say anything for a full minute. When she did speak, her voice was low and almost reverent. "What images I saw of it were horrific." She had tears in her eyes. "I had to look away."

I covered her hand with my own. What purgatory had we returned to, with people starving and dying in the streets, no money, no jobs and a country in ruin? For the first time, I was glad we had been down in the cave so I didn't have to watch our country being brought to its knees.

"What about the military?" Matt asked. "National Guard? Anything?"

Carlie looked tired. "Nothing. The president and vice president were killed in the initial attack, and what my uncle heard was that everybody from the Secretary of State to the Speaker of the House went into hiding. No one's heard from them since the bombing."

"So who the hell is running the country?"

"No one knows," Carlie answered. "It's like a ship without a captain."

"And the terrorists?" I asked.

"My uncle knows a few guys in the Army who said that intelligence is looking into it, but so far..." her voice trailed off.

"Jesus Christ," Matt said, and ran a hand over his face.

The bus engine slowed as we turned into a more well lit metropolitan area.

"When we get off the bus, hold onto me," Carlie instructed. "Keep your backpack pressed up against your chest, so no one can try and get in it."

"Where the hell does this bus let you off?" I asked.

"Somewhere we won't be staying long. Just keep moving. You don't have any money with you, do you?" We both shook our heads and she nodded. "Good. That makes it easier."

"What do you mean, easier?"

"They'll attack if they think you have cash."

I slid the Swiss Army knife from my bag and into my hand. I felt better holding it and I knew how to use a knife. Matt's hand squeezed my leg. "It's all right. I've got you."

I pursed my lips. "How about this? *I've* got *you.* Pretty boy from Palo Alto can get his ass kicked somewhere like this."

He snickered and turned to Carlie. "How are we getting to your uncle's place?"

"He's coming to pick us up, but we have to walk about two blocks so he can park somewhere that his car won't get mobbed. He should be there in about ten minutes to drive us back to the Hills."

"The Hills?"

"Cherry Hills. Southeast of Denver. Nice, upscale. You'll like it. You two will have your own bedroom."

I shot her a look and she amended her statement quickly. "I mean, you'll have to share a room like everyone else, if that's okay."

Matt poked me in the ribs. "Sounds like someone was gossiping while I was asleep."

Carlie winked at him. "She only told me the really good parts."

I shot her a look and she laughed as the bus slowed to a stop at the curb. "All right," she said to both of us. "This is our stop."

CHAPTER TEN

It was close to nine o'clock when Carlie's uncle pulled into his circular driveway in Cherry Hills. All I could do was gawk at the sheer size of the house, while her uncle Richard chatted on about business and the 'damned entrepreneurs' that seemed to think the attack on the U.S. was a chance to make money. Stepping from the car, it dawned on me why pulling up in front of this house didn't faze Matt at all. Of course not. He probably had lived in houses like this his entire life.

The entire front of it was made of stone. An enormous fountain stood in the middle, so large -that all six of us could have bathed in it back in the cave. It had two giant mahogany entry doors, with a giant black iron knocker in the middle.

I stood in front of it, staring, until Carlie came over to stand beside me. "What? You see something?"

"Uh, yeah, I see something. Your uncle's house is huge."

She smiled and took me by the arm. "C'mon."

Matt and Uncle Richard pulled our backpacks inside just as Ano came bounding down the stairs and flung herself at me. I had barely hugged her before she began turning around and around, talking so quickly I couldn't understand what she was saying.

"Ano," I said, "slow down. Where's Jazz?"

"Don't you hear what I'm telling you?" she nearly screamed. "My mom! My mom identified!"

"Ohmygod!" I shrieked with her, and hugged her back until my chest hurt. "Well? Where is she?"

"I have the address. I don't know whose it is, but..." her entire face beamed, "I don't care!"

I didn't want to ask about Grandma Vesper. I just couldn't. And so I hugged her again and rejoiced at the happy news that her mom had survived.

Jazz descended the stairs in bare feet, sipping a soda.

"Hey, girl." He hugged me when got to the bottom. His face was tired; as though he'd been through a war. He caught sight of Matt and pulled him into a hard embrace.

"Hey, man."

Jazz nodded towards the large great room straight ahead of us. "C'mon. We gotta talk."

When they left the room, I whispered to Ano, "Jazz's family?"

She closed her eyes and shook her head. "Jazz must've typed in his mom's name ten times."

"What about Matt's? How about the rest of his family? His mom? His brothers? What about them?"

"Jazz found John and Paul, but not Pete."

"And his mom?"

Ano's face had a slight smile. "We found his mom, June."

I repeated the name so I'd remember it when I met her. "June. June Skylar." I lowered my voice. "How about the rest of Jazz' family? His brothers?"

Ano looked in the direction the men had gone, keeping her voice low. "They lived in Brooklyn, and were like ten or fifteen miles from the first blast."

"*First* blast?"

Ano nodded. "All this information keeps coming in, like now they say there were three blasts in New York and not one. Same in the Bay area. It's crazy."

Now I know what Carlie meant about information overload. "Poor Jazz."

"Yeah. He's dealing with it really well. We wrote down the address that Matt's mom identified with so you and Matt could go there." She paused. "You *are* coming back with us to California, right?"

"Yeah. I'm coming."

"Hey," Carlie called as she walked back through the foyer where Ano and I were still standing. "C'mon up here and I'll show you your room."

I grabbed my backpack and headed up the stairs with her. The room she had Matt and me in was better than what you'd see at a five star hotel. A huge four poster bed sat in the middle of the room, which was richly decorated in browns, yellows and black. There was a flat screen TV along the wall and a bathroom that looked like it had been carved entirely out of marble. I carefully set my backpack down in the corner, not wanting to touch anything.

Carlie laughed and pushed me, and I fell sideways onto the bed and sank into the fluffy comforter. "C'mon, it's not that bad! You should have gotten here earlier and you'd have gotten the good bedrooms!"

"Um, actually, I was just thinking that you shouldn't have saved us the *best* bedroom. The others are *better* than this? No way."

Carlie had removed the grungy sweatshirt she'd picked us up in for a sheer tank top and shorts, and I wondered if she'd located her mom. "Hey," I said softly to her, "did you find your mom?"

Jazz's voice called up the stairs and Ano turned to both of us. "Be right back." She was gone quickly, and I sat down on the edge of the bed with Carlie.

"She ..." she took a deep breath. "She hasn't identified yet."

"Carlie, I'm sorry."

She pressed her lips together. "Thanks."

"Is Rich your mom's brother?"

"Yeah."

A thought occurred to me as I stared across the bed at her. "Did you look up anyone *besides* your mom?"

She looked down at her hands.

"Carlie?" Again, nothing. "Carlie, please. Did you look up his parents?"

Her eyebrow went up and she kept her voice low, in case Matt was coming up the stairs. "He stood in line the first time, after we got identified. He didn't come home that first night, just stayed in line and slept against the building."

I imagined Percy leaned against his backpack, waiting for the DMV to open again. "And?"

"The next morning we dropped Ano and Jazz off before taking me to the bus station, he was coming out of the DMV and..."

"Carlie, you have to tell me. Please."

"We took him. To the bus station, I mean. We waited there together until he caught his bus. Then I got on mine a half hour later."

I wanted to shake the answers out of her. "Where did his bus go?"

"Kate, one of his four brothers was identified in the computer."

"Only one?"

She nodded. Percy had been very clear in the cave. He was going to Virginia. But now, upon hearing that a brother was still alive, I wasn't so sure that he would follow through with that plan. "Do you know which brother?"

"He said his name, but I can't remember it." Her face was truly apologetic.

How can people hear things and then simply not remember? It made me crazy thinking about it, but I remained calm.

"All right," I said and scooted up on the bed and crossed my legs. "Percy has four brothers. They're all named after famous writers or poets."

She snickered. "You're kidding."

"I'm not, actually." I stared at her until she stopped giggling and forced herself to be serious.

"Sorry, Kate."

"No, it's fine. I'll figure it out." I took a deep breath. "His oldest brother is William."

"No, that wasn't it." And then she added, "Shakespeare, right?"

I ignored her comment, but she was correct. "Okay, second oldest was John."

"No, wasn't John, either." She paused. "Steinbeck?"

"No, Keats." Okay, it wasn't the oldest and it wasn't the second oldest. Then there was Percy, and then his younger brother. I tapped my head and went through memories. "Ernest!"

She thought for a moment. "Sounds familiar, but no, I don't think that was it. Sorry Kate, I suck at this."

"Yes, you do, but its fine."

"Wait. Percy. There's...a writer named Percy?"

"Poet." Her face was blank and I shook my head. "*Percy Shelley*?" Again the blank stare. "Just...don't hurt yourself. Concentrate."

"Did he write the—"

"Ssshhh." I closed my eyes and went back in time, trying to remember the conversation we'd had in lab about his brothers. We were typing our partner's blood that day. Percy's blood is AB positive. He told me his youngest brother hated needles. His youngest brother...

"Edgar."

"Edgar! That's it!" She pointed at me and snapped her fingers. "That's the one who was identified. How did you remember all...never mind."

I stood and paced, thinking out loud. "So, if Edgar is alive, and Percy's parents aren't, then Percy would have travelled to...did Edgar go to boarding school? I can't remember."

"How do you *know* all this stuff? I barely knew his last name."

"Thank God you show greater aptitude for medicine than men." I reached forward and grabbed her hands. "Carlie, tell me. Where did he go?"

Carlie set her mouth in a hard line. "I'm not going to tell you, Kate."

"Why the hell not?"

"Because you're with Matt now."

"So?"

"Kate, he's okay."

"How do you know that?"

Her face was sad as she watched my reaction. "You're still in love with him."

With one statement, she'd rendered me speechless. I couldn't respond without lying, and surely Carlie would know it was a lie. I couldn't look at her. She'd see it in a second just by looking in my eyes.

"Deny it," she said, almost as a challenge.

"I...I can't." Knowing she would see the truth anyway, I shed my armor for a moment to the only person I knew who could see what I saw in Percy. "I don't know how to...to be without him."

She opened her mouth to say something, then changed her mind and sighed instead.

"It's like, I know I'm with Matt. And I *care* about Matt." I looked over at her. "I really do."

"I believe you."

"But I think about spending the next...however long without," I whispered his name, "Percy?" I closed my eyes. "I can't do it. It'd be like asking you to stop doing medicine. You don't know how to be *you* without medicine."

Carlie was quiet for a moment. "I saw him kiss you at the depot," she said, and she looked down at her hands for a minute, her lips pressed together. "And I finally got how much you hurt those first few weeks in the Wind Cave. When you thought you'd lost him."

"Because it hurt you to see me kiss him."

"No. Because for once I saw him passionate about something besides science, and a little piece of me wished it would have been me that brought that out in him."

"Percy's never done that before. I don't think—"

"Kate, regardless of *why* he did it, he still did it with *you*. And not *me*."

"Listen, if you just tell me where he—"

"You guys need to come downstairs and get food if you're gonna eat," Ano said from the doorway, where she stood holding a soda in one hand. "What?"

"Nothing." Carlie slid from the bed and I tried to grab at her, to get her to stay. She paused at the door, while I was still scrambling to get off the bed. "Kate?"

I looked up as I half slid - half fell off the giant bed. "What?"

She swallowed hard, the look on her face pained. "New York."

CHAPTER ELEVEN

Seventy-two newly cloaked subs made up their combined fleet. Thousands of men were being prepped to board the subs, which would be loaded and armed to capacity. Before the subs could be launched, there were maps to review, attack plans to agree upon.

Their President and Vice President dead, the United States had hidden their next three leaders who could assume command of the country. The Jug-eum-ui Bundae had taken out the next in line and would not stop until all others shrank in fear from the thought of becoming the new leader of the United States. Their communications system unreliable, plants would be generating false hope that no further attacks would be made. The threats they had made to Canada and England seemed to be holding as the world watched the United States struggle to survive, and made no efforts to aid.

General Zhen reread the communication from North Korea. The Secretary of State had been found and executed in Pennsylvania. The Secretary of Treasury and the Secretary of Defense were being located, and would meet the same fate. Once the U.S. unconditionally surrendered, his troops would move in, executing a massive overthrow of one of the most powerful countries in the world.

Zhen knew that North Korea could not be trusted, and so his men had been instructed that, once on U.S. soil, there would be a coup. Russia's leader wisely found a remote hiding place in Siberia, though not remote enough that he was not being watched until the proper time. The leaders of the Middle East believed their locations were also safe, however, Zhen's men had taken great pains to have GPS world tracking devices planted on them before the last meeting concluded. Kim Jung-un, so arrogant in his belief that this battle was his to own and take honor from, paraded himself around Korea and continued to be visible to his country and the world. Zhen's eyes narrowed. This made him not only an easy target, but a welcome one.

The world would see North Korea as the aggressor, the instigator in this insurgency. There would be no one left to challenge China as it emerged the victor. Zhen closed his eyes. Years of sacrifice would soon yield the dividends of waiting. The time was close.

* * *

There was no bus that got anywhere near Warrensburg, the city that Edgar had listed when he'd identified. There was a bus that went to Albany, but that was the closest Percy was going to get. He had purchased a one way ticket to Albany, knowing he would have to navigate the remainder of the way by hitching a ride or on foot. He bought himself a sandwich and water at the only food vendor in the small station and then hid it inside of his pack so he could eat it in peace on the next bus. Eating food in plain sight was a good way to get found in an alley, especially given the caliber of people in the bus depots.

His head hurt from lack of food and water and he made a mental note to find somewhere at the next stop to get an aspirin. He ran handfuls of cool water over his face in the men's room and felt a twitch in his side where his stitched wound was. Taking a deep breath, he held a hand over it for a few moments. He thought it had long since healed, but occasionally it caused some pain and he wished he'd accepted Carlie's offer for Motrin before he'd left Denver.

Taking long strides and holding his pack in front of him with both hands, he all but sprinted to the Albany bus that sat waiting at the curb and found a seat towards the back. The sandwich was no less than two days old, but it was food and he knew that anything right now was better than nothing. It had been four days since he'd left Denver, and he wouldn't arrive in Albany until midnight tonight. A bad time to show up in the middle of freaking nowhere with nowhere to sleep but the streets.

He took out the piece of paper showing the address that Edgar had identified with. Where the hell was he staying? Why hadn't he gone to Philadelphia to be with their grandmother? He knew from the database at DMV that his grandmother was still alive, and certainly she would have cared for Edgar once there. Percy leaned his head back against the headrest and relaxed slightly as the door to the bus closed and the engine engaged. The seat next to him was mercifully empty and he wasted no time pulling the sandwich and water from his backpack. Half of it was gone in three bites and he mentally reminded himself to slow down or he'd be sick right after eating.

From across the aisle in the bus, a young girl around thirteen watched him eat. With a pang, he noticed she was only slightly younger than Edgar. A woman he assumed was her mother sat next to her, already asleep. The little girl's blonde hair was bluntly cut, and her right arm was completely covered in bandages that were badly in need of changing. After a moment, he realized she wasn't looking at *him*. She was completely and totally focused on the quarter of the sandwich he still held in his hand. Percy finished chewing the bite in his mouth and washed it down with half the water in the bottle. Sighing heavily, he turned to her and held out the fraction of sandwich he had left.

There was no hesitation. She snatched the sandwich from his hand and stuffed it into her mouth as fast as she could. He watched her until she'd finished and then accepted the half nod of thanks she gave him before leaning back against her mother. Outside his window, there were lights in the distance and he tried to focus on them. He knew that if he didn't sleep now he would be unable to find Edgar once he reached New York. He leaned his backpack against the window, angling his body as to cover most of it, and crossed his arms over his chest to try and sleep.

Only in sleep did he see her - and it wasn't *her* exactly, it was more like watching hundreds of snippets of movie trailers all spliced together. Her face in lab, so serious as she measured and poured from beaker to Bunsen. Her face the day he told her they'd been approved to go down to Wind Cave. The first time he'd seen her in something other than a lab coat. The night she'd kissed him for the first time. Her face as she changed his bandage in the cave - still so focused. Her face as he'd kissed her at the depot. The look on her face the last time they'd said goodbye. He had no idea when it had changed between them. One day, she was a lab partner, a friend to be sure, but really just someone as driven for answers in science as he was.

And then she'd kissed him.

He shifted in his seat, attempting to find a comfortable position, and felt his wound twinge. He grimaced and relaxed against the pack next to him. The minute Kate had kissed him, she had changed everything. He hadn't meant to kiss her back. Once their lips touched and she had wound her hands into his hair, he knew he had miscalculated her – in every way. He had nearly tripped on his way back into the cavern after kissing her, he'd been so stunned. Kate. Katie had kissed him and, to his utter amazement and shock, it was hot.

He hadn't been looking for a girlfriend when he'd met Carlie that night in lab. Hadn't been thinking about anything but completing his Masters and moving forward to his PhD. His relationships in the past hadn't ever been serious, and that had suited him fine. Women took entirely too much energy away from his goals, and he was single minded where those were concerned. Carlie was interesting and intelligent. They enjoyed each other's company. Her schedule at the hospital and his at the lab meant little or no time for those long drawn out talks women seemed to love so much about why his work took precedence over a relationship. It had been causal. Enjoyable. But three and a half weeks down in the cave with her was enough to know their temperaments weren't suited *at all*.

Kate was intelligent, driven, and single mindedly focused on her goal; one of the things that drew him to her in their first lab. She didn't possess any of the traits he so detested in most females; she wasn't giggly, flighty, and didn't wear inappropriate clothes to lab. When she'd asked to come to the advanced Chem lab, he'd thought nothing of it. As she continued to ask for more and more advanced work, he was pleased that she took such a keen interest in her chosen field. He should have seen what was happening; should have noticed the signs that she had begun to have feelings for him. But Kate, he mused, was much like him in that way. If she *did* have feelings for him, she wouldn't show it or allow it to interfere with her work. It was one of the realizations that caused him to conclude what a successful team they would make. They could both keep their personal lives separate.

Initially, the thought of Kate as a partner wouldn't have occurred to him. Not for a lack of physical attraction. To him, Kate had been young. Really young. To look at her, you wouldn't guess she was more than eighteen or nineteen, tops. He now knew she was turning twenty-two in a few months. September, actually. And was only a little more than two years younger than himself. From what he knew about her, she had barely any life experience outside of Stanford. He sighed. Had he known how she felt before they went down into the cave, he'd have never asked Carlie along. Then again, had he known, maybe a lot of things would have been different.

His jaw tightened as he thought of Kate with Matt. He'd been irritated when the Dean asked him to take Matt along as a 'personal favor'. He'd been even *less* pleased when Matt showed up with a friend – one more person for him to babysit on this expedition. And isn't that what he'd done? He'd managed to navigate the way through; find their way out. Survive for thirty days. And still, in the end, it seemed as if Matt had won. Or had he? Percy remembered seeing Kate in Fort Robinson at the bus depot as she'd turned to go, watched her take three steps away from the bus; her body language, everything screamed at him to come back. In a rare impetuous moment, he'd obeyed, and God...had she responded.

He was fairly sure she'd have a difficult time explaining her reaction to Matt, if she stayed long enough to do so. Matt was no good for Kate - he thought of her only as a possession. Good enough to show off, to marry and bear his children, but nothing beyond the superficial. For Matt, Kate would be a vehicle to complete the picture-perfect life; nothing more. Her intellect would be wasted, her curiosity worn down by endless cocktail parties and mommy-and-me classes for the next generation of perfect Skylar children.

He, on the other hand, knew that there was so much more to Kate than most people saw. Her intellect was just the beginning of her many qualities that really made her an ideal choice as a partner. He'd never considered marriage, especially not at this age. His parents had married young because it had been arranged. And, at the time of their death, they had been married over thirty years. With times as they were, marriage might be an option. His older brother John had agreed to an arranged marriage at twenty-five but had backed out before the invitations had even been engraved. His parents were horribly disappointed but in the end had understood when he chose, instead, to work on the stock market.

His eyes burned with the thought of his family. Only one of his four brothers remained. Why hadn't Edgar been with his parents when New York was hit? He was fifteen for Christ's sake...where could he have gone? On the map, Warrensburg was upstate, near Lake George. Had they sent him there for summer camp? It had been years since Percy had spent a full summer at home and had no idea when summer camps began or ended. He did know that school normally started in fall. September, if memory served. If this had happened in September instead of June, his two youngest brothers would have been away at boarding school. Safe. And he would have been at Stanford. And likely dead. What a difference a few months made.

A few months with Matt and Percy was sure Kate would come to her senses. A few months would go by and he would get a letter from her – then a stab of fear shot through him as he realized that the only address Kate had for him was in Virginia, with his uncle.

He hit his head on the frame of the backpack behind him, cursing his stupidity. He should have given Carlie a letter or something to give to Kate for him. In his haste to get to Edgar, he'd neglected that detail. He sighed. Once he found Edgar, he would send Kate a letter at...oh no. She wasn't going to stay at Carlie's uncle's house. By the time the letter reached her she'd be in California somewhere, with no way to find him. As sleep finally claimed him, a plan was forming in his mind – one that included a letter...and a promise.

Chapter Twelve

I kept my promise to Carrie and wrote her a short letter as soon as we got settled in Denver. A second letter went out at the end of that first exhausting week, after Matt and I had both been identified and had access to our bank accounts. I'd sent the last letter with Carlie's uncle on his way into the city, knowing it was the last time I'd get a chance to write until we reached California.

Uncle Rich's house was a complete disaster. Bags, backpacks, and clothes were everywhere as we all scrambled to pack everything and make it to the bus depot on time. Since Matt's and my trip would be more than two days and three buses, we had packed sandwiches, apples, and chips in our backpacks in an effort to keep expenses low.

Although Jazz and Ano's trip was a shorter distance than ours, it would take longer to get there due to the damage and lack of passable roads going in or out of the greater Los Angeles area. They'd both had enough experience hiking and surviving over the last month that they'd be in a better position than a lot of the people out there.

Carlie, however, hadn't said anything either way about coming back with us. Each time it had come up at dinner over the last two weeks she'd carefully sidestep the issue. With Ano and Jazz splitting off to Los Angeles, I needed to know Carlie would at least be close. Stanford Med Center might not be standing, but there had to be a hospital nearby.

I found her downstairs in the finished basement, reading another of her textbooks. Her leg was draped over the arm of the leather chair and she looked up as I came down the stairs.

"Hey!" she closed the book and smiled at me. "All set?"

I crouched down next to her chair. "I need to know."

"What?"

"Where you're going."

"I can't tell you what I don't know myself."

"Well, don't you have an idea?"

She sighed and rubbed the bridge of her nose. "Everything that could prove my residency is gone. My grades, my transcripts, everything. Think about this for a second, okay? I've spent the last two weeks sending off letters to schools in Pittsburg, Chicago, and Seattle."

"I thought Seattle was—"

"My uncle has a friend who used to sell pharmaceutical drugs and he says they've set up a temporary hospital outside the hot zone in Washington state. They're asking for everyone who has an MD to come. I just don't know if me going up there...no USMLE, no residency, you know, is going to work. What if I make that trip and they say, 'get outta here, kid' and I've made that trip for nothing?"

"How about University of Denver?"

"Okay, I'd be going from like a top ten medical school to not even in the top twenty-five. That's just...sad. Also, when I went to the University of Denver to talk to the administrator, she says that, because they're actually a college that hasn't been damaged that they're impacted. Students are flooding in to finish their degrees." She threw up her hands. "Why? Don't they understand they can't get in without money and there is no such thing as financial aid?"

"So how do you intend to pay for the rest of med school, then?"

"My uncle said he'd pay for it."

Must be nice. "Oh."

"Besides, now that the cash system is so much in question and doctors are in such high demand, the cost of med school has really dropped. It's a quarter of what it was last year."

"That's great."

I wondered suddenly how I'd pay for mine. Like the great psychic she was, Carlie read my face. "Um, other hospitals are actually taking on med students who will work their residency for free in exchange for med school and indentured servitude after the completion of their program." She tipped her head to the side. "You know anyone like that?"

I licked my lips. "I might. Where?"

"Penn State, Northwestern, and UC San Diego. And I heard from another second year resident that Boston U is also doing it. That's just a rumor though. You'd have to check it out."

I leaned my chin on my hands on the edge of the chair. "So where does that leave you?"

She shrugged. "Trying to find someone who knows someone from Seattle who can get me connected."

"Carlie, please. Come back with us."

"Why? There's nothing left back there. I've been to the DMV like a hundred times. If my mom was alive she'd have identified by now."

I heard Matt's heavy footsteps on the stairs and I stood. "Hey," he said, pointing with his thumb upstairs. "If we're gonna make that first bus we gotta go. C'mon."

Carlie got up with me and ascended the stairs. "I'll take you to the depot," she said. "From there, I think I'm going to have to find my own way."

This morning of all mornings, the bus depot was packed. Every day in Denver it got worse. As July became August, it had brought with it heat and more people flooding east from the West Coast, hoping to find better conditions.

True to her word, Carlie had come to see us off. Matt had bought us both a ticket; against my will I allowed him to pay for it – and only after we'd argued about it for six days straight. I had money in my account; the money from the sale of my dad's house in North Dakota. It had finally released from the trust once I turned eighteen. I never used it, as my scholarship and financial aid had really paid for everything I needed. Now I was drawing on it to survive. Jazz and Ano's bus left ten minutes before Matt's and mine, and was on the opposite end of the depot. We stood in the middle of the platform, all of us close together, none of us speaking, as if afraid to begin goodbyes at all.

Finally, Carlie stepped forward and hugged Jazz and Ano, wishing them a safe trip. Matt hugged Carlie and kissed her on the cheek, thanking her for everything and asking her to relay the message to her uncle.

She had tears in her eyes when she hugged me. "You remember everything we talked about," she whispered and pulled away gently. "You'll make an amazing doctor one day, Kate. But it doesn't come without sacrifice." Her eyes held the meaning that words could not and I nodded.

"I remember."

"Be safe and write me as soon as you get to California."

"I will."

I hugged Jazz hard, and him me, knowing it would be some time before I would see him again. "You take care of her." I said it sternly, and with the voice that indicated there was an ass whooping if the direction was disobeyed.

He smiled and nodded at me. "Will do."

Matt and Jazz embraced hard and Ano scooted to the side to hug me close. "Tell your mom I miss her," I said into her hair, because I didn't trust myself to say it while looking in her eyes.

"I will."

"Be careful."

She nodded, but neither one of us let go of the other. "Okay. You too."

"You make Jazz take good care of you." I rested my head on her shoulder for what seemed like the very last time ever and concentrated on the sound of her voice.

"I will. Don't *you* go off and do somethin' crazy."

I tried to laugh. "Like what?"

She hugged me tighter. "Like runnin' off to find him."

I didn't say anything for at least a minute. "Don't you go doing something crazy either."

Her throaty chuckle made my eyes burn. "Like what?"

"Like get married without me."

A smile lit up her face. "Like I could get married without a maid of honor!"

"Write me," I pleaded and she nodded.

"Soon as we get there. I've got Matt's mom's address and you've got mine, right?"

I patted the pocket of my backpack.

"And *real* letters," she teased. "None of your writing about the weather. Details!"

"I promise."

From above us on the loudspeaker, boarding for both buses was announced. "First call."

I'd known that day at the bus station in Fort Robinson that we wouldn't be together again as a group. From that moment on we'd be scattered across the country, like leaves that stay together on a tree through summer and are scattered on the ground in fall. However, knowing it and coming to that moment was causing me such grief that I felt actual, physical pain inside me. I wanted to grab all of them, and hold us all together...to keep us all from going the separate ways that life was pulling us.

And then second call was heard, and the threads of the fabric that had held me together for the last month tore apart.

Ano grabbed me again, hard. "I love you," she said fiercely and kissed me on the cheek before Jazz pulled her by the hand towards their departing bus.

"I know," I responded and allowed Jazz to pull her hand from mine.

"Baby, c'mon." Matt reached a hand out to me and I watched Ano and Jazz disappear into the crowd.

Carlie took a step back and handed each of us our packs in turn. "Go," she said, then descended the steps to the ground, disappearing around the corner in the sea of people pouring into the depot.

Matt was tugging on my hand towards our bus, nearly dragging me with him in an effort to get there. We arrived out of breath, found two seats together and sat, preparing for the thirty-hour ride to San Francisco. Matt leaned back in his seat and turned his head to look at me. "You okay?"

I was not okay. I was anything but okay. I'd said goodbye to Carrie and Charlie, to Percy, to Ano. I teared up and I could feel my bottom lip quiver. I concentrated on keeping my voice even. "I'm fine."

"It'll be okay," he promised, even though we both knew this was as far from anything he could control as there was. "We'll see them again soon."

I turned to look out the window. I felt alone in the world once again. Matt reached out and took my hand in his. Wrapping my fingers around his own, he kissed it.

"Hey," he said, "don't cry, baby. We're going home."

Chapter Thirteen

The closest we could get to Matt's mom was San Jose. Unbelievably, the freeways coming into California looked untouched. Normal. We went through Sacramento and south on I-5, avoiding the maze of Bay Area freeways that were surely impassable. We turned west on the 205, headed towards Dublin and began to see signs of damage. When we finally reached the 605, both of us were nearly pressed to the window. The bus never got over thirty miles an hour, and moved slowly, allowing us to see exactly what had become of the place we had both called home for so long.

The 280 East towards San Jose took only a few minutes, and we gathered our packs and sat anxiously waiting, holding hands side by side. The 'bus station' was nothing more than an old newspaper stand and ten or twelve old bus benches lined up outside it. We stepped off the bus onto the street on what used to be Keyes, and it was apparent that, even fifty miles from San Francisco, damage had been done here as well.

The businesses that had once bordered the streets were abandoned, the windows blown out and the doors wide open. Trash and debris littered the streets; cars that had been parked on the side of the road had been pushed up onto the curb and looked as though they'd been abandoned along with everything else.

I held my pack and walked with Matt towards the newspaper stand where a tall African American man sat inside, arms crossed over his chest. Only five people had gotten off the bus. It had continued on its way, leaving a long cloud of dust in its wake.

"Hey," Matt greeted the man inside the newspaper booth and looked around for a schedule. "Looking to go to Los Altos. Any buses going that direction?"

The man stroked his goatee. "Nope."

"Okay, what bus gets the closest?"

"No bus."

"There are no buses coming through here that go to Los Altos?"

"No moah buses. 'Dat bus you jus' get off of? 'Dat the only bus coming troo here. In or out."

I looked around us. We were literally in the middle of nowhere.

"Then what are you doing in the booth? Isn't this a bus station?"

"Yes."

"All right then...you're telling me—"

I touched Matt's arm and turned to look at the man, who had stood now to address Matt. "Is there any way to get to Los Altos, except on foot?"

A slow smile spread across the man's face and he pointed at me, but addressed Matt. "'Da lady ask 'da right question." He pulled a dirty piece of paper from underneath the board serving as his counter. "He-ah and he-ahh. 'Dese are de places we take you." He pointed behind him, to a car parked on the side of the street. Rust covered the entire right side of it, and it didn't look as if it was even running. "My cousin take you to Los Altos." He narrowed an eye at us. "For one hundred dollars."

"Forget this." Matt angrily pushed away from the counter. "A hundred dollars? It's fifteen miles, for Christ's sake!"

The man shrugged calmly. I crossed my arms over my chest, matching his demeanor. "Fifteen miles, fifteen dollars." I half expected him to get angry, but again he smiled.

"Beautiful girl know how to bargain. I tell you what. He take you for fifty."

I shook my head. "Beautiful girl knows she can probably walk down a few blocks and get it for twenty-five." I raised an eyebrow at him and the smile diminished some.

"It be dahk soon." The grin returned. Beautiful girl get caught in 'da dahk before she make it." When I said nothing, he nodded. "But I tell my cousin to do 'dis for forty." He slapped his hand down on the board, as if making his final offer.

I reached in my front pocket and pulled out a twenty and a ten and slapped them down as well, right in front of me and under my hand, so I could retract them quickly. "Thirty and tell your cousin he has two passengers to go to Los Altos."

He stood still for a moment, and I wondered whether he would stick to his guns or not. The other people had gotten off the bus and left, and he had no other prospective customers in sight. He sighed and called out to the man sleeping at the driver's seat. "Kallah! You go to Los Altos." He grinned and held his hand out for the thirty dollars. "For 'da pretty lady and..." he glanced over to Matt, "her valet."

I laughed and nodded to Matt, who walked over to the car and loaded our backpacks in the backseat, then waited for me to complete the transaction. I handed him the money and nodded my thanks, nearly running to the car to climb in the back seat. With a jolt, the car came to life and pulled away from the curb with a screech. It took a full two minutes before Matt spoke, and even then it was in a whisper.

"Where did you learn to negotiate like that?"

"Shopping with Ano."

He laughed out loud as the car swerved back and forth around debris, on back roads and side streets, taking us the long way through to Los Altos, to Matt's mother.

From the moment we pulled up in front of the address that Matt had written down, I realized I was in hell. The house was enormous, and had a daunting gate surrounding it. With a speaker at the curb. After Matt pulled our backpacks out and helped me from the back seat, Kallah sped away in his trashed Mazda. We stood, looking around at the houses, only half of which had lights on in them. Many had windows broken out and looked as though it had been looters and not the blast that had done it. Matt walked up and pushed the button on the intercom.

After the third try, I was about to give up and search for a house that might not have squatters living in it, when a voice was heard from the other end of the intercom. "What!"

Matt pressed the button to speak. "Um, I'm looking for June Skylar."

A full minute passed before we received a response. "Who's asking?"

Matt pressed the button and I could hear the choke up in his voice as he said it. "Her son."

Within seconds, the front door flung open and a woman I assumed to be his mother came hurrying out the front door. "Matt? Matty?"

She hit the gate, but it was locked. The man behind her hurried out with the key.

"Get this Goddamned thing open, Jim!"

The lock was opened and she flung her arms around Matt, nearly putting out my eye in the process. She pulled back and held him by the face. "Let me look at you. Oh, you're so skinny!" She turned to Jim, who was watching her embrace Matt. "Isn't he skinny? Oh, come in, come in!"

Matt pulled away for a second and reached for my hand. He pulled me closer and caught his mom by the elbow. "Mom? Mom! This is Kate."

Silence. Dead silence. She turned to Jim, then to me and finally back to Matt. "Oh!" Then, somewhat recovering, she nodded kindly and held her hand out to me to shake. "Thank you for bringing my son home! Jim," she said and inclined her head towards me, "a little something for the waif, I think."

My eyebrows shot upwards and I crossed my arms over my chest. When

Jim reached into his wallet, Matt held out a hand, stopping him. His face was upset. "No! Mom, Kate is my...Kate and I are together."

The waif? I could only assume she was referring to me. His mother turned, looked back at me in surprise, but said nothing. Jim looked up and down the street. "I think it best if we get in and discuss this inside."

"Yes," Matt's mother agreed. "Quite right, Jim." She pulled Matt into an embrace, his hand slipping from mine. "Come in here and tell me what's kept you! You should have called!"

With no other alternative, I picked up both our packs and thanked Jim as I passed through the gate. He closed it behind me and locked it with a snap.

Once inside, Jim helped me with the packs and he set them inside the door. I wondered if he was a friend or someone Matt knew. I held my hand out to him. "I'm Kate Moore." Jim just stood, not accepting my hand. "I go... went to Stanford with Matt, before the blast."

"Oh. Jim. Overstadt. Friend of Matt's parents." Only then did he shake my hand, and lead me into the house, trailing behind Matt and his mother.

The house, despite the outward loveliness, was quite dated on the inside. The counters were an older tile, and the floor a large Spanish looking tile that kind of matched. June sat Matt down at the kitchen table, pulled some food from the fridge, and set it on the counter.

"Mom..." Matt motioned for her to sit down and Jim stood in the doorway behind me, watching. "Mom, come and sit down with me."

She pulled more and more food from the refrigerator until nearly everything was on the counter. "Mom, hey..." Matt closed the refrigerator door and led her to the table, to sit across from him. He looked into her eyes and stroked the platinum hair back from her face. "Mom, what happened? Where's Dad?"

She shook her head for a moment, the same smile on her face as it had been since we'd arrived. "Your father?" her eyes were vacant and she looked around the kitchen and shrugged. "Well, he's around here somewhere." The smile returned and she stood and walked to the food on the counter. "I'm going to fix you a plate of food that will fatten you up! You and Pete, always too skinny! Don't they feed you at Stanford?"

Matt swallowed hard and I could see he was trying to reach his mom, who was clearly not all there. "Mom, leave the food." He came and stood next to her, stopped her from moving by holding her gently by the shoulders. He spoke slowly and carefully. "Mom, do you remember what happened to Dad?" She didn't respond and was looking somewhere over his left shoulder. "Dad, Mom. Where is Dad? Is he...is he dead?"

I took a cautious step into the kitchen, having hung back in the doorway with Jim. I had that sinking feeling you get when you know something is horribly, horribly wrong but you can't quite place your finger on what it is.

Looking at his mother's expression change from vacant to tortured, I knew that the person I saw in front of me was not June Skylar. At least, not anymore.

"There was…a ladies luncheon." She said it quietly, as if afraid someone would hear her. "For the Charity League in San Raphael. For the day." Her eyes welled up with tears. "He said, 'go and have fun.'" His mother's chest rose and fell as the life drained from her face. "He went into the city. To have lunch with Pete." Her eyes looked past him, remembering. "At first we thought it was an earthquake. And then another sound and a horrible rumbling. We felt this…gust. Like a terrible…" The tears began to fall down her cheeks.

Matt's hands dropped from around her shoulders and he looked at the floor.

"Everything blew over, and people were screaming…" her lower lip quivered and her mouth opened as if to scream but no sound came out. "They were screaming, Matty. I crawled to the house with Ruth. She was… she was right behind me." She paused and actually looked behind her, as if Ruth would still be there. Finding nothing but the refrigerator, she turned back to Matt, who was holding his fist against his mouth.

"Mom," he began, but it was useless. Matt might as well have not been there at all.

"When I looked back," her mouth stayed open, and the tears flowed freely down her cheeks, "I saw the skin on Ruth's…" she began to sink to the floor and Matt stepped forward and caught her in his arms.

Jim motioned to Matt to follow him and I stepped to the side to allow him to pass. They walked down the hallway to the last bedroom where Matt laid his mother on the bed. Jim reached the nightstand and grabbed a pill bottle from it, extracted one pill, and sat on the edge of the bed. She was crying inconsolably. "C'mon, June," he crooned. "What kind of friend am I if I let your husband come back from golf seeing you cry?"

The sobbing slowed and she accepted the water glass from him. "Golfing?"

"That's right. He and Robert, remember? Today's their golfing day."

"It is?" June shook her head and the sobbing ceased, and at once the veil lowered back over her face. "Oh yes," she said, and sniffled again.

Matt watched the scene from in front of me in the doorway, his mother – clearly not all there – being tended to by Jim, who was setting up this façade in order to keep her in some containable form. "Now, just take this *aspirin*," he said, handing her a large pill.

"Aspirin."

"That's right. For your headaches."

She took the pill with some water and he helped her lie back against the pillows. "Thank you, Jim."

Matt came forward and sat on the edge of the bed next to her and held her hand.

"Matty," she said, "Father will be home tomorrow. And you'll have to explain to him why you didn't call. We'll all have dinner at the club tomorrow night." A slight smile touched her lips and Matt wiped the tears from his face with the back of his hand.

"Okay, Mom. I'll see him tomorrow."

She patted his hand and closed her eyes. "I'm so glad you're home." She exhaled once and was asleep.

Jim led us back out into the living room, where he steered Matt into the large oversized chair in the corner. He walked to the bar and poured three drinks. "Here, this will help."

He handed both of us glasses filled half full of dark amber liquid, then sat opposite Matt in a large leather chair.

"How long has she been like that?" Matt asked.

Jim sighed. "Since I found her."

"When was that?"

Jim ran a hand over his face. "I made my way to Napa and found them all in the hospital there...horrible conditions. Matt, you can't even imagine."

Matt took another drink of the amber liquid. "And your wife? God, I'm sorry...um...Terri?"

"Toni."

"Right, Toni."

Jim took a drink out of his own glass and said nothing.

"I'm sorry," Matt said. "What about Ruth? What's the story there? Did... Ruth...did Ruth die?"

Jim let out a long breath. "I can't get the story out of her, and really, I don't think it'll do any good. According to the hospital where I found them, Ruth was dead a few minutes after the initial blast hit, and I don't know from what."

Matt nodded somberly and accepted Jim's gentle nod to take another drink.

"With Toni gone and your dad in the city," Jim said, "I brought her home here. Matt, she wouldn't have survived there."

"Thank you, Jim."

Jim stood and walked to the drawer of a large mahogany desk, withdrew two letters, and handed them to Matt. "I notified your brothers when I saw you hadn't identified. They're both coming here to see her and decide what to do."

"So, they know...?" Matt motioned towards the bedroom that his mother was in and Jim nodded.

"They know."

"When are they coming?"

"Those letters said they'd be here last week, so I expect them any day now."

"Is she always like that?" I asked.

"It's like every morning, something in her brain hits restart," Jim said. "She doesn't know how she got here, and I have to make up this song and dance about how she went to a party and had too much champagne."

He chuckled, and Matt joined in, but it was bitter. Matt held up the letters. "Again, Jim, thank you." He took another long sip of his drink. "For everything."

"You're welcome to stay here until your brothers come," Jim said. "After that, I'm going to shut up the house and go live with my daughter in Kentucky."

"We'll be gone as soon as we can," Matt assured him. "We don't want to inconvenience you any more than we already have."

"Thank you. There's a room at the top of the stairs and to the right, all the way at the end of the hall. You're welcome to use it." Downing the remainder of his drink, he stood, bid both of us goodnight, and retired upstairs to his bedroom.

In the eerie silence of the old house, we heard the click of his bedroom door shut behind him. Without a word, I walked to the chair where Matt sat, looking at the small amount of alcohol left in his glass. His shoulders slumped forward and he didn't react to my presence. Perching myself on the arm of the chair, I searched for something to say that could possibly diminish the depth of pain he was feeling right now. More than ever, I found myself missing Ano; her comforting words, her throaty voice. Ano could comfort anyone – no matter how ravaged from despair they were. Being that I lacked that quality, I reached for Matt's empty glass and replaced it with my own full one.

He nodded in acknowledgement, his voice breaking as he spoke. "Would it have been better if she'd died, too?"

I didn't believe he was searching for an answer, and so I gave none.

"I just know she wouldn't want to live like this." He drew a shuddering breath and I could tell, even in the dimly lit room that he was crying.

I reached out to him hesitantly and ran my fingers through the back of his hair. "Your brothers are coming," I said. "You'll get to be with your brothers really soon."

He took a long drink of the liquid, until over half of it was gone. He leaned forward, massaging the bridge of his nose with his fingers. "It's *all* gone," he whispered. "Everything is...it's just..."

There are times when you need to pull from your memories to help those in need. When I'd left my father's grave and been dropped back home, I went to his room, crawled onto his bed, and cried for three hours straight.

All I'd wanted was someone – anyone – to comfort me, to hold me and tell me...even if it was a lie, that everything was going to be all right. I took the empty glass from Matt's hand and, setting it on the floor beside the chair, slid into his lap. Wrapping my arms around him, I patted his back gently, as Ano always did with me. I rocked gently back and forth – I took that from Carrie – and whispered, "Sshhhh. It'll be all right."

CHAPTER FOURTEEN

Even with a lighter backpack than she'd had in the Wind Cave, three days of buses, walking, and sleeping in bus depots left Carlie exhausted. The last fifteen minutes of the ride to Bellevue, Washington felt like ten hours. At this point, she didn't care if they accepted her into the program; she would find somewhere that wasn't moving and sleep there – even if it was a gurney.

She had nothing to go on, and her uncle had told her she was on a fool's errand; no address, no name to contact, and no one she knew to help her out if she got in trouble. Being Carlie, she simply had to go. As she stood on the side of the street in Bellevue, however, she wasn't certain her uncle had been entirely wrong. Looking around her for a minute, she approached a woman sitting inside the small booth that served as a ticket kiosk for the bus station.

"Hi, do you know where the hospital is?"

The woman's red hair was unnaturally bright and her lips were saggy and wrinkled. "Which one?"

"The...um, one that replaced University of Seattle Med Center."

The woman shrugged. "No idea."

"Thanks." Leaving the safety zone of the bus station in Bellevue wasn't nearly as bad as Denver, she reasoned, and shouldered her backpack as opposed to holding it to her chest.

As soon as she got out of the bus depot alley, she walked west, knowing that, eventually she would find someone who might know where she could find the hospital. After wandering for an hour and a half, all Carlie got was lost. Finally, down a one way street, she saw a handmade sign for a coffee shop and nearly ran for it. It had obviously been a restaurant before the blast, with the Formica tables and plastic chairs scattered throughout the large dining area, and she chose a table closest to the door and sat.

A tall waitress came to her table, her face marred by a red scar that stretched from her forehead to her chin. Her nametag read, 'Ulma'.

She greeted Carlie hardly looking up from her pad. "Know what you want yet?"

"Um," Carlie pulled the menu from its holder on the table. "Coffee? For now?"

Ulma disappeared without a word, and Carlie looked around the dining room, not sure what she was waiting for, or who she could ask that might know where a hospital might be. The waitress came back with her coffee and set it down quickly in front of her when more customers came in. Carlie reached for the sugar and watched Ulma smile at a few of them and chat easily as they sat in one of the corner tables.

For an out of the way place, it actually got a lot of foot traffic. And, she thought with surprise, it had really good coffee. After two refills and nearly an hour, Ulma came over to where Carlie sat, clearly irritated that the only thing she'd ordered was coffee. She tore off a tab from her pad and laid it on the edge without a word. As Carlie reached for her wallet, the bell on the front door rang again, and in walked a tall, dark-haired man...wearing blue surgical scrubs. Carlie's mouth fell open at her good fortune, and Ulma – seeing the look on Carlie's face – followed her gaze.

"Ah, forget about it," she said in a conspiratorial whisper. "Works eighty hour weeks and...not...interested."

As if not hearing her, Carlie stood and walked to the doctor, hurrying before he sat down at a table. She could see the black circles under his eyes and bags forming under those. He looked to be around thirty-five, maybe older, and really handsome in that rugged Indiana Jones kind of way.

"Doctor," she said, and he sighed before turning to address her.

"I take one break a day. Go to the hospital and you'll get seen."

She touched his arm. "You don't understand, I'm—"

He finally turned towards her. His face was exhausted; nearly as much as hers. More, if possible. "Look, young lady—"

"Most people call me *Doctor*." She'd said it for the shock value, to get his attention. It worked. As soon as she said it, his expression changed.

"Oh, forgive me. *Doctor*...?"

"Mannis. Carlie. Pleased to meet you."

His eyes were a steel blue, too much silver in them to be...

"Can I help you, *Doctor* Mannis?"

"Right! Yes. I've been looking for the hospital. University Washington Med Center relocated and I'm here to apply to finish my....to see if they are accepting residents so I can—"

"Oh. You're a resident." He leaned against the counter, exhausted.

"Can I buy you a cup of coffee?" Carlie motioned to the table she'd been sitting at, where Ulma was still standing, amazed that she'd gotten the handsome doctor to talk. "You can sit and rest."

He paused for three seconds and finally conceded. "One cup."

He followed her to the table and Ulma looked on in disbelief when he sat down across from Carlie. "The usual," he said to Ulma with a smile and she nodded, eyebrows raised, and left them alone.

"I see you're a regular around here," Carlie remarked.

"Yep." He leaned back in his chair. "So, Mannis. Where'd you do undergrad and rotation?"

"Stanford."

It was his turn to be surprised and he whistled through his teeth. "I see."

"I wasn't there when the blast hit."

"Clearly."

"Now that Stanford's gone—"

"You're left without somewhere to finish your residency."

She nodded. "I didn't get your name, Doctor...?"

He smiled, showing a dimple in both cheeks. "David Windsor. Good to meet you."

"You too." Carlie took a sip and leaned forward. "So, is there a program here? Or did I just travel fifteen hundred miles for nothing?"

"Where'd you come from?"

"Denver."

He nodded, silently assessing her for a moment, and then accepted the steaming cup of coffee Ulma handed him. "You taken the USMLE yet?"

"No. Had a few weeks to go before I took it."

"Uh. Okay. Um, most of the residents in our program have already taken it."

"Oh. I see." Carlie stared down at her hands, wondering what the hell she was going to do now.

He sighed. "I'm going to regret this. I can talk to the chief, see if there's some way—"

Carlie's eyes lit up but he stopped her with his hand.

"I'm not saying anything, and I'm not promising anything."

"I know. Absolutely."

His face became hard. "This isn't Stanford. This is foxhole medicine." David's face turned serious. "This isn't 'stitch it pretty, neat and nice'. U Dub was a teaching hospital. This is a war zone, plain and simple. We're here to get people patched up, as fast as we can, so that bed can be used for someone who really needs it."

"Okay."

As if trying to scare her away, his voice got low and he asked, "The day after the blast, I called time of death on seventy-five people within the first half of my day. Seventy-five!"

Carlie blanched.

"That first week? We had bodies lying in the street outside the tents we'd set up – waiting to be seen. They *died* waiting to be seen. Y'understand?"

She nodded profusely, but stayed put.

"I had an attending doing amputations with no more sterile conditions than..." he looked around, "than we're in now." He paused and watched her features. "I lost most of my residents in the first two weeks because they couldn't handle it. Because the smell was so bad. Rotting flesh and blood and..." he paused, realizing his voice was raising and he stopped and ran a hand over his face. He tapped his coffee cup with his index finger. "This is the real thing, Mannis. Not what you learned at Stanford. There's no split lip case hiding behind curtain one. It's *all* real."

"I get it," Carlie said, her jaw set hard.

David checked his watch again. "How much experience did you have at Stanford with burn trauma?"

"A little."

"How much?"

"Um..." she struggled to remember, and pressed her lips together. "Less than a dozen within the last year. Mostly second degree. Only one graft, taken from the back and I watched, not assisted."

"Okay. Here's how it is. You've got your three basic traumas that come in off the street. Most common's your radiation burns; depending on how long they've been exposed and how bad they let it get, it will need excision of the tissue."

Carlie wished she had the small pad she used to keep in her lab coat pocket to take notes.

"Cut it out, clean it, patch 'em up and release them."

"Who do they follow up with? Don't they need—"

"Maybe you didn't hear where we're working. You're not in a fully functional hospital. We're a trauma station. Only."

She nodded. "Sorry. Right."

"There's a bus. Leaves twice a day from the trauma unit here that goes straight to a hospital in Bellingham that wasn't touched by this, that offers follow ups and traditional medical care. Your job, if you can take and pass the second part of the USMLE, is to make sure they're alive when they get on that bus."

"All right."

"Second most common's your open wound laceration. So much debris everywhere, people get cut digging around where their home used to be, hoping to find some shred of..." he shook his head. "Anyway."

She cleared her throat. "And the third most common?"

"Hmm?"

"You said there are three basic traumas."

"Oh, right, right, right." He ran a hand over his face. "Sorry. Been on for twenty-four straight. Not thinking as clear as I should." He took a long drink of coffee. "Third most common is what we call the dark spot."

"Sorry?"

David looked out the window for a moment. "People got nowhere to go, Mannis. They're sleeping in the streets, they're drinking water that's been contaminated with radiation and God knows what else. They ingest it and ..." it dawned on Carlie what the third type of trauma was, and she felt slightly sick.

"...and it eats away their organs until they bleed to death internally." His tone was bitter. "We call it a dark spot because on an ultrasound, it shows up as a large dark spot that spreads. Depending on the severity of the holes in their organs."

Carlie looked at him with concern. "What do you do for them? How do you triage them and get them..." David didn't say anything, just played with the handle on his coffee cup. "You...don't. Do you?"

His eyes, cold blue and hard, stared into hers. "We do what we can. Depending on how far along they are, we do what we can."

What he was saying went against everything they had taught her at Stanford, everything she'd learned in classroom training and clinical rotation. What he was saying was against her Hippocratic Oath; to do no harm. In her training, the failure to give care was considered doing harm. To fail to give people care, to watch them die and do nothing...she didn't know if she could simply sit back and watch it happen. The full realization of what she was stepping into had begun to hit her. What he was offering was the chance to – if she passed the USMLE – actually practice medicine. On people who desperately needed her skills. The thought of doing it absolutely terrified and exhilarated her at the same time.

"You got somewhere to stay, Mannis?"

"I was hoping to find the hospital and—"

"I get it. I get it." David took a long drink of the coffee. "I gotta get back." He stood and tossed two dollars on the table, despite her protests that it was her treat. He turned to go, flipped around, and raised an eyebrow at her. "Well? You comin?"

Chapter Fifteen

San Bernardino was the closest they could get to Riverside. From there, they hiked three miles through debris to find the next bus station. Where they'd been told to go, there was no station, no markers, no signs. And so, they kept walking, trying to stay in the roads as much as possible, picking their way through shattered glass and chunks of concrete from buildings and homes.

Los Angeles reportedly had had two bombs explode within it. Stepping carefully through the streets, it was hard to believe it was only two. Everything was covered in a thick layer of gray dust. As if the entire area had been too close to a volcano eruption, the dust had settled over the area like a blanket. From underneath collapsed buildings there were still traces of human suffering and Ano turned her face away as they passed. They had walked single file originally; now they walked side by side. The amount of human suffering and destruction formed the need for them to see another human next to them who was alive.

Travel was slow. They picked their way carefully through the thick layer of gray soot, placing their feet down carefully, not knowing what lay underneath each step. Progress was arduous. Around noon they sat down together and pulled out sandwiches they'd packed from their last stop on the bus.

"You doing all right?" Jazz asked Ano with genuine concern.

Ano looked out across the sea of desolation around them. "I guess."

"My dad came out here once to the West Coast to see me before he died."

Ano turned towards Jazz. He had an ease about him, a way of talking that made people want to hear what he had to say. Ano knew he would have made a good lawyer.

"You ever make it down here?" she asked him. "To L.A.?"

He took a bite of his sandwich. "No. No, we didn't. He didn't want to go anywhere or really do anything when he came out, which kind of frustrated me, you know?" He squinted in the extreme glare of the sun. "I kept trying to take him to see the Golden Gate or to a Giants game. In the end, all he wanted to do was just be with me."

"He must've been proud of you."

Jazz nodded and rinsed the sandwich down with some water, then handed his canteen to Ano. "I suppose. He never said much. He was one of those men who said a whole lot just by saying nothing."

"Yeah." She looked around them. "What do you think he'd say about where you are now? You think he'd tell you to go home?"

Jazz smiled, but it was filled with sadness. "No, he'd tell me that home is in your heart and your mind. And that my mom and brothers lived a good life."

Ano covered the hand that rested on his knee with her own. "And he'd be right."

They were quiet for a moment, both lost in their own thoughts, looking at the wreckage that surrounded them. Enormous pieces of concrete from fallen buildings littered the ground, pieces of rebar stuck out at odd angles. Nearby, a human arm was visible from beneath the wall of a collapsed building. Jazz closed his eyes and muttered a quick prayer.

"It's like the end of the world, isn't it?" Ano asked. "Nothing moving, everything collapsed. There's no sign of life here anymore. I mean, where'd all the people go?" She looked around as if she expected to see someone.

"We'll see people soon. We just have to keep walking is all. C'mon." Jazz stood and extended his hand to help her up, then they heard the sound of a car engine.

Swerving back and forth amongst the debris was an older car, covered in dents, scrapes and odd colored paint. It began to swerve to the side as it approached Jazz, but he held his arms up in the air and waved for the driver to stop. The car rolled to a stop about a hundred feet in front of him. The windshield was so filthy, it was nearly impossible to see inside. Jazz held a hand out to Ano to stay put and he approached the car.

The driver was about Jazz's age, but pale with black hair that stood up all over his head. His face was dirty and his eyes narrowed suspiciously as Jazz approached the car.

"Get back!"

Jazz stopped where he was, his hands up, as if in surrender. "All right man, I'm just looking for directions."

"Just stay where you are." The man's accent sounded Russian.

"I'm trying to get to Riverside," Jazz said, keeping his hands up where the Russian could see them.

"Why?"

"My girlfriend and I...we're trying to find her mom. Bus dropped us off in San Bernardino. They told us there was a transportation station somewhere near here. We been walkin' forever. You know where it is?"

The Russian looked at Jazz, then over to Ano, who stood up from where she'd been sitting on the piece of concrete to eat. Part of their lunch still sat uneaten on the concrete block they'd used as a table. "Det good food?"

Jazz's eyebrow went up and he nodded. "Yeah, it's good. We been eating it, so...you know."

The Russian licked his lips. "For the rest of the food 'dere, I give you directions."

Jazz looked back at Ano. "How about for the rest of our food, and..." he pulled a five dollar bill out of his pocket, "five bucks, you take us to Riverside?"

The Russian laughed harshly. "Five bucks don't get you to next block."

Because he looked like he might take off, Jazz held his hands up again. "Alright. *Ten.* And the food."

The Russian never took his eyes off Ano. "Where you go in Riverside?"

Jazz reached for his back pocket and, with two fingers, pulled the piece of paper from it. "Arlington Boulevard. You know how to get there?"

"Riverside Freeway. Still 'dere." The Russian looked to Jazz and again back to Ano and the food. "Bring 'da food, and *twenty* dollars."

Jazz motioned to Ano to come to him. "He says he can take us to Arlington to your mom for twenty bucks and...the rest of our lunch."

"You think he's...can we trust him?"

Jazz shook his head and spoke under his breath. "Probably not, but I'll take my chances at this point."

She gathered the remainder of their lunch in the plastic wrap it had come in while Jazz followed her with the backpacks. She approached the driver's side, handed the driver the lump of food, and got into the backseat. They all sat for a moment while the Russian stuffed the remainder of their sandwiches into his mouth. Leaning his head back on the headrest, he put the car into gear. It jolted to a start, swerving around debris to make it to the Riverside freeway.

"By d'way." he called out. "I'm Viktor."

"How'd you get a car running, Viktor?" Jazz asked him over the buzz of the motor and the wind coming through all four windows. "I mean, you don't see nearly anyone with a car."

"Yes!" Viktor said. "My cousin, he has car shop? In valley. Before 'dis happen. We all put...uh, together? Electric parts work now."

Making a wide left, they entered onto the San Bernardino freeway headed towards Riverside. The car's engine sounded like it was at maximum power and the speedometer read thirty miles an hour. They swerved back and forth through the cars littering the freeway. Pieces of freeway were missing and rebar stuck up like birthday candles from the concrete. Some of the cars were on their side, most were simply pushed up against the guard rail. Viktor pointed to the sign ahead of them, still hanging from the metal pole. "Arlington, ah?"

Jazz nodded. "Yeah! Yeah that's it!"

The little car screamed forward and took the off ramp, which thankfully, was clear. At the bottom of the ramp Viktor turned left. "What number?"

They drove down a wide boulevard with businesses bordering either side. Jazz looked at the paper in his hand. "2030."

Back and forth they swayed, Viktor swerving between piles of brick or mortar in the street and more abandoned vehicles. The little car hit several small pieces of debris as it flew along. Ano thought she might be sick and tried to roll down the window while gripping the door handle for support.

Thankfully, the little car slowed and pulled in front of a check cashing store.

Ano sank back against the seat and looked out her window. The place looked abandoned. "A check cashing place? For real?"

Viktor looked around. "Yes, 'dis for real. Twenty-thirty Arlington."

Jazz handed him the twenty dollars and they gathered their backpacks and stepped out. The little car made a U-turn and sped back towards the highway, onto the off ramp, going the wrong direction.

Ano approached the front door, which was locked. It was one of about five buildings on that street that had sustained only moderate damage. The bars on the windows were still intact but the brick border had crumbled a bit. She banged on the window and tried to look in, but saw nothing.

"Shit." She turned to Jazz. "What the hell are we gonna do now? Why would she identify with this address if she wasn't here?"

Her back to the window, she didn't see the face appear. It disappeared a second later.

Looking straight at the window, Jazz saw it and came forward, yelling. "Hey! Lady! Hey!" He ran to the door, banged on it with his palm. "Please! We're looking for someone! Open up, please?"

"You see someone?" Ano turned around and pounded with him. "Hello? Open up!"

From behind the closed door came the reply. "Go away!"

Ano was just about out of hope, and she leaned against the door, her face pressed to the filthy glass. "Please. I'm looking for my mom."

Jazz quit banging when they heard no response. He turned his back to the window and sighed.

"Your momma Eunice Vesper?" a muffled voice from inside asked.

Ano flipped around, her face and hands pressed against the glass. "No, that's my grandma! That's my grandma! Is she here?" Taking a step back from the window, Ano began to scream out, "Grandma! It's Ano!"

They heard a click, the door cracked open about two inches, and an elderly face peered out at them. "Who you?"

Ano stepped in front of the crack, ready to strong arm her way in, if necessary. "Anobelle Johnson. My mom's—"

"Michelle Johnson."

Ano nodded eagerly. "That's right! Is she here?"

The door opened an inch more. "Who's he?"

"This is my...this is..."

"I'm her boyfriend. Jazz Taylor, ma'am."

Ano smiled at Jazz, and then looked back to the face that peeked at them through the three inches in the door. She didn't say anything for a few minutes, and from behind her, Ano heard a throaty voice so familiar she almost cried. "Lively Cross! Either you open that Goddamned door to my granddaughter or so help me God I'm gonna get up off this cot and whup up your old ass!"

Ano began to laugh and cry at the same time and literally pushed her way through the door; then stopped dead. Five cots were positioned side by side in what used to be the waiting room of the check cashing store. On the middle of the five, Ano's grandmother was struggling to sit up, and Ano rushed to her side.

"Grandma!" Ano began to cry hard as she flung herself into her grandmother's arms and rested her head against her large chest, sobbing. Her lovely, slim arms wrapped around the older woman's waist.

"Oh, hush now," her grandmother told her, rubbing her back and rocking back and forth. "Ssssh. Hush now, e'thing's gonna be a'right."

"I was so worried!" Ano sobbed. Her grandmother smoothed the tears from Ano's cheeks. "We didn't see that you'd identified, and then we saw that Mom had..." a sudden thought occurred to her and she looked around. "Where's...where's Mom?"

Her grandmother shushed her again. "She'll be back in a while, now. Jus' gone to find food, is all."

Ano looked around, finally seeing the other three people with them. "What are you doing here? And why didn't you identify?"

"Well," her grandmother said, and coughed hard for a few minutes, "I hadn't been breathin' too good and the DMV is a ways. Only had enough for one trip." She looked around at the others. "And ev'y body here needed to go and somebody needed to stay." She coughed again and Ano wished that Carlie was here to listen to her grandmother's lungs.

"Have you seen a doctor?"

From behind her, Lively's scratchy voice sounded. "Ain't no doctor gonna come here, and we ain't gonna go there!" she crossed her arms over her chest, as if to make a point. "Too many people sick and dyin' in those places. Doctor's don' know what the hell they doin'."

Ano turned back to her grandmother, who had taken her hand and was stroking it. "I'm so glad to see you." Her voice caught. "When we heard L.A.'d been hit, I thought..."

Grandma Vesper nodded. "I know, I know. Now the good Lord had a plan for me and your momma and we jus' fine."

"Why were you here instead of home?"

Grandma Vesper pointed to the man lying on the last cot in a row. "Bradford needed a ride downtown." She whispered to Ano, "Had to cash his Social Security check."

"So, you drove him?"

"Mmmhmmm. Your momma drove us down here, 'cause this was close to his son's house. We were gonna have lunch there after we stopped here." She clucked her tongue. "Never even left the front door."

Ano looked over to where Bradford lay, motionless on the cot. "Is he okay?" His body was covered entirely with a blanket and his chest was barely moving.

Her grandmother covered Ano's hand with her own. "He was the first one out the door when it hit."

She nodded solemnly and Grandma Vesper's voice cracked slightly. "It was like someone blew e'vything one direction, real fast." She looked into Ano's face. "You know?"

Ano nodded, even though she didn't know, and couldn't imagine.

"Bradford got hit by a shopping cart...jus' blew into him like he was nuthin'. After the second blast, that's when we found him. She patted Ano's hand. "We know he's not long for our world."

As if aware that people were talking about him, Bradford drew a rasping breath. Grandma Vesper reached up and stroked Ano's hair and smiled at her beautiful granddaughter.

"Your momma been so worried 'bout you! Down there in that *damn cave*..." she pointed a finger at Ano. "I tol' you not to go down there!"

"I know."

"An' I tol' you som'pin was gonna happen."

Ano nodded. "I know."

"I had a feelin'! An' I told you and Miss Kate on the day you left that—"

"If we hadn't been in the cave," Jazz said, "we would have been at Stanford. And...worse off. So, I'm glad she went. I'm glad we both did."

Grandma Vesper's eyebrows both went up. She looked at Jazz and then back at Ano. "Whut'd you bring home from that cave, chile?"

Ano laughed her deep throaty laugh and she held her hand out to Jazz. He took it and came to sit down next to Ano on the foot of Grandma Vesper's cot. "Grandma, this is Jazz Taylor. Jazz," she squeezed her grandmother's hand. "*This* is my grandma."

"Pleased to meet you, Ms. Vesper," he said, and held out a hand to her grandmother who took it and smiled an incredibly wide smile.

"Well, call me Grandma Vesper, *Jazz,*" she said, still smiling. Out of the corner of her mouth she asked, "What's he do?"

Ano smiled, tears forming in her eyes and said the thing she never thought she'd get to say. "Grandma, he's a preacher man."

CHAPTER SIXTEEN

"I want to stop. Can't we stop and rest?"

Edgar's voice had begun to grate on him as they trudged along the interstate.

"No," Percy said through gritted teeth. "We have to keep moving."

"Why?" Edgar complained. "Percy...stop. My feet hurt."

Percy resisted the urge to raise his voice to his brother, and instead stopped and allowed him to sit for another minute.

"I'm thirsty."

Percy removed the canteen from the strap on his hip and handed it to his brother. "Don't drink too much," he warned. "You'll get a stitch in your side."

Despite Percy's caution, his younger brother drink thirstily from his canteen until Percy pulled it from his lips.

"Enough."

Edgar looked around, his curly hair a rat's nest and his freckles darker than ever with the heat. "Are we almost there?"

Now Percy knew why lions ate their young, and why his mother had literally threatened his father with divorce if they had any more children.

He sighed. "No. Another few miles or so."

Even with the camp caretaker bringing them as far as Lake George it hadn't helped. None of the phones were reaching Philadelphia. The blasts from New York had knocked out all lines that could connect them, and Percy knew there'd be no reception until they were within Pennsylvania state lines. Maybe not even then. Hitchhiking was dangerous. They'd been doing it for nearly three days and Percy was tired. Neither of them was sleeping well and they were conserving their food. A sign about five miles back had said Newark was within twenty-five miles and Percy hoped that they might secure a ride the rest of the way into Pennsylvania from there.

"C'mon," he urged his brother. "We'll walk side by side this time."

Edgar stood, and fell into step beside Percy, whose tall frame and long legs made it difficult for him to keep up. Every few steps he would have to sprint, but Percy wasn't going to slow his step. They needed to make it to Philly.

"You gonna tell me what happened or not?"

Percy had been thankful that the camp counselors hadn't told the kids what had happened, but was having a difficult time not telling Edgar now that it was just the two of them. He stayed silent, wondering what to say to him. What could he say to the brother nearly ten years younger than himself? The child that William had nicknamed 'Oops' until his mother had made him stop. He smiled as he remembered his mother's face; trying not to laugh, slapping William on the shoulder. Edgar had no mother. The thought made him wince.

His grandmother would know how to raise him. She'd raised five boys herself – his father included – and put up with his grandfather all those years. Surely she'd get Edgar into the best boarding school there was in Philadelphia. Edgar would be fine. Percy nodded as he reaffirmed his decision to take Edgar to their grandmother's.

"Percy?" Edgar's voice squeaked at the end, causing Percy to smile.

"When's your voice going to change all the way?" he asked, and gave his brother a shove.

"Father said his didn't change all the way till he was twenty."

Percy swallowed. Hard. "Oh, yeah?"

"Yeah." They walked in silence for a few minutes. "Is Mother meeting us at Gigi's?"

Edgar had called his grandmother Gigi his entire life. No one else dared call his grandmother by her given name except Edgar. Knowing it would be her last grandchild, she spoiled Edgar horribly, a fact that had been much lamented by his mother. The youngest of five boys, his father had always been the favorite. His grandmother's oldest sons had both died in the Korean War, the third oldest she'd lost to the church. His father's older brother had an arranged marriage to a woman much older than himself and they'd chosen to have no children. And so, out of five sons, their father was the only one who provided his grandmother with another brood of five boys to look after. And look after them she had.

"No," Percy replied. "She's not meeting us." The last few words stuck in his throat and he knew this secret wasn't going to make it until Philly. However, he was going to drag it out as long as he could.

"I *know* something happened," Edgar said.

"Really?" Percy held out his thumb as a car passed them on the road without even slowing down. "How?"

"Heard some of the counselors talking one night when we snuck out to

MICHELA MONTGOMERY

get into the girls' camp."

Percy smirked at this. "I assumed that 'lights out' at Forrest Pines meant, you know, *lights out.*"

Edgar snickered. "The lights *were* out."

"All right, so what'd you hear?"

Edgar sprinted a few steps to keep up and shrugged his pack onto his shoulders again. "That someone bombed the U.S." He looked up at Percy as they walked. "Did they?"

Percy didn't say anything for a minute. "Yeah, Ed. Yeah, they did."

"Where?"

His mother was good at answering all of Edgar's questions. Unfailingly patient, his mother had raised five boys nearly completely on her own. His father, like many self-made men in New York, had ridden the real estate market at its height – and left the child rearing and domestic duties to Percy's mother. William, the oldest, followed his father's footsteps by majoring in business and going after his MBA. His older brother John worked on Wall Street for Merrill Lynch for years. Last Christmas he'd brought home that girl...what was her name? She worked at...Saks?

"Percy!"

His brother was nearly running to keep up with him. He slowed his step.

"You going tell me what happened or not?"

His mother should be here to do this. She was always better at breaking bad news. He hadn't seen Edgar in nearly a year; last Christmas, just after he'd turned fifteen. He seemed so much taller.

"You've grown."

Edgar smiled widely. "Mother says I'll be taller than Grandpa Warner."

"Did she?"

"Yes. He was six feet seven."

"He was six foot *four,*" Percy corrected. His mother and grandmother had shared the gift of exaggeration where his grandfather was concerned.

"How tall are you?"

"Six-two."

Percy walked backwards with his thumb out as another car passed them on the freeway.

"How tall is John?"

His brother John was the spitting image of his grandfather; and the only one of the five boys that hadn't gotten the ruddy, curly red hair that seemed to plague each of them from about birth through high school.

"John was...John is..." His face burned and he was angry. Angry at what was happening. Angry that his plan was dissolving before his eyes. Angry that his future was uncertain – in every way. And angry that, instead of getting Edgar home to his parents, he was taking him to their grandmother's house. Alone. "John...the last time I saw him," he said, "was six-three." He gritted his teeth. Fifteen. Edgar had lost both of his parents at fifteen. An orphan. What does that do to a...

He stopped dead on the side of the freeway, mid-thought. "Son of a bitch."

Edgar took two steps back from his brother and pointed at him, covering a smile. "You're not supposed to curse in front of me!"

Like a freight train, the realization of the parallels hit him. "Son of a bitch!" he repeated, to no one in particular. For a minute, Percy stood there, on the side of the road, hands on his hips, thinking. No, impossible. The only person who knew how this felt, the person who would now have the most in common with his brother— and him— was three thousand miles across the country.

Glad for the chance to stop, Edgar looked across at his older brother. "What's wrong?"

There was no way to explain to Edgar what connection Percy had just made. No way he could tell him anything about a personal situation that, truth be told, Percy himself didn't quite understand. Still pondering, Percy began to walk. His brother trundled along beside him like a puppy, volleying questions the whole time.

"How much longer?"

Irritated at the interruption in his thoughts, Percy snapped, "About ten minutes shorter every time you ask!" He muttered under his breath, "I'd have killed everyone down in that cave if they'd have asked me this often."

Energy suddenly renewed, Edgar's face lit up. "Tell me about the cave!" Again his voice broke at the end and Percy smiled.

He sighed, glad for the distraction. "What'd you want to know?"

"Was it cool? Did it have scorpions in it like *The Mummy*? Were there huge spiders that crawled all over and the webs got...oooh! Percy! Have you seen the New Indiana Jones movie?"

His brother's line of questioning was comparable to having a conversation with someone with ADD. He wasn't quite sure which question to answer, so he took the last one first. "No, I haven't."

"I did. Mother took me and Valance to see it when we got home from Avon."

Avon was his brother's boarding school. Valance, his brother's best friend since...oh, God.

"Did Val go to Forest Pines with you?"

"No, why?"

"No reason."

"He usually spends summers in the Hamptons with his grandmother."

Percy actually exhaled. Thank God. Edgar wouldn't have lost everyone. He still had a brother, a grandmother, and possibly a best friend. They walked on, accompanied by Edgar's incessant chatter, and Percy found himself wondering if Kate had had the benefit of a friend. Any friend so that he wouldn't think of her...completely alone at the same age his brother was. He was physically sick just thinking about it.

"...this trick he does with his thumb where he..."

Percy rejoined the conversation. "Who is this?"

He answered, exasperated. "Pete! The head counselor!"

Percy looked at his brother admonishingly. "Do not," he said sternly," take that tone with me."

Edgar lowered his head. "Yes, Percy."

They walked in silence for a few hundred feet. Percy noticed Edgar shifting his pack back and forth. "Stop that," he snapped, and for a few minutes, Edgar obeyed. But a few hundred feet more and he did it again. Percy stopped, so frustrated at the interruption he was ready to snap. "What is wrong?" he asked, his tone loud and full of bite.

Edgar looked like he was going to cry and he looked down at the ground. The freckles on his arms showed brightly even as the afternoon sun had begun to fade in the sky. "There's something under my strap that's pinching my shoulder," he said, and Percy took a deep breath to calm down.

"Let me see." He stepped toward his brother and helped him slip the pack off his pack. Percy examined the straps of the brand new backpack carefully. Obviously, his mother had purchased it just before he'd been sent to Forest Pines this year. It was a good pack, and a sturdy one. "I don't see anything wrong with it. It's fine." As he was handing it back to his brother, he noticed some spots on the shoulders of his shirt. "Edgar," he said, and reached for his brother. "Come here."

Edgar had been standing quietly in front of Percy while he inspected the shoulder straps. He came towards Percy, head down. Percy set Edgar's pack on the highway and looked down at the spots of blood decorating his shoulders.

"Sorry, Percy."

"Hold still," he said, and put his hands underneath this brother's shirt, pulling it over his head. Once removed, he inspected the blisters that had formed over his shoulders from carrying the heavy backpack for too long of a distance. Percy cursed under his breath and pulled the shirt back on over Edgar's head. He had nothing to clean the blisters, nothing to disinfect them with. He was ill equipped to deal with any of this.

Shifting Edgar's pack to strap it over his own he said, "I'll carry your pack for a while."

Edgar shook his head. "It's fine, Percy. I can do it."

"I've got it." Percy leaned down, grasped the strap of Edgar's pack, and pulled it upwards toward his shoulder. "Now let's–" The pain in his stitched wound was sharp this time, nearly doubling him over and making him cry out and lean against Edgar.

"Percy!" Edgar cried.

Percy straightened and wiped the sweat on his forehead. "No," he assured him. "I'm fine." It took a few moments before Percy caught his breath.

Another car approached and, in an act of sheer desperation, Percy waved both hands over his head, as if flagging down a plane. In a true act of mercy, the truck slowed to a stop; an elderly couple in the small cab.

"Where you headed?" the man asked Percy.

The pain in his side was still there, and he was out of breath when he answered, "Philadelphia." He glanced at Edgar. "With my little brother."

The man pointed to the bed of the truck. "Hop in. We'll take you as far as we can."

Percy had never been so glad for a ride in his life as he was at that instant. "Thank you!" he nearly cried, and walked to the back where he opened the tailgate and had Edgar help him slide the packs from his shoulder before he could crawl in himself.

Once in, Edgar reached over, closed the tailgate tightly, and leaned back against the bed next to Percy. "You okay?" he asked.

The pain was subsiding and Percy was able to draw in a deep breath. "Better now."

They rode in silence for a few minutes until Percy knew he had run out of time. "Edgar," he said solemnly, "there's something I need to tell you."

CHAPTER SEVENTEEN

The few private minutes I got each day were either spent writing a letter or studying the medical book Carlie had tucked in my pack before we left Denver. I'd written to Carrie nearly every few days in the two weeks we'd been at Jim's house. Oddly, it was easier for me to tell her things in letters that I couldn't in person. And so, on each page of my letters, I poured out my heart. I wrote about what had happened since we'd left Fort Robinson, and then told her about leaving Ano. I told her about finding Matt's mother and returning to where I'd lived at Stanford.

The building that had been my home for the last four years was gone; literally only the brick foundation of the building was left. Not one ounce of evidence that I'd existed remained. We'd actually seen people we knew. It was awkward to share stories with people who looked at Matt and me together as if we were a pair of mismatched socks. And of course, I told Carrie about Percy, and how his only brother Edgar was alive and that he'd gone to New York. I hadn't said any more than that. I knew that, being so insightful, Carrie would understand.

In my letters to Ano I tried to give her as many details as possible about what had happened to the campus; the surrounding places we'd been together, and the amount of damage in the city itself. Matt and I had ventured as far north as Daly City one day, but from there it was pretty much impassable. On campus, the administration building was the only thing besides the clock tower that came away with minimal damage. I was able to talk to the admissions office clerk, who was trying unsuccessfully to reboot all the computers. Clearly, changing my major at that point wasn't a topic I felt would be high on her priority list, and so I didn't broach it.

In my letters to Carlie, I always told her about how far I'd gone in the book she gave me, what I was learning, and questions I had regarding the material. I took volumes of notes in the two spare notebooks from my pack, and referred to them as if giving myself an examination on what I'd already studied.

The letter I had started a hundred times but never completed was the letter to Percy. Since he wasn't in Virginia and that was the only address I had, it did me little good to consider sending it. However, that didn't stop me from writing it. Sometimes it was filled with all the questions he would have hated: *How are you? Are you all right? How is your brother? What are you doing?* Sometimes, the letter was filled with things I would never have the courage to write but thought about constantly. His eyes. His smile. His voice. His touch. The things I kept very quiet to myself, but thought about on my way to and from the postal station two miles from Jim's house. Every day.

Jim was a hospitable man, and by the time Matt's brothers had arrived had even begun to relax around me. John Skylar arrived first, weighted down with a large rollaway suitcase despite having taken nearly two weeks and fourteen buses to arrive at Jim's home. I'd never seen Matt's father, but June told me (in a more lucid moment) that John was the spitting image of her husband. John had been at Harvard when New York was hit and gave us more details on how the East Coast fared than I would have liked.

Second oldest, John was taller than Matt by a good three inches, and a solid fifty pounds heavier. I could see how he played rugby at Stanford, and how he'd be very good at it. I liked John immensely; his sense of humor was off color and his laugh was larger than life. He came with me on my first few trips to the postal station and we talked the entire way there and back. He was easy to talk to, intelligent, and had me laughing nearly the entire way.

The youngest Skylar was Paul, Matt's little brother in every way. Paul resembled June in both stature and looks. Slight build and not an inch over five foot eight, sandy blond hair and, like all the Skylar boys, blue eyes. There was something about Paul I simply didn't like, but I couldn't put my finger on it. He told us he'd changed his major again, just before the attack, and he laughed about how this might have caused his father to kill him for spending another year at Notre Dame. I didn't like his shifty eyes, or the way he stared at me without saying a word. The way he spoke to me, the way he treated me, with a disdain and contempt that was never said out loud. I would be happy when I wasn't around Paul any more.

Since the arrival of his brothers, Matt's mood had improved considerably, and I saw him joke with John several times throughout the day. Most of their day was spent coordinating where to go and what to do once we left here. His mother's bank account, which was considerable, would have to be used to pay for her care, somewhere close to one of the brothers. But which one? Many heated discussions and options had filled our evening dinner table as they discussed both South Bend as well as Boston as potential future homes for their mother since both John and Paul both had roots in a city and Matt didn't. I didn't like how Paul gave Matt grief over the fact that we didn't exactly have a plan and I'd brought it up to Matt one night after everyone had gone to bed.

Even in the dark I could see his face turn hard as he responded, "He's my brother, Kate. One of two I have left. He's my *family*." He'd rolled over in bed, his back to me, and gone to sleep.

As the days went on and plans went forward to move Matt's mother to Boston instead of South Bend – Paul's flightiness having been sighted as the reason for the decision – Matt and I talked less and less. I was isolated there at Jim's house. I had no one. My days were lonely and I missed being able to talk to a woman whose memory didn't reset every morning she awoke. Also, since I *was* the only woman, I had been assigned the role of entertaining Matt's mother during the day while the men went over finances and tried to find their mother a care home in Boston. My only coveted time alone was on my daily trips to the post station, when I took as long as I could there and back to mail my letters.

"Hey, Brad, just two to mail today." I handed him a letter for Carrie and a letter for Ano and turned to go.

"Hey, Kate? Hang on. Got something for you." He walked back and removed three envelopes from a bin and brought them back to me at the counter. "These are addressed to you and not the boys. Enjoy."

We'd been getting a few responses from hospitals in Boston with information regarding long term care. Before John had left Boston he'd requested any boarding information be sent to Jim's address. But these three letters were addressed to me, and I stood there holding them for a long time before thanking Brad and walking back out to the road. Carrie, Ano, and Carlie had written me, and I debated ripping them open right there and reading them. I reasoned that by the time I read all three it would be dark and Matt would worry. Tucking them in the waistband of my jeans, I nearly skipped back to Jim's house.

Noiselessly, I opened the side door and tiptoed through the hall, hoping to make it up the stairs and read the letters in private when I heard the voices coming from the kitchen. Paul's voice was angry and raised.

"Why're you always defending her?"

"Paul, stop." John's voice was unmistakable.

"No, I wanna know. Someone's attached herself to you because you have money, because of who you are, and I'd like to know—"

"You don't know her." Matt's response sounded tired, and I leaned against the bottom banister for support.

"Just listen to me for a second." Paul's voice lowered and I could hear most, but not all of what he was saying. "Come back with me. You can finish…

and then everything will go back to normal. Get rid of the extra baggage and—"

My heart was beating like a jackhammer and I leaned in to hear more of the conversation.

"...free to do what you want. God, just get rid of her already! Even John said she isn't right for you!"

My cheeks burned at this, because I had liked John so much.

"That is not what I said," John corrected.

"Alright, well, whatever," Paul conceded. "We've got a plan. What's hers? To follow you around and spend our parents' money? Is she hoping to maybe cash in on this?"

"Shut up!" Matt said, and I heard his chair scoot back from the table. "Don't talk about her like that!"

John's voice was calm, but strong. "Paul, shut up and sit down. Matt, sit back down." I heard two chairs scoot against the tile floor. "Matt," John began carefully, "I like Kate. She's a nice girl. But what's your plan, here? I mean, is *she* really what you want?"

"Exactly." Paul agreed, and I felt sick. I began to ascend the stairs.

"I...I don't know. I mean, Kate is amazing. Neither of you really know her."

"Neither do you," Paul said in that nasal voice of his. "All you know is she's a science major with no family."

"I spent a month with her. Trust me, I know her."

John sighed. "A month, in God knows what conditions. You'd fall for anyone in that circumstance."

"That's not it!" Matt's voice lowered. "She followed me here because—"

"That's convenient, right? She latched herself onto you on the road to an easy life!"

"Shut up, Paul. You're wrong."

"All right," John said. "Maybe. But where is this going? I've seen you with a lot of girls. I mean, don't get me wrong, she's pretty."

"Yeah, if you like vanilla pudding," Paul said, and my eyes narrowed.

"But man, she is not *anything* like what I thought you'd end up with."

Paul actually chuckled. "No shit. If you'd have brought her to Christmas dinner, people'd think you hired another maid." He laughed out loud and I felt like I was going to vomit.

I made it to the top of the stairs and stood there, hearing the last of their conversation wafting up to where I stood.

"We're leaving for Boston in three days," John said. "I'm not telling you what to do but I think you should get some space from her and come back with me to Boston for a while."

"I'm not leaving her."

"Leaving her is the only thing that makes sense."

"John's right. Dump her. Jim's gonna leave soon. She'll find *somewhere* to go."

Matt's voice was softer. "You don't get it. I...can't leave her here. She has no one."

"Sooner or later," came Paul's response, "little orphan Annie's gonna get old. The Midwest is full of hot women dying to get their hands on someone like you and me. Even John."

"Fuck you."

Paul laughed and I turned to go. I'd heard enough. I entered the bedroom I shared with Matt, the door clicking softly shut behind me. Had I stayed at the top of the stairs a minute longer, I might have seen Jim standing below the stairs in the hallway listening as well.

Once in the bedroom, I pulled my backpack from underneath the bed. I stuffed the few outfits I owned into it and shoved it back under the bed. My heart was beating like a rabbit and I focused on making a plan. As I bent over, the three letters I had shoved in my waistband fell out and onto the floor. I tore open the letter from Ano. It was filled with news of her mother and grandmother and plans to take them both back to New Orleans to live with her uncle and his family. She left me the address and sent her love.

I folded Ano's letter back into its envelope and hid it within the pages of the anatomy book that I'd been reading. The second letter was from Carrie, and I pulled it from its sheath as well, drinking in every word. Mostly her news was about the progress Charlie was making and the new boys they'd hired to help them on the farm. She talked about how sorry she was to hear about Matt's mother, and what a burden this could place on the heart of a child. At the end she signed it, '*Be happy, Love, Carrie.*'

As much as I had needed letters from Ano and Carrie, neither held any comfort for me tonight. I tore open Carlie's letter and two scraps of paper fell out onto the bed. I read the letter first.

> *Kate,*
>
> *It's about two in the morning here and I've been on rounds for thirty hours, so if this letter doesn't make good sense, you know why. Sorry to hear about what's going on there with Matt's mom. You're strong and I know you'll get through it.*
>
> *I've passed the USMLE (part 2) and am now doing residency here at the trauma center in Bellevue. The hours are long*

and the chief attending here is tough on us. Half the time I hate it and swear I'm going to quit and go to a cushy job in the Midwest and the other half I'm learning too much to think about it. Got the letter you sent Uncle Rich. The address here at the hospital isn't a good one, but I'm staying with a bunch of the residents, so...use the return address on this letter, okay?

Enclosed is the information we talked about for Penn State and Northwestern. UC San Diego shut down its program according to a resident here who was down there about ten days ago. Both have accelerated programs for new incoming victims (sorry, that's you) and would give you the "in" you'll need. I'd go for Penn personally. It's closer to NY and you have a greater need there than anywhere else. I know anything that will get you closer to NY is a good thing, right?

I'll tell you more about what's going on here in my next letter. I'd answer the two pages of questions you sent, but I was too busy laughing to finish reading them. My attending found them incredibly perceptive and wants to offer you a job after you've completed clinical rounds. Pause for laughter. I'm off to get three hours of sleep on a cot. Love to you and Matt.

Carlie

I read it twice before turning over the small pieces of paper in my hand. Both had addresses and contacts names. I smoothed the one for Penn State against my leg. I tucked it all back into the envelope and slid that letter into the book as well.

Pulling a piece of paper from my writing tablet, I wrote a few lines and signed it at the bottom. I grabbed one of the envelopes I'd purchased from the postal station and tucked in the note, scrawling Matt's name across the front. It was getting dark and I knew it wasn't safe to leave until early tomorrow morning. Mentally, I planned how to pack without him hearing me, and I slid the letter for him underneath my pillow so he wouldn't see it when he came in for bed. As if on cue, the door opened and he appeared in the doorway.

I looked up with a resolute expression on my face.

"Hey. Didn't hear you come in." His face looked worried, and I wagered it was because he wouldn't have wanted me hearing his plans to go back to the Midwest to find Miss All-American.

"Just got here." I blinked, but said nothing.

"Oh." His expression relaxed some. "We're fixing dinner, wanna come down?"

"Not hungry. Thanks, though."

I looked at his face and felt betrayed, in the most extreme sense of the word. Not just because I had slept with him, or because I had trusted that he was, in fact, different than I had perceived him to be. But because I had chosen him, and in doing so, lost the one man I had loved for three years. I had made the wrong choice.

He stood next to the bed, looking at me, not saying anything for a few seconds. "Do you want me to bring a tray up here and we can eat together?"

"No, you should eat with your brothers and your mom. Your *family*." Although I didn't mean for the inflection to be quite so pronounced, it came out that way nevertheless.

"Kate, about that. I know I was short with you the other night. About Paul…"

"Don't worry about it. I got over it."

He stared at me. Even if he tried to read the expression on my face, he couldn't have. I'd wiped away any trace of pain and buried it. "I just want you to know that Paul, he says stupid shit. It doesn't mean anything. It's… it's just how he is."

I nodded once. "Okay."

He walked across the room and reached out to take my hand and, as if my reflexes for self-preservation had kicked in, I jerked my hand back before he could touch it.

His eyebrows knit together. "We're back to this?"

"No."

"I can see you're upset with me about the other night, and—"

My voice was toneless and even. "No, I'm not. Everything is fine. I'm just tired and I think I'll read a little and go to bed."

He looked unsure if he could trust what I was saying. Knowing he was going to take more convincing, I swallowed the lump in my throat and lied. "We'll talk about it tomorrow morning."

This seemed to relieve him a little, and his face relaxed. "Okay." He reached up to touch my face and I steeled myself for his touch. The feel of his fingers against my cheek nearly had me in tears, but I pressed my lips together in a smile. "Tomorrow morning, then?"

I smiled again, burying the lie deep in my heart. He retreated from the bedroom, leaving me alone to pack my remaining few items as discreetly as possible before bed.

I didn't need to set the alarm; I hadn't really fallen asleep. The sleep I did have was restless and I tossed and turned until the clock on the nightstand read three a.m. As quietly as possible, I slipped from the covers and pulled my backpack out from under the bed. I pulled on my jeans and the shirt Carrie had given me then lifted the pack onto my shoulders. Before I left the bedroom, I pulled the letter I'd written out from under my pillow and set it next to Matt. I watched him sleeping for the last time, and felt something between extreme pain and terrible longing grip my heart.

I closed the door behind me and tiptoed down the stairs, stopping at the door to the kitchen. No one would notice if I took an apple or two, and it was going to be such a long trip to Philly.

"Already packed you some food," came a soft voice from behind me. I gasped and swung around and came face to face with Jim. He was in his pajamas, his craggy old face tired in the light of the kitchen.

"I'm so...I didn't mean to wake you," I said lamely.

"No, I don't suppose you meant to wake anyone, did you?"

I didn't know if his intent was to expose me for leaving, or to help get me out of his house. "I'll just be on my way," I said, backing from the kitchen.

"Hang on," he said, and reached into the cupboard to retrieve a pillowcase, which bulged with food. He handed it to me. "Going to be a mighty long trip. Wherever you're going."

I nodded and accepted the pillowcase from him. Swinging my pack down from my back, I stuffed it inside and zipped it back up. "Thank you, Jim."

I turned to go, but he stopped me again. "Paul always was a horse's ass."

There was no way for me to respond to that, except to nod.

"Matt's a good man. He knows what he wants."

"I'm sure he does." I wanted to add, *And it doesn't include me*, but simple pride prohibited me from arguing the point.

Seeing that I was not to be swayed from leaving, he offered, "Got a bike in the garage. It's old, but I pumped up the tires last night and it works. It'll get you to the bus station faster than if you're on foot."

Walking the entire fifteen miles on foot was daunting, but I had counted on hailing down one of the makeshift cabs I saw everyday on my way to the post station. "I can't return it to you," I said, and he held up a hand.

"Not asking for it to be returned." He crooked a finger and led me into the garage, where an older bike sat waiting on the side. He opened up the side door and we stepped out into the cool morning air.

"Thank you, again, Jim. For everything," I said and swung a leg over the bike. It had been years since I'd ridden, and I tested out my balance by lifting up one foot. It was fine. I'd remember soon enough.

"You sure you won't wait until he wakes up? Gonna be hell to pay when he finds out you're gone."

I looked at his kind face without a word. Jim nodded in acknowledgement of my decision.

"God's speed, then."

"Thank you." A little shaky, I pushed off; unaccustomed to the weight of my pack and balancing on a bike. I weaved a little as I headed down his driveway to the end of the street, disappearing around the curve at the end.

CHAPTER EIGHTEEN

Carlie never knew whether the day was going to be a good one or not. On a good day, she actually got to save more lives than she lost. On a good day, she got to send nearly all the bodies on a bus to Bellingham and watch them disappear with a puff of exhaust.

"Mannis!"

That day wasn't today.

"Three, four, five, breathe!" She looked to the monitor next to her and shook her head, beginning compressions again. "One, two, three, four, five, breathe!" She listened for the sound that meant this little girl would live to see age six. Flatline.

"Mannis, *now!*"

She cursed. "Time of death, eighteen thirty-five." The nurse next to her pulled the sheet up over the child she had been working on for the last fifteen minutes. She reached David and snapped off the pair of gloves she'd been using, pulling a fresh pair from the box that was taped to the pole supporting part of their triage station.

"I'm here, what've we got?"

David barely glanced at her as he screamed orders at the nurses and staff around him. "Grade two laceration to the femoral artery. Hold pressure here!" he said, grabbing her hand and pressing it against the bloody leg in front of her. "I need a battle pack if we're gonna stop the bleeding and save the leg."

"It's deeper or longer than you think," she said, looking into the wound. She called to the nurse next to her, "Cut these off him! His pants? Now! That's it, cut upwards."

As David tore open the packet of battle solvent, Carlie reached up past the laceration, pressing her fingers hard in between his joint and his groin. She looked up to David. "Got it." Her bloody, gloved hand outstretched to the nurse, she asked, "Clamp?"

Maria handed her the clamp and Carlie clamped down the artery.

"Bus is leaving," David advised her under his breath.

"He can't go now. I just got it clamped."

"Mannis, last bus out tonight. Let's get him on it. They can finish what we started here on the bus."

"The hell they can. Before we transfer him, we should—"

David poured the battle triage package onto the gaping wound and pressed down against the leg until it the bleeding slowed. "Where's my stretcher?" David yelled and two men came running towards him.

"I'm not finished!"

"Yes you are."

They transferred him from gurney to stretcher, and Carlie watched them pull the man into the last slot on the bus to Bellingham. Gravel shot out from the wheels and the bus disappeared into the blackness.

She snapped off her gloves and threw them into the yellow waste bag. David stopped her on her way back inside. "What the hell were you doing?"

"Clamping off the leg!"

"No, before that. I was calling you for five minutes to assist before you came. What the hell were you doing?"

"An entire warehouse collapsed this morning, Dr. Windsor," Carlie said, her tone short. "I was tending to one of the twelve people who managed to survive it."

She walked into the temporary building, peeling the bloody apron from her and throwing it in the contaminated laundry she passed in the hall. When she passed one of the exam rooms, she heard screaming. One of the clinical residents came towards her from behind the curtain. "I think it's...I think you need to..."

Carlie pushed past him and into the exam room. On the table was a girl around seventeen bleeding profusely from a laceration on her face. Carlie stepped into the room and reached for the arms of the girl, who swung at Carlie as she got closer. "Miss, you need to calm down." The girl swung at Carlie again.

"Thomas, get an orderly." Thomas nodded and was gone. Carlie snapped on another pair of surgical gloves, walked to a cart near the screaming girl and pulled a small syringe from it and a bottle underneath. She was pulling several cc's into the syringe when the orderly arrived and helped Thomas hold the young woman down.

Holding the girl's forearm, she talked to Thomas in a calm voice. "Intramuscular injection, mixture of Methohexital and glucose, approximately two and a half cc's." Carlie inserted the syringe into the arm of the patient.

As the patient's body relaxed he asked, "Shouldn't I use the cubital vein and inject—"

"Not for this solution." Carlie allowed them to recline the girl, who was now drifting into a twilight sleep and nodded to Thomas. "Finish her stitches. And make them small. We don't want it to scar any more than we have to."

She discarded the empty syringe and walked out from behind the curtain.

"May I have a word?" David fell into step with her as she walked down the hall towards the cupboard they used for an on-call room.

"Just one?"

"Dr. Mannis."

She stopped when she reached the door, his arm barring her way. "That's two, actually." She stood, too tired to cross her arms over her chest and regarded him, a tower in front of her. He hadn't shaved in at least two days, and his dark brown hair went a hundred different ways from being under a surgical cap most of the morning.

"Dr. Windsor?" she would have raised an eyebrow, but she lacked the energy to do so.

He sighed and spoke to her in a quiet tone. "When we are in an emergent situation like this morning, it is imperative for you to accurately assess whether a patient will benefit from continued heroic measures or...not."

"She *could* have survived, and I made the call."

"You made it based on emotion."

Carlie's eyes narrowed. "Respectfully, sir, I disagree." She ducked under his arm and pushed her way into the on-call room, pausing for a moment before collapsing onto the only soft bed in the hospital, one of her legs draped over the side. She felt dizzy and slightly sick. The room was spinning. Her eyes closed.

The door swung open and David entered. "I'll say this one last thing and then let you rest for an hour," he said and then stopped.

Carlie wanted to respond. She wanted to yell at him and tell him to go to hell. Something was wrong. She simply couldn't. She couldn't lift any of her limbs. The entire room spun and suddenly went black.

"Dr. Mannis."

No reaction.

"Carlie!" He pressed his knuckles against her sternum, hard, and she didn't react. He stood quickly and called out the door, "Nancy, get me a gurney, now!"

* * *

Quiet. An eerie quiet filled her ears. She remembered walking into the on-call room and the entire room spinning. Her eyes opened to the room around her. Brick walls with some really bad paintings hung on them. Carlie looked down at herself; she was in bed, still in her scrubs.

On top of the covers, right next to her, was Dr. David Windsor, still in his blue surgical scrubs, sound asleep. She struggled to sit up and waited for the dizziness to return. The room didn't spin, but her body felt incredibly heavy and she fell back among the pillows.

"You're awake."

She looked next to her and saw David rousing. "It would appear so."

He sat up and reached over to take her pulse. She was quiet for a moment until he finished. He managed a weak smile. "Better."

"You drugging your residents now to win arguments?"

He smirked at her and ran a hand through his hair. "No. Not recently."

"What happened?"

Gently, he pulled a strand of hair back from her face. "Combat Stress Reaction."

"What is that?"

"More common in battle-type situations. But, well, you know," he motioned towards the window, "sometimes it feels like we *are* at war."

A crushing wave of emotion rolled through her and Carlie teared up. "What the *hell* is happening to me?" she asked, wiping at her eyes. "I don't... this isn't me." Embarrassed, she sniffled and David handed her a tissue from the nightstand.

"It's shell shock," he said, his voice soft. "Common for first time soldiers, and brought on by lack of sleep and extreme stressful situations over a long period of time."

"I'm not a *soldier,*" Carlie said, wiping at her eyes. Every emotion possible flowed through her and she fought to control it.

David smirked at her. "*I* was," he said, and pulled the covers up around her chest. "And I know the signs."

She turned her wrist over to look at the time but her watch was missing. "I was supposed to be at the—"

"We're both on mandatory R&R for the next twelve hours."

"Is there something I should take? A medicine?" She began to cry again. "Goddamnit!"

David laughed and crossed his arms over his chest. "No, there's nothing for this except rest, and allowing your body to come down." He moved to get off the bed.

"Please?" she asked and held him by the wrist. "Don't go."

"All right." He sat back down next to her. "I can make us some breakfast and you can take a shower."

She looked around. "This is your place?"

"Yeah. I know you've been staying with a few of the residents at that communal *hole in the wall,*" he said, "but I knew you wouldn't get any rest there, so I brought you here." His expression changed to a serious one. "If you're uncomfortable, I can—"

"No, no. Thank you, Dr. Windsor."

One side of his mouth curved into a smile. "I think you can call me David."

"All right. David." Carlie sat up and tried to swing her legs over the edge of the bed. Her limbs felt heavy, even after six hours of sleep.

David moved to her side of the bed and lifted her feet back onto the mattress. "Stay put."

He leaned over her to help her back into bed and she could see his chest through the v-neck of his scrubs. Impulsively, she reached a hand out to touch him. The minute her hand touched his skin, she looked at his face and withdrew it.

"I'm sorry," she said and rolled away.

He sat on the edge of the bed and pressed his thumb against his eyes. "Um...no, it's very common to have...you can expect your emotions over the next ten to twelve hours to be erratic and..." She was still turned away from him and he gently rolled her to face him. "Dr. Mannis."

She shook her head like a fifteen year old but his voice stayed soft.

"Carlie." The sound of him saying her name forced her to look at him and he leaned close to her. "It's all right. It wasn't fatal."

They both laughed at his joke and she apologized again. "I can't explain and I doubt it's the Combat Stress...whatever..."

"Reaction."

"...but I feel like I'm not in control. And I hate that."

David touched her face gently. "You'll be fine." He smiled once again and moved to get up off the bed.

"Doct...David?"

He turned to her. "Yeah?" he sat back down on the edge of the bed.

"I need to ask you to do something for me."

"All right."

Her face became serious and she looked like she might cry again. "It might be...unpleasant for you."

"Like I don't do *'unpleasant'* things all day long?" he sighed. "What?"

She sat up slightly, leaning on her elbow, and reached her hand out again, to touch the base of his neck. Her palm flattened against his chest and she scooted down to be closer to him. He was watching her, without saying a word. Carlie slid her hand slowly, carefully underneath the shirt of his scrubs, over his chest. She closed her eyes.

"I knew it would feel like that," she said. Her eyes opened again and he saw the expression on David's face. "What?"

A sardonic grin appeared and he said "I'm waiting for the *unpleasant* part."

She leaned forward, pulled her hand out from under his shirt and slid it behind his neck. "I wasn't done." She leaned forward and pulled him to her, touching her lips to his. "Will you," she asked, and gently bit his bottom lip, "kiss me back?"

"Is that a good idea?" he murmured against her mouth.

She smiled. "Probably not."

Turning his head, he covered her mouth with his own and pressed her back against the pillows, the heat from his mouth filling her. His hand still around the back of her neck, he kissed down to her collarbone. Carlie lifted the bottom of his scrub top over his head and slid her hands down the hard line of his chest.

"Carlie," he said softly, "we shouldn't do this."

"I know." Her hands wound up towards his hair, which had grown longer in the month she'd been at the trauma center, and pulled him to her. "But I need it so badly."

He rolled onto his back, taking her with him and opened his mouth against hers, surrendering whatever arguments he had to the contrary. Her mouth moved down his body, tasting his chest, her fingers digging into his forearms. Finding a barrier in the bottoms to his surgical scrubs, she deftly pulled them over his hips and gasped at the sheer size of him.

David kicked off his remaining clothes and watched Carlie's reaction. Rolling onto his side, he slid a finger underneath the thin sleeve of her shirt. "I think turnabout is fair?"

With the skilled hands of a surgeon, he removed her clothes, and soon they were lying in a pile next to his, on the side of the bed.

"Where were we?" he teased, and lowered his head to her neck. He slid his arm underneath her and wrapped it firmly around her backside.

As if the rational side of her brain had simply disconnected, Carlie moved against him without reservation. David's hands touched her everywhere and she closed her eyes. His chest was so firm and warm and she pressed against it, testing the reality of him next to her. His entire body felt solid next to hers and she moved to explore him with her mouth.

"Oh...God, Mannis..."

She raised her head from him for a moment, a blush spreading across her cheeks. "Carlie. Not Mannis."

Her tongue and mouth tasted him for the first time and he let out a loud groan. Rewarded by the sound of his pleasure, she wrapped one hand around the base of him and teased the rest with her lips and tongue. For several minutes she enjoyed the sound of him, the taste of him. This was the connection she'd never had with Percy – with anyone, really – in so long. And, almost desperately now, she needed it.

Surprising her by turning the tables and rolling her onto her back, David pulled her into the middle of the bed, his body solid and heavy above her. She accepted the weight of him, groaned as he pressed their hips together for the first time.

"You can make as much noise as you want," he coaxed. "The building is empty except for me and one other tenant."

With that encouragement, they rolled onto their sides and he slid his hand along the incline of her body. David wasn't in a hurry; he was excessive in the thoroughness of pleasuring her. With the skilled hands of a surgeon, his fingers journeyed lower and exerted subtle, gentle pressure, causing Carlie to break apart from their kiss and gasp. Her back arched, and her hands wound into his hair. His thumb rotated slowly, his fingers inching simultaneously inside her until her breath was coming in short gasps and she was begging him for release.

He rolled on top of her and entered her quickly with a firm stroke. Carlie's voice ripped through the apartment in a mixture between a hard cry and a gasp. Her fingers dug into his shoulder, and she enjoyed the flexibility that one leg around him afforded her. She moved against him, enjoying the sensation of his thrusts. David lowered his head to her neck tenderly, the contradiction of his thrusting and his kisses overwhelming her.

She fought against the release that was so close she could almost touch it. "David," she moaned, "oh, God. Please."

Still inside her, he sat up and wrapped her legs around his waist. The sudden change in position shifted him deeper inside her and Carlie cried out. David's hand on her back pressed them against each other tightly and he coaxed her, "Move your hips forward." He took a shallow breath, beads of perspiration having formed on his chest. "Now," he said, and lifted her up gently by her bottom, "use your legs…and…" he set her bottom down on him; hard. Her cry echoed through the empty apartment.

Carlie needed no further encouragement. Bracing her hands against his chest, she moved against him with fervor, his hands around her waist – lifting and pressing her down on top of him, moving both of them towards climax. Unable to maintain control any longer, David set her down hard on top of him until they climaxed in unison.

CHAPTER NINETEEN

Four days after Bradford died, they left Los Angeles. Between Jazz, Ano, her mother, and the money Bradford had left, they were able to pay passage to New Orleans for the five of them, Lively included. The first two legs of the journey weren't bad. In fact, Ano was occupied writing a long letter to Kate until they left California.

"What're you tellin' her?" Jazz asked, peeking over to the letter that Ano discreetly covered with her hand.

She smiled and raised an eyebrow to Jazz. "*Everything.*"

He laughed at this, mainly because it did no good to argue with Ano, and secondly, she was in such a good mood since they had found both her mother and grandmother that he happily played along.

Jazz liked Ano's mother Michelle. Protective where her daughter was concerned, she wasn't about to let Jazz in until she was satisfied that he wasn't going to hurt her. All of her teasing and testing was good natured, and Jazz took all of the ribbing well.

By the forth bus ride, somewhere in the middle of New Mexico, Lively began to grate on everyone's nerves and had to be separated from Grandma Vesper, who had threatened to relocate parts of her anatomy if she didn't pipe down. Ano's mother and grandmother were sniping at each other for close to two hours, and by the time they changed buses in El Paso, Ano was ready to *walk* the rest of the way to New Orleans, as long as it was in silence.

Jazz found her leaned against some lockers, standing in the shade while the bus refueled. "Hey."

She tried to smile, but it came out looking pained. "So help me, God..." she began and he held up a hand in acknowledgement of the problems. "If Lively wasn't an old woman?"

Jazz laughed and nodded. "A'right?" He laughed and they were quiet for a moment. "It'll get better." He rubbed his hands on her upper arms. "She's gonna fall asleep pretty soon. She always does 'round this time."

"If she doesn't, Grandma's gonna put her lights out. Permanently!" They both laughed for a minute. "Hey," she began, "I wanna ask you something. You don't have to answer me if you don't want to."

Jazz looked down at her, a hot breeze blowing against them. "What's up?"

She looked out across the street at the city that appeared almost normal, completely untouched by the events of months past. Cars drove by, the sound of ambulances sounded in the distance. Life, as a whole, seemed normal here.

"Do you *want* to live in New Orleans?"

Jazz didn't say anything. His eyes scanned the bus depot and he pressed his lips together.

"Jazz?"

"No."

"Then why didn't you say anything?" she asked, exasperated with him.

He shrugged. "Because! I knew you wanted to be with your mom and your grandma! Because I don't have any family and..."

She grabbed the front of his shirt and pulled him to her. "What?"

He leaned in, enjoying the closeness of her. "Because," he finished, "I wanna be wherever you are." He smirked. "Even if that means New Orleans is where I hang my hat."

She traced a finger around the features of his face and he closed his eyes. "You are a handsome man, Jazz Taylor."

"Mmmmhmm."

She almost added something, then thought better of it. Her heart, where men were concerned, often got ahead of itself. Something Kate reminded her of constantly. Unfortunately, she was right. Where Jazz was concerned, she had no self-control. That also meant there was a greater potential for hurt if it didn't work out. Jazz was the man that all women want; the one who would hold your bag while you tried on shoes without looking like a tool, the one who would look so good in a suit at a party that all your single girls would be next to him just to get a good look, and the one who would rub your feet after a hard day and listen to you without criticizing. Yes, Jazz was the perfect man.

He opened his eyes and caught her looking at him. "What are you thinking about?"

She laughed, low and throaty. "Nothing."

He leaned in and kissed her lightly. "You're angry because I didn't want to live in Louisiana."

She pulled away. "No! No, I don't wanna live there either. I'm..." she stared off into the distance. "I don't know where to go now, and...it makes me anxious."

"Makes me anxious too. How'm I going to make a living? How'm I going to go from being a lawyer, you know, the only thing I've done for two years, to *seminary*."

Ano leaned in to kiss him again. "I don't know." Thinking seriously about what he'd said, she asked, "How long is Seminary school?"

"'Bout the same as a Masters. Two years." She touched the tops of his ears and he squirmed, grabbed her finger playfully. "Quit, now."

"Do you know any grad schools that offer that as a concentration?"

"The one my dad went to is in Louisville."

"*Kentucky?*"

He nodded. "Southern Baptist Theological Seminary."

Ano's features tightened, as they always did when she was concentrating hard on something. "How far is Kentucky from New Orleans?"

"About seven...maybe eight hundred miles. Long way, baby."

Jazz hadn't learned yet that Ano was a formidable force once she got under way. Her brows furrowed again and he touched them with his finger. She smiled up at him.

"We could do it," she said hesitantly. "If you still want it."

"What d'you mean, '*if I still want it*'?"

"You've been planning your whole life to be a lawyer. Working for two years to finish law school. Corporate law. Right?"

"Right."

"Look," she said, tucking a long strand of hair behind her ear, I just don't want you to look back ten years from now, and regret, you know, not doing it."

Jazz half smiled at her, then turned and looked out over the city. "It seems normal *here*," he said, "but it's a different world *out there*." He waited for Ano to say something, but she didn't. "When I was at Stanford, I knew what I wanted, y'understand? I knew who I was. What was expected of me." He hit his fist in his hand with each point, as if to drive it home.

"And you don't now?" Ano asked.

He turned to her, his face serious. "I love the law," he said. "Love it. Love hearing about it. Love studying it. But," he smoothed his thumb over her cheek. "I just don't see the need anymore. Corporate law. It's like...what's the point, y'know?"

Ano nodded, but wasn't quite convinced. "Jazz, the country will recover. It won't always be what we see today."

"I know that."

"I don't want you to give up on a law degree if that's what's going to make you happy."

He pressed his lips together for a minute and closed his eyes. When he opened them, she was staring at him, waiting for him to finish. "What I see now, making a difference in people's *lives*," he said with meaning, "is being a man who can guide them. A man who can show them that we are not abandoned. I could stay in corporate law and take the bar. Then get a job with a firm that will be so knee deep in litigation over what's happened in this country that I'll be filing pre-emptive motions till the cows come home." She giggled and he touched the side of her lips with his index finger. "But I won't be home to go to block parties with you, or take you out to dinner on your birthday. I won't see our baby take her first step, or see her first tooth come in. I'll be working to tear things down. I don't think this country needs more tearing down."

Ano had tears in her eyes. She understood.

"It's easier to decide this now at twenty-three than at forty-three when we have four kids and a mortgage."

She wiped her eyes with the back of her hand and laughed out loud at him. "You're crazy talking...four kids my...*four* kids? I'm not gonna...FOUR?"

Jazz held his hands up in mock surrender. "Or three."

"*One*. Maybe."

He leaned down and kissed the top of her nose. "Two, and you agree to be open regarding discussions for more."

Ano wrapped her arms around his neck and fairly purred in his ear, "Practice makes perfect, counsel. I'll agree to *practice* making more."

Jazz kissed her hungrily, and wrapped his arms around her trim waist. "I know it was only a week, but if I had to go one more minute not being able to touch you at night..." he sighed heavily, "...I was about to go out of my damned mind."

Her throaty laugh made him smile and she nibbled the tender lobe of his ear. "Kind of makes me hungry for that bed in Carlie's uncle's house."

He found the tender spot on her neck that she loved for him to kiss and he paused there, making her wait. "Or the shower..." he pushed against her gently, biting the part of her neck that drove her insane.

"If you're in the seminary, will we have to stop...you know..."

He grinned mischievously. "I was *conceived* while my dad was in seminary school."

"Okay, but...." Ano pushed against his chest when he leaned in to steal a kiss, "your parents were married."

He shrugged. "So? We'll get married."

His ears would ring for a full twenty-four hours for the yell that erupted in his ear.

"*What*?" Ano screeched. "You do *not* just say it like that to a woman! Boy, have you lost your mind?"

"What did I say? What, you don't want to get married?"

"It isn't that I don't want to get *married*, it's that I want to get *married*."

Now it was Jazz's turn to be confused. "I thought...that's what I just..."

"No. Married. With a church, and bridesmaids, and a cake and a huge dress and flowers, with the candelabras and—"

"Woman do you know how much this is gonna cost?"

"I do not want to get married for the sake of convenience, or because it's easier for you in seminary school to be married as opposed to 'dating'."

"I didn't—"

"Eht!" she held up her slender index finger to him. "I want to get married in front of my family and..." she stopped before she said *friends*, realizing that most of the friends she'd had were now more than likely dead.

Ano lowered her head and he tipped it up by her chin.

"If you want a big church wedding and the dress..."

She looked timidly at him. "You know how weird it is to be talking about marriage with a man I only met three months ago?"

Jazz smiled widely, and Ano fell in love with him all over again. "Yeah, I do. Been thinking the same thing, myself." He looked out over the shimmering El Paso heat, and then back to her. "But here I am."

Ano looked up at him; his solid, six foot frame against her lithe five nine. "Once we get settled we can check into seminary school."

"Maybe see if there's anywhere close that offers a Masters in Psychology."

Ano grinned. "That would be good."

He pinned her against the lockers as they heard first call from the bus driver, and he entwined his fingers through hers. It took all her self-control to not wrap her legs around him right there at the bus station.

"We better go," he said, and kissed her deeply.

"Mmmhmm," she said, kissing him back. "Yeah."

"On the next damned bus for seven hours with the damned *Love Boat!*" Lively said right next to them, and Jazz nearly dropped Ano with the shock of seeing Lively's face that close to theirs.

Ano had to physically bar his way to get to her and Lively shook her head, shuffling away from them. Jazz' jaw was tight and he pointed to her, his mouth set in a hard line. "That...!"

Ano held a hand up to him to silence him. They heard Lively mutter something about filth as she shuffled down to the bus. "I know, but she's an old woman."

"She's not going to get any older if she keeps doin' that!"

Ano muffled a smile with her hand.

"I was about to do the world a favor!"

"Now you know we couldn't leave her in L.A."

"Girl, she would have been in *no danger!*" He bit his lip, swallowing his anger. "That woman is the most unpleasant, foul, irritating—"

"Give me one more kiss to last the next seven hours."

Jazz leaned against her, opening his mouth against hers. He lifted her up slightly, his hands nearly spanning her waist, and she gasped his name.

"You keep doin' that and we're gonna find out if the walls in the bathroom on that bus really are soundproof," he warned.

Before he could get a second kiss, Michelle and Grandma Vesper rounded the corner. "There they are, c'mon you two!" Michelle called. "Where you guys been? Ugh, Lively wanted to find this...hey, Ano, what's wrong?"

Ano tucked a strand of long hair behind her ear. "Nothing."

"She jus' tired, is all." Grandma Vesper patted her on the back and looked to Jazz. "I take this young man and he set next to me some o' the way!"

Jazz eyes filled with fear at the thought of being stuck with Grandma Vesper for seven hours, listening to story after story and acting interested instead of sleeping. Ano saw his expression and patted her grandmother on the back.

"It's all right Grandma, I'd rather you sit with me. I can tell you more about the cave."

She fell into step with Grandma Vesper and Jazz walked by Ano's mother back to where the bus waited. Lively's voice could already be heard – from all the way at the bottom of the bus steps. Ano grabbed the handle to climb aboard the bus but then she spun around, causing Jazz to catch her in his arms.

"You better get some protein when we stop next time," she warned him softly in his ear.

"Yeah?" he asked, and grinned. "Why?"

"It's a long time until seminary."

CHAPTER TWENTY

"Percy, for goodness sake, sit down," his grandmother admonished, and Percy sat at the chair directly opposite of her. "Edgar," she said with a softer tone, "go and fetch me the post."

Edgar left to go down to the large mailbox at the street.

Percy drummed his long fingers on the table while he waited. His grandmother looked over to his hand, then back to the game of backgammon she and Edgar had engaged in prior to the interruption for the mail.

"We could simply dispense with the formality of having Edgar go get it and let you sit, street side, until the post is delivered each day." She said it without looking at him, and he turned his face away in case his cheeks flushed; a trait relating to the red hair that he particularly hated. The only benefit was that, as he grew older, his hair became darker brown and less red. The horrid occasional blushing remained.

Edgar came through the door, letters in hand. His grandmother held her hand out to take them, and it took nearly all of Percy's self-control not to snatch them from her.

"Edgar, I do believe it's your turn, dear."

She set the letters in her lap and watched Edgar roll, clapping animatedly as he did so. "Good for you," she said, and he slid five of his chips back into the home position.

Knowing she would draw this out as long as possible, if nothing more than to have Percy down in the main living portion of the house rather than his room – where he spent most of his time lately – Percy coughed gently into his hand and interrupted the game. "May I look at the mail? To see if I've received anything?"

"Gigi," Edgar prodded, knowing it was torturing his brother to have to wait, "your turn."

Their grandmother smiled at him. "I know it is. Just a moment, dearest."

She retrieved the letters from her lap, flipped through them, and returned them to her lap. "Edgar, go and ask Sasha to fix us tea early this afternoon, will you?"

He rolled his eyes but obeyed, and left the large room with the awkwardness of a boy who hasn't quite realized his body had left boyhood behind. Percy's grandmother patted the edge of Edgar's seat and waited while Percy moved to take his brother's place.

"From whom are you expecting a letter?" she asked, not looking up at him immediately.

He cleared his throat. "A friend. A friend who has information for me on someone I was with down in the cave."

"Is this the reason for the shortness with Edgar...and myself?"

Percy regarded his grandmother carefully. At eighty, she was still a force to be reckoned with. Perfectly coiffed even in these times, her chin length white hair was never out of place. Her clothes always seemed to Percy to look as though she'd just had them pressed and cleaned seconds before you'd seen her. Her skills of observation after raising five boys were nothing less than clairvoyant.

"I'm sorry, and...it is."

She looked directly up at him. "What are you waiting here for?" she asked.

Percy looked at his hands. "I wanted to make sure Edgar is—"

"Edgar will be fine. It's nearly September, and Avon starts up again after Labor Day."

"Then I will keep my promise to him and stay until then, and escort him back to Avon."

"I offered to get him into Hill, here in Pennsylvania."

Percy sighed. "He wants to go back. I understand it's familiar to him. He's a sophomore, his friends are still there. Might...all still be there."

"We're lucky Avon is still open."

"I know," Percy agreed.

His grandmother didn't press the issue, but rubbed her hands together as she did when she was thinking about something. She'd lost another son; out of her five boys, three had died. Out of five grandsons, she had only two left. And both were leaving her in a few weeks. Percy wished he could convince Edgar to stay, but how could he when, if in the same position as Edgar, he would make the same decision?

"Where will you go?" Her voice trembled, and Percy wondered if it was age or emotion that made it do so.

Resolve made, he raised his head and addressed his grandmother clearly. "Virginia."

"And, if you should get a letter? What then?"

He couldn't very well snatch the letters from her lap, but it was twisting his insides to not know if she had any information for him. "I suppose," he said calmly, "that it would depend on what information that letter provided me."

Gigi sat back in her chair, which is to say that she tipped slightly; as long as he'd known his grandmother, her back had never rested against a chair. Ever. She considered it poor manners and extremely bad posture. Many summers of teaching – and firm reprimands - had ingrained that in his brain. "What's her name?"

Percy's brows came together. "The friend that I'm expecting the letter from?"

"No. The young lady that has you so in knots."

"I'm not in knots."

"Then may I ask why your fists are clenched and you've looked to the letters in my lap three times since we began this conversation?"

Percy unclenched his hands and smoothed the legs of his pants. He debated on telling his grandmother anything. Before this they hadn't spoken since Christmas of last year, and even then it had been a kiss on the cheek and normal pleasantries. She was elderly, and had no knowledge of—

"Camilla and I often wondered when you'd finally fall in love," Gigi said. "She used to worry about you so. Used to wish you'd come home telling her you'd failed a class at Stanford because of a girl. We used to wish you'd spent more time chasing women into bed than into study hall."

Percy's mouth hung open and he shut it with a snap. "You and my mother used to talk about—"

A twinkle sparkled in her eyes. "I wasn't always seventy-nine," she said with a wink, and Percy actually smiled back. "What is her name, please?"

Percy sighed. He was going to have to admit it, out loud. "Kate."

Her eyebrows went up. "Just Kate?"

"Kate Moore."

"Strong name. Good family?"

Percy massaged his temples with his hand. "She's...she has no family, Gigi." He took a chance using her given name, as Edgar did, and it didn't seem to offend her.

She was quiet for a moment, studying Percy carefully. "Is she in trouble, this Kate?"

"I don't know."

"I see." Her aged fingers moved the heavy backgammon pieces around for a few moments.

Percy simply couldn't take it anymore. "Grandmother, please," he implored and she looked through the letters in her lap.

"There are none from any *Kate*," she said, "but here is one addressed to you." She handed him a letter from the bottom of the stack from her lap. He stood immediately, pausing to kiss her on the cheek before nearly sprinting to the stairs. "Percy," she called, and he halted mid-step.

"Yes?"

She turned towards him and smiled slightly. "If you'd like, invite this friend of yours, this *Kate* to come. You could stay a while. I'd like the company very much."

He returned the smile and nodded. "Yes ma'am." Once in his room, he tore the letter open, nearly shredding the envelope in his haste to do so. The one page letter was written neatly, and in small print.

> Percy,
>
> I was so pleased to get your letter. I am glad you found your brother and so sorry to hear the news of your parents and other siblings. Charlie and I think of you often and pray for you every night. As for Kate's address, I have it, but by the time you receive this I'm afraid it will do you no good.
>
> Matt's mother was found in an altered state, and they must move her to a care or home hospital within the next two weeks, according to Kate's last letter. As soon as I hear from her again and receive a good address I will forward it to you in Philadelphia.
>
> Be well,
>
> Carrie
>
> P.S. Although you didn't ask in your letter, I know that Kate wonders how you are...and thinks of you often.

Percy read the letter no fewer than five times before folding it back up and tucking it into his shirt pocket. Kate would be leaving California, or had already, with Matt and his mother. He pulled the scraps of envelope from the ground and searched for the postmark. The letter had taken three weeks to get to him. Kate was clearly still with Matt. He was wasting his time. Carrie had said she thought of him often. Kate would never say that. Even if it was true, which he wouldn't consider right now, that was something personal that Kate wouldn't have told anyone. Not even him, most likely.

He had delayed going to Virginia for nearly five weeks hoping to get word back about Kate, and in the end was simply fooling himself. He walked to his bed, pulled his old, familiar backpack out from under it. He knelt there for a moment, considering his options. Logically, there was nothing else to do. He wasn't the type of man who would continue to care for a woman who showed no interest in him. He walked to his dresser and removed the new clothes that he'd purchased since arriving at Gigi's and threw them onto the open backpack.

When three drawers had been entirely emptied, he reached down to lift the backpack onto the bed. As soon as he lifted, it was as if a knife had been thrust into his abdomen and a scream tore from his chest. He dropped the backpack onto the floor and fell to his knees. His hand pressed against the old wound on his abdomen, which hurt nearly as bad as it had when it had happened in Wind Cave. Beads of sweat formed on his forehead and upper lip as he struggled to sit up. Unable to do so, he tried to crawl to the door of his bedroom. Thankfully, footsteps sounded on the stairs and Edgar burst into his room, followed by Gigi. The room was spinning and he felt nauseous, as if he would vomit.

"Percy!" Gigi was on her knees at his side, yelling for Edgar to call Phillip immediately. "Is it that spot again? The one that's been hurting you?"

Percy nodded, unable to speak.

Phillip ran into the room and Gigi ordered him to pull the car around.

"We're going to go to the hospital," she said as calmly as she could and Percy shook his head vehemently, afraid if he opened his mouth to speak he would throw up. He gritted his teeth against the pain that was ripping through the lower half of his body.

Edgar's face was white with fear. "Percy?"

Gigi hushed him from the floor. "We're taking Percy to the hospital, and he's going to be fine." Her voice was strong, but her eyes were filled with the fear of losing another grandchild, this time right in front of her eyes.

Phillip returned to scoop Percy up off the floor. His hand grazed Percy's hipbone and Percy let out a scream once again. Pushing Phillip away he collapsed on the floor, breathing hard.

"Oh God..." he gasped, holding his side and dripping sweat. "It hurts so badly."

More carefully, Phillip leaned down and picked Percy up, struggled down the stairs under the weight of him, and deposited him into the back seat of the car. Gigi and Edgar were close behind him, following down the steps. Sliding Percy's head into her lap, Gigi directed Phillip, "I don't care how you get us there, just *go*!"

The BMW left the circular drive and accelerated. Gigi stroked Percy's face. Within moments, Percy surrendered to the blackness and passed out.

Chapter Twenty-One

"As I said, all of you will be accompanying one attending on rounds tonight, for one twelve hour shift as part of your classroom training." Dr. Unger looked at the group of them as if he was cross. "You will complete one shift for every four weeks of classroom training. You will not speak unless asked. You will not sit unless told to. You will not talk to the patients or give any indication that you exist unless I tell you. Is that clear?"

A chorus of *yeses* was heard from the group of twelve med students that had been given this hospital as their assignment. There were three other hospitals involved, and Kate's classmates had been divided into thirds for their first foray into an actual hospital environment.

Dr. Unger looked to be about fifty, with a large, round, bald head and a mustache that made his upper lip nearly disappear. Shaking his head at the group, he led them down to the ER, and all of them followed obediently behind him.

He slid open one curtain and they all crowded into one corner of the small area. Dr. Unger handed a chart to Kyle, who stood next to Kate in the new white doctor's coats that they'd all been issued tonight before coming.

"Kyle, what symptoms did Mrs. Rodriguez present with?"

Kyle's hand shook as he read the chart notes and quickly summarized the symptoms. He looked up at Dr. Unger and handed him back the chart.

"From these symptoms, what tests should we use to diagnose the problem?"

From around him, three people began to speak. His eyes snapped up and they were all immediately silent until he called on one of them. "Tate."

"Blood panel, ECG, and chest x-ray."

Dr. Unger nodded and looked at the rest of them. "And if those scans yield nothing? Hmmmm? Then what?"

No one spoke. "You. Jennifer."

"Janet."

"Whatever."

"Um..." she stood, silent for a moment, thinking, and Dr. Unger crossed his arms over his chest.

"Your patient is dying, Miss, while you stand around and say, 'Um'." He turned to me. "Kate, if those tests yield nothing. Then what?"

We were all silent for a few moments. "You've been studying the heart for the last week, people!"

I lifted my chin. "Run another blood panel with different parameters."

He nodded and turned away from me slightly. "To test for what?"

"To test the Creatine Kinase fraction, and the Troponin levels."

Dr. Unger put the chart back into the slot at the foot of the patient's bed and looked at Tye, who was the tallest and also the quietest in our group. "And if those levels are increased, Tom, what is that indicative of, and what course of treatment would you recommend?"

"It's Tye, sir."

Dr. Unger's eyes narrowed.

"It...is indicative of myocardial infarction, and I'd recommend a course of medications to dissolve any blockage that had formed." He hastened to add, "After I'd confirmed the blockage through a dye test."

For the next four hours, Dr. Unger led us all through the halls of the ER, and then into the trauma center. Philadelphia, unlike many cities, actually had ambulance service; one of the reasons we were getting this unusual glimpse this early in our classroom training. Some of my classmates had been at this longer than I had; and I was lucky to have joined the Penn State program at all.

Dr. Unger pulled aside another curtain where we stood back and watched a trauma team triage the young man on the table. I gasped and covered my mouth with my hand.

"Incisional hernia," one of the female doctors said above the noise on the monitors. "Possible strangulation of the large intestine. Get me an ultrasound machine in here! Curtain three!"

I began to shake. "The stitches didn't hold."

"I'm sorry, Kate, did you speak?"

I nodded mutely and took three steps forward into the room into the path of the doctor who was calling for the ultrasound machine. "He had stitches. In his lower right abdomen. Nine internal and..." I trembled at the sight of him unconscious on the table, "twenty external."

Dr. Unger's voice was loud right beside me. "And how do you know that?"

"Because," I fairly whispered, "I helped put them there."

The last four hours of my shift felt like an eternity, only made easier by the fact that I knew Percy was in surgery for a portion of that, and working in the ER I was able to determine when he was out of the OR and in recovery. Once released, I nearly ran to his room on the fourth floor. It meant I would miss the bus going back to the dormitory, but I was happy to spend the precious money on an actual cab to go back later tonight.

It hadn't occurred to me entering his room that there might be people with him. I had to check myself when I saw an elderly woman and a young man standing at his bedside. I stopped, then turned to look at Percy lying in bed, eyes closed, still sleeping off the effects of the surgery. Hesitantly, I straightened and smoothed my white coat down as I walked into his room and over to the bedside.

"Doctor," the older woman addressed me, "would you see if there is a nurse that can check my grandson's IV? It's causing him some pain."

His voice croaked out, but it was getting stronger. And so unmistakably his. "It's fine, Gigi."

Percy's eyes fluttered open and he shook his head slightly, as if his eyes were playing a trick on him. I could barely trust my ability to say his name without smiling. He was alive. And in front of me.

"Hey, Percy."

His hand, attached to an IV, went to his head and then down to touch his incision. "I'm...you're not...you look so much like..."

I smiled, my stomach doing somersaults. "I'm part of the accelerated medical program at Penn State. For about three weeks now."

"Three weeks." I could tell he was still groggy, and he moved his wrist the wrong direction and winced.

I reached up, lowered his arm for him and checked the IV on the back of his hand. Placing two fingers on his neck, I took his pulse. He was quiet for a moment, but reached his hand up to touch mine.

"Kate." He laced his fingers through mine, an incredibly intimate touch for us.

"I can get a nurse for you, if the IV hurts your hand," I offered, but he said nothing.

"You're...here..." he said again, as if worried he was in some kind of anesthesia induced hallucination.

I nodded, still not trusting myself to smooth his hair off his forehead as I so wanted to do. His eyes closed again, as he mumbled something about Carrie being wrong. I looked up to the woman I now knew to be his grandmother and the young man who in all likelihood was Edgar.

Reluctantly, I pulled my hand from Percy's. I had no idea what I should say to them. I reminded myself silently that I did not have such a great track record at meeting families, and winced at the memory.

Percy's grandmother was the first to speak. "I'm Gigi Warner." She turned to the young man at her elbow, who looked exactly like Percy, only younger and with more freckles. "And this is Edgar, Percy's youngest brother." She paused, her face not at all unkind, and extended her hand to me.

"Kate Moore," I said, accepting her hand with a nod.

"Did you operate on my brother?" Edgar asked me.

"No, I didn't. I'm not..." I glanced curiously at Gigi to see how she reacted to what I was saying. "...exactly a doctor yet. I'm a med student."

"Did they let you watch?"

I couldn't help myself from smiling. This is what Percy looked like as a teenager? I had the oddest urge to laugh.

"Will he be okay?"

"Yes. I talked with Doctor Wagner downstairs," I told Edgar. "Your brother is going to be just fine."

"How do you know my grandson?" His grandmother's expression was a mixture of curiosity and anticipation, as if she'd just solved a puzzle or found something wonderful. Her hair was a lovely white-silver and was bluntly cut right at the chin. From the size of the diamonds that glinted from her hands and her ears, I'd say she was likely from high society. Like Matt's family. Instantly, I felt strangulated.

"We were in the cave together. I was helping him with research on...well, research." My heart began to race and I struggled to slow my breathing.

"You were in the cave with him. When the attacks happened."

My heart was going to explode it was beating so hard. My mouth felt as though it was filled with cotton. "Yes. That's correct." *Breathe slower, I reminded myself silently.*

She looked from her grandson to my face curiously. "And you've been here since then?"

I struggled to get enough air. "I'm...no. I had to help a friend find his mother."

"Did you find her?"

Pain squeezed my heart at the thought of Matt, but I nodded. "Yes. We did."

"Did you go to Stanford with Percy?" Edgar asked.

"Um, yes. I did. We went to Stanford together."

His grandmother put her hand to her heart. "Have you been back?"

"Yes. I have."

Edgar's face showed awe, whereas Gigi's showed only concern. "How was it?"

I remembered going to Stanford with Matt, spending the day with him, holding hands with him walking across what used to be the path to the bookstore. I remembered all of this, and wished there was something I could put in my heart that would wipe away the memories as easily as the bombs had wiped away my world.

"I found it...much altered." My heart was still pounding and I was sure everyone could hear it. It sounded so loud to me.

She nodded silently, and Edgar looked from her face to mine without speaking. His face, I thought, was so much like Percy's it was frightening. Same straight nose, same strong chin. But missing the intense look Percy always seemed to wear. Edgar's face looked so young. And yet, like everyone nowadays, his face showed sadness.

"So you've been here for three weeks?" Percy's grandmother— Gigi, she'd said— asked.

"Yes." A bead of sweat trickled down my back and I knew I had to get out of here. Quickly.

"For medical school?"

"That's the plan, yes."

"How long is the program?"

My throat was dry and my tongue felt like cotton. "Normally I'd do classroom work for two years and clinical rotation for two, but given the circumstances they've condensed it down into a three year, instead of a four year program."

"I see."

I took a step backwards. "I should get back," I said lamely. "It was nice to meet you both."

"And you, dear."

"I have to..." I pointed my thumb towards the door, "...to go. It was nice to meet both of you."

As I turned to flee, I heard Percy's grandmother ask, "We will see you again, won't we?" She motioned down to Percy, who still lay in bed, asleep. "He's admitted through Sunday, they said. I know he'll want to talk with you more."

"Yes. Tomorrow I have classes until seven, but..." I glanced at Percy's face; the face I'd seen in my mind hundreds of times since that day in Denver, "I'll come back before he's discharged."

I turned and fled, not stopping until I'd reached the grass in front of the hospital, taking in large gulps of air as if I'd been running a marathon. I bent over, hands rested against my knees, and concentrated on slowing my heart rate. When I could breathe again, I wiped the sweat from my forehead and stood up straight, walking in circles until the beats of my heart didn't feel like a hammer in my chest.

Finally able to take a breath without pain, I looked back up to the granite side of the hospital where, four floors up, Percy lay in a hospital bed...waiting.

CHAPTER TWENTY-TWO

Carrie walked back into the house with the mail and wiped her hands on a dishtowel before taking it to the kitchen table to read. Her letters from Kate were something she looked forward to each week, although it had been several weeks since she'd gotten one.

Her smile faded, however, as she read the letter. Tears formed in her eyes by the end of the first page. She wiped the tears from her cheeks as she read Kate's words, shaking her head sadly. She sat, looking around the kitchen. She folded the letter back into its envelope and, having no other way to cope, Carrie sat and had a good cry.

She turned back to the counter and set to making a chicken pot pie for supper. She'd shelled peas this morning, and had plenty of carrots. After she'd slid the pie into the oven, she looked around, her hands literally itching. She pulled out the flour and began making homemade bread. She mixed it in her large yellow bowl, the one with a chip in the side, with a vengeance. Kneading it, she pounded it with her fist, hard. The back screen door slammed and Charlie walked in with a part to one of the tractors in his hand.

"I'm gonna need to go into town tomorrow. See if Hillson's can even get this for me anymore. It's been a..." he stopped dead as he watched her pounding the mound of bread. "That bread attack somebody?"

"No."

"Well," he said, and scratched his head for a moment. "It's gonna press charges."

"Just making supper."

Charlie normally wasn't a man who messed with a woman when she was emotional. Truth be told, he'd rather be run over with his own tractor than endure a 'heartfelt discussion' or watch Carrie shed a tear. However, her face told a story that her voice just couldn't, and he set the tractor part down on the table and crossed the kitchen to take her in his arms.

"Hey now," he said softly, in the voice that rumbled in his chest. Carrie leaned up against him. "What's got all this goin' on? One of the boys?"

She wiped her eyes with her hand. "No."

Charlie sighed. "Kate?"

Carrie nodded and let out a little sob.

"She okay?"

She shook her head and Charlie sighed. At this rate, it would take all night.

"She left California." Carrie wiped her face with the damp dishcloth and sniffled. "Because she heard Matt and his brothers talkin' about her in the kitchen."

"All right."

She took a shuddering breath. "She heard him say...he said..." and again she took a shuddering breath, "that he was going to get rid of her. Leave her there. Alone. That he was going off to find someone else, someone suitable. Someone *better*."

He blew out a breath in a whistle and pushed the straw hat back on his head. Carrie leaned against the counter and crossed her arms over her chest. Her face became stern, like it used to when one of the boys tromped through the house with muddy boots.

"He has no idea!" She sniffed loudly, her nose stuffed up from all the crying. "No idea how bad he hurt her by..." She turned around to the raw bread dough lying on the counter and gave it a thump with her fist, "...by what he did. *No idea.*"

Charlie was always a rational man. It was one of the things she loved about him. Unfortunately, he was also *a man*. Since she had no other women close by she could talk to, Charlie had to listen. After thirty years, he was really good at listening.

"I'm sure that Kate's gonna do fine," he said soothingly. "Maybe she didn't hear him right." Carrie turned to him with a stricken look on her face and Charlie held up his hands in mock surrender. "All right, I don't know what happened." He wrapped his arms around her waist and rested his chin on her shoulder. "She's a strong girl."

"She's strong 'cause she's had to be!" She pointed, as if Matt was standing right outside. "'Cause of people like *him* that hurt her and make her feel like she idn't good enough for the likes of him." She pounded the bread with her fist once again.

Charlie was a smart man. Smart enough to know when a woman needed time to work things out. *This* was one of those times.

"Okay. Well, I'm gonna get back out to the fields. Got those boys working hard. I could use another set of hands. We'll be ready for winter wheat."

Carrie nodded, but didn't say anything for a minute, and Charlie turned to go. "I just wish..." she said, her back still to him, "that she was here. That she'd come back. I'd take care of her."

Charlie exhaled. So this is what it boiled down to. Carrie was lonely. And someone had hurt a child that Carrie had clearly fallen in love with. He nodded, finally understanding. "Well, write her a letter. Ask her to come."

Carrie stopped kneading. "There's no room for her. This house is mighty small." "Once the crop comes in, we'll be able to ask most any price we want for it and get it, I 'spect. So we could build her a little house. Near ours." He paused. "If you want. Till then she could stay in the cottage."

Carrie turned and fairly jumped into his arms. He hugged her hard and then set her on the floor. "Don't know what there is for her back here," he said. "She was doin' something in science, wasn't she?"

Carrie nodded, a smile now on her face. "Yes, but she's on her way to Philadelphia now, she said. To go to med school."

"How long ago was that?"

Carrie flipped her letter over. "Three weeks."

"Nothin' like that out here."

"I know, but she's only doing it cause Matt hurt her. And she's searching for something that'll keep her so busy she won't notice how bad it hurts."

Charlie sighed. "She's there by now. Wait another week or so. You'll get another letter with a good address in Philly."

Carrie stopped. "Philadelphia." Carrie turned to Charlie, her hand out. "Oh my Lord."

"What?"

"She's in *Philadelphia*."

Charlie shrugged. "And?"

Carrie laughed out loud. "Well, I'll be damned."

Charlie leaned against the counter. From behind him, the phone rang.

"Now, who the hell is calling us?" Charlie reached back and pulled the receiver from the hook. "Yeah, hello?"

Charlie made a few 'uh-huh's' and then nodded once. "I'll be there in about an hour. You just *stay put*." He hung up the phone and looked at his wife.

"Well?" Carrie asked. "Who was it?"

Charlie crossed the kitchen and picked up the part to his tractor from the table, and the keys that hung from a hook on the wall. "I'll be gone the better part of two hours. But I'll be back."

"Charlie Blackhawk, you come back here and tell me who called!" But Charlie was halfway down the drive as she stood at the front door and called after him, "What about supper?"

"Keep it warm, I'll be hungry when I get back!" he called and drove quickly down the long drive that led to their house.

Carrie stood on the porch, hands on hips, wondering who in the world could have called. Walking back in towards the kitchen, she leaned against the counter and stared out over the field, wishing Kate was there.

Nearly three hours later, Charlie pulled the truck down the long drive that led to his house. He drove slowly, prolonging the inevitable. "I'm saying she's not gonna take this well. From you or from me," he said to his passenger.

"I know."

The house was in sight, and he took his foot completely off the gas and let the truck roll into its spot. The lights were on, and he could tell the boys had packed in the tools from the field and gone home for the night. "I'm not even sure if she'll let you stay."

"I didn't know where else to go."

Charlie waited until the truck coasted to a stop, then shifted it into park. "All right, best to get it over with, then."

They both got out of the truck and walked up to the front porch. Carrie, anxiously awaiting Charlie's return, opened the screen door to greet him. Her smile faded when Charlie moved to the side, revealing their new houseguest. Her mouth formed a hard line and her brown eyes became stormy. She crossed her arms over her chest.

"Now before you get upset," Charlie began, holding a hand out to her, "you need to listen."

She looked from Charlie to their guest, then back to Charlie. The expression on her face was as cold as stone, proving she had no intention of hearing anyone out tonight. She moved to the side, allowing Charlie to come into the house. "Supper's on the table," she said to him as he passed.

She stepped into their guest's path, barring his way. She stared into his face, her eyes cold, and her voice low and angry. "I'll let you into my house... for *tonight*."

"Thank you."

"Tomorrow you go."

"Yes, ma'am." Matt nodded and swung the pack down from his back when Carrie stepped aside for him to pass.

CHAPTER TWENTY-THREE

They'd spent most of the day in bed, showered together, and then eaten dinner before falling into an exhausted sleep, their legs intertwined under the covers. When Carlie awoke the next morning, it was from the sound of the rain drumming on the window. She rolled over, barely aware of the empty spot in bed next to her. Panic flooded her when she realized it was morning, and likely way past the twelve hours that Dave had allowed her to recuperate. She bolted upright in bed, frantically searching for the alarm clock.

On the nightstand, the digital clock had a piece of paper taped to it, with a note. It read:

Stay in Bed. Relax. I'll be back early.
Doctor's orders.
David

The clock read 9AM. David had gone into the hospital at least two hours ago. She wrestled with her conscience for a few moments before deciding, for once, to heed someone else's advice and actually listen to her body, which was still tired. Sliding her legs to the side of the bed, she stood and walked to the kitchen, her bare feet cold on the hardwood floor in David's apartment. His kitchen cupboards were nearly bare, his fridge emptied of most everything edible last night when they'd made omelets for dinner.

She sighed and felt her stomach rumble. They were going to actually need food if she was going to stay there, even for the rest of the night. The heel to a loaf of wheat bread was wrapped in a plastic bag on the counter and she tore off half, eating it as she walked to his bathroom. For a loft, David's place was huge. It occupied the entire fourth floor of the building, and at one time, might have had a nice view.

Carlie turned on the shower and kicked her clothes into a corner. Her hair had grown long since she'd last cut it, and it took forever to wash. She stepped into the shower and allowed the hot water to wash the remaining stress from her body. David's shampoo smelled wonderful, and she took her time washing herself in the steaming water. When she'd lived with the other residents, her showers were under five minutes and normally tepid, at best. Carlie closed her eyes and sagged against the tile wall, suddenly tired again. Turning off the water and wrapping a towel around herself, her tired legs carried her to the bed. Not even bothering to dry her hair, she pulled the covers over herself and allowed the warmth from the comforter to lull her into a dreamless sleep.

By the time she awoke the second time, the rain had stopped and the clock on David's nightstand read 5:05. She'd slept for another eight hours. Her stomach, cramping slightly, was demanding food. She got up, her hair still damp, and slipped back into her jeans. The only top she'd been wearing when David brought her here was her scrubs, and she couldn't bring herself to put it back on.

Aware that it was likely crossing a boundary, she went to the dresser and found an undershirt and an oversized cashmere sweater and pulled them on, rolling up the sleeves. The sweater was cozy and warm, and Carlie felt more at ease in it than she had in a long time. Luckily, David had brought her bag with her from the hospital, and she flipped it open for cash. Fifty-five dollars. That wasn't going to buy very much, and she would need somewhere to get money. She sighed. Logistical problems filled her head on everything from where to get food to how to lock the front door.

As if by divine intervention, the front door opened and David walked through it, arms full of two bags of groceries. She hopped up from the floor where she'd been examining the contents of her purse to greet him. He closed the door behind him and dead bolted it, sliding the groceries onto the counter as she sidled up next to him.

He smiled at her. "Up and about I see."

She looked at the floor, her feet bare below her jeans. "I just woke up."

His smile reached the corners of his eyes and he touched her nose with his fingertip. "Good." Seeing her in his sweater, he stepped back and nodded. "Looks good on you."

She wrapped her arms around herself. "I took a shower and wanted something to wear besides my scrubs…"

"It's too small for me anyway, and it looks better on you."

Carlie had the urge to kiss him, but didn't know if last night had been kindness, exhaustion, or a combination of the two. Either way, David was unpacking food from the bags and her mouth began to water. His scrubs were still on, and she felt like she should repay him for letting her recuperate all day. She took the block of cheese from his hands, set it on the counter and turned him to face her. She tugged at the drawstring on his surgical pants. "Why don't you go take a hot shower? I'll cook dinner."

"You know how to cook?"

She shrugged. "Among other things."

David smiled at her again. Glad to relinquish the kitchen duties to her – and more likely to take advantage of a hot shower, he nodded and headed towards the master bath, tugging his surgical scrubs over his head.

There was plenty of food in the bags he'd brought, along with a bottle of wine. Carlie cut off pieces of bread and cheese and ate slowly while she fixed dinner for both of them.

An hour later, David emerged from the bathroom, freshly shaven. "You're not going to be hungry for whatever smells so good in the oven."

She finished chewing a piece of bread and nodded. "Yes, I will."

He pulled a long sleeved rugby shirt on over his head and ran a hand through his damp hair. "What's for dinner?"

"Makeshift chicken Kiev, steamed vegetables and the rest of the French bread."

He lifted up the bottle of wine. "You didn't open it?"

"Couldn't find the thingie."

He reached into a cupboard above her and produced a bottle opener, proceeded to uncork the bottle, and poured two generous glasses for them both. From outside, the rain started again, and made soft *tink, tink, tink* sounds against the windows.

Carlie wanted to talk to him about something other than medicine, but was dying to know how his day was. She fidgeted slightly, until finally, he laughed out loud.

"Ask! You're dying to ask, so go on!"

"Alright, how was it today?"

David took a deep drink of his wine and accepted when she offered him a piece of buttered bread. "Went well, actually. Better than yesterday. No collapses, nothing catastrophic."

She nodded, relieved. Had the day been a bad one, she would have felt horribly guilty that she was at home sleeping. "I'm so glad." She sipped her wine for a minute. "Thank you. For today, for everything. I didn't realize how tired I was."

"Thought you'd try and come in."

She bit into another piece of cheese. "Mmm, no, I took a shower this morning and...I swear, I almost didn't make it back to bed I was so tired."

He nodded, his face suddenly grave. "It's a serious thing, Carlie. Nothing to mess with. You exhaust your body and, in the conditions we're in, you're asking for organs to begin to shut down."

The wine warmed her and she nodded her head. "How do you know about the combat fatigue whatever? You said you were a soldier?"

He didn't answer her, but took her hand and led her to the couch, as if it was the most natural thing on Earth. They relaxed into the plush sofa and he pulled her feet into his lap. The rain pelted the window softly and they sat in silence for a few minutes. She closed her eyes and leaned her head back. This was too easy. Too comfortable. She'd never been this way with anyone in her life.

"You never told me the story of where you were. When the blast hit San Fran," he said, and she raised her head to look at him.

"Oh. It's not, you know, that interesting."

"So bore me."

He wasn't going to answer her question about being a soldier. "All right, um, I was in South Dakota. In a cave."

"A cave?"

"Yeah."

"And that's not interesting?"

She laughed. "You weren't there. It was anything *but* interesting."

"Why the hell were *you* there?"

The correct answer was the truth. She'd had a boyfriend at the time and followed him as...an adventure. However, thinking it and saying it were different. "A friend of mine was finishing his thesis, and a group of us went with him."

"How many is 'a group'?"

"Six," she said, taking another drink and pulling his feet to rest in her lap.

"Jesus. How long were you down there?"

She thought for a moment. "Nearly thirty days." She let a beat pass and added, "We didn't know the blast had hit at all. Percy—that's my friend— he's a scientist. He knew radiation readings were higher the closer we got to the surface. So we stayed down there. All of us. Until we ran out of food."

David studied her closely. The room was getting darker and he left the couch to crouch in front of the fireplace and light a fake log on the grate. "Haven't used one of these in about a year and a half, so I'm not sure if it'll light or not." He walked back, lit the candles on the coffee table, and sat back down on the couch with her. "So, you heard about it when you emerged?"

She nodded and sipped her wine. "Where were you?"

"I should have been at the Med Center that day, but I had a patient who was due to deliver any day and she went into labor while she was in Anacortes. I wasn't on rounds that day and I drove up to deliver the baby."

"How far is Anacortes from Seattle?"

"About eighty miles. Far enough to feel the blast, but barely within the nuclear fallout radius of the one that hit Seattle." He paused. "You go back?"

"Where, Stanford?"

He nodded. "Yeah. After you came up from the cave."

"No. No, I...my mom lived in the city. Right...you know, next to the Bay Bridge."

"Jesus."

"Yeah." She played with the edge of his sock, rubbing his foot absentmindedly. "Couldn't do it. I don't know, maybe it's the coward in me."

"You're anything but a coward, Carlie," he said firmly.

"Either way, I didn't go back. She's never identified even though part of me keeps hoping she was, you know, out of the city for the day. Something."

"What did she do?"

"She was an artist," Carlie said, as if it pained her even to say the words out loud. From the kitchen, the oven beeped and they both got up to get dinner.

For a while, the two subjects they didn't want to discuss hung in the air, and dinner was relatively quiet. Never able to contain her curiosity for long, Carlie set her fork down and stared at David for a few seconds before she asked.

"Tell me about when you were a soldier."

Surprisingly, he didn't rebuke her, and he didn't say no. He sighed heavily and poured more wine in each of their glasses. Outside, the light sprinkle had grown into showers. David leaned back in his chair. "I was stupid and eighteen. Joined the Army."

"And?"

"And you're too young to hear it."

Her eyebrows shot up. "Excuse me?"

"You heard me."

"I was hoping you had a momentary embolism and lapse in rational thought." She tipped her head to the side. "How old are *you*?"

He laughed out loud at the question. "Don't you know you're not supposed to ask a man his age?"

"That only applies to women. How. Old. Are. You?"

"I was in med school when you were in...I'm guessing junior high?"

"All right, I'll research the answer myself," she said and stood, crossed quickly to the counter to his wallet lying next to his keys. He tried to snatch it before she got there, but was unsuccessful. She held it up out of his reach as he wound an arm around her waist. "You're thirty-seven." She released the wallet and he pulled her into his lap.

"Which puts me at...I'm guessing fifteen years older than you?"

She made a face and pushed against his chest. "Twelve."

"Ah, twelve, *much* better," he said sarcastically.

"So, you were eighteen," she said as he turned her around in his arms, "and stupid. We've established that."

"Thank you."

Carlie kissed his neck and bit his earlobe. "And then?"

The smile on his face was sad, and it made her stop playing for a minute. "My mother forced my older brother to join. To keep an eye on me."

She covered her mouth with her hand and he nodded. "It was the first Desert Storm. He died. I didn't." He tossed his napkin up on the table, turned his attention back to her. "I didn't re-enlist, I went to med school." His eyes hardened and he turned away from her. "My mom hasn't spoken to me in seventeen years."

"Where did she live?"

"L.A."

Carlie blew out a breath and ran a hand through his hair. Saying she was sorry wasn't going to help, and Dave wasn't a man who would accept abject pity from anyone, whether or not it was intended that way. Knowing that, she laid her head against his chest, and he wrapped his arms around her, kissing the top of her head.

CHAPTER TWENTY-FOUR

In areas where there had been less damage, TV and radio stations were still broadcasting. By the time they reached Ano's uncle's house, they were ready for some modern conveniences. New Orleans had a television station and three radio stations that still broadcasted. While Ano cooked with her mother, grandmother, and aunt, Jazz and the rest of the men 'held court' in her uncle's garage, listening to the news and discussing what was going on.

Dinner the third night of their stay was unusually quiet and Ano looked around to the men at the table. They were all somber, unlike the last two dinners where everyone's spirits were jovial. Halfway through the dinner, Ano's uncle cleared his throat and addressed the whole table.

"Been waiting for an appropriate time to bring this up, and talk to ya'll 'bout somethin' we heard on the radio s'afternoon." His southern accent was pronounced, but everyone at the table stopped eating to listen. He cleared his throat, and looked down at his plate for a moment before continuing. "We been monitorin' the lines, thinkin' that the things we been hearin' are just rumors. Bad rumors."

Ano looked to Jazz next to her, and he wore the same worried expression her uncle did.

Her aunt touched her uncle's hand. "Maybe now isn't the best time."

"Time's runnin' short. Folks got to hear it. Didn't get no warnin' las' time!" His voice was shaking, and Ano couldn't tell whether he was angry or frightened. He looked up at each of them sitting around his table. "U.S. government left us...las' person to take office over for the President got hisself shot."

Ano hadn't known this, but hearing it spoken out loud like this made her shiver. Who had taken the president's place? Clearly the president and vice president had been killed. Who had taken their place? The Secretary of State would have been in Washington, DC when the bomb went off. Who then?

"An' now they saying that there's another attack comin'. Comin' in on foot and by plane. Finish off what they started."

No one around the table spoke. Ano's hands had gone cold, and she had perspiration beading up on her upper lip. Jazz, next to her, didn't move.

"When?" Grandma Vesper's voice sounded like a strong bell from across the table, and her uncle responded.

"Some say next week. Some say a month. Don' know."

Ano had a million questions for her uncle. She felt like she was being slowly strangled. Her entire way of life, everything she'd been brought up to believe was in question. In danger. Her future. Gone.

She finally found her voice. "Where is the government? Who is protecting our borders? We've surely got militia left in the United States."

Her uncle sighed. "Ano, the government left us unprotected. Sent more men overseas just before the attacks. Some fifty thousand. Like..." he struggled to explain it in simple terms, "like someone knew what was goin' on afore we did."

"So we have no soldiers?" She found that impossible to believe.

This time, her oldest cousin Christee spoke. He lived a few blocks over and had been with the men every day, listening to the news. "Baby girl, it's not that we don't have soldiers somewhere in the country, a'right? It's jus' there's no one to organize them. Uncle Robert's right. No one gonna stand up to be President now and try an' lead us into a war we can't fight. A war we can't win."

She felt tears coming, and Jazz's hand slipped into her own. A war. Not a war on TV or in the news, but a war fought on the very soil they claimed as their own. "Don't we have..."

Her uncle quieted her with his hand. "Men greater than us are tryin' to figure this out. Somewhere. I have to believe they are."

"Or runnin' for cover!" Nate said loudly. Papa Nate was her Uncle Robert's father, and at least eighty years old.

"So," Grandma Vesper said, "what do we do?"

Uncle Robert sighed. "We all been talkin' 'bout it. Figurin' out a way for all of us to survive. If the phone was workin' we'd call Pete."

Pete was the oldest brother, and a retired Command Sergeant Major in the National Guard. She hadn't seen her uncle since she was in grade school.

"Phone ain't workin'," Papa Nate reminded him.

"I know, Pop." He sighed and looked at the thirteen faces around his table. "We got an idea though. Seems Jazz remembers hearin' something about buyin' guns or rifles when they were travlin' to Denver."

"An' we figure to fight this fight, we need ammunition. And something to protect o'selves with this time." Nods from all around. "If they comin', they'll be doin' it from e'vywhere. No tellin' where they comin' from."

Finally, Jazz spoke. Ano was amazed that his voice was strong and young sounding among all the older men that surrounded the table. "We need to move away from here. Get somewhere safer. If they attack the borders first we can have some lead in time. Time to protect ourselves. Find safety. Fight back."

"I'm not goin' anywhere," her aunt said stubbornly. "If there's a fight, I'll stay put right here, shoulder to shoulder wit' my neighbors."

Ano listened to the discussion on whether leaving or staying was the best decision.

"Are you sure that this is really happening? That there is no...that the military..." her voice trailed off and sounded small.

The table became quiet once again and her uncle nodded. "We're sure, Ano."

"Who else knows?"

"That's the trick, see," her cousin said. "They got most of our communications down. It's like they have us isolated. We can't band together without communication. It's like we're shooting in the dark."

"So we're just going to sit here and—"

"No, Ano," Jazz said, squeezing her hand. "We're not going to just sit here. We're going to find somewhere to buy some guns. And we're going to fight back."

On the full-sized mattress in the spare room at her aunt's house, Ano lay on her back, looking up at the ceiling. She couldn't sleep. Oddly enough, it wasn't just the thoughts of the invasion, or losing her family again that kept her awake. It wasn't the unspoken threat of violence in her own country, possibly her own city that had her lying awake. It was fear. Pure, unadulterated fear of what they were facing kept her from falling asleep. An hour later, Jazz opened the door quietly, careful not to wake her.

"You can turn on the light," she said. "I'm not asleep."

He kicked off his shoes and crossed to lie, stomach down, on the bed next to her in the dark. "You okay?"

"No," she answered plainly. "I'm not."

"I know. I know."

"You believe them? What you're hearing? On the radio, and, I mean, doesn't the whole country know about this? Could it be a fake threat?" her voice rose slightly. "I find it difficult to believe we have no one who can fight for us in the country!"

Jazz slid towards her, silencing her lips with his finger pressed to them. "You need to listen to me. They been telling me what's goin' on and I didn't believe it till I heard it for myself. They got a radio in there and been contracting people from all over. People aren't gonna wait for the government to see if they can bring the soldiers back to help us fight. Baby, this isn't a battle we can fight like it's a game of chess, from thousands of miles away. We been relying on men and women we've never met to protect us. We can't do it anymore. We gotta fight for ourselves."

Ano felt like she was going to cry. "So," she asked, "where do we go? What did you all decide?"

"We're not in agreement," Jazz said. "They want to stay, and I think heading for the Midwest is safest position right now. It didn't get hit as badly as other states the first time, it's safer, as you and I clearly know. We have a better chance of getting rifles and ammunition as we pass through places that haven't been hit as badly."

He stopped and waited for her to absorb the information.

"Where would we go?"

"I don't know. Haven't gotten that far yet."

"I see."

"There's something else." He sighed.

Ano waited, but when he didn't say anything, she prodded him. "What?"

Jazz sat up and took her hands in his own. He sighed, looked down at his lap, then finally into her eyes. "I think that we should get married."

For a second, she thought she hadn't heard him right. "Wh...wha...?"

"I know it's not what you want. It's not the fancy restaurant with a ring box and me on one knee. I'll get down on one knee if you want, but this is just me asking you...from my heart. I don't want to go into this without you. And...I have no family left." Ano could tell he was close to tears. "I lost..." he sniffed and she sat up to face him, knees touching.

"I know, baby."

"I'll fight for this country. And I'm proud to do it." He straightened slightly. "Like my father served this country proudly."

Ano wiped the tears from her eyes.

"But, if I do it," he said, "I do it with my *wife* by my side."

Ano's tears – those of joy and fear – came out in a sob, and she covered her mouth with her hand. From inside his pocket, Jazz pulled a small diamond ring, and she gasped.

"Now, don't go getting too excited," he said, "it's from your Grandma."

"Jazz, my Grandma doesn't wear a ring."

He laughed. "I know. She had it on a chain around her neck. Said it's been too small for twenty years but she jus' kept it close to her heart." He shrugged. "She said your grandfather gave it to her when they were married."

Ano was crying freely now. Her grandfather had died when Ano was a very small girl; maybe five or six. She had few memories of him, except that he smelled like pipe tobacco and had strong arms and a warm laugh. And that Grandma Vesper had loved him dearly.

"I asked your uncle's permission tonight. I would've asked your dad if ... you know."

She nodded and laughed through her tears. "I know."

He held the ring out in front of him, hopped off the bed, and ceremoniously walked around, got down on one knee beside the bed. Ano was laughing and crying at the same time. He reached for her hand.

"I love you," Jazz said, and Ano thought it was odd that he'd never said it so loud and out in the open as right that minute. "Even if the rest of my life is only a month, I want to spend that time with you. Ano, will you marry me?"

CHAPTER TWENTY-FIVE

The cement safe-room felt colder than it had an hour ago. The small cot in the corner and the military light that dangled from the ceiling gave it a 1940's appearance. He paced the floor as he had for the last ten days. By now, he wondered why he hadn't worn a trench in the floor, he'd gone over it so many times. The small table in the middle of the room held maps, his passport, and a variety of documents that he hadn't bothered to read or sign...yet. He knew, however, it was his obligation— his duty—to do so.

Curtis Thompson was not a strong man. He'd been put into office by his father, a career politician before him. A member of the House for years, his father had convinced him to run for governor the year before he was to retire. Curtis never anticipated he'd win. But he had won, and then within five years assumed his father's seat. Appointed ten years later to the President's cabinet, Curtis had often wondered how he came to be at the position he enjoyed. Many of the decisions he made were not his own. The votes he cast were lost in the others who lobbied with more influence. Multiple bad decisions and indiscretions kept quiet by turning his cheek to the illegal acts of other members of the House or Senate. It was a dirty, dirty business.

Pacing the room, Curtis finally recognized the gravity of his actions. The paltry sum of his life's accomplishments overwhelmed him as he considered signing the documents on the table. He glanced at his watch. One more hour. He had no more business being Commander in Chief than his predecessor, who had lasted less than five hours in the position. Sweat beaded on his forehead and he wondered how long he would last. An even worse thought entered his mind; that he would survive and be expected to lead the country through this horror.

His father had been governor of Texas for many years, and Curtis heard the angry voice in his head calling him a coward and telling him to sign the document. Curtis, in the only moment of courage he would ever experience, deliberately walked to the table and signed the document. Once completed, he sighed with relief and tossed the pen into the middle of the table. A single sound from the other side of the door caused his heart to stop.

The door opened and two men dressed in black appeared. Both carried assault rifles and had hoods covering most of their faces. Seeing them, Curtis sank to his knees to pray for his life. Three shots rang out within seconds of their entering the room, before Curtis' knees even hit the floor. The documents from the table were gathered and stuffed into a secure bag and carried away as Curtis' blood ran down the drain in the corner of the small cement room.

* * *

"Nurse," Percy's doctor called out without looking behind him, "hand me the package of gauze pads over on the counter."

I walked into the room and pulled the box from the counter. "I'm not the nurse, but I'll be glad to assist, doctor."

He glanced at me as he pulled the last of the bandage off and stood, discarding it next to him. "Sorry, Doctor ah..." he looked for the name on my coat and found none.

"Just Kate, for now."

He accepted the pads and nodded at me. "You're one of the new 'pledges'. From Penn."

"'New *victim*' I believe is the most commonly turned phrase."

He laughed. "Well, if our patient doesn't mind you assisting me, this *is* a teaching hospital."

Percy's voice was hoarse, but he assented. "I don't mind."

"All right then."

I peeked around the back of his doctor to catch a glimpse of Percy and saw only the top of the dark, reddish brown mass of curls. I waited patiently until the doctor completed cleaning, re-bandaging, and taping the wound. He returned the bed to its original reclining position.

"I think I can let you go home a day early," he said. "How about tomorrow?"

Percy didn't say anything. His eyes were locked on mine.

Signing the chart, the doctor hung it back on its place at the foot of Percy's bed and motioned to me. "Shall we?"

"Oh, I-I," I stuttered. "I'm...I just completed my shift."

"I see." He looked from me to Percy and back to me again. "Well, then," he smiled and pointed at Percy. "I'll be back in tomorrow morning to discharge you."

Neither Percy nor I said anything until we heard the door swish closed behind the doctor. I hadn't meant to exclude his grandmother and brother, and I turned to her with a smile, wondering if she would remember me. "It's nice to see you again, Mrs. Warner," I said, and she waved off my greeting.

"Gigi, please."

"All right...Gigi."

"We're so glad you could come, Kate."

"Hello, Edgar," I called to the young figure slumped crosswise in the hospital chair, and he nodded vaguely in my direction.

"Well," Gigi said, and stood quickly, "visiting hours are over and we should be getting back. Edgar?" She reached for her grandson and waited for him to finish shutting off his electronic game before standing and offering her his arm.

"Oh, you don't have to go!" I said, now feeling guilty that I was cutting their visit short.

Gigi smiled at Percy, who nodded at her that it was all right to leave. "We'll be back tomorrow," she said. She looked at Percy and then at me. "Until then, I know he's in excellent hands."

I wasn't sure if that was meant as a compliment to the hospital or to me, and so I thanked her. Edgar gave a tired wave to Percy as they departed, and before I knew it we were alone.

I'd had so many dreams about Percy while I was in California that being with him right now seemed surreal. Just in case it was a dream – surely the most realistic one I'd ever had – my eyes drank in his face, his hands lying on top of his blanket, the expression he wore. It was a mixture of relief and... something odd. Something new. And very un-Percy.

"Are you comfortable?" I moved above him to turn the light down one click.

He nodded, his eyes remaining fixed on mine. "Yes, thank you."

I walked around his bed to the other side where his dinner sat on a tray, untouched. "Not hungry?"

"Not especially."

There were two small bags sitting next to his hospital tray, and I motioned to them. "Presents?"

"Scones," he informed me. "From my Grandmother's cook."

My mouth watered at the thought of homemade food and I remembered Carrie's kitchen and how it always smelled as if she was baking when you walked into it.

"Please have one," he offered, and reached up to open one of the bags.

I held up a hand politely. "No, that's okay."

He sighed, exasperated with me, and pulled one from the bag. Finally, the old Percy. "You look like you haven't eaten a meal since we left the cave. Here," he said, pulling a sugared strawberry scone from the bag. "Have one. It'll make Sasha happy to know someone's enjoying her food."

I hadn't eaten since this morning, having given up dinner to catch the shuttle to make it before eight, and I gratefully accepted the scone. "Thank you." I split it in half and put half on his tray. "Split it with me," I told him. "You'll need to eat something if you're getting discharged tomorrow. Look healthy."

He nodded in silent assent and I took a large bite of the scone, which seemed to all but melt in my mouth. I closed my eyes. God, how I missed home cooked food.

"You've lost weight. Didn't he feed you out in California?" Percy's tone had a bite to it.

I tried not to choke on the scone, and averted my eyes from his face.

The mention of Matt hurt, and he retracted instantly. "Sorry, Kate. That wasn't fair."

We ate in silence for a few minutes, until I moved to a subject that was more neutral. "Tell me how you found Edgar."

For the next hour, I sat on the edge of his bed and he told me about finding Edgar at camp, and making it to Philadelphia. We talked about the buses, the damage in New York, and the plans to send Edgar back to Avon in a week. He'd carefully avoided asking about California, and I was grateful. I wouldn't be able to share that with him; with anyone except Carrie, and then only in writing, which I wasn't even sure she'd receive.

"Have you heard from Ano?" he asked, and I knew then that he was avoiding asking what had caused me to abandon Matt and come to Philadelphia. It wasn't like Percy to push; one more thing about his personality I was grateful for.

"She wrote me a letter about a month ago," I said, starting the second scone he offered me, "and she and Jazz were moving her grandma and mom back to New Orleans to be with family."

"They're both alive?" he asked incredulously.

"Yeah, weird, right? Just a twist of fate." I shrugged and then mentioned Carlie, not knowing how he'd feel hearing news about his ex-girlfriend. "Carlie's doing well," I said, and looked up after I'd said it, gauging his reaction. He caught me, and we both laughed out loud.

"What, you'd like a reaction from me?" he joked, and I was grateful to see a real smile on his face.

"No..."

"Forget it, *Doctor* Moore," he said. "I know you too well. It's okay, go ahead. How is Carlie?"

"She's good. Working in a trauma center in Bellevue."

"Washington?"

"Yeah. U Dub Med Center closed and they kind of created this for urgent medical care in the area. She works, like, a hundred hours a week."

"Ah, so nothing's changed."

I smirked and raised an eyebrow, but took another bite of the scone instead of making a snappy comeback. Percy handed me his water cup, which I accepted with a grateful nod. Fairly sure I was making a pig of myself, but unable to stop, I took another bite. I realized Percy was watching me eat and hastened to change the subject.

"Your grandmother..."

"Gigi."

"Yes, Gigi. You live with her? You and Edgar?"

"We do. She's like to keep Edgar here, in Philadelphia with her." He pressed his lips together and closed his eyes for a moment.

"What do you think?"

"My mother was always the one who made these decisions. If I were Edgar, I'd likely make the same decision he is. To go back to what's familiar."

I imagined the weight that was on Percy's shoulders. He'd merely traded one responsibility for another. In the cave he was responsible for the five of us. Now he was responsible for Edgar and his grandmother. I was only responsible for me.

"That's a difficult decision," I said.

"Don't placate me, please."

"I'm not." I set the last part of the scone down on the table next to his bed and dusted off my hands. "I'm saying I've never had to face anything like that, and I'm sure it's a difficult decision."

Percy narrowed his eyes to look at me, as if making a decision. "When we were walking to Philadelphia, I was struck by the similarity of the situations."

"Which?"

His eyes met mine. "Edgars and yours."

At first, I didn't catch on, and then, as I realized what he was saying, I shook my head. "But I'm...no, you see, Edgar is..." Everything I was about to say sounded pitiful and self-serving.

"You became an orphan at fifteen, did you not?"

"Sixteen."

"Edgar is fifteen. He's lost both parents as well. It struck me while we were walking how..." his voice softened, "how similar our lives are."

I laughed out loud without meaning to, and the shock of it caused him to frown. As much as I tried, I couldn't keep a twinge of bitterness from my voice. "Your life and mine. Similar." I looked out the window. "Not hardly."

"I realize I still have family, and you—"

"Have none," I cut in. "You're right. I have no one." I wanted to bite back the tone in my voice, to not be angry at Percy for what he could not help. I didn't want to lump him in the same category that I'd put Matt in, and yet, seeing the reality of what his family was poured salt in a newly opened wound. "Your life is much different than mine. And no matter how similar we may seem, when people look at me they will always see an orphan who came from nothing. Who *has* nothing." I straightened my shoulders. "But I am more than that."

A look of pure, unadulterated hatred covered Percy's face. He leaned towards me, his voice low. "What the hell did he do to you?"

What he said shocked me nearly as how he'd said it. I shook my head, feigning ignorance. "I don't know what you're talking about."

"I may have been blind for three years to what you felt for me Kate, but I'm not blind to what you *feel*. I can see it on your face, hear it in your voice." His tone was accusatory. "What the hell happened?"

I slipped from the edge of his bed and straightened my jacket. "Nothing. I wanted to continue studying, and Matt didn't. Quite simply."

"Bullshit."

I'd never heard Percy curse before, and my mouth dropped. "Excuse me?"

"You heard me. You can't lie to save your life, Kate. Not even when you told Professor Montobel why you were thirty minutes late for the lab where we had to dissect those rats. Remember?""I was...I...that was..."

"Yes, go on!" he said, egging me on. "Tell me. Matt wanted to stay in the city, is that the story?"

He couldn't possibly know the truth. How would he know? Unfortunately, he was right. I couldn't lie well. Okay, I couldn't lie at all. Regardless, I was going to give it a shot, to save my pride. I raised my chin again. "That's right. We found his mother and he wanted to stay with her and his brothers."

Percy crossed his arms over his chest and nodded slowly. "And that's the truth?"

I swallowed. Hard. I hadn't lied to Percy. Ever. Nor knowingly deceived him. However, I couldn't very well tell him what had happened either. There was no middle ground. My mind searched for a plausible story, something close to the truth that he would believe. Then, in all its brilliance, it hit me. "Like you said, playing house got old." *For him.*

"That's the reason you left him. In Los Altos. Alone."

"Ye..." I stopped. "Percy?"

"Yes, Kate?"

I leaned against his bed with my hip, breathing hard. "How did you know we were in Los Altos?"

Percy pressed his lips together. "Hmm. Funny story, actually." He paused, feigning a slight smile on his lips. "Would you like to recant your story now that you know I know where you were?"

My heart was beginning to pound again. *Carrie.* The letter I'd sent her. Oh, God. She wouldn't have told Percy, would she? I had to know. "C...

Carrie?"

He nodded and I turned my back to him, my humiliation complete. "Carrie told you what happened?" My insides hurt just at the thought of Percy knowing the depth of rejection I had experienced. I hit the window with my fist and leaned my head against its coolness.

"Kate! Stop!" he called from behind me.

I spun around. "What did she tell you?" Had she told him everything? Every horrible detail of why Matt had wanted to discard me? I couldn't endure the thought of Percy knowing. My eyes were desperate. This was too much emotion for him, and I was sure that, after this, I would need to leave. "Please," I said, trying to calm down. "Just tell me and then I'll go."

"She said you and Matt were moving his mother to a home. That she wasn't...well. And that you'd be leaving Los Altos soon."

Relief flooded through me. I blew out a huge breath and nodded to him, embarrassed that I'd had an emotional outburst, especially in front of him. "Oh." I tried to stop the thumping in my chest. "I...I'm...sorry," I said lamely.

"What else would she have told me?"

I took a step towards the door. "Nothing. I overreacted. I apologize."

"Kate, don't go."

I looked back at him. "I have to, or I'll miss the shuttle. I shouldn't have stayed so long."

"Wait one minute. Please."

I felt ridiculous, but I had no good excuse for my actions. I couldn't very well tell him why I'd reacted that way.

"Please," he implored.

Slowly, I walked back to his bedside. I was able to control my voice now. "I can get you some more water before I go."

"I don't want more water." He took a deep breath. "I didn't mean to upset you."

"Really, I'm fine."He reached down and touched the back of my hand. "Kate, what would Carrie have told me?"

I shrugged, my expression bland. "Nothing. It doesn't matter."

He sighed and his brows knit together. "It does matter. A great deal. To me."

It wasn't that easy for me. And I needed air. "I'm sorry. I overreacted. Everything's all right now."

"You..." he said, his voice that baritone I had missed so much, "are anything but all right."

"Sorry, Percy. I really am fine now."

His voice was low and soft, and my heart calmed, just hearing it. "Whatever he did," Percy said, stroking the back of my hand gently, "or whatever he said to hurt you..."

"Nothing. He didn't *do* anything."

Percy sighed and looked down to where his hand was touching mine. "One day," he said slowly, "you *will* tell me what he did to make you leave."

Not likely. "Of course." I wanted to go, but his touch had me anchored.

"I'm being discharged tomorrow."

"Yes, I know."

"My grandmother mentioned that she'd like you to come over to the house. For a visit."

Being back in a situation where I would be judged for my lack of pedigree? Forget it. "I have class."

"Next Saturday?"

"Lab."

Percy sighed and raised an eyebrow. "Next Sunday?"

Crap. I tried to search for a reasonable explanation and found none. He knew it. I was stalling, my mouth open, searching for an answer he would accept, and nothing was coming to mind.

He was smiling at me. "You're too flustered to lie to me. I'll send a car to pick you up. You're at the housing on campus?"

"Building G."

"Nine-thirty too early?"

"No."

"Good. The car will be there at nine-thirty to pick you up."

There was no goodbye kiss or awkward farewell. I ducked out of his hospital room, strode down the hallway, consumed with the thoughts of what had happened, and of seeing him in eight days.

CHAPTER TWENTY-SIX

"You gonna make him take his supper out there like last night?" Charlie asked.

Carrie stood watching Matt through the window in the kitchen while he worked with the other three field hands they'd hired to help plant the winter wheat. It was just after midday and the sun was hotter than it had been the day before.

"Not sure." She dried the plates off and restacked them in the cupboard.

"I best go back out. Help the boys," Charlie said.

"All right if I take the truck?"

Charlie put his hat back on, then nodded at his wife. "Yep. Need somethin' in town?"

"Some more sugar, is all. And butter. If *he* stays around, I'll need to bring in more eggs from the coop."

Charlie sniggered quietly. "All right. Will you pick up the mail while you're there? I'm still waitin' to hear back from Carsen's in Nebraska if they've got that tractor part or not."

"Will do." Pulling the keys from the hook, Carrie walked down the front, climbed in the truck, and pulled out of the drive. The whole way into town she thought about Matt. And Kate. She wondered what could have made Matt do such a thing to Kate, what could have gotten into his head to let his brothers talk that way about her. Despite what Charlie said, she wasn't ready to hear his reasoning behind it. She wasn't even sure he'd told Charlie, but if he had, Charlie had kept it quiet, which was fine with her.

Now Kate was back in Pennsylvania. With Percy? Had she gone there to find him? From her last letter, she hadn't known where he was. Those two were like magnets that couldn't get the ends lined up. If they could... would the ends be the ones that pulled towards each other? Or repelled? Carrie didn't know. She'd written a letter to Percy, which she had tucked in the pocket of her overalls, and had planned on mailing it today. She pulled in front of the post station and parked, then climbed the steps to wait at the counter.

"Heya, Carrie."

"Tom."

He went into the back for a moment to check for their mail and then stopped halfway up and tore a piece of paper from a machine that looked like a really old electric typewriter. "Brand new. First one to come through this way! Can you believe it? We'll find ways of communicating long distance after all!"

"What is it?"

"Part telegram, part telegraph. This one's for you!"

She stared at him for a moment. "For me?"

Tom smiled and handed her the telegram. "Yep. All the way from Philadelphia."

Philadelphia. Was it from Kate? Excited and flustered, Carrie accepted the piece of paper. The message was short but clear:

```
To:  Carrie Blackhawk, South Dakota
From:  P. Warner, Philadelphia PA
Message:What did he do to her that made her
leave?
```

She read it over, five times, and then the request for an answer, post paid. They had found each other. Somehow, Kate had found Percy. Knowing her as he did, Percy knew that Kate was hurt. Carrie knew that Kate was too proud to tell him. However, this was Kate's story to tell, not hers.

"Something wrong?"

Obviously, Tom had read it, he'd been the one to take the code and type it out onto the paper for her. "Um...no," she said, and contemplated what to say in response. Clearly, the letter wasn't going to be needed anymore, and she folded it to put back in her pocket.

"Reply is post paid up to five lines," Tom said, impressed. "That's a big deal. These are expensive to send!"

Carrie nodded mutely, considering what she should do. They'd found each other, of that much his message was clear. But Kate had trusted her enough to pour her heart out in a letter. On the other hand, if Kate wasn't telling him, maybe she had shut down again. The thought made her heart ache. She could hear Charlie's words as if he'd been standing right next to her: *You're interfering!*

Did Kate need a push? Did Percy need to hear what had happened to help her get through it? Carrie didn't know him well enough to know what he would do with the information. She did know that the last man who had Kate's heart had hurt her, and with that in mind, she made her decision.

"Tom, I want to send a reply."

Tom licked the end of his pencil and grabbed a pad of paper. She hated doing things this way, but it was so much faster than mail.

She took the pad and pen from him. "I'll write it. You send it."

Tom waited until she was done and took the paper, reading it back to her. Carrie confirmed the message and thanked Tom before getting back in her truck to go to the store. Tonight, she was going to have a talk with Matt.

Tom sent the code for all five lines of a response to the post station near Society Hill, Pennsylvania. It read:

```
Kate will tell you in time
Her heart is broken badly
Keep her safe and love who she is
Be safe be happy send her my love
Carrie
```

Matt was just grateful not to be eating in the stifling barn, and even happier that Carrie had finally allowed him inside the house. He'd lost weight over the last month, and tried not to shovel food in from the never ending supply in front of him. Carrie was an amazing cook. Fried chicken, mashed potatoes, oh, and her biscuits! She piled another spoonful of potatoes on his plate and accepted his nod and half-mouth-full thanks.

She waited until he was nearly done eating before she levied her first question at him, conscious that he wasn't actually done, so he wouldn't get up and leave without seeming incredibly rude.

"You get your mom somewhere for folks to take care of her?"

The fork stopped halfway to his mouth, and he lowered his arm. Charlie stopped eating as well, then a smile tugged at the corner of his mouth and he resumed eating. Carrie would take care of this and work through it. And God help Matt while she did.

Matt wiped his mouth. "Yes, we did."

"We?" She paused. "You and your... *brothers*?"

It was the way she'd said the word *brothers* that clued Matt into the fact that Kate had either sent her a letter and told her everything, or she'd stopped by here on her way to...where?

"Yes, me and my two brothers. How did you—"

"She all settled in Boston?" Carrie's eyebrows went up, cluing Matt into the fact that she already knew most everything and he was going to fill in the blanks of what she didn't know. Or die trying.

"Carrie…" he began.

"It's a yes or no question, young man."

"Yes. She's all settled in Boston."

"How long did you stay there getting the *lay of the land* before you headed back here?" Her tone was sarcastic and he caught it. There was also something else. Pain. She was hurt. Hurt, disappointed, and…his worst fear was confirmed. He'd broken Kate's heart, and she'd told the only woman who'd shown her the kindness of a mother. Carrie wanted a pound of flesh from him, for Kate.

He leaned back in his chair and thought for a minute before speaking. Anything he said was going to come out sounding bad. He looked to Charlie, who was concentrating so hard on buttering his biscuit that he'd likely grow nearsighted.

"Carrie, please listen. I came here right after making sure my mom was settled. I didn't stay in Boston, I didn't get the…the *lay of the land.*"

"Why'd you come? You hopin' she'd come back here to lick her wounds and you'd pick her back up, dust her off and," she shrugged exaggeratedly, "what?"

"I went crazy when she disappeared."

Carrie pursed her lips and didn't look at him. "You went crazy."

"That's right."

She turned to Charlie. "He went crazy."

Charlie inclined his head, but – wisely – said nothing.

"You went so crazy that you went after her."

"Well," Matt said, "no, because—"

"You went *so crazy* after waking up and finding her note that—"

"How do you know about—"

"—that you got up and ran to the bus stop? Got in a cab?"

Matt sighed. "No. I didn't."

"You didn't." Carrie looked at Charlie. "He didn't." She tapped her finger on the edge of the table and then asked Charlie, "What would you do if you woke up and found me gone?"

Knowing what was good for him, Charlie answered, "I'd find you."

She turned back to Matt, who was shaking his head.

"I didn't know where she was going!"

"How many bus stations did she tell me there were in town? One?"

Matt leaned his head forward into his hands while Charlie watched Carrie's interrogation in silence. He knew to get in between her and Matt now would be like getting between a Pit Bull and a steak; highly unadvisable.

"I should have gone after her."

She held up her index finger to him, not ready to let it go quite yet. "Should have? *Should have?* Then why the hell didn't you?"

"Because! By the time I woke up and found her note, I didn't know how long it had been since she'd gone! I thought—"

"You thought that not losing face in front of your brothers was more important than losing the woman you loved."

"No!" Matt nearly shoved the chair back, and Charlie leaned back in his chair, a warning look on his face that he'd best sit down and check his tone while talking to his wife. Matt sat back down and his tone softened. "No. That's not it."

"If that wasn't it, then what was it?"

Matt sighed and his tone became desperate. "I woke up and found her note, and I went crazy. I had no way to make it to the bus station on foot. It's fifteen miles! And there's no guarantee that a cab would come by! Fifteen miles would have taken me most of the morning on foot."

"Once you'd reached the bus station, they'd have told you where Kate went! She was easy to recognize."

"Sure, if you get the same person who was there at whatever time Kate got there! If not, then you're just—"

"Pissin' in the wind," Charlie piped in. Carrie shot him an annoyed look – and Matt, a grateful one.

"You get to Boston, drop your mom off, and come here." Carrie paused. "Why?"

Matt sighed. "Because this was the only place I knew she would come if she was hurt."

"*If? If* she was hurt?"

"I didn't mean that my brothers didn't hurt her! I only meant that I didn't know where else she'd be!"

"Wait," Carrie held out her hand to him, "if your *brothers* hurt her? Your brothers. Not you?"

"Carrie, I have to know what she told you."

"She told me about a conversation she'd heard between you and your brothers on the staircase. Something about 'excess baggage' and bringing home a maid ring a bell?"

"I never said that!" Matt said defensively.

Her tone was so quiet he had to lean in to hear her. "If you didn't disagree, to Kate, it's as good as you saying it yourself."

"I told my brothers I loved her. I told them I wanted Kate!"

"She didn't tell me any of that in her letter."

"Well, maybe she didn't hear the entire thing."

"I think she heard quite enough."

Matt's face was tortured. "Carrie, if I told you how sorry I was...how much I loved Kate and want her back. If you know where she is..."

Carrie didn't say a word. Charlie had finished his supper and was busy examining his fork.

"You know." Matt caught his breath. "You know where she is!"

Carrie sat in silence, staring at her hands in her lap.

"Carrie, please! Tell me where she is! I'll do penance for the rest of my life, I'll—"

"I can't tell you."

"Wha...*why*?" Matt ran a hand through his hair, perched on the edge of his chair. "I had to get my mom situated. I had to—"

"This isn't about your mom, or how much time you took."

"Then what? You don't believe me? I made a mistake, Carrie. Haven't you ever made a mistake that you wished to God you could take back?"

Her face had finally softened and she looked at him. "Yes I have."

"Okay, then. I have to find her. I have to get her back. You know where she is Carrie, I know you do."

She nodded. "I know where she is."

Matt's face broke out in a smile. "Then tell me. Tell me and I'll make it better. I'll go to her and beg if I have to."

Carrie stared at him from red-rimmed, dry eyes. "She's *broken*, Matt. You *broke* her."

A heavy moment of silence filled the room. Matt sat down in the chair with a thud and his head slid forward into his hands. "Oh God."

Her tone wasn't accusatory, and she didn't tell him the details to hurt him, but Carrie believed that sometimes the truth did its own kind of cleansing, harsh or not. "Kate didn't come here. After your brothers decided she wasn't...up to par," she paused, "she couldn't. She was ashamed, Matt. Ashamed of herself, of what your family thought of her, whether or not you agreed with them."

His face came up and he looked at her, his eyes bloodshot; a man possessed.

"I wished she would have come here," Carrie said. "I'd have taken her in and...I don't know... Doesn't matter now. She's safe."

"Where?"

The tone of his voice made Charlie hurt for him. It was clear that he loved her; had remorse for how things had happened. But Charlie knew what was coming.

Carrie closed her eyes. "Med school."

"What? Where?" When she didn't respond, he pled, "Please, Carrie?"

"She's on a new path, Matt. Somewhere safe. Somewhere she might be able to heal."

After a horrible, lengthy pause, Charlie got up and crossed to the liquor cabinet and poured a short glass of whiskey.

"She...she's *on a new path?*" Matt echoed.

"Yes."

His chest rose and fell as he considered the meaning behind this. "Alone?" Carrie shrugged.

Matt shook his head, as if trying to clear it. "Did she meet someone? Is that it? She met some other guy, and..." His face colored and then, slowly, it dawned on him. "Percy. *Percy* found her."

The statement, with all its finality, rang out in the kitchen. Charlie set the glass in front of Matt and cleared his dinner plate away. Carrie didn't take her eyes off him. "More like fate took a hand," Carrie explained. "She didn't go seeking him out, Matt."

He face was like solid granite. "No." He stood and turned away from her, then back to face her, begging for a different response. "No, it's...no! She can't be! He didn't even know where she was!"

"Then maybe it was meant to be," Carrie said gently.

Matt looked to Charlie for help, but, finding none, turned back to Carrie. "He doesn't love her! Not like I do!"

"That's for her heart to decide." Carrie delivered her final blow with crystal clarity. "For her and Percy to figure out...together."

CHAPTER TWENTY-SEVEN

In the few months that Carlie had been at the trauma center, they'd never had the chief call a staff meeting. In fact, as a new resident, she'd never been to any organized gathering of all the medical staff. So this morning, as they all huddled in the largest room the trauma center offered, Carlie was nervous.

There were no loudspeakers or microphones; the chief would have to shout to be heard by all the medical personnel in the room. He stood on top of a large box of supplies at the front of the gathering, and a hush fell over all of them.

"This is going to be a quick meeting," he said, his strong voice booming over them. "This morning, I received a disturbing transmission from the chief of surgery at Tri-County hospital in Eastern Washington."

Carlie looked to David, who had come to stand beside her, cup of coffee in hand.

"It seems there are now rumors of a second attack that may be coming to the U.S."

A collective gasp and some cries of fear echoed throughout the group. Carlie set her mouth in a hard line and waited next to David.

"I know that most of you have families that are scattered across the states, and, in response to this message, I'm releasing you. Any of you who want to go are free to do so, with no detrimental ramifications. I'm damned proud of the work we do here every day." He cleared his throat. "Each and every one of you is responsible for saving the lives of the people left here after the blast. And, for that, I thank you. Seattle owes you a great debt."

No one spoke, and for a moment Carlie wondered if that was all. He didn't move, so she stayed where she was, needing to hear the remainder of his message.

"For those of you who make the choice to stay..." he paused, and the line of his mouth turned down, as if telling them this was distasteful to him, "I cannot guarantee your safety. We were a target in the first attack. No one knows what this second attack will entail." The room was deathly silent. "The transmission I received indicated the timing of the attack is uncertain, but it is believed to be less than a month away." He raised his chin and looked at the staff around him. "I urge you not to waste time. Go as soon as you can to your families. Protect them. Keep them safe. God help us all."

The chief stepped down and the room became a mass of activity. People pushed past her and Carlie pulled her arms in to protect herself as she moved through the crowd to the doors leading to the main trauma ward. The mass exodus was to the rear, where it was as if the floodgates had opened and people poured out to gather their things and go home, to seek safety.

David caught up to her and took her by the arm, pulled her into the on-call room, the only room that wasn't being flooded with people. The sound of silence in the room was deafening.

"What are you doing?"

Carlie took a step back from him. "Going to work. What did it look like?"

"Didn't you hear the chief?" His face was tense, his blue eyes flashed.

"I was standing next to you. Clearly, I heard the message, same as you."

"Then get the hell out of here!"

"I have no family left."

David took a step towards her. "Your uncle. The one in Denver? Still want to tell me you have no family?"

Carlie crossed her arms over her chest. "What am I supposed to do in Denver? Cower under a bed and hope to Christ they don't bomb or invade? Or pray I'm a lucky one that gets shot or raped and left for dead, but somehow survive?" She raised an eyebrow at him, seeing that her speech had rendered him mute. "I don't work that way. If I'm going to die then it's going to be doing what I was born to do. It's going to be working to save the lives of Americans who did nothing but live free in a country they believed in. It's not going to be hiding hundreds of miles away hoping to God that someone saves me." She was breathing hard; partly from adrenaline, partly from fear.

David swore under his breath, his face inches from hers. "You're a damned fool."

Carlie smiled a genuine smile and cocked her eyebrow. "Takes one to know one."

David knew there was no way to convince her. The woman was the most stubborn individual he'd ever encountered.

"Fine. If you're going to stay, I'm going to teach you how to shoot a gun," he said.

"I don't have a gun."

He smiled. "I do."

"Are we going to *share* said gun?"

David chuckled and smoothed her hair away of her face. "I have more than one."

"Ammunition?"

He nodded. "Lots."

"I don't suppose now would be a good time to tell you I've never liked guns."

"Most doctors don't. Carlie, what the chief said this morning doesn't surprise me."

"Did you know about this?"

"No, of course not. However, I suspected that the bombs were only the first stage of an attack."

Carlie suppressed the fear that rose in her throat. "The first stage?"

"They've all but cleared a path for themselves to arrive in the very cities they destroyed. The least resistance will be there, the least number of people to oppose them upon arrival. Strategically speaking, it's the way they're most likely to come."

"Where are our armies? The Navy, the National Guard? Who the hell is going to help us fight these bastards?"

"The President sent over another wave of troops to the Middle East," David said, "just before the first attack. By the time word was out, there would have been nothing they could do."

"Why don't they come back now?" she asked.

"They must be deployed. There has to be someone directing them. Someone leading them. Otherwise, my God, they'd be shooting in the dark."

"David," she said, trying to understand, "we have militia. Supposedly the greatest one in the world. Is it possible that somewhere, *someone* is leading them? That they'll—"

"Come save us?" he cut in. His voice was low and she realized how naive a notion it was that the military would ride in on a white horse and save the American people in a blaze of glory. "It's a possibility. A narrow one. I'm not in the military anymore, so I don't know."

"Since the chief justice, the one who died taking over the presidency, is dead, what now? Who is going to lead the U.S.? Or are we on our own?"

David sighed. "If someone is now in charge, no one will know about it. They'll be trying to keep it as quiet as possible to avoid a repeat performance of what happened last week. And if someone is in charge who knows what to do and how to organize militias, then they could recall the troops from the Middle East and deploy them along the U.S. border with firepower."

"You think that would be enough to deter them?"

"No. There *will* be a war, Carlie. The men who planned this attack, they're not interested in a 'show of strength'. It'll take more than threats to send them packing."

"What will it take?"

The pain showed in his eyes. "Death. Ours or theirs."

Carlie shivered, even though she wasn't cold. "So even if we had soldiers—"

"There would still be fighting. There would still be an attack. They believe if they can break into America's borders and destroy it, then they will have achieved something. Some, I don't know, freaking sick kudos in heaven or some such nonsense."

"I don't get it," she said. "I just don't get it."

"Don't try to make sense out of war. You'll go crazy."

Carlie reached up to him and touched the stubble on his chin. "Were you scared when you went to the Middle East?"

David slid a hand around her waist and the other around the nape of her neck, looking directly into her eyes. "I was young," he said. "Eighteen. I'd never been further than a couple hundred miles from home. I was terrified."

Glad that he'd been honest with her, Carlie held onto him by the shoulders, enjoying the solid feel of him.

"I'm not terrified this time. Do you want to know why?"

She nodded eagerly. Anything that could assuage her fears was worth hearing.

"Because I didn't know what to expect then. I do now. The sound of machine gun fire doesn't scare me. The sound of men dying around me is...what we do every day. When it comes this time, I'll be prepared. I'll be armed. For whatever happens." His mouth was at her ear, and his whisper was almost pleading. "*Now* will you go?"

Carlie smiled and slid her hands underneath his scrubs along the line of his chest and around his round shoulders. "No."

He pressed her up against the wall, his mouth covering hers. Carlie dug her fingers into his shoulders and wrapped her legs around him as he kissed her hard. "I can be very convincing when I want to be."

"I'm staying right here. With you."

He sobered. "All right then. I'll prepare you. For whatever will happen."

The pounding in her heart was nothing compared to the pounding in her head. A war was coming. And death was coming with it.

Chapter Twenty-Eight

It had been over eight years since I'd worn a dress. Possibly longer. One of the other clinical residents in my program had loaned me the dress as a favor, with the promise that I would help her complete the chemical biology paper by next Wednesday. Since I finished it the night it was assigned, it seemed to be a fair trade. I looked at myself in the mirror on the back of the door and winced. I looked like a kid dressed up in my mom's clothes. That, and my boobs didn't even begin to fill out the dress near as well as hers did.

"Holy shit, Kate!" Simone looked up from her bed where she pored over one of the egregiously thick textbooks from anatomy. "Ohmygod you look gorgeous!" Of the five other girls who shared my large housing commune, Simone was by far the nicest.

I tucked a strand of hair behind my ear. "I can't wear this."

She hopped up to tighten the straps of the dress over each shoulder. "Yes, you can."

I looked at my reflection in the mirror and grimaced. "I look ridiculous in this dress!"

She stood behind me and peered at my figure. "Are you kidding? With your figure? Show it off! Who is this guy, anyway?"

"Someone I knew at Stanford."

She giggled, which Simone did pretty much before she said anything. Looking at her, you'd never guess she was pre-med. Frizzy blonde hair and enormous blue eyes, she had a kind, motherly appearance, even at twenty-five. In fact, she pretty much mothered all of us. "Is this someone a... *someone*?"

Her questions, although sweet, made me miss Ano. I'd written to her weeks ago when I arrived at Penn and had given her the address to the University dorm I was staying in. I hadn't heard back yet, and I missed her. Today, of all days, I needed her advice. "Simone, it's a long story."

"Well, long story or not, he's going to flip when he sees you in this. You look completely different."

I faked a smile, thanked her, and checked my watch. I had exactly ten minutes to make it downstairs before the car Percy had sent for me showed up. I turned to go.

"Wait!" she fairly shrieked. "Stop!" she walked over to me and tugged at my wrist. "You can't wear this big clunky old thing," she said, unsnapped my watch, and set it on my desk.

"I like that watch." I massaged my wrist. I hadn't taken that off since Matt gave it to me when we got to San Francisco. I felt naked without it. Or, perhaps *alone,* as it was the last reminder of him. Simone stepped back and examined me once more. She tapped her mouth with her finger.

"You need a purse."

"Simone, I have to go."

She rummaged around in her closet for a black purse to match. Finding one, she nodded and handed it to me. "Put in your keys, a lip gloss and your—"

"I don't wear lip gloss."

She rolled her eyes in a 'do I have to do everything?' kind of way and unzipped the purse. "Voila. Lip gloss."

I smiled and kind of marveled at how prepared she was. "Thanks."

"Now," she said dropping my keys into my purse, "go."

"Thank you."

"I want a full report tonight!"

I waved as our door slammed shut behind me and I nearly ran three flights of stairs down to pass the office.

"Hey, Kate!"

Rob was that annoying front office guy that never let you pass without making either a comment or asking you a question that seemed completely self-evident. That, and he smelled like hamburgers. Those two things kept me from going to the office very often.

"Yeah?" I paused, which is to say I kept walking, but slowed, and he held up his index finger for me and walked back to the mail slots.

"Got something for you!" he called out and I turned my wrist over and cursed the fact that Simone had made me leave my watch. "Came in on Friday," he called from the back, "but I haven't seen you, so..."

"Rob, I'm kind of in a hurry, so I'll get it later, okay?"

He returned with a blue and red envelope marked 'Urgent, Electronic Post' on the front.

"What the hell is that?" I asked.

"New. Just started coming. Telegrams! You know, like in the old days? Amazing what they think of."

I tore the seal from the package and reached inside to remove the small typewritten message. It read:

```
From: New Orleans, LA; Port Orleans Parish
To: K. Moore, Pennsylvania Univ. Student
housing, Bldg. G

Told you I wouldn't do it without my maid of
honor
September 20 Bayshore Baptist Church New
Orleans LA
Got your letter I'm worried Send immediate
reply
Ano
```

For a minute, I couldn't breathe. I stood, reading the transmission over and over. Ano was getting married. She couldn't do it without me. She needed me there. Her maid of honor. To marry Jazz. My heart was going to explode. I looked up at the clock above Rob's head. 9:40.

"Shit!" I ran, telegram in hand, out the door to the front lot where a black car sat waiting for me and a driver standing next to the rear passenger door.

I was glad I had the next hour to think through Ano's telegram and compose myself before seeing Percy. Wrong again. When the driver opened the door, I saw Percy's long legs stretched out in the back and let out an exasperated sigh. Of all the times I needed to be alone just to think! I climbed into the back seat next to him and the driver closed the door behind me.

I'd seen Percy in a lab coat hundreds, no thousands of times. I'd seen him in jeans and hiking shorts. I'd seen him in his boxer shorts and a t-shirt in the morning. However, I'd never seen him dressed as he was tonight. Dress slacks and a button down shirt, his tie askew, he had the look of a prep school boy gone bad. He looked...amazing. My heart nearly stopped.

"H...hi."

Percy barely seemed to notice that I'd spoken. His eyes were looking me over as if I was someone else.

"You're..." he swallowed and I realized our knees were almost touching, "lovely."

Percy had told me I was competent, that I was brilliant and that I had a gift for science. However, until that moment, he'd never commented on my physical appearance at all.

"Thank you," I said shakily.

"I don't think I've ever seen you in a dress before."

"I thought that since it is Sunday, and I didn't know if..." I looked down at myself and smoothed the hem down over my legs.

"It's very appropriate. I was going to change after church, but I wanted to see you."

It was hardly the time to point out that he would have seen me when I arrived at his grandmother's house, and so instead I tried to remember the coaching Simone had given me.

"I'm glad." I sounded like an idiot, but Percy actually smiled when I said it so I couldn't have botched it too badly. "I've never seen you in a suit before," I said, trying really hard to resist the urge to reach up and touch his neck where the top button of his dress shirt was undone. "You look...really good."

"Thanks," he said, but his eyes followed the length of my body and now settled on my bare legs, which were exposed above the knee when I sat down in this dress. God, I felt naked. How did women get used to not wearing jeans and Converse?

I shifted in my seat, still holding the telegram from Ano. I'd clutched it so hard it was wrinkled horribly and I smoothed it out and tucked it back inside the heavy envelope it had come in.

"Mail?" he asked curiously.

I looked down at the envelope. "It's from Ano."

His face brightened considerably and took on a conversational tone. "How is she?"

I struggled to say it without either wincing or having a panic attack. "Getting married, actually."

His eyebrows both raised and he didn't speak for several minutes. I tried to smile, but it came out looking forced, so I let it fade from my face.

"I see. Is that an invitation?"

I nodded and tried my hand at smiling again. I had a little more success this time, and hoped it came across as believable. "It is."

"When's the happy date?"

I pulled the telegram from the heavy envelope and re-read the date. "September twentieth."

"You're going, of course." He wasn't asking. He knew, without me even speaking, that I wouldn't miss her wedding date for anything.

"Oh, absolutely." Logistically speaking I wasn't sure how I was going to skip all those classes without ramifications from my teachers. I'd find a way to make it work. Death in the family...something like that. With Ano getting married, it felt true.

"I could go with you...if you wanted. We could take my grandmother's car instead of the bus."

I'm sure my surprised expression must have given me away, and he added, "She has another car. A Range Rover. Something without a driver."

I laughed softly, hesitant about accepting. This was uncharted territory with Percy. I didn't know what he wanted for us. Hell, I didn't know what *I* wanted for us. I was still stinging over Matt.

I realized I hadn't given an answer, and I shrugged. "That's a long way. I don't even know how long it is, but at least a few days' travel to get there."

"All right, we'll discuss it."

I decided to change subjects. "Did you think about what to say to Edgar about going to Avon?"

Percy's face took on a serious tone and he rested his arm over his knee. "I did, but I'm not certain."

"I gave it some thought yesterday."

He raised an eyebrow at me. "Thought you were in a lab yesterday."

"I was."

"Then you should have been paying attention," he admonished me with a slight smile.

"I *was* paying attention."

"Would you be so kind as to tell me what you covered in lab, then?" he said in that professor tone I loved so much.

"I'd be happy to." I closed my eyes for a moment. "Angina, or Angina Pectoris, is described by the patient as temporary heart discomfort when the heart is not getting enough blood. Ischemia will occur, which results in a greater risk to the heart muscle. Diagnosis of Angina Pectoris is commonly—"

"All right, all right," he said, and I opened my eyes. "You cheated."

"I can't help it."

A smile tugged at the corner of his mouth. "It's kind of attractive."

It was confirmed. Men were idiots. My neurotic blessing (or curse, in my opinion) was 'attractive' in his eyes.

"Hardly."

"What did you come up with for the Edgar issue?"

"I thought about Edgar being your only surviving brother."

"Yes."

"And even though I don't have any surviving relatives, if I did, I'd want them as close as possible." I looked at him directly. "To keep them safe."

His brows were knit together and he was concentrating on what I'd said. He nodded his head slightly. "So you would enroll him in a school here in Philadelphia?"

"I would. To keep him close. If something else happened and you couldn't get to him..." I wondered if I'd overstepped my bounds.

Percy was looking at my face now, and he nodded again, as if seeing my point. "Yes," he agreed. "It's not as easy to get to him now as it once was."

"He will understand," I said, more gently than I meant to, and Percy turned to me so that our knees were now officially touching.

He draped an arm on the seat behind me. "I agree with your assessment of the situation," he said carefully.

He was close. Really close. The hand in his lap was nearly touching my leg. He leaned in so that his face was inches from mine. The arm on the back of the seat came around my shoulder and I found myself leaning into him. I'd wanted to touch Percy since I'd seen him in that hospital bed, seen him hundreds of times in my sleep since he left me in Fort Robinson, and replayed that morning in the cave over and over in my mind. Right now, with him in front of me, I couldn't move.

His index finger touched my knee and traced a small circle over and over. I closed my eyes. If I looked up, I was a goner, and there would be no going back. As if he could read my mind, Percy reached over and tilted my face up by my chin. I opened my eyes and was caught instantly by Percy's gaze. It was mesmerizing. I could barely breathe. His hand slid from my chin to behind my neck and he leaned towards me. With agonizing slowness, his lips grazed my jaw and I closed my eyes. His teeth opened gently against my neck and ear, nipping their way so gently towards my lips that the anticipation actually hurt.

Unlike the first time we'd kissed where I was the aggressor, this time Percy had the advantage, and he was using it to the fullest extent possible. Sliding my hand from his chest to his hair, I ran a hand through it; something I'd wanted to do for way too long. As if waiting for my touch to encourage him, Percy found my mouth and kissed it. Thoroughly.

He opened his mouth and deepened the kiss, flicking his tongue against mine. Turning towards him, I returned the kiss, my hands and mouth now unable to control themselves. I took his bottom lip into my mouth and he groaned. His hand slipped behind my knee and pulled my leg over his lap so that I was sitting against him, facing him.

"You just had surgery. We should be careful."

"We will be. Later."

He held me to him, in a kiss that was taking on a life of its own, and I pressed my hips against him and heard him groan again. He broke away from the kiss and his teeth and lips followed the incline of my neck and throat. Sliding from behind my knee up the outside of my bare thigh under my dress, his hands gripped my behind and pressed me down against him. I tipped my head back, moaning softly, and one of his hands pulled my strap down over my shoulder and kiss where it had been.

I had no idea when I'd gotten dressed that Percy would be seeing me half naked for the first time. But as he pulled the other strap down and the too-large top of the dress slipped down to my hips, I crossed my arms over myself in an effort to cover what I hadn't intended on revealing. Percy gently uncrossed my arms and intertwined our fingers together. He shook his head as if awestruck and lowered his head to the base of my throat. I wrapped my arms around the back of his neck and threaded my fingers through his thick hair. His hands moved to cover my breasts and he leaned me backwards, his mouth following his hands; his teeth and lips teasing me until I had to bite my lip to avoid crying out.

He pulled me to him, his mouth covering mine in a kiss that made me forget my name. I had no idea that Percy – *my* Percy – was like this. Simultaneously I wondered if he had been this way with Carlie. Their encounter in the tunnel that day had sounded so much more...clinical.

My fingers found their way to the buttons on his dress shirt and I pulled the tie from around his neck and discarded it on the seat next to us. I took his bottom lip into my mouth and bit down gently, then opened my mouth against his once again. I slid his shirt from his shoulders revealing his firm chest. I had wanted to touch his chest so badly for so long I couldn't help myself. Flattening my palms against it, I smoothed my hands over the scattering of dark hair and lines of definition. He was so beautiful. I trailed my fingers down from the base of his throat to his flat stomach. His arms went around to my back and he pressed me to him, our bare skin finally touching, and the sensation set me on fire.

"Oh God, I want you," he breathed against my hair and I almost cried at the sound of the phrase. Something I'd waited over three years to hear, something I thought would never come from his lips had finally happened. Percy knew all of me; who I was, who I wanted to be, where I came from. And oddly enough, he still wanted me.

Opening my mouth against his, I kissed him again. I could no more tell him the truth of my feelings than the man in the moon. Couldn't tell him I'd adored him – akin to hero worship – my entire undergraduate career. However, I could answer him, and hope that he would see the rest in my eyes.

"I want you too," I said breathlessly.

He leaned towards me and slid a hand under my dress once again, then the car began to slow. We stopped dead, both of us knowing we would likely be exposed by the driver in a matter of moments. Faster than I thought possible, I slid from his lap onto the seat next to him and struggled to pull the dress straps back over my shoulders. Only seconds later, with him attempting to jerk it out from underneath me did I realize I was sitting on his shirt and tie. Finished with adjusting the straps of my dress, I helped him pull his arms through the sleeves of his shirt and button up the front.

We were actually laughing hard towards the end; at getting re-dressed so quickly, at having the threat of being discovered by Phillip the driver, and at the thought of exiting the car looking like we'd both been mauled by mad gypsies. He slipped the tie around his neck as the car pulled to a stop and tied it fast. I finished buttoning his shirt as best I could and before the door could be opened, he pulled me to him for a last kiss.

I have no idea what we looked like emerging from the backseat. Only, the expression on both Edgar's face and – although she hid it immediately – Gigi's, was enough to tell me we weren't fooling anyone.

"What *happened* to you?" Edgar asked as Percy exited the car from right behind me and we stood in front of the large white house that towered above me like a castle.

Percy ran a hand through his hair that looked like he'd just woken up. "Nothing. I picked up Kate from school."

"Cause you look like—"

"Edgar," Gigi said from the base of the steps, "go in and make sure Sasha has the Devonshire cream I like so much set out for tea."

He grumbled slightly, and giggled when he passed me, but climbed the front steps and did as he was told. I felt Percy smoothing the back of my hair as nonchalantly as he could so it didn't look like a rat's nest.

Gigi stepped forward and took my hand, and I smiled at her. "Thank you for having me," I said nervously, although I'm sure it showed in my face. "You have a lovely home." I'd heard Carlie say it to Carrie, and thought it sounded nice, so I added it on.

She squeezed my hand warmly. "I trust you had a...pleasant ride here with my grandson?"

I was barely able to keep a straight face. "I did, thank you."

She motioned for me to ascend the steps and I did so as Percy offered Gigi his arm. Behind me, Percy answered her question as well.

"We had a pleasant visit. Catching up on old news."

I entered the house and stepped into the large foyer, so I didn't see her pat him on the shoulder and whispered discreetly, "Dear, your shirt is on inside out."

I had never had a formal tea. Truth be told, I didn't really care for tea – iced or any other. However, the tea we had that afternoon was simply decadent. Edgar and Percy acted as if it was commonplace to have people simply waiting at your elbow to reach something for you or put new food on your plate. I hadn't eaten breakfast before I left, and by the time the first tray of food was uncovered and offered to me, my stomach was growling so loud I had to press my hand against it to keep it from being heard.

I knew enough to only have one helping of everything, but I took advantage of every dish offered. By the time we finished, it was half past noon and Gigi asked me to take a walk in the garden. While I was wondering whether I was supposed to come around and offer her my arm as Percy had, she surprised me by telling the men to keep their seats and walking towards the rear doors to the garden without benefit of support. She did take my arm when we descended the steps towards the rose garden and as she pointed out each variety of rose, I tried to nod and act interested. As I'd told Carrie once, I wasn't skilled at the act of growing things, unless a Petrie dish counted.

"This one here, this is Eleanor. Named after the former first lady."

"Ah!" I said, and tried not to sound like an idiot. "It's beautiful."

"You studied with Percy at Stanford."

It was more of a statement than a question, but I nodded and answered, "Yes, I did."

She pointed to the stone bench under a tree in the distance. "And you were in the Master's program there. *With* Percy?"

He hadn't told her about me.

Oh, God. This could be painful.

Had Percy told her anything at all? "No, I had just finished my undergraduate degree when the whole group of us went to Wind Cave. For Percy."

We strolled leisurely in silence. It was bright outside, and muggy, but there was a breeze. "You went there to help him?"

I looked down at my feet as we walked and tried to think of a way to answer her question truthfully. "Yes. Percy and I had planned to go just the two of us, then it became this pilgrimage of sorts. And before we knew it, there were six of us."

We were nearly at the bench. "He hasn't told me much of what went on down in the cave. Only that you were all able to survive for the thirty days after the blast, and then came up."

It wasn't in Percy's nature to give the gory details of what had happened. Being his grandmother, though, she deserved to know and so as we reached the bench and I helped her sit, I told her. "He was nothing short of heroic," I said, knowing I was sounding a little lovesick.

"Heroic?" Her eyebrows went up. "Really? Go on."

"He navigated for all of us through the tunnels, to water sources throughout the caves. It was such a burden – having the responsibility of the five of us weighing down on him," I said. Gigi she patted the area next to her and I sat, looking back out over the garden. "He accepted it, as he always does. Just took the challenge and conquered it. Saw all of us through safely." I turned to her and smiled shyly. "He got us home."

"Were you close friends at Stanford?" she probed and I could tell where she was going with this.

I fidgeted a little. "I'm...well, we...worked together every day. In class, and labs, and I helped him with all of his research projects." I wouldn't have called us friends, but come to think of it, I didn't know if Percy had any close friends. Rather than take a passive role in the conversation, I decided to find out a little more about Percy. "What was Percy like growing up?"

"Shorter," she said, and we both laughed. "Ah, Percy. He always seemed to have an idea. Always the one with a plan, with...a direction. His mother used to say that he was always moving, but at least he was always moving forward."

I wondered if I should ask about his mother or if it was too tender; too new and painful. "Is Percy like his mother? Does he take after her a great deal?"

My question didn't seem to bother her, but her voice trembled as she responded. "He is like Camilla in so many ways," she said. "His gracefulness, his demeanor. He is so unlike Robert, my son. Robert could fill a room with his roar." She patted my knee gently. "And Percy isn't prone to roaring. But I'm sure you know that." She winked at me and smiled again.

I wasn't quite sure what she meant by it, but I smiled back nonetheless.

"He was always quieter, always thinking. Camilla and I so hoped he would meet someone at college; bring her home. But, year after year..." she shrugged, "he would come home alone."

I didn't say anything. Was it possible that Percy hadn't known I was in love with him because he'd never really been in love himself? Was it too much to believe that he was now falling in love with me? I was quiet, thinking over what she'd said...lost in my own thoughts.

"Percy says you have no family to speak of."

This is where I was inevitably going to fail. My shoulders sagged. "No, I don't."

"When did you lose your parents?"

I hated telling people this. Mainly because it normally invoked pity, which I detested, and secondarily because it didn't really matter when they died. They were gone. I was alone. "My mother died of cancer when I was four, and my father died when I was sixteen."

"You have no siblings, grandparents, and no other family?" The same questions everyone asked.

I gave the same answer I always gave. "No, none."

I waited for it. The 'I'm so sorry' or the 'how horrible!' or something like that followed by a very long, very uncomfortable silence. *Wait for it. Three, two, one...*

"I lost my father when I was ten."

Okay, that wasn't what I'd expected. "Ten?"

"Mmmhmm." She pointed to the other side of the garden. "Come. Let's walk." I helped her stand and she took my arm this time. "My mother died of breast cancer when I was seventeen. Just a few years after Daddy."

I thought it was kind of weird that at eighty she still referred to him as 'Daddy'. "You were in Philadelphia?"

She laughed. "Oh, my no! I grew up on the south side of Chicago. The poorer side, truth be told!" She laughed as if she'd told a great joke and I smiled. "And then, I met this man on a trip to New York. I'd followed some girls there for a secretary class; left my four siblings at home while I went to earn a certificate." She leaned into me and squeezed my arm as if telling me a secret. "Spent my last three dollars of tip money on a new dress. The girls all thought it would be fun to go to this club that night. We were all no more than twenty. So young and so naive. This man in a black suit came over and asked me to dance. Well, I said no because my feet were pinched in the shoes I was wearing. I'd borrowed them from a girlfriend of mine and they were a size too small."

I was so engrossed in her story that I didn't notice we were headed back toward the house.

"A few minutes after I'd said no, he came back over and invited us to dinner. All three of us, can you imagine?" she laughed, lost for a moment. "He paid for a cab to take us to a restaurant, we all had dinner and then he asked me for my number back in Chicago. Told me I was prettier than a movie star." She leaned towards me and whispered, "Silver tongued devil till the day he died."

"He sounds like an amazing man."

"He was. We had five sons together who were all strong men." We walked down a row of topiaries, each one more elaborate than the next.

"Percy's father?"

"Robert was always my favorite. You're not supposed to admit you have a favorite as a mother, I know, but Robert was mine." We kept walking, a faint smile on her lips. "He was my only son who had children, you know."

"Really?" Out of five boys, that was a little hard to believe.

"Yes, but oh, how I love his boys." Her lower lip trembled. "I love them still, even..." her voice trailed off and she squeezed my arm.

I wanted to change the subject, to bring it back to something less melancholy. "Edgar reminds me of Percy so much."

She laughed out loud at this; a real laugh, and it warmed my heart. "Don't let Percy hear you say that! He thinks Edgar should be more serious, more studious, more..."

"More something."

"Yes. But I think Edgar is what Percy would be like without the seriousness to bind him. I admit to being partial to Edgar. He is my baby; my last grandchild." She paused. "That is, until I have *great*-grandchildren."

It was so subtle I nearly hadn't caught it; the reference to having children. I laughed nervously. "That's a while off, I think. Edgar is only sixteen."

"Yes, but Percy is twenty-four. A year younger than Robert was when he proposed to Camilla. A year later, William was born. You never know where life will take you."

That's the truth, I thought, and helped her up the steps toward the back landing. She stopped halfway up and looked out over the enormous garden. She touched my chin gently. "I see why he was going crazy not hearing from you."

Percy had been crazy? Not hearing from...me?

She smiled at me warmly. "Come back and see me," she said. "Often."

"I would like that," I said, and really meant it.

"I have the feeling," Gigi whispered with a conspiratorial wink, "that we will be great friends."

All I could do was smile as we ascended the rest of the steps towards Percy and Edgar, waiting for us to return.

CHAPTER TWENTY-NINE

"Wake up, Ano. Damn, girl am I gonna have to get a cup o' cold water?"

From underneath her pillow came the muffled reply, "I'm up."

Jazz harrumphed around the room for a few moments, shutting drawers in the bathroom loudly, dropping his shoes next to the bed until the face of his bride-to-be emerged out from underneath the covers and pillows in the middle of the bed.

"What is so all fired important," she said, her eyes still closed, "that you would wake me this early?"

Jazz sat on the edge of the bed and rubbed her back to help wake her up. "It's ten-thirty."

Her head came up so fast he had to sit back to avoid being head butted. "*Ten-thirty*?" Ano half slid, half crawled out of bed and turned on the shower. "I'm late, I'm late!"

Jazz nodded. "I know."

She peeked a head around the bathroom door before she stepped into the shower. "Why didn't you wake me up sooner?"

It would be useless to tell her that he'd considered both nitro glycerin and dynamite to rouse her from her near-comatose state, and so he shrugged and laughed. "I'll set the alarm louder next time."

Downstairs, the entire household was alive with activity. Both Ano's grandmother and mother were cooking for the rehearsal dinner tomorrow night and her aunts were still sitting at the dining room table, busy making bows for the end of each of the pews. Even Ano's uncles and cousins, who had initially been averse to such a hasty marriage, were now getting into it and helping. Most of the men were over at the church making sure there would be enough chairs and tables for the reception.

Jazz walked through the kitchen on his way to borrow Ano's uncle's car and received both a slap on the wrist from Ano's mom when he grabbed a deviled egg and a pat on the behind from her grandma as he accepted the keys from her uncle. Despite all his trying, Jazz had been unable to locate Matt to be his best man. From Ano's reaction when he told her, Matt's absence wouldn't be missed. Jazz wasn't sure what had happened between Matt and Kate, but it had to be bad. Ano refused to even talk about it, even with him. The meager information she'd given him, between a few tears and carefully whispered curse words referencing Matt, of course, was that Kate had left him and never wanted to see him again.

He'd known Matt for two years, and in that time, they'd become close friends. Jazz knew he was different than most of the guys Matt hung out with, and that suited him fine. He hadn't ever been the kind of man who needed to be part of a fraternity; it just wasn't him. Matt seemed to respect the fact that Jazz didn't kowtow to him just because he was a *Skylar*. They both shared a love of the law, a love of baseball, and beautiful women. Which was why, when Matt came into their tort class one day star struck over meeting...well, *seeing* this girl no one believed it. No one, including Jazz.

For as much as he had dated, Matt had a strong reputation as either a player or a ladies man. He dated women several times, took them to expensive restaurants, the theater or a show, then simply moved on. He never really spent enough time with any one girl to get close to her, and thus had no real trail of broken hearts behind him. Including his. That is, until he'd met Kate.

Jazz looked down at the map that Ano's uncle had drawn him to get to the bank and turned down the next street. He had no idea what could have gone so wrong between Matt and Kate that had Ano so torn up, other than Matt simply doing what Matt did best; move on. Without Kate. It simply didn't add up. Matt was crazy happy with her, he'd said. 'Different than any other girl I've ever been with', Matt had told him in Denver. And Jazz, for once, had wondered if Matt could have finally fallen in love with a girl who wasn't preoccupied with dating a Skylar.

He had the address where Matt had been staying in Los Altos, but Ano had told him – in hurt, clipped tones— that Matt wasn't there anymore and she had no idea where he was. He would have liked to have known if Matt was okay, at least; if his mom had gotten the care she needed and that everything in his world was all right. Without an address, it was hopeless. Jazz' brother would have been one of his groomsmen if things were different...and he tried not to think about it. He tried not to think of his mother as Mother of the Groom, or the fact that he would have been the first of all the Taylor children to be married. Now, not only was he the first, he was the last...and only.

He stepped on the gas harder than he needed to, and had to work to slow himself down. Ano talked to him all the time about his grief, his anger, his pain. He was tired of talking about it. And now, something else loomed out there on the horizon; something threatening not only his present, but his future. He gripped the steering wheel hard, pulled into a parking spot at the bank, and grabbed his identity card.

No one knew that the only kind twist of fate that had been dealt to Jazz had occurred just prior to him leaving for the Wind Cave. His grant and his loan money had come through and he'd deposited both checks the week before they'd left so he could cut the checks for summer session and fall tuition when he got back to Palo Alto. They'd never returned, of course. And because the money had been from Stafford loans and the other half from the U.S. government, it had gone into his account immediately. When they'd identified, Jazz wondered if that money would still be there. His bank had somehow survived as one of the ten financial institutions that didn't go under. So in Denver, while Ano had stood in line waiting for the machines to check on her mother's and grandmother's identity, he'd checked his balance. $32,042.14 had printed on the slip that the clerk handed to him.

Now, however, it concerned him. Was it real money? All the money folks had had in other banks was real and they sure *lost* it! His, as far as the financial institution was concerned, was real. Jazz walked into the bank, presented his identity card, and slid his request for a withdrawal to the teller. He'd learned to write it down so that no one standing near you could hear that you were getting cash and try to shoot you for it on your way back out to the car. The teller counted the money and slipped it into a clean white envelope. Quickly, he nodded his thanks and returned to Ano's uncle's car.

When he passed the post station on his way back to the house, he considered inviting his only two living relatives – his Uncle Martin and his Aunt Lena – to the wedding. He'd discussed it with Ano, but in the end, had decided against it. He wasn't close with either of them and was fairly sure they wouldn't make the several thousand mile trip down to New Orleans to watch a nephew that they hadn't seen since he was seven get married. He'd looked up friends he'd had at NYU and had sent three of them letters, but only one had written back; his friend Chris, who had lost his wife in the first blast and really was in no condition to travel anywhere.

He hadn't told Ano that being separated from Matt was killing him. Matt, was his only living friend. And although Jazz was growing close to a few of Ano's cousins, Matt represented a life that he wanted to remember. A life he wasn't quite sure he was ready to leave behind. A life that still had a hold of him, no matter how he tried to turn his back on it. He still wanted to be twenty-three. He still wanted to be in college – happy, young, ready for life to begin. However, as he looked around him each day, the only thing that remained of that life was fading. Meeting Ano had been the best thing that had ever happened to him. Beautiful, smart, fiery...damn, but he was crazy for that woman. His mom would have loved her. He and Ano made sense in a world gone wrong. Her family had accepted him in; eased the pain he felt over the loss of everything.

Marrying her was the most impulsive thing he'd ever done, but he trusted the decision. He knew she was his when they'd been at Carrie and Charlie's, when he saw her doing dishes and cooking with all the women at the sink and it just struck him like lightning.

Wait. Carrie's house.

He made a U-turn at the next light and headed back to the post station without pausing to reconsider. Ano would kill him. Kate was due to arrive that night, so it was too late for him to get an answer back before the wedding. It was a long shot, at best. He knew that Kate had written to Carrie though, and had likely told her where Matt had gone after they'd left Los Altos, if they'd even left together. If Carrie would send Jazz a telegram back with Matt's whereabouts, he could at least find him.

Jazz hopped out of the car and fairly ran into the postal station, knowing it could backfire on him. However, the risk of losing the last thread of his old life was too great. He would have to pray the Carrie knew where Matt was.

"There he is! Hey, baby, what took you so long?" Ano was seated in the middle of the kitchen, ribbon all over the table, the floor, herself.

Jazz laughed at the scene. "Nothing. Last minute wedding stuff." He tossed her uncle his keys. "Thanks, Robert."

"No problem, son. Got it all taken care of?"

"Not all of it. I still have some details to finish."

Uncle Robert nodded. "Well then, lemme know when ya'll need it again."

"Will do."

Ano was picking out a color of nail polish from about fifty different bottles on the table in front of her. Her cousin Julie did nails and was giving Ano a manicure and pedicure tonight after Kate arrived.

"Hey," he said to her, "when's Kate's train comin' in?"

She pointed to another bottle, then wrinkled her nose when she saw it up close. "In about an hour. Why?"

Jazz looked around at the kitchen crawling with women and leaned in close to Ano. "Can I talk to you for a minute?"

"Sure." She pulled a light pink bottle from the end. "This one. Girl, don't you have me painted like a two dollar—"

"Ano."

She looked up to him, saw his face serious and suddenly, the room fell quiet. Her face blushed with worry. "Sure, Jazz. Julie, I'll be right back." Pulling the ribbons from around her neck and arms, she stood and deposited them on the kitchen table.

"E'vthing ah'right, Jazz?"

"S'just fine, Grandma." They walked past everyone on their way upstairs to their room.

Once inside, he closed the door and leaned against it. Ano's expression was a mixture of terror and fear. "What's wrong?"

"I have to tell you something."

Ano looked like she was going to cry, but she nodded her head. "All right. Whatever you need to say, I will understand." She sat down on the edge of the bed with her counselor face on. "These things get called off all the time," she said and patted the side of the bed next to her for him to sit.

"What?" Jazz laughed out loud and she raised an eyebrow at him.

"Are you crazy? I still wanna marry you, I just need to tell you something!" He leapt at her on the bed, pushing her back onto her back and kissed her neck. "The women in your family overreact entirely too easily."

"Do not say, 'we need to talk' in that voice to me when I'm marinating twenty pounds of shrimp downstairs!" she yelled at him. "Y'almost gave me a heart attack!" She slapped him on the shoulder and he continued to laugh.

"I *do* need to talk to you," he said, and rolled to the side of her, onto his back. He massaged his head. "I did something today, and I don't wanna start off keeping secrets from each other so I'm just going to tell you."

"Uh-huh."

Jazz looked at Ano with her lovely brown eyes and full mouth. That wide smile and throaty laugh that could easily drive him happily crazy for the rest of his life. It was best if he just blurted it out. Got it over with.

"I sent Carrie and Charlie a telegram today."

Ano blinked, nodded slightly, and tried not to appear obvious that she was examining her nail polish color while he talked. "Mmmm-hmmm."

"I told them we're getting married."

She smiled, still waiting for the bullet. "Okay."

Say it fast, he told himself. "I asked them if they knew where Matt was."

"You did WHAT!"

Jazz was sure that Ano's voice was easily heard at their church, some seven miles away. In fact, his ears were still ringing a few seconds after she said it. "Baby, you—"

She was up off the bed and pacing in front of him. "Don't you '*baby*' me! What possessed you to do that? Didn't I tell you that...that I don't know where he is?"

"Yeah, and that's why I thought maybe Kate had—"

"Kate doesn't want to see him, Jazz!"

He grabbed her wrist as she passed him, and raised his voice to her for the first time. "Yeah, but *I do*!"

Her mouth opened and her expression went blank. He let her hand drop and looked down at the floor.

"If this is about you having a best man—"

"It isn't that." He finally looked up at her again. "Everyone I know, from home to college, everyone, is...gone."

Ano came to sit on the edge of the bed once again with him. "And you wanted someone there who was...just yours. Besides me."

He snickered. "Besides you. Yeah."

She nodded, but didn't say anything for a long minute. "Matt's your boy. I understand that." When Jazz didn't respond, she went on. "But he hurt my girl." She pursed her lips and closed her eyes. "Cut her deep, Jazz."

"What'd he do? Ano, you gotta tell me."

In spite of the fact that she was trained to be a counselor, when it came to Kate, Ano was a mother lion. Love her and you'd survive. Hurt her...and look out. Jazz suspected that because Ano had been Matt's biggest supporter and had all but pushed Kate at him in the cave, that she somehow felt responsible for the pain Kate now felt.

"I'm going tell you," she said. "And no matter what I say, you can't defend him or make excuses for him."

Jazz nodded. "All right."

She took a deep breath. "They were in Palo Alto together. His brothers, uh, they told Matt to ditch her." She said it quietly, and didn't look at Jazz. "Told him that she wasn't the kind of girl be belonged with. That she was an orphan, not good enough for Matt. That," her voice caught in her throat, "she only wanted him for his money. Something like that."

"Oh, man."

Ano sniffed and straightened. "She didn't tell me the whole story. It's not Kate." She rolled her eyes. "You know."

"Yeah."

"She left him, and now she's trying to heal."

Jazz took her hand in his. "I'm not defending him," he clarified, "I'm asking."

"Ask."

He took a deep breath. "That's what Matt's *brothers* said."

Ano inclined her head at the obvious nature of his statement. "Yeah?"

"What did *Matt* say?"

Ano got a sad smile on her face. "Nothing. He didn't say anything."

Jazz blew out a breath in a whoosh. "Doesn't make sense."

"I know, but Kate wouldn't make it up, Jazz."

"No, baby, I'm not saying that. I just wonder if Kate heard the whole thing? Or if—"

She pointed a finger at him. "You said you wouldn't defend him!"

He held up his hands in surrender. "You're right. You're right."

"And anyway, she's with, you know..." She pursed her lips and rolled her eyes.

"Percy. Damn, you can say his name!"

She looked at him incredulously. "I know his name! I'll say it! Percy! She's with Percy now."

"Wow. You managed to do that without hardly any hand gestures or anything."

She hit him on the chest. "Shut up."

"Good Lord, woman."

"Three years, Jazz. *Three years* I watched her throw herself at that man! And he was oblivious to her!"

Jazz snickered. "And now he's not."

"Well," she said, crossing her legs, "it's about Goddamned time. And he'd better treat her well while he's here or so help me, if my Grandma sees him step one foot—"

He pulled her to him by her hand and kissed her. "I get it. I get it." Pulling her onto the bed with him, he rolled over the top of her and kissed her deeply.

"You're gonna mess up my hair," she said playfully, and wrapped her legs around his waist.

Jazz pressed his entire body against hers and whispered in her ear, "I'm gonna do a whole lot more than that."

She raised an eyebrow and laughed that unmistakable Ano laugh. "Why, Mr. Taylor!" She wrapped her arms around his neck and flicked her tongue against his throat. He growled and she giggled.

A loud pounding on the door made them both jump. "Child you best not be engaging in any...pre-marital activity!" Grandma Vesper's voice was deep and throaty from the other side of the door, and they both started laughing silently against each other. "If I have to come in there, it's not gonna be pretty!"

"Um, okay! Thank you!" Ano called as Jazz laughed against her neck. "I'm coming out!"

"An' tell that man in there that he best be getting' ready to drive to the train to pick up my Miss Kate!"

"Oh, shit!" Ano nearly threw Jazz onto the floor in her haste to get up. "Kate! Kate's train! Jazz, c'mon!"

CHAPTER THIRTY

Last minute anything, in my opinion, is rarely good. Because I'd waited until the last minute to decide on a mode of transportation, the only seats left on the train to New Orleans were coach, and not a sleeping car. Also, because I'd finally relented and allowed Percy to accompany me, we were lucky to get two seats together at all. From the short telegram Jazz had sent me I knew that they'd be picking us up at the train station and taking us back to Ano's aunt's house.

Percy had suggested getting a hotel, which I'd informed him would be seen as impossibly rude by Ano's mother and grandmother, whom I hadn't seen in close to a year. Last Christmas, to be exact. Although what I'd told him was technically true, I really wanted to stay with Ano, to be close to her one last time before she belonged more to someone else than she did to me. It was silly, childish, and sentimental. A very small part of me was also scared of having a hotel room with Percy; alone, with nothing at all stopping us from being together. That day in his grandmother's car was the closest we'd ever been to having sex. Since that day, I'd been in class, on rounds, or Percy had visited me at school for a late dinner or to talk. We'd kissed goodnight the few times I'd returned to my commune to find everyone asleep or out in lab or rounds, but nothing further.

He didn't believe in causal touching. He wasn't the type to hold your hand or put his arm around you for no reason. Matt, on the other hand, had been quick to touch. Holding hands, arm wrapped around my waist as we walked, even something as simple as tucking a strand of hair behind my ear. His hands were nearly always on me. And as much as it pained me to admit, I had actually come to like being touched by him. I hated the fact that a part of me still missed it.

I had carefully avoided most of Percy's covert attempts to get information about Los Altos and Matt out of me. Mostly I answered with vague generalizations, or shrugged and told him I didn't remember. The humiliation of actually telling him out loud why I was considered undesirable by another man was so abhorrent to me that felt physically ill contemplating it. I expected Percy to eventually move on. It wasn't like him to belabor a point. But he didn't, and we continued this inane dance around the real questions he wanted to ask and the real answers I could never give. It was Capra-esque in its irony.

After twenty-two hours on a train, half of it spent studying for my cardiovascular exam the week after I returned, I closed my book and leaned my head back against my headrest. I was finally going to see Ano again, and then say goodbye two days later. In a rather weak, self-pitying moment, I lamented the fact that my life had been filled with a lot of goodbyes lately. And how was Jazz going to take the fact that I was coming without Matt? They were best friends. Wasn't he a little bit...

My eyes flew open. *Matt was best friends with Jazz. Best friends. Oh God. Was Matt going to be Jazz' best man?* The thought of seeing Matt again made me physically sick with dread. I was bringing Percy, and how was that going to look if...

"You haven't slept a wink since we left. At least *pretend* to rest." Percy's voice was close to my ear, but his eyes were closed and his arms were crossed over his chest.

My face relaxed just at the sound of his voice and I leaned back against my headrest. "All right."

"You finished studying?"

"Yes."

"Mmmhmm," he said, eyes still closed. "So you're prepared for the exam."

"Yes."

"You're concerned about passing it?"

My eyebrows knit together. "No."

He turned towards me in his seat, which left his face inches from mine. "Then what is so occupying your thoughts that's making you unhappy?"

"I'm not unhappy."

"Will you allow conjecture on the subject?"

"Of course."

"Your best friend is getting married and you feel some type of ethereal loss through that relationship. Add to it that you're not certain if Matt is going to be at the ceremony, and it makes this situation...difficult at best."

I was kind of amazed that he'd said it out loud, but also relieved. The conductor announced arrival in New Orleans in twenty minutes. I didn't want to rationalize my feelings of loss about Ano getting married, and so I did what I was good at. I deflected.

"I think she's too young to get married."

Percy shrugged. "Twenty-two isn't what is used to be."

I almost laughed out loud it sounded so funny coming from him. "And Ano would have told me if Matt was going to be here." My hand flew to my mouth when the words came out.

Percy's eyes clicked open and he turned to me. "Really, why?"

I silently berated myself for speaking when I was exhausted. "Because..." I tried to think quickly, and all that came to mind was cardiovascular tissue degeneration.

"You're too tired to lie to me," he said smoothly and laughed gently.

I hit my head against the headrest. Damn him for knowing me as well as he did! "Well, Matt's not going to be there." *Oh, please, let me be right.*

"If he is," Percy said, his eyes closed again, "he won't be bothering you."

I narrowed my eyes. "Is that why you came? Because you thought Matt would be here?"

Percy looked at me with a benign smile on his face. "Of course not. I came to be with you, and enjoy your company. I have no reason to see or speak with Matt. The only thing that would cause me to have anything to discuss with Matt is if he had caused pain to someone I care for. And then we would have to have another *chat.*" His eyebrow rose at me. "Our last chat concerning that subject did not end well."

I remembered their last 'chat' in the cave had ended with Matt sustaining a black eye and very badly split lip. Although Percy had fared better, I still did not envision round two going well. Nor did I have any desire to be the cause of a Neanderthal show of power by two men I... I stopped the thought before I could finish. I didn't...couldn't...love Matt. I had to stop thinking of him as he was in the cave. My instincts had been correct all along. A man like Matt Skylar had been interested in me for one thing. Like a naive schoolgirl, I'd fallen for him. That made me gullible, and pretty much like every other lemming he'd ever dated at Stanford. I was going to forget him in time. Forget his touch, and forget his taste. I closed my eyes. I was going to forget how it felt, just for that brief period of time, to feel as though I belonged to someone who actually wanted me.

The train slowed, approaching the station. Percy and I gathered our things from around us and prepared to disembark. Adrenaline at the thought of seeing Ano had my heart racing, and it took an effort at self-control to keep from pushing through the crowd to get out into the station.

"Did they say where they were meeting us?" Percy asked as we were herded through the aisle towards the exit.

I tried to be heard above the other hundreds of voices around us. "No, just that she would meet us here." Holding my backpack by the straps I followed Percy off the train. When he got to the ground he lifted his arms up to me as if to lift me down. I hopped off the train myself, despite a raised eyebrow from Percy.

"Really?" I asked him. "Lifting a human from a train weeks after you've had surgery?" He sighed, but said nothing. I smiled in silent victory.

From across the platform, I heard a voice, familiar and in a near scream, calling my name. I turned just in time to see Ano...my Ano, running to me full force. Somehow knowing I would drop my pack in a second to reach her, Percy grabbed my pack and I ran towards her, our two bodies meeting in something between a hug and a body slam.

"Oh my God! Look at your hair!" she said, touching my head. "It's so long!"

I touched my hair, and then hers. "Look how beautiful you are! You look so happy."

She grinned and a dimple showed up in her right cheek, as always when she smiled widely. "I am."

We embraced and touched foreheads, our arms gripping each other so tightly that it hurt. I simply couldn't let go. "I'm so glad you're here," she whispered. And then, our circle of confidence engaged, she added, "I'm so sorry, baby girl."

I nodded, not wanting to think about any of what I'd written her in my last letter. "S'okay." Before Percy could hear I made a request that only she could understand. "Not now, okay?"

"Later, though?"

I nodded and we released each other, Jazz and Percy appearing on scene next to us both.

"Hey, Percy!" Jazz reached out and shook Percy's hand.

"Congratulations," Percy said.

"Thanks," Jazz said with a nod of his head. "C'mon, baby, let's get back."

"Okay, okay!" Ano grabbed my arm and turned me towards the waiting car and I reached for my bag from Percy.

"I've got it," he said, and prepared to sling it up onto his shoulder.

My hand pushed down on the frame and I raised an eyebrow at him. "Again? Need I remind you what the doctor said?"

"No need. I have one in front of me who seems to have memorized his entire discharge summary."

"Cooperate, please." I lifted my pack up onto my shoulder and walked side by side with Ano back to the car.

"What was that about?" she asked so only I could hear.

"I'll tell ya later."

* * *

It was nothing short of pandemonium when we arrived back at Ano's aunt's house. Grandma Vesper kissed me over and over and embraced me no fewer than ten times. Ano's mother Michelle had her arm around my waist for about the first half hour and kept patting me and hugging me to her telling me how much she had missed me. I met more cousins than I thought was possible to have in one family, and kept track of maybe three of the twenty names.

Everyone seemed to want to feed me. A large plate was slid into my hands, already piled with food. Our packs were literally pulled from us the moment we arrived. Jazz seemed comfortable introducing Percy around the room while Ano told a funny story about the two of us when we were in Stanford. It seemed, at least for tonight, that we could go back in time to college, that we could pretend that life was simple and we were all still carefree, and that the wedding day after tomorrow was nothing but the result of young love and not necessity of the times.

As always with Ano's family, it was warm, inviting, and happy, with about fifty people talking all at once. Wedged on the couch between Ano's mom and Grandma Vesper, I saw Percy holding a plate piled as high as mine with food. All the men were asking him about the cave and he was actually trying to respond to the questions being fired at him. In between men telling him to "Eat up, boy!" he gave answers that both interested and intrigued Ano's relatives.

"An' jus' look at you!" Grandma Vesper squeezed my elbow. "You lose any more weight, I'm gonna come up there to that med school and feed you m'self!" She barely looked towards Percy, but pointed a finger at him with a mock warning. "Boy, you start feedin' this chile!"

He grinned. "Yes, ma'am."

She kissed me on the head again. "You brought her down into that cave and saved my baby." She rocked back and forth, and I sensed a really tight hug in my immediate future. "And we...we all..." tears formed in her eyes, "jus' thank God you made her go." She kissed me on the head again and nodded towards my plate. "Eat, now! Gonna make Grandma cry? You gotta eat!"

Ano scooted onto the ottoman in front of us, her eyes wide at the plate of food in my hands. "Damn, girl! You thinking of feedin' the free world?"

"For real."

Ano's uncle had opened a large bottle of wine and was pouring it into wine glasses and plastic cups for the fifty-some people that were crowded into the living room and kitchen of his home.

"E'vyone?" he said, and I saw Ano's aunt with an identical bottle filling glasses on the other side of the room. A cup full of deep red wine was passed to me. "I'm gonna let my soon-to-be nephew say a prayer tonight." He looked around the room and found Jazz, who, despite his protests, reluctantly agreed.

"Dear Lord, we thank you for the safe passage of our dear friends. Their presence here is deeply appreciated. The love in this room is deeply felt. I want to thank you for the love of my wife-to-be..."

A few cheers and catcalls were made from the cousins.

"...and for her family who has taken me in as if I was their own." Jazz paused for a moment, and his voice trembled. "I want to say a prayer for those not with us tonight, for they are sorely missed. Missed, but not forgotten. They are with us tonight, and with us always in our hearts."

There were murmurs of 'uh-huh' and 'mm-hmmm' from around the room.

"God, bless us as we journey on, as we push past our fear, as we journey into the future, and as we embrace a brave new world on the horizon. Praise in Jesus' name. Amen."

What seemed like several hundred 'amen's were heard from around the room, including mine, and then we all drank deeply of the wine in our cups. I possibly should have reconsidered wine before eating more food, but I was with Ano. I was among family. I was next to Grandma and Michelle, and really, I was home.

CHAPTER THIRTY-ONE

"No, now I've got about three pies to make and I need flour." Carrie scolded both Charlie and Matt, who were sharing a private joke leaning against the front bumper of the truck. "Honestly, you two are worse than a couple of old women."

She teased them, but enjoyed seeing Charlie in such a good mood lately. Having Matt here was turning out to be a blessing in disguise. One of their workers had just up and left last week, and Matt had jumped in, eager to ease the burden on them. It seemed to Carrie that it was as if he was doing penance every day, paying for his arrogance, punishing himself for losing Kate.

Since that night, he never spoke about it, and never asked Carrie other than the most basic questions. How was she? Had she gotten a letter recently? Was she eating enough?

Knowing his internal struggle and the pain the truth was going to cause him, Carrie answered the questions she could; ignored the ones she couldn't. She'd received a letter from Kate about a week after Matt had arrived, full of news about med school, and not really more than a paragraph about Percy. Taking pity on him one night, she'd read him a little of Kate's letter, where she described her rounds at the hospital (she omitted the name for obvious reasons) and the attending she'd been watching allowed her to help him stitch a wound for the first time. The elation of having done it correctly came through clearly in her letter.

After she'd read a little to him, he'd said, "She seems happy," but his voice had been sad and he'd gone to bed moments later.

The absence of a letter from Kate over the last few weeks had eased the tension between them some and Carrie was always happy when she saw Charlie and Matt coming in from the field with the tractor, dust billowing behind them. The first of the rain was supposed to come this weekend, which would be good for the soil. Before the rain could come, they were going to a barn raising at Edel's farm where all the men would contribute to rebuild a barn that had been destroyed months before the blast hit and never rebuilt due to the bank closing and lack of funds. The women would all bring food and the few families actually remaining in Fall River could began to rebuild a community, despite the rumors they were hearing about another surge of attacks.

Carrie was making three pies, and needed another few pounds of flour from the store. For reasons still unknown to her, both men had insisted on coming along to town. How could she get any work done with them hanging on her like a couple of old hens?

"All right," she scolded, "now go." She handed a letter folded in half to Charlie and pleaded with him to keep it folded until he handed it to Tom at the post station. "Go see if we've got word yet about that part for the tractor, would you?"

Charlie hated it when she put him in the middle of lying to Matt. It was clear from the scowl on his face that, although he wouldn't let Matt see the address on the letter to Kate, he was unhappy at having to do it. Matt pretended not to notice and stuck his hands in his pockets as he and Charlie walked the three blocks to the postal station.

"I'll mail that for you," Matt offered, but his hands remained in his pockets.

"No thanks," Charlie's answered gruffly.

"Sait's got his tobacco store opened back up, I see," Matt commented as they passed.

"Mmmhmm."

"I'm betting they have some fine pipe tobacco."

Charlie chuckled. "And if I came back with an ounce of it I'd be in the doghouse, same as you."

They walked in silence for a few minutes until the post station was in sight. Matt's voice was nearly pleading. "Charlie, please."

He exhaled. Goddamn he hated this. He'd wanted to give the kid the address the first night, but Carrie had made him promise, and he would never, ever break a promise he'd made to his wife. Not for Matt, not for anyone. And damn, if she didn't know it. "Can't do it, Chief."

He knew Matt could have ransacked the house and probably found a letter from Kate. Could have done a hundred dishonest things to get it but didn't. The fact that he stayed in spite of the daily torture made Charlie love him, just a little. The fact that he stayed and worked like a son of a bitch in the fields every day made Charlie love him even more. The sight of his face every time the post came and it didn't have a letter from Kate pained Charlie more and more each day. But once Carrie had made her mind up about something, it was done.

"Afternoon Tom." Charlie handed the folded letter to Tom, who didn't unfold it until he was well out of sight and then he tossed it into the bin for outgoing mail.

"Hey, hang on there!" he said when Charlie turned around to leave. "Got another electric post for Carrie!"

"Another?" Charlie looked surprised. "Didn't know she got one before."

"Oh, yeah." Tom came back with the slip of paper in his hand and handed it to Charlie. "From different folks, though."

Charlie stood and read it over for a moment, then folded it in half. *Goddamn it.* Matt, who was trying not to be obvious about wanting to see who it was from, pleaded with his eyes.

"Return post paid," Tom reminded Charlie. "You wanna send a response?"

"I'll ask Carrie 'bout it," Charlie said gruffly and stalked out of the station, Matt hot on his heels.

"You gonna tell me what's in that telegram?"

Charlie hadn't needed a smoke in twenty years as badly as he needed one now, but he walked right past the newly reopened smoke shop. "Nope."

"Is it from her?"

Thankfully, he could be honest in his response. "Nope."

Taller than Charlie by a good three inches, Matt still struggled to keep up with his stride towards the store where Carrie stood waiting next to the truck. "Is she okay?"

Charlie stopped a hundred feet from the truck and looked at Matt, hard. "You gotta trust me that I'm going to talk to Carrie tonight." He was breathing hard. "Okay?"

Matt nodded and a grateful smile spread across his face. "Okay. Thanks, Charlie."

"I might not get you anything, Chief."

"I know."

They made it to the truck and Matt took the groceries from Carrie and opened her door, earning him a shaking head from Charlie. He rode in the bed of the truck the whole way home, waited through dinner for Charlie to say something, and finally after Matt had cleared and done dishes, Charlie spoke to Matt.

"Go'on out to the cottage, Matt. Me and Carrie gotta have a talk."

There was smoke on Matt's heels as he left. "Yessir."

Carrie watched him go and turned to Charlie with a smile. "What's that all about?"

Grim expression on his face, Charlie reached in his pocket and retracted the telegram she'd received from New Orleans from Jazz. Carrie read it over several times and then shook her head.

"Well, Goddamn it."

He nodded once. "S'what I said."

"What do I do, Charlie? I can't lie to Jazz. He wants to know where Matt is, I'll tell him! Or, I'll send him a telegram tomorrow."

Charlie released a breath. "Thank God. So we can tell the boy that—"

"No. If we tell Matt about this," she held up the telegram, "he'll know that Kate's there in New Orleans."

"And?"

"And if Kate's there, don't you think he'll try and go down there to find her?"

"I do."

She held up her hands, exasperated. "And that's okay with you?"

Charlie knelt by Carrie's feet and looked up into her face. His whole life, he'd only loved one woman. As they'd grown older, she never said a word about his thickening middle, or the lines that deepened around his eyes each year. She'd raised their two boys into fine men, and probably missed seeing them more than she'd care to admit. But he knew she was wont to meddle in the lives of others from time to time, and this was no exception.

"Honey, he's hurt," Charlie said, in pain himself. "And keeping it from him isn't making him regret it any more. Now, maybe he'll get to her in time, and maybe he won't, but he loves her, an' I believe that. He deserves the chance to go and make it right."

He could see his argument was winning her over and so he delivered one final phrase that he knew would do it.

"You gotta *let him* be happy."

Her eyes came up to meet his and she nodded, albeit reluctantly. "All right. I'll send a reply tomorrow."

Charlie stood and walked towards the door. "All right." He called out towards the cottage, although he knew Matt wouldn't have gone inside. "Come in here, boy."

"What're you doing?"

Charlie chuckled. "Making him happier than he's been in nearly three weeks."

From the front cottage porch, Matt stood and jogged over to Charlie. "Yeah?"

He nodded towards the house. "Get in here."

Matt was inside within seconds, looking anxiously from Carrie to Charlie. When he couldn't wait for Carrie anymore, Charlie prodded her. "Read it to him, honey."

Carrie unfolded the telegram from her lap and read:

From:214 Rugvale Road, New Orleans, LA
To: 55 Shoreline Hwy, Fall River, SD, Carrie

```
Blackhawk
Need information location of Matt Skylar
If you know where he is please provide ASAP
Ano and I are being married September 20
Any information will help
Jazz Taylor
>immediate reply requested, post paid<
```

For three full seconds Matt didn't move. Then he looked first at Charlie, and then to Carrie, who sat waiting for his reaction.

"Jazz is getting married," he said. And then, as it dawned on him, he walked to Charlie and gripped him on the shoulders. "Jazz is getting *married*!" he nearly screamed.

"I know," Charlie said, although he had a smile a mile wide.

Matt began to pace. "Which means Ano asked Kate to be her maid of honor, which means *Kate's gonna be in New Orleans on September 20th*."

Charlie nodded. "Yep."

Matt turned one way, then another. He turned to Charlie, out of breath. "Can you drive me to the bus station?"

"Bus don't leave Fort Robinson till the morning," Charlie said. "And I'd give you my truck but I need it for work."

Matt seemed possessed. "What the...how can I get to her?"

Carrie was the only calm one in the room. "Matt, you can catch a bus tomorrow, and—"

"No, no! I need to..." he paced in front of them, "I really need to get to her."

"There's an Amtrak station, 'bout five hours west in Wheatland."

"The one in Wyoming?" Carrie asked.

Charlie nodded and Matt looked to Carrie. "Does the bus in Fort Robinson go to Wheatland?"

"Forget the bus, boy! I'll drive you there! We'll leave tonight!"

Carrie stood. "Charlie, really. Now, tomorrow morning—"

The expression on Matt's face stopped her. "All right," she conceded. "Take him to the bus."

Matt jumped high in the air and touched the ceiling with a whoop. "Charlie," he pointed back to him as he walked towards the back door, "I'm comin' back here to help you grow that wheat!"

"I'm countin' on it, boy!"

"And I'm bringin' Kate back with me!" he let out another whoop out as his feet hit the dirt and he ran to pack some clothes before they left.

Charlie grabbed his keys from the hook and stood behind Carrie. She was awfully quiet. Never a good sign. "I had to," he explained. "It was killin' me."

"She'll never take him back. She's been hurt too bad."

He pressed his lips together and came to kneel again by her side, groaning as he did so. "Momma, getting too Goddanged old to crouch down like this. Too hard to get back up!" Carrie smiled and he lowered his voice. "If she won't, then it's up to *her* to tell him."

"It'll hurt her all over again to tell him!"

"I know, and it simply kills you to let another man live his own life." This comment earned him a pressed lip frown from his wife. "Send back a reply tomorrow, tell Jazz that Matt's on his way and to expect a call."

"You think he'll make it in time?"

Charlie sighed. "Gonna be close. I dunno."

"I'll send it."

"Thank you."

Matt bounded into the room, still stuffing clothes in and zipping up the side. "You ready? Let's go! Let's go!"

They both kissed Carrie on their way out the door, amidst her requests for driving safely to Charlie and sending word that he'd arrived safely to Matt. She watched them go, her heart aching. A little for Kate because she knew how deeply she'd loved Matt...and how badly he'd hurt her. A little for Matt for the pain that losing Kate had caused him. And a little for herself and Charlie – for the loss of them all.

CHAPTER THIRTY-TWO

"Now tilt it down, just slightly. That's it. Now squeeze."

The sound of Carlie's gun firing echoed against the ruins that surrounded them. David checked to make sure she hit her mark, then asked, "You feel the difference that time?"

She nodded and lowered her gun. "Yeah."

David checked his watch. "All right, it's time, c'mon. It'll be dark soon."

She helped him pack away their weapons and they walked home, not speaking. Two weeks of target practice, of shooting anything that wasn't nailed down to improve her aim, was growing old. They walked together in companionable silence for a few minutes on the way back to his flat. Since the mass exodus that had taken place a few weeks ago, only three other residents remained at the trauma ward besides herself, and they'd chosen to move to a smaller (and safer) apartment than the one they'd shared as a group of twelve.

Without nearly any discussion, David had moved her things into his flat, where she'd apparently taken up permanent residence. Their life together fit together so well; two people who shared the exact same goals and dreams for the future, if that future existed. With the word of a new attack spreading, people were fleeing the area and the days at the trauma center became slow. And so, their days became comforting in their predictability. Few real traumas came in, and they were able to go home together nearly each night while another shift took over. On the rare day off, David taught her to fight. He taught her to shoot, both stationary and moving targets. As September drew to a close, more people appeared to be leaving each day; headed for safe ground, headed for shelter without the threat of invasion. And yet, she and David stayed.

After dinner had been cleared and the dishes done, she came over to recline against him on the couch. Life was easy with David. He was completely unlike any man she'd ever met; passionate, knowledgeable, and singularly dedicated to the task of saving lives.

"I want to give you something."

She sat up and turned to face him, his face somber. Having just taken a shower, her hair was damp and she tucked a strand behind her ear. "Okay."

"I debated whether to give you this or not."

"What is it?"

He reached in his pocket and produced a small plastic tube, no longer than a half inch in length. Carlie reached for it and examined the pill inside of the small plastic tube.

"Uh, you shouldn't have?"

"It's..."

"I know what it is."

He was quiet for a moment, and didn't try and explain. Carlie sat next to him, holding the pill, shaking her head.

"Wouldn't it be easier," she asked, "to put a gun to my head? Less painful. Less traumatic."

David nodded solemnly. "A gun can be taken from you easily. You can be disarmed." He looked into her eyes. "What then?"

"The likelihood is that they would just shoot me, not torture me. I have little or no useful information or—"

"There are worse things than..." He couldn't continue for a moment. "I've seen men, soldiers from other armies, do things that...the women would have been better off dead." He reached over and closed her fingers around the plastic tube. "Promise you'll keep it with you. Just in case."

"I don't believe in suicide."

"You would. If you'd seen what I've seen."

Carlie placed the small tube on the coffee table next to the couch and leaned close to him. "Usually, a couple has to be married in order for the man to want to kill his mate. Aren't we progressing kind of fast?"

"You're making light of this, and it's not a laughing matter."

"That's the only way I can deal with this right now. I'm doing this part on my terms. I'm desensitizing myself to what's going on." She tucked her legs underneath her and faced him. "I'm staying at a trauma unit that's likely going to be invaded within weeks by enemy soldiers. I'm staying in the hopes that – on the chance that the U.S. actually does have soldiers that show up, we can help patch them together and still manage to not get shot in the process." She took a breath. "I'm sleeping with the chief attending..." he started to interrupt and she held her index finger up, "who is by far the sexiest man I've ever been with."

"Thank you."

"Wasn't done." Carlie cleared her throat. "I'm learning to fight, shoot a gun, and take a man's life should he try to take mine first. Meanwhile, during the day, I'm learning to *save* lives, patch people together and send them back up so they, too, can get gunned down within two weeks' time. Lastly, my... boyfriend...gave me a suicide pill to make matters easy if I should be taken against my will."

They both sat in silence and, having exhausted most of her talking points, she sighed.

"If the irony of this situation doesn't occur to you," she said blandly, "then I'm recommending a head CT first thing tomorrow morning."

He turned to face her. "Your...boyfriend?"

"Well," she grinned, "yeah. I'm...well, yeah."

He raised an eyebrow at her. "Aren't I a little old to be a 'boyfriend'?"

"You're not too old for everything that's gone along with it lately."

He chuckled. "You have entirely too much healthy sexual energy for one person."

She leaned towards him on all fours, and kissed him squarely on the mouth. "I've been told that before." She pressed him back against the pillows and moved to straddle his lap. Her hands tugged at the bottom of his shirt and moved to unbutton his jeans.

"Carlie," he said, and pushed against her to lean forward. Her mouth was teasing his and she paused to pull his bottom lip into her mouth. "No. We—"

"I warn you," she said mockingly. "I've been trained in the fine art of combat, and I'm not afraid to use it." She continued her assault on his neck and jawline until he restrained her by the wrists, holding them to her sides. She wriggled and squirmed against his grasp.

"Show me some of that combat training," he said, his voice low in her ear.

She pulled back, unsure if he actually meant it or not. His face was deadly serious, so she shook her head. "Ouch. No."

His hands were like vises around her wrists. "Carlie, I've got you restrained. Now break free."

The harder she struggled against him, the tighter his grip got. Seesawing towards her, he pushed her back against the cushions until he came to rest on top of her. "Get free," he commanded again, but his body was heavy, and try and she might to break his grasp, she couldn't. Her wrists were beginning to hurt.

"Ouch! David, I can't."

She knew he was trying to teach her a lesson, one she didn't care to learn tonight. Not realizing the consequence of her action, she maneuvered her knees between them quickly and pushed him to the side, off the couch and directly onto the coffee table, shattering it underneath him.

"Oh, my God!" her wrists released, she moved to help him. Shards of wood were all around him, but David wasn't hurt. He dove at her and she dodged to the side, avoiding his grasp and moving quickly towards the kitchen.

He caught her ankle and she went down hard on her knees and elbows to the hardwood floor. He flipped her over and had her legs pinned when she lashed out with her knuckles as he'd taught her, catching him squarely in the throat. He gagged and released her. She slid on her hands and knees again towards the kitchen, only to have her hair grabbed from the back and pulled backwards once again to the ground.

A war cry came from her throat as she reached back to scratch and claw at him, but he stayed securely out of her range. From behind her he restrained her wrists behind her back and pulled her to a standing position, pushing her against the wall. Her feet were bare and she struggled to find an instep she could injure, but he kept his feet out of range. The wall was cold against her cheek and she could feel herself weakening. More than fear, she felt anger, and she slid her right elbow out and up, striking his jaw with a crack.

He didn't release her, but his hold on her lessened and she spun, one arm still behind her and lifted her knee up between his legs. His knee came down simultaneously, blocking her attack, and she tried again – harder this time until she'd wrestled free from his grasp and was on the attack as opposed to the defense. Her punches would clearly be nothing to him, which was why she dove and rolled out of his reach into the kitchen. She grabbed the counter to help her up and found what she'd been seeking all along. As he caught up with her, she spun, long handled butcher knife in hand.

"I win."

Her chest was heaving, as was his, and he had blood coming from the edge of his lip where she'd elbowed him. He stood, holding his hands up in mock surrender. She didn't lower the knife until he backed out of the kitchen and sat down at the kitchen table, holding his ribs.

David leaned against the table, his brows knit together in irritation. Carlie shook in anger. "That wasn't funny."

"I didn't intend for it to be."

She set the knife reluctantly on the counter. "I didn't like that."

"I didn't do it for fun." She walked over to him, not ready to forgive him quite yet.

"Your lip is bleeding."

He raised his eyebrows causally and reclined in the kitchen chair, his long legs stretching out in front of him. "Yeah, it is."

She massaged her elbow and wrists, where light blue marks were beginning to form. "You hurt me."

He stood and she took an instinctive step backwards. He held his hands up in surrender. "I'm sorry I hurt you."

Carlie looked down to the floor. David took another cautious step towards her.

"I need you to know this *isn't* fun. It's not a game. It's not 'target practice'. And I needed you to understand how very serious I am about you leaving."

"You did this so I'd leave? You'd rather I leave and go hide somewhere than—"

His voice rose above hers. "I'd rather you were safe! I'd rather I didn't have to give you cyanide capsules, for Christ's sake! Carlie, in all likelihood, we're not going to survive if the attack is unopposed."

"Then why are you staying? You think I have a death wish?"

"No. Because I think, if I love my freedom then I should be willing to fight for it, and yes, to die for it. I have the training of a soldier. I *was* a soldier. And if we have no active duty soldiers to stand the line, then I'll take out as many of theirs as I can and possibly save one or two of ours before I die."

"And you think I would be safer hiding somewhere else - letting men die for the same freedom I enjoy every day?" She pressed her lips together. "Hardly seems fair."

David tried to chuckle, but then winced and held a hand to his rib where he'd fallen on the coffee table. "There is no fair in war. Or didn't they teach you that in pre-med?"

She crossed the kitchen and motioned to his arm. "Lift." He raised his right arm over his head for her to feel along his ribcage. "It's not broken." He lowered his arm. "And I'm not leaving."

David hung his head, and then raised it to look at her once again. "Would you be staying if it wasn't for me?"

A slight smile played across her lips and she raised an eyebrow at him. "That's an awfully conceited question to ask."

Carlie crossed to the refrigerator, pulled an ice pack from it and hummed lightly as she leaned in and pressed it against his face. "What would you say if I told you that you were my reason for doing a lot of things lately?"

His face softened. "I'd say you were a fool. And in good company."

She allowed him to put his arms around her and kiss her lips gently. "I shouldn't forgive you," she said, and resisted the urge to poke him in the ribs.

They studied the wreck that they'd made of the living room; table in shards, chairs tipped over...and both began to laugh.

"You're insane."

He nodded. "I'll grant you that."

Carlie gingerly rubbed along her wrist where the red had turned light blue. He gently turned her wrist over and kissed the pulse point. Her eyes closed when his lips touched her.

"David..." she said softly, and his eyes met hers.

His lips worked their way up her arm to her elbow where she'd fallen.

"Does it hurt here?"

Carlie nodded and allowed herself to be turned around as he smoothed her mane of chocolate brown hair over one shoulder. "How about this?" he breathed, and with aching tenderness made his way up the top of spine to the base of her skull.

With one hand against her abdomen he pulled her to him, his other hand sliding underneath her shirt. "Tell me where it hurts," he teased.

"Everywhere." "Well then," he said, and in a single, swift motion he scooped her into his arms and carried her to the bed. "Let's play doctor."

CHAPTER THIRTY-THREE

Jacques Bertrand II was the most beloved Prime Minister in decades. Revered by the people for his level-headed decisions, Jacques considered himself a man of the people. Raised in a working-class home, he valued loyalty and hard work above all else. His great love for his country only endeared the people to him more; he held the future of Canada in his hands and never forgot the weight of that responsibility.

The entire second floor of his Gatineau Park residence was off limits to all Canadian personnel but him. He ascended the stairs and was greeted by three Navy Seals armed with M-16s and combat equipped.

"Mister Prime Minister," the first Seal greeted him and saluted, which Jacques answered.

Jacques waited while his retina was scanned before being allowed onto the second floor. Once there, he was accompanied by one of the Seals into the back Master bedroom that had been modified within the last three weeks. At the door, another check was made; the Seal retreated as Jacques was allowed to enter.

"Monsieur Bertrand."

Jacques stepped forward and embraced the man for whom all the secrecy was necessary. "Mister Secretary."

Jacques sat across from Albert Riley and accepted the cup of tea that was handed to him. "Once again, gracious thanks for your hospitality."

Jacques dropped two sugar cubes into his own cup before sipping his tea. "Accepted, but not necessary. Canada is your home for as long as you require the-" he paused for a moment while he searched for the word. "Seclusion."

A heavily armed Seal entered accompanying a woman carrying a stack of papers. She paused and whispered something in Albert's ear. As Albert listened to her, his face hardened and his eyes closed. When she had delivered her message, she left - the Seal securing the door behind them.

"Curtis Thompson was found executed in the safe house in Pennsylvania."

Monsieur Bertrand sighed and set his teacup down. "I am sorry."

Secretary Riley paused. "Leaking his location was the most difficult thing I've ever had to do."

"But his sacrifice ensured your safe passage," Monsieur Bertrand reminded him. "And Canada values your faith that we can ensure your safety. Ours is a bilateral relationship that extends far beyond trade. The future of our country's economic stability depend on America surviving this...crisis."

Albert Riley stood and walked to the window, which had been equipped with three-inch glass clad polycarbonate; the strongest bulletproof glass known to man. "The deployment began last night, and our fleet will be in position within the week."

"And the intelligence we spoke of?"

Secretary Riley stood looking out over the scenic Quebec landscape. "Our only concern is that we are defending against an enemy which has no enemies."

"Every serpent has a sword that can destroy it," Monsieur Bertrand assured him. "Our combined forces must work to find the weak spot of this...particular serpent."

The door opened and a group of men accompanied by six Navy Seals entered the room. Monsieur Bertrand stood, as did Secretary Riley.

The Chief Justice of the United States stepped forward as the door was secured behind them. His face held immense relief at seeing the Secretary of Defense alive and well.

Albert smoothed his shirt as he stood, and shook hands with the Chief Justice.

"Should we-" He glanced at Monsieur Bertrand and then back to Secretary Riley. "Proceed?"

Secretary Riley nodded. "We are among friends."

The Chief Justice lowered his voice. "This will be the first time a President has been sworn in on foreign soil." He pulled a worn bible from his pocket and wiped the sweat from his brow. "Secretary Riley, please repeat after me. I do solemnly swear..."

* * *

The rehearsal dinner had lasted long into the night, leaving us too tired and tipsy to do anything but climb the stairs and fall into an exhausted heap. Before the morning sun had a chance to peek through the shades, I lay awake thinking; staring at Ano sleeping next to me – knowing this was the last time we would wake together as single girls. Tomorrow morning when Ano awoke, she would do so as someone's wife and, one day as someone's mother. The thought of Ano having a baby made me feel jealous, and so I discontinued that train of thought immediately.

"It is entirely too early for you to be thinkin' whatever it is you're thinkin' that makes your nose go all funny like that," Ano said, her voice scratchy, and I rolled over to look at her.

"Wow. You're awake."

"Yeah."

"And I didn't have to, like, kick you or anything."

Her throaty laugh echoed off the walls. "Shut it. Didn't sleep that deep. You know."

We wouldn't get another chance to talk before she got married, and she was my best friend. I had to say something. "Ano, I have to ask."

"So ask."

"Do you really love him?"

Her large brown eyes stared back at me, brimming in happiness and she nodded. "Enough to marry him?"

She sighed. "What's *enough*?"

As much as I'd love to have an answer for her, I didn't. I shrugged on my side, still staring at her face. "I don't know. Are you still going for your Masters?"

"Of course. But with everything going on, it's complicated."

"Do you think Jazz is happy not being a lawyer?"

"He says he is."

"You don't believe him?"

"It's not that. It's just...we're still so young and everything is so new. He might decide in a few years to go back to it. I don't know."

I hesitated asking her this, but I had to know. "Ano, are you happy?"

"With Jazz?"

"No, I mean...just...you know, everything. Where your life is going right now. You'll be twenty-two with a husband in the seminary. Maybe. And then trying to get a Masters. And—"

"And before you know it, a baby comes along..." she laughed. "That what you're gonna say?"

I nodded.

"Look, my mom already had this talk with me."

"Really? Your mom doesn't want you marrying Jazz?"

"I just don't think she wanted it to happen like *this*. And, you know, at twenty-two."

"But you're ready."

She nodded and grinned. "I'm ready. It doesn't scare me. I could wait. Two years, heck, ten years! Jazz is who I'll want." She looked into my eyes. "Does that make sense?"

Of course I could understand that. It wasn't that I'd imagined myself marrying anyone, but if I had even entertained the thought, it was always Percy I saw in my mind. Not that I hadn't ever really considered the thought of marrying Matt. Well, not many thoughts, at least. But I knew I was too young, and...there had been something missing with Matt. Really missing.

Ano scooted closer to me, and her voice went lower. "I wanna know what happened."

I groaned and buried my face in my pillow, pounding on it. "No, not now!"

"Yes!" she said fiercely. "You have to tell me!" She pushed me gently to the side and uncovered my head.

"Why would you wanna hear that? Today of all days?"

"Because I do."

"Save that answer for later today," I said sarcastically. "You'll need it."

She pursed her lips and smoothed the hair from my eyes. "Spill."

"Ano, I...I can't."

She scooted even closer. "Why not."

My face burned. "Because...I...got over it is why."

"Yeah!" she scoffed. "You got over it."

"I did!"

"As long as I've known you, you haven't 'gotten over' anything!" Her voice softened. "Katie, please. Just tell me."

"I tell you and you tell Jazz, and then—"

"No, no," she said, her index finger raised between us. "This is between you and me."

I sighed. "I'm going to say this once, and then we're never gonna talk about it again. Ever."

She held up her hand. "I swear."

"Ever!" I said with emphasis. "Deal?"

"Cross my heart."

"Okay. I was coming home from the post office and I came in kind of quiet so I could go upstairs and read my letters. I heard Matt in the kitchen with his brothers, and they were talking about moving their mom to Boston to a hospital. His brother Paul—"

"That's the one you didn't like?"

"Yeah. Paul said something to Matt like, 'why don't you just dump her. She's only after your money.'"

That earned a head shake and clucking of the tongue from Ano.

"And then I hear John telling Matt that they're leaving for Boston in a couple of days and that he should just leave me there. In Los Altos. Alone. And come back with them." The bile rose up in my throat. "And that there were a lot of hot women waiting to get their hands on guys like Matt where they came from."

Ano closed her eyes for a second and reached for my hand under the covers. "What did Matt say to all this?"

I shrugged, making sure I kept my voice even. "Nothing. Paul said..." I tried to laugh, but it came out harshly, "that if Matt had brought me home, people would have thought..."

"Tell me," she urged. "Get it out. Then it's over."

"That people would have thought...that he'd brought home another maid."

"*What!* What did Matt say to that?"

My chin tilted up just slightly. "Nothing."

"NOTHING?" The string of adjectives that Ano strung together was too long to remember, but it was foul – and referenced several of Matt's body parts. And a meat cleaver. She pulled me to her and I rested my head against her soft shoulder. We lay there, comfortable next to each other, knowing that words would pale in comparison to the comfort she was giving me just by hugging me. Just by being Ano.

"How about...you know, Captain Comfort downstairs?"

I broke into a grin. "You couldn't leave it alone, could you?"

"I had to go there."

"Well, I told you at dinner last night about the wound, and the ER, right?"

"Mmmhmm."

"So, we've started spending, you know, time together since then."

Ano raised a perfectly arched eyebrow at me. "Time?"

"Yeah."

She examined her nails and ran her tongue over her teeth, then looked back at me. "Girl, how stupid do you think I am?"

"We haven't."

"Oh, please!"

"No, Ano, we haven't! Really."

She scanned my face. "Oh. My. God." The look on her face was something between admiration and pity. "Why the hell not? He stares at you all the damned time!"

"Oh, he does not!"

"Yeah he does!"

I blushed a little at the thought of Percy even feeling a tiny bit of how I had felt about him for the last several years. "I don't know if I'm ready to. I just left Matt, and everything is still new with Percy..."

Ano's voice, soft and right next to me, struck on the very thing I couldn't say out loud. "You're still in love with Matt."

"Sometimes I still feel so strongly for him it hurts." The pain I'd been hiding behind was really close to spilling out.

"You can say the word," she said gently.

"I don't understand," I said. "Percy is everything! He's...everything! And I think that he feels something for me."

"Clearly." Ano played with the end of her thick braid over her shoulder. "Do you still feel the same way about him?"

"Ano," I lamented, "when I was with Matt, all I could think about was how Percy was. Some days he's *all* I thought about. But..."

"But then?" Ano prompted.

"But then Matt hurt me so badly. I should hate him! Hate him!" I pounded the mattress between us to illustrate my point.

"But you don't?"

"I can't hate him. When I'm with Percy, it's like...like I can't breathe. I finally have him. And I'm so happy." My eyes looked at her hopefully. "That's good, right?"

"Why did you choose Matt?"

That was so long ago that I struggled to remember. "I'm not sure."

"All right. When you kissed Percy at the train station, did you want him to stay?"

No question. "Yes."

"More than Matt?"

"You don't understand. They are so different."

Ano scoffed. "No, trust me. I believe you."

"Why don't you like Percy?"

Ano thought for a moment and watched me play with the row of buttons of the edge of her nightgown. "I didn't say I didn't like him."

"Please!"

She laughed. "All right, I can't believe you were right there for *three years* and..." her eyes opened wide, "nothing! Then suddenly, Matt shows interest in you and—"

I gritted my teeth together. "That's not exactly when he started liking me."

"Well, whenever he started. I just wanna make sure he won't hurt you."

"Yeah, me too." I flipped her thick braid of hair back over her shoulder. "But today isn't about me, or Matt, or Percy. Today is about you and Jazz."

Ano's face completely lit up.

"Now that I've told you, we're done talking about it, right?"

"Right."

"We gotta get up," I said, glancing over her shoulder to look at the clock. "You're getting married today!"

The dress Ano had chosen for me to wear was actually really pretty and unlike most bridesmaid dresses, *could* actually be worn again. Hitting me just below the knee, the cranberry red dress clung to every single (slight) curve I had. Thank God Grandma Vesper knew how to sew. She'd had to spend part of the day yesterday taking in the bust and pulling up the straps. I had no shoes that matched, so I was borrowing black heels that belonged to her cousin Cammie, no, Caliope...well, one of her cousins.

By the time three o'clock came, the men had abandoned the house long before Ano and I came downstairs. Our hair and makeup was done and Ano's uncle had brought the car around for the bridal party. Somehow, we all squeezed in together. The entire drive to the church took less than ten minutes. I sat and just stared at Ano. With her wedding dress on, she looked like she'd stepped off the pages of *Vogue*. The dress was actually her cousin Georgette's, whose wedding had been last June. The entire gown was white Italian silk, with hundreds of real pearls sewn onto the bodice and train. It was strapless, and fit Ano as if it had been made for her. The veil was borrowed as well, and sat on my lap in its box to be put on in the bride's room at the church. I wasn't the one getting married and I was still nervous.

When we stepped out of the car, I could see why Jazz and Ano had chosen to get married here. If you've ever seen the movies where the church looks like a postcard? That's their church. White with a bell tower and a clock, the church reminded me of a Norman Rockwell painting. Only my best friend was getting married in this one. There were a few straggling guests standing out in front of the church, and they 'awww'ed at Ano as we walked around the church to the side, where the bride's room was. Once inside, I stepped out of the way and let Grandma and Michelle take over. The veil had to be placed just so. Her hair was slightly out of place. She was fluffed, pulled, and tightened, until there was nothing left for anyone to do. She was perfect. The photographer, a friend of the family, captured it all and then asked us to come into the courtyard for candid shots.

Christee, Ano's oldest cousin, had agreed to be Jazz's best man. He stood next to Uncle Robert in his suit, looking happy but uncomfortable in the humidity. We all stepped out into the courtyard where Ano was whisked away by the photographer and the rest of us stood, waiting to be called for our turn with the bride.

From right behind me, Percy's voice sounded in my ear. "You shouldn't look this lovely, you know. It's not fair to outshine the bride. Haven't you heard that?"

"Uh-huh."

I was surprised when he stepped forward and slid an arm around my waist. "This is quite the dress," he said, still admiring it.

"Thanks. Ano picked it out."

He nodded but didn't stop looking.

"It's just a dress."

"Not on you."

I blushed at the compliment. "Thank you."

He moved his hands down the sides of the dress, still looking down at me.

"Mr. Warner," I said, in my most authoritative voice, "are you paying attention to the lab or the young lady in front of you?"

He laughed at my attempt to mimic his 'professor' voice. "Most assuredly, the lady." His face was more relaxed than it had been in a long time.

"I'd hate to keep you after class," I whispered as his face came towards mine.

"Mmmm. I've been..." he kissed my lips lightly, "a very poor student lately."

I was enjoying our banter. "It would be a pity if I had to fail you."

"Do you offer extra credit?"

Percy was being openly affectionate; something I'd never seen in him until now. Sliding my hands up his shoulders, I looked into his face. "I evaluate it on a case by case basis."

His grin was incredibly infectious and his voice, once again, was low against my ear. "I'm incredibly motivated to earn a passing grade."

I raised an eyebrow at him and pursed my lips, as I'd seen Ano do hundreds of times. "Then I think—"

"Hey, Christee?" Brinden came running around the corner. "Christee!"

"Right here, man, what's up?"

"Where's Jazz?"

"Groom's room with preacher. Why?"

Brinden waved him off. "There's somebody here says he needs to see him. Somethin' 'bout an emergency." He ran back around towards the front of the church in search and Jazz and the hair on the back of my neck stood up.

Percy's smile didn't falter, but his arm slipped from around me. "I'll go make sure the groom is okay."

The photographer was calling to me and Percy pointed towards Ano. "Go. Smile and be beautiful. Everything is fine."

Percy almost ran to the front of the church where he was reasonably sure the emergency was nothing more than the arrival of a certain unwanted guest.

CHAPTER THIRTY-FOUR

Percy rounded the corner and heard the raised voices coming from the church steps.

"No, you don't understand! That's what I'm trying to tell you!"

"Listen, I didn't get her telegram. I didn't...damn it, man! I didn't know where you were, y'understand?"

"Yes! I get it! But I'm here! I made it. I know I'm not wearing a tuxedo but—"

"She won't see you. I'm telling you, much as I hate to say this, you gotta go."

Percy could hear Matt's voice, nearly shouting at Jazz. "*What*? I came over two thousand miles to see you get married! I'm not gonna leave!"

"I been trying to find you for weeks to be my best man."

"Well, I'm here!"

Jazz laughed. "I can't! Not now. Ten minutes before the ceremony?"

"I'll be honorary best man then."

They embraced. "I'm glad you made it, man," Jazz said. "I'm sorry 'bout everything. With Kate."

"It's not over yet," Matt stated.

"You sure 'bout that?"

"Yeah. Wait...why? What did she tell you?"

Jazz tried to keep his tone even, but Percy could hear he was getting upset. "Nothing. Ano won't tell me what happened, just that she left you. But look, that isn't the—"

"Please! Please, Jazz. Just for one minute. I'm begging you to just listen."

Percy could hear Jazz exhale. "Fine."

Percy pressed himself against the side of the church and listened. He knew he should leave. However, he also knew this would likely be his only opportunity to hear – from the source – what had occurred between Kate and Matt. He wasn't going anywhere.

"My brothers were both in town and we were trying to decide where to put my mom. So Paul said something about how he doesn't see me and Kate together, and John tells me..."

"Yeah?" Jazz prompted.

"Okay, he tells me to just leave her there in Los Altos and go back to Boston with him. But I told them...I told them I wanted to be with Kate!"

Jazz was quiet for a minute. "There was more, though, right?" Matt didn't respond. "I know Ano, and she wouldn't freak out like she did if there wasn't somethin' more. C'mon, man. Don't bullshit me."

"Paul made a comment...about how Kate was only after me for my money. And—"

"There's more?"

"He compared Kate to one of our maids. Something like that."

Jazz whistled. "And you told Kate all this?"

"No."

"Then how did she hear it?"

"She was in the next room," Matt said weakly. "She pretty much heard everything."

Percy's hands were balled into fists at his sides. He had never wanted to kill another human being the way he wanted to kill Matt Skylar at this moment. Of course Kate wouldn't have told him. He was fairly sure she wouldn't even have told Ano the whole story. He was also sure that Matt was downplaying it in his favor. Percy hoped Jazz knew the same thing.

"Man, I can see you're in a bad way. I feel for you, but if I let you in there Ano's gonna kill me, Kate's gonna leave, and this is my *wedding day*."

"You don't understand," Matt said desperately. "I *have* to see her!"

Jazz's voice lowered, but not enough so that Percy couldn't hear him. "She didn't come alone!"

"Wha...what? What do you mean she didn't *come alone?* Who the hell is she with?"

The response was silence. From around the corner, Percy smiled.

"PERCY?"

"Listen," Jazz said quietly, "she looks really happy."

Matt's voice was angry. "She'll *never* be happy with him! You know how he is! He's only—"

Percy heard one of the doors to the church open and a voice called to Jazz. "Hey, man. They're ready to start. You comin'?"

"Yeah, yeah, on my way." The door closed and Jazz sighed. "All right. Enter through the back of the church when everyone's already sitting down. Don't make a scene!"

"Thanks, brother, I owe you one."

"You're gonna owe me more than that if Ano catches you here. Now stay here till after the weddin' march."

"Okay, and…congrats, man."

The doors opened again, and Percy knew Jazz had gone in. It would do him little good to pummel Matt in the front of the church, and he would make too much noise. Running fast around, Percy slipped in through a side door and into the pew behind Ano's mother as Pachabel's Canon began to play.

Kate and Christee entered the church. Thank God her eyes were fixed at the altar as she walked down the aisle. When she passed Michelle and Grandma Vesper, Kate looked at Percy, who winked at her and smiled. He was a head taller than anyone else around him, and was fairly certain he'd be easily spotted by Matt, who had better keep his promise to Jazz by staying in the back of the church.

Kate was Ano's only attendant. The wedding march began to play, and all eyes turned to the back of the church, where the doors opened and Ano appeared on her uncle's arm. Glad for the opportunity to turn around and search for Matt inconspicuously, Percy saw him in the last seat of the last pew in the last row of the church. Thankfully, as Ano passed him, she was smiling so brightly on her uncle's arm, she didn't pause or notice.

But when Ano passed Matt, he turned towards the front of the church and locked eyes with Percy. A look of pure hatred passed over Matt's face as they stared at one another. Percy kept his expression bland, and raised an eyebrow in challenge to Matt, who was now aware that Percy was alerted to his presence. Ano made it to the altar, and the only thing he feared was Matt trying to get Kate's attention during the ceremony. He could handle Matt privately before the reception. As long as Matt didn't get anywhere near Kate, there would be no problems.

The church was quiet and all eyes were on Ano and Jazz.

"Friends, family, please be seated." Everyone sat. Kate stood beside Ano at the altar, with her uncle still holding tightly to Ano's arm.

"On this joyous occasion, we pause to thank the loved ones who have raised these two children. And so we ask, in Jesus' name, who gives this woman to be married to this man?"

Michelle stepped forward, and Ano's uncle reluctantly released Ano's arm. "Her mother and I do." The pastor inclined his head and Ano's mother touched Ano's face and kissed her cheek through the veil before she sat in the front pew beside Uncle Robert.

Ano extended her hand for Jazz to take. Both of them ascended the first step up toward the altar together, side by side.

"I know we've all heard about love at first sight," the pastor said, "but tonight, we are in it midst. Ano and Jazz may be young, but in Jazz' words, they have loved a lifetime already."

Percy studied Kate carefully, saw her lower lip quiver just slightly. In all the years he'd known her, he realized that he'd only seen her cry once. He could tell, looking at her now, that she was fighting back the urge.

"With every shadow comes a ray of sunshine," the pastor was saying, and Percy tried to focus on the ceremony instead of the expression on Kate's face. "And in our troubled times, we look on Jazz and Ano and know that God's love and mercy is all around us, binding us together, telling us to love." The pastor motioned to Ano and Jazz. "Children, have you come here before God and these witnesses to pledge your lives to one another?"

Ano and Jazz answered in unison, "We have."

"Then kneel now, and receive the blessings of almighty Lord our God."

Ano handed her bouquet to Kate, who moved quickly to straighten Ano's train to fall perfectly behind her as she knelt. Percy's eyes never left Kate's frame, so slight and delicate standing next to Ano – knowing that at that moment, Kate's heart was breaking as she stood beside her best friend.

"We come to our Lord as children, and only in God's love do we grow. Marriage is about the binding of two souls for eternity, in the holy sacrament of marriage." The pastor took a step down to stand beside them as they knelt. "Children, take each other's hands."

Jazz took Ano's hands in his and the pastor put his hands on theirs.

"You are here together. Look at each other, now. Although you can both stand separately, you are bound together by your hands. And although you love differently, you share a common love for each other. You each came to this altar from a different path – Jazz from the side and Ano right down the middle. In life, you will approach many things from different angles, but you must always meet together...at the end. That is how you will make it through every trial that life brings you," he said, holding their hands together, "with strength and courage, and the love that brought you here today. Don't ever forget it."

The pastor took a step backward and motioned for Ano and Jazz to rise. "Jazz, if it is your intention to be married to this woman, repeat these words to her now."

Jazz turned toward Ano and cleared his throat, repeating the words that the pastor said.

"Ano, I come here today to give you all that I am. Everything I have is yours. We will grow together, from this day forward as man and wife. With God's help, I promise to be the best husband to you that I can be. I will love you, honor you, and keep you for now and always, in sickness and in health, and forsaking all others I will be faithful to you for all the days of my life, so help me God."

Percy heard Jazz's voice quaver at the end. His shoulder's straightened and he cleared his throat. Ano was crying unabashedly when she repeated her vows to him.

"Jazz, I come here today to give you all that I am. Everything I have is yours. We will grow together, from this day forward as man and wife. With God's help, I promise to be the best wife to you that I can be. I will love you, honor you, and keep you for now and always, in sickness and in health, and forsaking all others I will be faithful to you for all the days of my life, so help me God."

Kate pressed a tissue to her cheeks and turned her head away from the couple. As he watched Ano and Jazz, Percy felt something that he hadn't felt in a long time; possibly ever. Staring at Kate, he felt more than protective. More than just affection. More than not wanting to see her hurt because of Ano's wedding. It was...

"Jazz, do you have a ring for Ano?"

Jazz nodded and his voice broke as he answered, "I do." He turned and took the ring from Christee, who stood next to him.

"Slip it on Ano's finger and repeat after me."

Jazz took Ano's hand in his and slipped the ring on as he repeated the pastor's words, "Let this ring be a constant reminder of the love I feel for you. Look on it as a symbol of my love and faithfulness. It has no beginning, no middle, and no end."

"Ano, do you have a ring for Jazz?"

Ano wiped her eyes and nodded. "Yes, I do." Kate handed her a gold band. When she took the ring from Kate, Percy saw Ano squeeze Kate's hand.

"Ano, place the ring on Jazz' hand and repeat after me."

"Jazz, let this ring be a constant reminder of the love I feel for you. Look on it as a symbol of my love and faithfulness. It has no beginning, no middle, and no end."

They stood together, holding hands at the altar and the pastor said something quietly to the both of them and placed his hands on their heads. They bowed their heads together for a moment.

Raising his head again to look at the congregation, he announced, "Jesus has brought this man and woman together in His house. They have joined together with their hands, the pledging of their vows and the exchanging of their rings. With the power vested in me by the State of Louisiana and Almighty God, I now pronounce that they are man and wife!"

The congregation erupted with cheers. The pastor quieted them for a moment with his hands and said to Jazz, "You may kiss your wife."

Jazz lifted Ano's veil and drew her close for their first kiss as man and wife. Amidst cheering, cat calls, and joyous applause from all around, Jazz and Ano kept kissing.

Breaking apart, Ano took her bouquet from Kate, touched her cheek, and started back down the aisle... with her husband.

CHAPTER THIRTY-FIVE

I'd never been to a wedding before, so really, I hadn't known what to expect. I couldn't imagine anything being more beautiful than Ano's though. I silently congratulated myself on making it through the ceremony without crying...too much. I had held it together right up until they said their vows. And then, somehow, it was too much. The first tear fell and it was as if I couldn't keep them from flowing.

Thank God one of Ano's cousins did make-up for a living, and managed to cover up my red eyes before pictures. Ano's relatives had gone all out for the decorations and everything glittered with little white twinkle lights. After the sun went down, it looked like a thousand stars had come out. The gazebo in the courtyard twinkled as Ano and Jazz had their pictures taken before moving into the reception.

"That's a good color on you."

I spun to find Percy leaning up against the pillar of the gazebo. He walked toward me and handed me a glass of champagne.

"Thanks." I accepted the glass and drank deeply.

"Easy, there," he cautioned. "You might want to take champagne a little slower than water."

I smirked at him and took another long sip. The bubbles tingled on my tongue and it went to my head immediately. The tension seemed to ease from my body and I closed my eyes. "Mmmm," I said. "I like champagne."

He caught me lightly around the waist. "Really?"

I looked up into his face. Strong and handsome, straight nose and a strong chin. I had adored that face from the first moment I'd set eyes on it. Every time I was this close to him, his face was enough to render me speechless. I suppressed a smile.

"What are you thinking?" he asked and stroked along my neck and cheek.

I laughed self-consciously. "I was thinking about when we were at

Charlie and Carrie's house. When you met me out at the barn," I reminded him, "and I almost fell."

His face was next to mine and I could feel his breath against my cheek. He took my champagne glass and set it down on the railing. "I caught you."

I slid a hand into his hair. "Yes you did."

Percy kissed me lightly, then tightened his grip around me as his kiss deepened. "Kate," he said, breaking away from our kiss. "I want to tell you something."

"Girl, don't you make Grandma come out there and turn the hose on you!" Grandma Vesper's voice called loudly from the door of the reception hall. "An' you tell that handsome young man to bring you in here and feed you! Don't you make Grandma worry!"

We both laughed and Percy called back, "I'm bringing her in!"

"All right, then!" She retreated into the hall, muttering all the way, "Bring her out there without a sweater on. She catch her death o' cold and be out there kissin' instead of in here where she should be warm! Give him a piece of my mind if he don't take care of Miss Kate the way he should."

"I think we should go in," he said, giving me an enormous grin, "before she comes back out to give me a *piece of her mind*."

"You wouldn't survive that." I said, and was only halfway joking.

The reception hall was covered in miniature white lights, and white silk was draped along the ceiling and walls in honor of the occasion. It looked like heaven. The hall was flooded with people, tables, food and champagne. Ano's family had done a beautiful job.

I was full after the first plate of food that Percy brought me, piled high with more than I could eat in a week. By the second plate, I was convinced that he was under orders to continue feeding me from Grandma Vesper. Each time Percy disappeared, another set of Ano's cousins slid into his place at the table and chattered on about the wedding and how beautiful Ano looked. By the time Percy returned for the fourth time, his plate only half full, I began to get suspicious.

"Where are you disappearing to?"

"Food table. The shrimp is wonderful. Here." He handed me another glass of champagne.

I watched Ano glide across the dance floor with Jazz, and sadness crept into my heart. Ano was married. And now I was alone. Really alone.

From beside me, Percy must have sensed my mood. "Care to dance?"

"No, I'm fine right here."

All right, I'll admit. I've never danced in my life. Wasn't asked to any school dances, never made it to prom, and my dad wouldn't have known how to teach me to dance if I'd paid him.

Percy took my hand. "We'll go slow. C'mon."

He led me to the dance floor and his arm encircled my waist. Guiding me with his hand in the small of my back, Percy swayed with me to the music.

"What are you thinking of right now?" he asked in my ear.

"I'm thinking how good you look in this suit, if you must know."

"You sure it's not too much champagne that's making you talk like that?"

"It might be."

"Well, can I get you another glass?" he teased and I laughed. He spun me around once and kissed the nape of my neck.

"Any more and you won't be able to keep me awake on the train."

His hand on my back slid down to my behind and he looked into my eyes. "I have other things in mind for the train ride to keep you awake."

"Yeah, in those two little seats we've got, it'll be a miracle to turn around, let alone—"

"I got us a sleeping car."

I pulled away, surprised. "You did? When?"

He laughed at my reaction. "Yesterday. When you and Ano were getting your nails done."

"Percy, thank you! Another twenty-one hours in a horrible little seat and...wait. A...a sleeping car?"

He nodded and our eyes locked. "A *sleeping* car."

Warmth crept through my body at the thought of the next twenty-one hours alone with Percy in a bed. No school, no homework, no interruptions. No...*sleeping*. Wrapping my arms around his neck once again, I let my lips touch his ear gently before whispering back, "Then you've wasted your money most profoundly."

He squeezed me gently and pressed me closer to him. The song ended and Percy led me back to our table. He looked around us nervously.

"Everything okay?" I asked.

He nodded, but continued to look around. "Just fine. I'm going outside for a second. I think I see Ano's uncle out there." He smiled. "Another glass of champagne while I'm up?"

"No, thank you."

I saw Ano making the rounds of tables, greeting people, and accepting kisses from everyone. She was simply beautiful. Three of Ano's cousins slid into the seats around me, but I wasn't in the mood for conversation. I wanted a few moments to think.

I walked to the bar and poured myself a glass of water, then slid into a seat at an empty table.

"Hello, Kate."

A sick feeling spread through me. I knew that voice. I kept facing forward and clutched the water glass on the table in front of me. It wasn't him. It couldn't be. Ano had promised.

"Please, Kate," he implored. "Look at me."

Because I'm a fool, I turned. "Hello, Matt."

I hated how good he looked. Hated the rugged handsomeness that came so naturally to him. He looked like he'd just come in from working in the field. His face was tanner than I remembered it. He pulled out a chair and sat next to me. "You don't mind, do you?"

I very much minded, but didn't think my response would matter. I looked out over the dance floor because staring at Matt hurt my eyes. And my heart. I looked out at Ano, silently imploring her to look my way. To send Jazz over to rescue me. Her back was to me. I was on my own. And drowning.

"Please look at me."

"Percy'll be back. Any minute."

"I think he'll be busy for a little while."

I'd had too much champagne to be neutral. Been too happy to feign indifference now. "I should go see where he is."

Matt reached out to me, but I pulled away faster than he could react. I felt the heat returning to my face and I needed to get air. I stood up from the table, my chair fell over, and I walked past it on my way out into the near-empty courtyard. Large gulps of air seemed to help and I concentrated on slowing my breathing.

Matt's voice followed me out into the evening air. "I have to explain," he said, pleading. "Please, let me explain."

"You don't owe me anything." I walked one direction, looking for Percy and found the area dark and empty. The shoes I had on were still too large and I slipped them off for ease of escape.

"I don't blame you for being angry."

"What a comfort." The opposite direction had a latched gate, too high for me to hop over in this dress. My heart was pounding. I couldn't be trapped. It was too cruel.

"Your note..." he stepped in front of me, blocking my path, "...destroyed me."

He was right in front of me, and I had no way out but back to the reception; through him.

"What do you want, Matt?"

"Kate, if I told you how sorry I was... My brothers...and what they said, they had no right! I should have said it sooner to them, and to you."

"Said what?"

He took a step forward; I retreated a step. "I told them I loved you. That I have a plan for us. It's a good plan, Kate." He hung his head for a second and looked behind him as if afraid someone was sneaking up on him. "I've been staying with Carrie and Charlie for the last month or so. Carrie's been keeping your location from me. She wouldn't tell me where she's been sending letters or..." he took a step closer and reached out to me for my hand, "where you are. I do know you're in med school now."

I recoiled when his hand touched mine.

"Don't do that," he said, a little too sternly. "I'm sorry. I've been awake for three days trying to get here, just to get the chance to see you. To get the chance to tell you that I want you back, Kate. I'll do anything."

I couldn't say anything. Didn't say anything. He reached his hand out to me again, this time sliding it along the slope of my waist. I ground my teeth together. Paul's words echoed in my mind. I tried to take a step backwards but his hand held me fast.

"You used to like it when I held you. Please..." His face softened and he pulled me towards him.

I lifted my eyes to his face. "No. I don't belong with you."

"What?"

I raised my eyes to his. "I said *no*. The note I left you...I meant it."

"How can you say that?"

"Because it's true!" I took his hand and removed his from my waist. "Your brothers wanted to you leave me there! Alone in Los Altos with nothing."

"But I wouldn't have!"

"It doesn't matter. Because even if I came back with you tonight, even if I came back to you, I would always be... what was it Paul called me? *Little Orphan Annie*?"

Even in the dark I could see his face turn red. "You can't blame me because of something my brothers said."

"I'm not. I'm blaming you for what you *didn't* say. What you *should have* said to them that night."

"And what should I have said?"

I hoped he couldn't hear the catch in my voice as I responded. "You should have said that you cared for me. And then told them both to go to hell." My knees were shaking now and I felt sick.

Suddenly he was next to me, his voice against my ear. "I *did*, baby. Right after they finished, I told them that I loved you."

I pulled away, shaking my head. "No, you didn't...I heard you."

His face actually showed hope. "You didn't hear all of it, sweetheart. I told them I wasn't going to leave you. That I loved you...that you were all I wanted. So help me God."

I turned away from him. He was lying. He'd say anything at this point. Maybe he'd even gone back to Idaho or Indiana or wherever Paul was from and sown his oats by now. Either way, it couldn't be true.

"Oh, God. Please, Kate!" His head came in to rest against my neck and I felt his breath. "I love you. Please believe me." His hands touched my shoulders and slid down the length of my dress to rest on my waist. "You're so incredibly beautiful in this dress."

I couldn't breathe. His hands were so familiar.

"Please," he implored. "You have to believe me." His lips touched my neck. Something in his voice told me that he was telling the truth. "Kate..." His voice was rough and I pushed away the comfort that hearing it was giving me, even after all this time.

Everything right now was so confusing, I had to have space and time to think. "Matt, you can't just come back here and..." I turned and tried to push past him, but his arms were on either side of me. "Let me through. I'm going back in to the reception."

Matt wouldn't budge. "Let me come see you tonight. You're staying at Ano's aunt's house?"

"I'm going back to Philadelphia tonight."

"Philadelphia." He exhaled and his face relaxed. "Let me write you there...I'll come see you. I can—"

"No." I pushed against his chest, solid in front of me. "You can't. If you do, I'll—"

"You'll what?" he said, and his face came close to mine. "Tell me. You'll listen? Or you'll remember?"

I was angry and hurt, and didn't want to stand here being reminded of what had happened. I waited, knowing if I lifted my eyes up to his, we would kiss. My throat was closing up. "I've got to get back. I've got to—"

"She's got to make a toast," Percy finished. There behind Matt, standing in his blue suit, was Percy. I almost flung myself into his arms. He offered me a hand, which I took, and led me around Matt. "Go in, Kate," he said, his voice velvet smooth. "I'll be in before more champagne is poured."

I stood rooted to the spot. "No. I'm not leaving."

Percy didn't take his eyes off Matt and there was pure hatred in his expression. "Matt and I need to catch up. I don't think we ever finished our chat."

Matt pushed the sleeve of his shirt up his forearm. "No. We didn't, now that you mention it." He took a step closer to Percy. "It'd be a shame if our *chat* got blood on that fancy shirt."

"Stop it," I said, stepping between them, but Percy's strong hands glided easily around my waist and moved me aside as if I weighed nothing.

He was chest to chest with Matt. "I don't intend to get any of *your* blood on my shirt, thanks. You have your *own* shirt to bleed on." He smiled. "Like last time."

Matt's fist grabbed a handful of Percy's shirt and when I opened my mouth to protest, we heard a loud voice from behind us.

"Aw hell no! I know ya'll aren't doin' this at my *wedding*." Ano appeared in the doorway, her dress taking up the entire double doors, and she stepped into the courtyard. An eyebrow was raised and she stood with a hand on her hip, looking at Matt, Percy, and me.

"You." She pointed to me. "Get your Maid of Honor butt back in there and get a glass of champagne for the toast. And no stories about that night in the library, either."

Ano turned to Percy. "You. Get back inside and set your ass down in a chair and watch your woman make a fool outta me with her speech." Reluctantly, Percy nodded, took a step back and smoothed down the front of his shirt where Matt had grabbed him.

"And you," she said, shaking her head at Matt. "The only thing keepin' you alive at this point is the fact that my husband loves you like a brother. The only brother he's got left. So get your sorry self back in there, at a *different* table, and eat something. Go skulkin' around someone else's girl. Leave my girl Kate alone. Period. You hear me?"

Matt nodded. "Yes."

"Then what are ya'll waiting for? Move!"

At that moment, as we all three filed back into the rec hall, we knew, one day Ano would be a great mom.

After the last 'thank you for coming' had been said and the last hug had been given, Ano and Jazz left the reception to head back to her Aunt's house to pick up their bags and head to the train station for a two-day honeymoon in Florida – a surprise from Jazz. Given the impending threat of attack, no one thought it was wise but Jazz insisted and finally won his case against all arguments to the contrary.

Percy, Matt, and I would follow them home in Christee's car, where Percy and I would retrieve our bags and head to the train station ourselves for our long ride back to Philadelphia. Jazz had spoken to Ano's aunt and uncle about letting Matt stay there and rest before heading back to South Dakota and they had graciously agreed.

With Grandma, Michelle, and Christee in the front seat, Percy sat wedged between Matt and me for the seven minute ride back to Ano's uncle's house. I knew as we pulled away from the curb that it would be the longest seven minutes of my life. Thankfully, Grandma Vesper kept a one-sided stream of conversation going about everything from Brinden's overindulgence in alcohol to the wonderful tasting sweet potato pie. I listened, remembering how much I missed both Grandma Vesper and Michelle. And how now, everything had changed.

Pulling up in front of the house, I was going to wait for Matt to get his pack from the trunk, but Percy motioned for me to come inside with him. "They'll be a minute. C'mon, let's get our bags. We need to get going or none of us will make our trains."

I agreed, mostly because I would have to say goodbye to Matt in a few minutes, and postponing it was making it harder. Ano and Jazz were ready, their bags around them in the living room when we opened the front door.

"I see Mr. and Mrs. Taylor are ready!" Ano's mom cried and ran in to hug Ano for the hundredth time that night.

"Hey man," Jazz said to Percy. "Y'all wanna help me get our bags in the trunk of my cousin's car? I got yours here with our stuff."

Percy and I had packed before we left for the wedding, knowing time would be short. I waited to hug Ano, letting her mother and grandmother fuss over her for a few minutes before she left on her honeymoon.

"Now, you 'member," Grandma Vesper pointed her index finger at her granddaughter and took on a stern look, "anything happen y'all get y'self somewhere safe. Fast, an'—"

"I know. I know. We'll be all right."

Michelle hugged her daughter with tears in her eyes and smoothed one of the large curls that had come loose from atop her head. Her voice shook a little. "You are so beautiful."

"Guys," she laughed, and hugged them both, "I'm not joining the Peace Corps. I'll be home in two days. I'm fine!" Ano turned to me for help. "Maid of Honor?"

I laughed and Grandma Vesper opened up one arm of the communal hug for me to enter, which I did. Both arms went around my waist and I squeezed them back, shutting my eyes tight against the tears that had threatened to pour out all night.

"An' you!" Grandma released us all and pointed now to me, and I grinned back at her. "You don' start eatin' right and takin' care o' yo'self, Grandma gonna bring you back down here an' fatten you up!"

"Okay, I promise."

Michelle hugged me hard. "Now, you listen," she said in my ear. "Jus' cause I got one girl married doesn't mean I don't still have two baby girls to care for." I nodded, and swallowed back a tear. "You take care of your heart." Her voice went to a whisper; not that the men would have heard her over the loading of luggage back and forth, but just that they were words of advice meant only for me. "You'll know when it's right."

I nodded again and she kissed my cheek, then released me.

"Girls," Jazz called, "we gotta go! Mom," he came and hugged Michelle tightly and it was a little weird to hear him call her 'Mom', same as I did. "Thank you so much."

"You take care of my baby girl."

"I will." He turned to his right. "Grandma."

"Oh honey, give Grandma a hug." I think we all heard Jazz's ribs crack a little when Grandma Vesper gave Jazz one of her hugs, and he kissed her on the cheek as he reached for Ano's hand.

"We love you all. See you in a couple days." They ran out the front door and I waited while Percy hugged both Michelle and, to a more cautious degree, Grandma Vesper.

Matt was standing by the curb with his pack saying goodbye to Jazz as we walked up. Matt kissed Ano on the cheek and hugged her and then turned to us. Percy stood stoically beside me while Jazz and Ano got in the car. Matt stepped towards me for an awkward goodbye.

"I have your address now, so I'll write you."

I had no idea what to say. Looking at him was killing me.

"I'm staying at Carrie and Charlie's house, so if you need anything..."

Percy snorted, pressed his lips together, and turned to check on Christee, who started the engine. "Car's ready."

I looked at Matt. I couldn't just walk away, leaving him standing there holding my address. He looked tired. Worn out. Tortured. I had the insane urge to turn his collar down, which was flipped under the wrong way.

"Take better care of yourself."

"Carrie's feeding me, so..." he shrugged. "I'm helping Charlie. With the wheat."

"That's good."

"Kate." Percy tapped his watch, a sign that we'd be late for our train, and the chance to say goodbye Ano and Jazz.

Matt glared at Percy.

I swallowed hard and gave a slight wave of my hand. "Okay. G'bye, Matt."

"Wait!" He took a step towards me as I turned to go, but Percy stepped between us; clearly not allowing him access to me again. "Kate," he said softly, even though he directed a venomous glance in Percy's direction, "at least hug me goodbye."

Percy laughed, but I didn't see any harm in it. It was, after all, just a hug.

"It's okay," I told Percy, and saw Matt's slight triumphant smile as I crossed the distance between us.

He wrapped his arms around my waist, knowing that Percy was watching every move he made. Had one of his hands gone any lower than my hip, I'm quite certain Percy would have removed the offending appendage with no compunction. I rested my head against his shoulder and felt his body relax. His hands ran up and down my back a few times and I reached up and turned his collar the right way, and gently touched his cheek.

"I'll miss you," he said. "I'll come see you soon."

I released him, but his arms held my waist gently. The hug had exceeded the time limit that was appropriate, and Percy's patience with Matt had evaporated.

"Okay. Let's go," Percy tried again, and I had to push against Matt to get him to release me.

I slid into the front seat next to Christee and Percy climbed in next to me and closed the door. I raised a hand in a wave to Matt and the car pulled away from the curb.

CHAPTER THIRTY-SIX

Midnight on a Saturday night and the train depot was nearly deserted. I was thankful for that; I didn't think I had the energy at this point to fight through the crowds after what I'd been through tonight. We went to Jazz and Ano's train first. Percy and I would have at least thirty minutes to get to our train after theirs departed.

Kind man that he was, Jazz gave Ano and me some space to say a proper goodbye. Aside from Ano's hair and makeup, you'd never guess that Ano and Jazz had gotten married tonight. They'd both changed into jeans and t-shirts at her aunt's house and looked like young kids on summer break. I stood next to her, not knowing what to say.

"I don't want this to be sad," she said, and nodded sternly at me. "So I brought you something." She reached in her large bag and produced a long box. "Here."

"You didn't have to get me a present."

"Maid of Honor, baby! That's one of the perks!"

"I thought the perks were supposed to be sleeping with one of the hot groomsmen after the wedding."

Ano's eyes darted over to Percy, who stood talking and laughing with Jazz fifty feet away. "Well he wasn't a groomsman, but something tells me that you won't have to worry about that, either."

I laughed and opened my mouth in mock surprise.

"Open it!" she urged.

Inside the long box was a lovely, short strand of pearls. My breath caught in my throat and I clutched them to my chest.

Her eyes were bright. "You remember?"

I examined them, lying across the palm of my hand, in awe. "Of course I remember."

During our first year at Stanford, Ano and I had gotten on an old movie kick and somehow ended up watching *Breakfast at Tiffany's* about a hundred times in one weekend. At one point, somewhere between midnight and passing out from exhaustion, I'd informed her that I'd always imagined owning a strand of pearls like Audrey Hepburn had worn. The kind you get from your mother, passed down from generation to generation. Timeless and elegant. And, although I hadn't said it at the time, what I'd meant was... like the pearls had once belonged to someone special.

I clutched them to my chest, and happy tears spilled out over my cheeks. "Thank you." I hugged her fiercely and kissed her cheek. "It's the best gift I've ever received." And I meant it. If I thought I could get away with it, I'd wear them on rounds.

"Well, stop crying, 'cause there's more."

"There'd better not be," I scolded, but she produced another box tied with a small red bow.

"Happy birthday."

I thought she'd forgotten. My birthday was September twenty-second, two days from now. "I won't see you for your birthday, and I haven't missed one yet, so here you go."

Pulling the ribbon off the box and flipping open the top I looked down at a small 4 X 6 silver picture frame. The six faces smiling back at me made me catch my breath. "Where did you...?"

"Before we went down. Remember? I had that disposable camera with me and the ranger took our picture. He said, 'Take a picture. Just one...'"

"...for posterity."

"That's right."

I fingered the photo, the six of us standing next to one another and yet all from such completely different places, each going down with our own agenda. Percy, on the end stood tall with no smile. I think he was irritated at the guy for having the picture taken at all. Matt, his arms crossed, leaning with Jazz against the large rock next to the entrance. Carlie stood close to Percy, a sweatshirt tied around her waist, her hand resting on her pack. I found myself right in the middle, half smiling with my arm around Ano, her grinning like a fool at the camera.

"Thank you," I choked out, and closed the lid on the box as the whistle from the train sounded next to us. "Wait!" I reached in my pack and pulled out a square box and handed it to Ano.

"I told you, no wedding gift!"

"I really suck at following instructions."

She gave me an exasperated look and opened the lid. I hadn't had time to wrap it or even put a ribbon around it. She pulled off the lid and looked down into the box, then back up at me. "You made this? For real? With school and everything you got going on?"

"Carrie taught me how. Before I left."

She pulled the small wall hanging out from the box and smoothed her fingers over it, tears streaming from her eyes. "I said no crying, ya'll!" She stamped her foot in mock anger, but didn't take her eyes off the gift.

Jazz came over to stand beside her. "Hey, baby. We gotta go. Hey! What's that?"

Ano couldn't speak. She sniffed, tears rolling down her cheeks.

"It's a wedding gift," I said.

"Oh," he said, looking down in the box. "You make that, Kate?"

"Yeah."

He nodded, not understanding the significance of it. He looked at Ano. "What's wrong?"

She clutched it to her heart. "Nothing. Nothing's wrong." She lunged forward and grabbed me into a fierce hug, her tears wetting my cheek. "I love it. Thank you."

"Put that on the wall in *your* house," I said. And, because I knew that my time with her was short, I said the only words I could manage to choke out. "Be happy."

The whistle sounded again and she kissed my cheek, accepted another congratulations from Percy, and headed with Jazz toward their train. They waved to us once more before disappearing inside.

Within the box was a small wall hanging. The colors were brighter than the original; the one that had hung on the wall in her mother's house for as long as Ano had been alive. The words I'd stitched were the same: *God Grant Me: Serenity - to accept the things I cannot change; Courage – to change the things I can; and Wisdom – to know the difference.*

Percy took my pack from my hands. When he told me he'd upgraded us to a sleeping car, what he hadn't told me was that he'd upgraded to a sleeping *suite.*

I looked around us. "Percy, I have to pay you back for this."

He pulled the bed out, reclining it fully. The train whistle blew, and I stood, leaning against the door for a second while he fussed about the room, pulling down extra pillows and adjusting the temperature.

"Percy," I said again, thinking he hadn't heard me. Before I could say his name a third time, he was beside me, his face irritated.

"I wanted to do this. For *us.* This has nothing to do with money, or me having money, or anything ridiculous. It was about our comfort riding home. Together." His fact softened. "Okay?"

"Okay."

Issue resolved, he kicked off his shoes and loosened his tie. His face was tired, and he sat down on the edge of the bed. "Ano tell you about what they're hearing? About more attacks?"

I kicked off my shoes and leaned against the edge of the bed next to him. "Yeah. I told her we were hearing a few rumors, but nothing like what her uncle heard. You think there's any truth to it?"

He was quiet for a moment, and then turned to me, his face serious. "I think there's a good possibility. It worries me. I think," he said cautiously, "that I'll send a telegram to my uncle in Virginia when we get back to Philly. He may not be able to tell me much. But if there's danger, he'll simply advise us to get somewhere safe." He reclined onto his elbow and massaged his temples. "Which we will do."

"Your grandmother and Edgar will be fine. They know you'll keep them safe."

"And you."

"I'll be fine, too."

He chuckled. "What I meant was, we'll *all* get somewhere safe." He paused, allowing the meaning to sink in. "You didn't really think I would leave you behind, did you?"

I caught his inflection and my face colored. Oh God. He knew. I played with the hem of my dress, my eyes cast downward.

"How much did you hear?" He didn't answer, and so I asked again, my voice low. "In the courtyard. Between me and Matt. How much did you hear?"

For a long, horrible moment, he didn't say anything. The train began to move, and I steadied myself against the slow swaying. "Enough," he answered. "Enough to hate him more than I thought possible."

Now he knew what Matt's family thought of me, knew why I'd left. I can't imagine what *he* thought of me now that he knew what a complete and utter fool I was to follow Matt Skylar back to Stanford like some lovesick moronic...

"Kate?"

Percy slid his legs over the edge of the bed and reached for me, but I moved away before his hand connected. "I'm going to go splash a little water on my face," I said, and stumbled with the movement of the train.

Percy's hands caught me as I lurched forward, and he held me while I righted myself. He wasn't letting go, and I couldn't exactly wrench from his grasp. At least, not in *this* dress. I kept my head down, avoiding his gaze.

His hand slid from my elbow to my hand and I allowed myself to be pulled backwards, back onto the bed. Looking out the window I saw lights flash past us. My head was turned away from him and my hair fell over part of my face, out of the clip Ano's cousin had placed at the nape of my neck. Gently, I felt him reach up and release my hair from the clip, the rest of it tumbling out and over my shoulders. His long fingers ran through it and he set the clip on the table next to the bed.

There was nothing he could say. He knew it, and so did I. Percy had long abhorred women in class who played for men like Matt. Women who came to class in heels and full makeup, or who showed more leg than a Vegas showgirl under their lab coat. And now, I would be lumped into the category with those women. A category of females that held no interest for men like Percy.

"I don't know what you're thinking," Percy chuckled. "It's hard because if I can't see your face, I can't...."

I nodded, but couldn't turn. My face was hot with embarrassment.

"Kate, do you think that what I heard will change anything?" His hand reached for my chin and I turned my head further away from him.

I'd left a place where I was nothing, traveled hundreds of miles to put it behind me, gone to a prestigious college for a respectable degree. And Paul's comment stripped all that away from me and make me feel like that same girl who'd shown up at Stanford, seventeen, alone and painfully shy.

He slid to the floor and physically turned me by the legs to face him. "Look at me," he commanded in a stern voice, and like always, I obeyed.

My eyes met Percy's. I didn't see admonition, reproach, or even disdain. I saw...I didn't recognize the look on his face.

He smiled. "You're overthinking it."

"I'm thinking," I said cautiously, "that I don't know why you'd even bother with me after..."

His face darkened. "Because I'm so shallow as to care what someone like Matt Skylar's brother thinks?"

"No! No. Because—"

"Because I wouldn't want to be with you after you'd chosen him instead of me?"

My mouth hung open. I couldn't believe he'd said it out loud.

Undaunted, he went on. "Or because I wouldn't want to be with you after you'd already been with Matt."

Okay, that hadn't occurred to me in quite that way, but now that he mentioned it...

He slid his hands behind my knees and pulled me towards him. "Is that what you were thinking?"

I nodded mutely. Partly because he was right, and partly because I couldn't believe he'd actually verbalized my worst fears.

"What I wanted," he said, sliding his hands along the sides of my dress, "was for him to stop touching you. To stop talking to you." He leaned in to me and I could smell the faint scent of his cologne. "What I felt was so territorial," he looked into my eyes, "it wasn't...healthy."

He reached up and smoothed the hair from my eyes once again. The rocking motion of the train moved him forward against me, and a smile played at the corners of his lips. "I want you so badly right now," he whispered, his lips close to my jaw, "that it hurts."

"Still? Even though—"

"Kate, don't you know?"

Taking my hand in his, he pressed my hand gently against his cheek. His eyes met mine. The truth of what he was feeling was there, as always, in his eyes. I shook my head, not wanting to believe it.

He nodded in confirmation. "Yes."

Closing the gap between us, Percy trailed kisses along my jawline and down my neck. His hands slid over the front of my dress and then down to rest on my bare legs. I had seen it in his eyes. Percy was in love with me. Finally. I pulled at the tie around his neck and, unsuccessful in slipping it off, hastily tugged him towards me for a kiss.

Percy loosened his tie and unbuttoned the first few buttons of his shirt. "Not tonight," he said. "I'm not going to rush this, Kate. I've waited too long to have you."

He leaned towards me, his mouth grazing the line of my jaw, my neck, the slope of my shoulder. His hand slid to the nape of my neck, then down to unzip the back of my dress. I closed my eyes as his hand slipped between the fabric and my skin. Crawling up next to me on the bed, he slipped the dress over my hips and allowed me to unbutton his shirt the rest of the way down. Discarding the tie, dress, and shirt off the edge of the bed, he came to recline next to me, bare from the chest up.

My eyes drank him in and I trailed my fingers over the hard ridges of his chest, the line of his collarbone, the angular slope of his stomach. As if savoring my exploration, he watched my face intently...his eyes capturing each emotion as I felt it. Percy's hand slid up the line of my body, one hand coming up to cover my breast. He lowered his head to my chest, his lips and teeth making it impossible for me to concentrate.

"I don't want anyone touching you," he said, as if to reiterate his point, "but me." His mouth came down on mine, and I willingly surrendered. My hands roamed over his chest, feeling the muscles down to his abdomen.

I wanted to feel him, all of him, and my hands pulled at his dress slacks. Smiling at my impatience, he unfastened his belt with one hand and kicked his pants off the bed. He moved his hand to rest against me, his thumb pressing gently downward. Rolling against him, I opened my mouth and his tongue flicked against mine. I kissed his neck. Where his movements were calculated, slow, mine were heated and irrational. I had three years of repressed passion coming at me full force.

"Do you remember where I touched you in the cave?" he asked, his hand moving down the length of me. His fingers found my warmth and pressed... oh, so firmly. He whispered incoherent endearments in my ear, and I heard the sound of my own voice moan his name with need.

Because he'd touched me like this back in the cave, I knew the explosion his hand could bring – and I craved it. I needed it. I needed him. Slipping everything else on him to the ground, he leaned against me, covering my mouth in a kiss. His hands were pure power; nearly paralyzing in the pleasure they brought.

The light in the cabin was dim but I pulled back enough to look at him; his entire body was bare and ready, right there against me. I ran my hand down the length of his body, enjoying the sight of him. He reached for my hand, needing my touch as badly as I needed his. He wrapped my hand around him, exhaling in pleasure, and I began to move my hand rhythmically.

His finger slid inside me. I moaned and arched my back, his thumb still exerting pressure where I could feel my blood pumping in a heated, rhythmic beat. Our mouths moved over each other, drifting only briefly to taste the skin of a neck or ear before returning to each other once again. His fingers moved against me more firmly, and my breaths came in gasps. My body knew what it needed and I reached for his hand, pressing myself harder against it. I could feel release coming at a breakneck pace.

I cried out and came hard against his hand, all decorum discarded. Barely waiting for my breathing to slow, I pushed him onto his back. Teasing my way from his chest down past his abdomen, I allowed my lips and tongue free reign. When my mouth tasted him for the first time, he called out my name, his voice rough. My hand gripped the base of him while my tongue and lips slid along him rhythmically. His head thrashed from side to side, his hands clenched in my hair.

There were no gentle caresses; no words said in cautious passion. This was a forest fire.

Pulling me until I lay on top of him, his tongue thrust against mine and I answered it with equal fervor. His hand slid behind my knees and pulled me forward until I was straddling him. His voice was velvet smooth in my ear. "Is this what you imagined us doing in lab?"

My affection for him no longer a secret, I pulled his mouth to mine, tasting the heat from his tongue and letting it fill me. "Yes."

"Kate," he groaned, need filling his voice, "I've wanted you for so long."

Finally able to say it without fear of rejection, I breathed into his ear, "Then take me."

In a single, swift movement, he rolled on top of me, thrusting inside me for the first time. A cry tore from my chest that was half gasp, half yell.

Our fingers intertwined above my head, I wrapped my legs around him and felt him fill me with each stroke. We moved together, perspiration making our bodies slick against each other.

The same release that had come with his hand was coming again, this time so much more powerful that I cried out in need. He rolled to his side, sliding my leg over his hip so that he was inside me and his hand could touch me simultaneously. He was driving me insane with pleasure. I whispered to him incoherently, calling him, begging him to give me all of him, needing him to join me.

His hips rising harder with each stroke, Percy owned me. Each thrust brought me closer to the edge, until I was calling out his name. Three years of wanting him and needing his touch had been unleashed, and our bodies slammed against each other, holding nothing back. I could feel Percy in every inch of me and yet I still needed more. Wrapping my legs around his waist I lifted my hips to his.

"Percy," I called hoarsely. "Oh, please." My fingers dug into his shoulders and I let go of my last bit of control. We slammed against each other, our voices mingling with the explosion we both felt.

Afterward, we lay bare, our legs still wrapped around each other, Percy still inside me. I could feel his heart pounding in his chest. I kissed his chest and tasted his skin, my eyes closing in post-coital bliss. Percy's arms were still around me, caressing me, holding me. I'd waited over three years to be with him like this, and the reality of it was so much better than I'd ever imagined.

Surprising me for the hundredth time that day, Percy pressed his lips to my forehead and uttered the words that I had waited for him to say to Carlie that day in the tunnel. The words I'd dreamed about hearing but never had. The words I doubted he'd ever said to any woman; save his mother.

"I love you."

CHAPTER THIRTY-SEVEN

Since his announcement more than a month ago, the chief basically stayed in the trauma unit during the day. They rationalized that it was because he was happier being useful, but they all knew that it was because the entire unit was deserted, save their small band of rebels. Over the waistband of her scrubs, Carlie had one of David's guns strapped to her hip. She'd become used to the weight and the feel of it now, although it seemed an oxymoron to be administering medical treatment with a Glock hiding under wraps.

David and Carlie entered the trauma ward and greeted Ynez and Maria, and the chief motioned for them to come with him. Once safely behind the door of his office, he didn't bother with protocol of sitting behind his desk; he was addressing them as peers.

"Got a cousin in the Navy. Says we'll be under attack within the week."

Carlie's heart stopped. It was over. All the waiting, praying, preparing. All the second-guessing and hoping that it somehow wouldn't come to pass was over. The war was here. She couldn't breathe.

"He tell you we'd have any friendly fire?" David asked.

The chief massaged his chin, which looked like it hadn't seen a razor in a week. "Can't tell me. Of course."

Carlie raised a finger into the air. "Sorry, ah...*friendly fire*?"

"U.S. troops. No one knows where they are. It's like...military silence."

Her voice was agitated, but she tried to keep her tone respectful. "How can no one know where one of the most powerful armies in the world is?"

The chief chuckled, and David smiled too. It irritated her that her question seemed to amuse them. "Oh, someone knows. But no one's saying. If you and I know then the enemy knows. Trust me, that would be devastating."

"So..." Carlie looked from one man to the other, "we are going to be invaded? I mean, does anyone know where they're going to attack first?"

"East Coast's the most likely," David said. "They hit New York hard. I'd say that's first."

"They've had time to get men over to the West Coast by now," the chief said. "I'd wager there're a couple thousand men sitting in the Sound as we speak."

"Wait, our Sound?" Carlie asked, incredulous. "Here, off the coast?"

David's voice was quiet; patient. "Yes, Carlie."

The chief looked directly at David. "You're packing. Correct?"

David lifted up the shirt of his scrubs, showing the holster of one of his guns. Only Carlie knew that he kept another one strapped to his lower leg.

He motioned to Carlie as if she wasn't able to speak for herself. "How about her?"

David lifted the edge of her shirt revealing a holster similar to his own. The chief nodded his assent. "I've got three strapped to the underside of Maria's desk and one in Ynez' top drawer."

Carlie's eyes grew wide as she listened to them discussing the trauma ward like an armory.

"We should have something in Surgery One and Surgery Two," David advised him.

"I've had Todd and Ian bring all the spare linens and supplies they could from the back. I planned on barricading the rear bay doors so there's no way someone could gain entry from the rear."

David nodded. "Good plan."

The chief sighed and looked at them both. "I just thought you should know. Gonna be quiet here today. Streets are empty, shops have all but closed up. You two have enough food at your place to make it a week?"

"Did surplus shopping a few weeks ago. We're fine."

"Never thought it would end this way," The chief said gravely.

No one in the room was going to say that it wasn't over till it's over. There were no heroic statements to be made because, Carlie rationalized, none of them would have believed them.

She went about her daily routine on autopilot; not focusing on counting or ticking off how many jars of penicillin she was marking down, straightening the crash carts despite Tom's protests that he'd had a nurse do that a month ago.

In her mind, Carlie was somewhere else. She was ten years in the future, comfortable with a private practice, a cushy office in an upscale neighborhood. She was married, with at least four kids, taking time on weekends for soccer games and dentist appointments. Carlie refused to allow herself to cry. Because, in her world, she called her mom each Sunday to talk about their week, and on every call her mom would listen to Carlie talk about the practice and the kids, and then would inevitably tell her about a new piece she was working on for a gallery in the city. In the world Carlie created, the war had ended before it had begun, without a shot being fired. Without a bomb going off. Without one soul being lost.

Standing in the cage counting vials of medicine, she carelessly walked too close to the edge where it had been joined together. The sharp metal edge sliced through her coat sleeve and into her arm. She looked down as the sleeve of her coat flushed with red. "Shit!"

The cage had been constructed quickly, as had most of the trauma ward, and it was her inattention that had caused her to get too close to the area that everyone knew was dangerous. They'd fixed it several times, but cutting it back had apparently only made it sharper.

Carlie kept gentle pressure against the wound and walked calmly to trauma one where she slid the curtain closed around her and opened the top two trays for sutures. Removing her coat required her to release her arm, and as she did so, small splatters of blood hit the floor around her.

She grabbed a syringe of lidocaine and bent her arm at the elbow in order to get a better angle for the injection. She winced only slightly at the first injection. The second was better, and she noted it clotted fairly quickly. She noted the time so that she'd know when it was safe to begin stitching herself and cursed herself again for the carelessness.

"Looks like we've got a bleeder," David said from behind her, opening the curtain and walking to the exam table across from her. He patted the table and motioned for her to get up. "C'mon. Lemme see."

He looked at the torn jacket draped over the edge of the exam table. "Catch your arm on the cage?"

She nodded. "Mmmhmm."

He disposed of her syringe and helped lay her arm out with sterile drapes for irrigation and sutures. "You don't need all that," she chastised him. "Save it for someone who needs it. I was going to put a few sutures in it and forget about it."

"Good plan," David said. "You planning on getting septic today or tomorrow?"

Under her breath she muttered, "Like it'll matter."

David leaned back to look at her. "You having second thoughts?"

"No."

"I know how to get you out of the city. I can do it tonight. You'll be on a bus for—"

"Just stitch up the Goddamned thing, David!" Carlie snapped, close to tears.

He donned surgical gloves and pulled the suture kit from the second drawer, tore it open, and laid it out next to her without a word. "I ever tell you," he said causally, as if she wasn't about to come unglued, "why I became a doctor?"

She shook her head and her long ponytail swayed behind her head.

"When I first shipped out, I was on the front lines. Really bad stuff. Saw a lot of things most eighteen year olds don't ever want to see in their lifetimes." He began to clean the torn skin on her arm. "So this one day, we're out on patrol and we get a report of a car bomb that's gone off really close to us. We get there, and there's this guy lying on the ground. He's Iraqi. And everything..." David motioned to his stomach and middle, "is basically gone. We're screaming for a medic and putting the guy on a stretcher and I'm running alongside the stretcher, M-16 in my hands. We get back to the camp and this doctor, this surgeon, spends like two hours trying to save this Iraqi guy's life."

He was quiet for a moment while he carefully stitched her arm. "I see the doc later that night, smokin' outside the mess hall and I ask him what happened. He says, 'nah, guy didn't make it'. And I said, you know, something like, 'what a waste'."

Carlie was caught up in the story now, listening as he finished stitching her and began to bandage her wound.

"He said, 'Don't ever fucking say that to me again. I'm an Army doctor. Saving a life is what I try to do, no matter what flag that person hoists.'"

David finished taping Carlie's arm, snapped off his gloves and reclined, hands resting on his knees. "So I guess what I'm saying is this: you've made your decision to stay. If you're able to save a life, then you've achieved your goal. You've fulfilled your purpose as a doctor. Don't regret the decision now that you're thinking about all the things you could do if this had never happened."

Carlie nodded, feeling humbled, though not really comforted by his speech. "I feel cheated. Like...if this war wouldn't have happened, if they wouldn't have attacked the U.S. then—"

"You'd be back in your nice, cushy lab at Stanford looking at pristine samples under a microscope and not sitting here waiting to be killed."

"Yeah."

"You *have* been cheated. And you *should* be mad," David said. "You've got every right to be." He leaned in towards her. "Channel that. Because when the battle begins, and you don't know the difference between the sound of enemy fire and friendly fire, you'll need that hatred filling you to survive. If it's fear inside you, you're dead."

Carlie finally admitted what had been on her mind all day. "Right now, it's fear."

"There's nothing wrong with that. But when the shit hits the fan, which it will very soon, you need to get mad. Not *crazy* mad, but mad enough so that you can make fast decisions based on survival, not based on the fear of dying."

"Okay."

He looked at his watch. "We're going to need to go home early. Get good sleep so our hours can change."

"Hours change? What'd you mean?"

He sighed. "Carlie, first attacks don't normally come in the middle of the day."

"Oh."

"Let's go home."

She sighed and hopped down from the exam table. "No practice tonight?"

"No, I think we've had enough target practice. Besides, it's not safe to discharge a weapon anywhere right now."

He followed her out of the exam room. "Will you do me a favor on the way home?" she asked.

"Okay. What?"

"I want to go through to the city one last time. Before the sun goes down? To look over the Sound."

He paused for a moment before responding. "We can borrow Maria's car but we won't make it all the way up to the Sound tonight. Seattle, maybe. Puget Sound, no. And you have to promise you'll just look and we'll go."

Carlie nodded. "I promise."

Where downtown Seattle used to be was now mostly reduced to rubble, however, a few of the highways were passable so that if you made it to one of the higher elevations, you could look over that portion of the Sound closest to Seattle. David maneuvered Maria's car as close as possible so that Carlie could see the water, but not so close that the debris posed an immediate danger.

She got out of the car, wrapped her arms around herself, and walked to the edge of the overpass. It was peaceful, unless you knew what was coming. David looked around them for a few moments and then came to stand behind her, wrapping his arms around her and resting his chin on the top of her head.

"Do you believe the chief?" she asked. "Do you think that we have men out there right now?"

David debated saying what he really believed as opposed to what Carlie wanted to hear. "I think that the U.S. is putting men...armies in place where they feel we are at the biggest threat of invasion."

"Do you think that includes Seattle?"

He looked down into her face and then out across the water where the sun was still reflecting off the surface. "I think Seattle will be seen as a point of invasion potential."

In Carlie's mind, she could see the platoon boats coming and the men landing on American soil. She could hear the gunfire and the bombs explode, see the sky turn orange and blood red.

Behind her, David could see it too. He turned her around and pressed her face into his shoulder. "Don't look," he said. "It'll be over soon."

CHAPTER THIRTY-EIGHT

"Well," Carrie said, refilling Charlie's coffee cup and staring out the window towards the fields, "I'm worried." She wrapped an arm across her middle. "He *still* hasn't told you what happened?"

Charlie took another bite of eggs and shook his head. "Nope."

Truth was, he'd expected Matt to come home empty-handed, so the fact that he'd come back without Kate hadn't surprised either Carrie or him too much. However, the fact that he'd been silent for three whole days was nearly killing Carrie, and was beginning to worry him.

It wasn't good for a man that young to anchor himself to one girl like this. Wasn't healthy. Plus, and Charlie would never admit this out loud, what if Carrie was right? What if he'd hurt Kate so badly that she'd moved on? If Kate *was* with Percy – and truthfully Charlie had nothing against it one way or the other – then Matt needed to move on.

"Can you ask him?"

Charlie sighed. One of the many things he loved about Carrie was her ability and fascination with 'fixing' other people's lives. More specifically, their love lives. He shook his head and stood, taking one last drink of his coffee.

"I'll be out most o' the morning, Mother. Part for the tractor s'posed to come in to the post today. I'll go pick it up in town."

"Take the boy with you. Do him good to go into town. "Oh," she added, "and pick up the post while you're there. I'm expecting a letter from Kate."

"Will do."

"And..." she was still going, and he was nearly out the back door.

He turned and sighed, slightly irritated. "Yeah?"

She smiled. "Take him his breakfast." She held a small basket out to Charlie and he accepted it, mumbling the whole way out to the barn.

Charlie found Matt on his back, underneath the tractor, the only visible part of him his legs sticking out from underneath where he was working. He set the basket down on the ground next to the tractor. "Breakfast from Carrie. You send any more food back in there an' she'll come out here and feed you herself."

Matt slid out from under the tractor, a slight grin on his face. He wiped his hands on the cloth hanging from the pocket of his jeans. "Okay. Thanks."

He carried the basket up to sit on one of the hay bales, uncovered it, and bit into the flaky biscuit within. For a few minutes, Matt ate and Charlie poked around the engine of the tractor.

"You pull the carburetor off?"

Matt nodded. "Yep."

Charlie nodded. He'd actually done a fairly good job of it. For never having worked on a tractor before.

"I think it's ready for that part," Matt said, and stuck an entire piece of sausage in his mouth.

Charlie relaxed at the sight of him eating. At least he wasn't trying to starve himself. "Gotta go into town and pick it up today."

Matt stopped eating. "Is it in? Tom's got it?"

Charlie nodded and leaned over under the hood. "Yup. Talked to him last night."

"Mind if I go with you? I...gotta mail a letter."

"A letter, huh?"

The size of Matt's smile increased. "Yeah."

"This letter wouldn't be going to Philadelphia, would it?"

Matt was quiet for a minute, and took another bite of his biscuit. After a long pause, he nodded.

"You writing each other? Workin' it all out?"

Matt shrugged. He didn't know, after saying goodbye to her, if they were going to work it out. It was clear from the way Percy had acted around her that he had fallen for her. Finally. The realization of that and the confirmation from Ano after she and Jazz got back from their honeymoon was hurting him so much that he didn't know whether to pursue it or give up.

"Boys finished up the seedin' last night. I 'spect we could go into town and mail that letter this morning. We'll pick up the part, have the tractor running by supper. If you're up to coming."

Matt nodded, but there wasn't the enthusiasm there once had been in his reaction. He stood and dusted off his hands.

Charlie pointed to the basket. "Bring it along. It'd better be empty by the time we get home if you don't wanna hear it from Carrie."

The ride into town was quiet. Too quiet. Charlie cleared his throat a lot, tried a couple of times to talk about the weather, but Matt had finished his breakfast in relative silence. After picking up the part and Matt silently handing Tom the letter to Kate, they got back in the truck for the ride home. Key in the ignition, Charlie sat back, looked across the truck cab to Matt, who was staring out the window. "She hurt you back?"

Pulled from his reverie, Matt looked at Charlie. "What?"

"Only two reasons a man stays quiet as long as you have. One, he just lost his crop. And our crops are gonna come in just fine, so that leaves number two." He stared at Matt, hard. "You lost your woman."

Matt didn't say anything for a long while, and Charlie just sat in the cab, waiting for him to respond. It wasn't Charlie's way to push.

"She...ah...fell in love. I think. With another guy."

"With that fella Percy? The one that was here?"

Matt's face showed surprise. "How'd you..." he threw his hands up in frustration. "Carrie. 'Course."

"Now, hang on, don't get like that with Carrie. She found out 'bout Percy long after it'd already happened. They just happened to be in the same place at the same time. "It happens, chief."

It didn't happen. Had never happened. To him, that is. "He's not right for her."

"So says you."

Matt turned his face towards Charlie, his eyes flashing with anger. "Yeah, so says me! He's not, all right?"

Charlie chuckled, held his hands up in mock surrender. "Okay, all right. I'm sure the other guy said the same thing about you."

Matt didn't respond. After a few minutes thinking about Charlie's comment, he nodded curtly.

"You're gonna have to face facts, here. You might have to let her go."

Surprisingly, Matt nodded slightly. "I know."

"You might have to move on. Move forward."

Matt shrugged. "I don't think there is any way I can. Without her."

Charlie sighed. He'd never had to have this talk with either one of his boys, and he was glad of it. Never any good with matters of the heart. That was Carrie's department.

"You gotta try. All this mopin' around. Not good. For you or her."

"I keep thinking, you know, if I just wait! Or give her enough time, or explain what happened."

Charlie tapped the steering wheel and looked out the front window. "Sometimes that works, an' sometimes it doesn't."

Matt worked the muscle in his jaw. "You think I shouldn't have written her?"

"Depends."

"On?"

"On whatcha said. On how ya said it. If you told her you're sorry." he nodded to himself. "That'd likely be okay. If you told her the other fella doesn't love her? That he's no good for her? Then I'd say you shot yourself in the foot. You got the bad habit of callin' a horse's ass a horse's ass."

"What does that mean?"

Charlie chuckled and started the truck. "Means that you say what's on your mind. Tell it like it is, whether or not you should."

Matt hit his head backwards on the headrest several times. "I couldn't help myself." His fists clenched at his side and Charlie thought he looked like he needed to hit something. "I see them together and...the way he touches her and I just wanna wipe that smug freaking smile off his face!"

Charlie laughed. "Ain't love grand?"

"Arrgh!!"

"You should talk to Carrie 'bout this. She's much better at it than me."

Matt snorted. "Yeah. She thinks this is all my fault. Probably thinks I deserve to lose her."

"She's not like that, Matt. She cares 'bout you and doesn't wanna see you in any pain. You just hit a nerve, with what happened with Kate."

"Kate wrote her all the time. In Denver, and at my mom's house."

Charlie nodded. "I know. Minute she got the post, it was like the sun had come up in her face and for days she'd be happy. Read her letters over and over."

Matt smiled. "Kate, too."

"Carrie, she misses our boys. You know...men aren't...well they don't take to motherin' like a girl does. They get to a certain age, why, they pretty much have their wives to nag after them."

Matt laughed.

"Don't need one more female peckin' at them 'bout how they're doin'."

"Kate...she, you know, never had that."

Charlie nodded. "I know. And I think Carrie never havin' a girl had something to do with it. Always wanted one."

"What happened?"

"Ah, back then, you get to a certain age you just stop havin' babies. We were nearly thirty when we got married, then thirty-three with Ralph and Mark came along two years later. Back then, you just didn't have kids past a certain age."

"I want to have four. Like my parents did."

Charlie laughed. "She know this?"

"Nah. I didn't want to scare her."

"Probly best that you didn't! It scares the hell outta me! Four kids. You're kinda young to be thinking about having kids just yet."

"Not with everything goin' on," Matt said. "That's why Jazz and Ano got married so fast. Jazz says there's gonna be another attack."

"Wha....what?" The truck slowed as Charlie took his foot off the accelerator and looked over at Matt.

Matt told him about Ano's uncles and what they'd heard on the radio for the last month or so and Charlie whistled through his teeth.

"So, if they're right and there is a war coming, then the demand for U.S. products – reliable ones – will go up. Milk, wheat...you know." Matt turned towards Charlie, his face serious with the explanation of his plan. "With big business out of the way, there's bound to be a market more geared for the independent farmer. Land's been vacated by corporations. Man could work that land, or buy acres from someone who's moving on, pretty cheap. Work it, raise a family on it."

Charlie nodded. "You're assuming you'll survive the next attack."

"If it's fought on land I will."

"You got a gun I don't know about, chief?"

Matt chuckled. "No, I don't. But by the time the fighting makes its way to us, I will."

"Well, I'll tell you something," Charlie said as they pulled into the drive. "Down in the cellar I've got about three cases of rifles, guns and ammunition." He put the truck in park and turned to Matt, deadly serious. "You ever fire a gun?"

"Sure, but only at skeet."

Charlie laughed at this, and the sound of his laughter filled the truck. He ruffled Matt's hair as they exited the truck and walked towards the house. "Sounds like a real fine plan you got there."

Matt nodded at Charlie. "I just need the land."

"And the woman," he chided.

"I've got someone in mind," Matt said softly, and he walked side by side with Charlie, who was still laughing about shooting skeet.

CHAPTER THIRTY-NINE

"I'm gonna go outta my damned mind," Jazz whispered to Ano, lying in bed facing each other.

"I know," Ano said, trying to calm him down, "but where're we gonna go? I hate to say it, but...baby, what's the plan? We can't leave 'till we know if there'll be another attack. I can't leave my mom and grandma."

"We'll turn Lively over to the enemy," he whispered and Ano smothered a laugh with her pillow. "They'll surrender without a damned shot bein' fired!"

"Stop!" she said, giggling.

"How about if we moved with them? Went to seminary with them?"

"You crazy?"

"No, listen."

Ano scooted closer to him. "I hear you. But how are my mom and my grandma gonna live? My grandma was on social security and my mom's company is gone."

Jazz shrugged. "They gotta have medical billing..." he thought about what he was saying and rubbed his face, "...or something like it where we're going."

She sighed. They'd been talking about this for the past week and she was tired of discussing it and not resolving it, and tired of trying to figure out a way for them to leave New Orleans.

"I'm sure she could, I don't know, find something. That's not the point."

Jazz hated fighting with Ano about this, and yet, that's all they'd been doing since the day they'd returned from their honeymoon. "Your uncle says any day now."

"I know."

"And after it's over..."

Ano reached for his hand and found it under the covers, pulled it towards her, and placed it on her waist. "Let's not talk about it anymore."

"What's wrong?"

"I just don't wanna talk about what could happen if we don't..."

"Don't you talk like that," Jazz said, his voice soft, but firm. "We're gonna make it through this just fine. All of us."

Ano nodded but said nothing. He pulled her towards him and kissed her gently. "Ano." No response. "An?"

Faint sniffing was heard between them and he pulled her chin up towards him to look into her face. "What's wrong? You scared?"

"Course I'm scared, ya fool!" her voice was irritated and he smiled at her in the darkness. "And I'm sick of havin' no privacy, and of being afraid someone's gonna hear us when we..."

He silenced her mouth with a kiss and pressed her body against his. Jazz slid on top of her, her legs wrapping around him. The bed creaked softly as he moved against her. Ano broke away from the kiss and pushed him to the side, making a frustrated sound.

What the hell could he do? They couldn't very well leave with the attack coming any day. They couldn't go to seminary until they knew if more bombs would be going off. And they clearly couldn't continue to stay there without going completely crazy.

"All right," he said. "I have an idea."

"What?"

"We'll wait a week. If nothing happens in the next week we'll send a telegram to seminary, see if they have married housing available. Something with two bedrooms. And if they do, we'll move with Grandma and your mom..." she opened her mouth to protest and he pressed a finger to her lips, "...and we'll help her find a job out there. Close to us."

"What about Lively?"

He shrugged. "There's bound to be an old people's home on the way there."

"Jazz Taylor!"

He laughed and she joined him, hitting his chest with her fists. He covered her mouth with a kiss and she moaned against him.

"You can't press that fine body up next to me each night and not expect me to do somethin' about it."

She raised an eyebrow at him. "Then you'd better practice bein' more quiet."

"Impossible." He kissed her again, slowly, and she closed her eyes.

"I have an idea," she whispered.

"Mmmhmm?"

"We could turn on the shower like last night, and—"

"Uh-uh. Noooo." Jazz all but pushed her away and she looked at him in shock.

"Why not?"

"Because," he said, his teeth clenched, "then tomorrow morning when I come downstairs, Lively's gonna ask me about my stomach ache."

"Your   what?"

"Yeah! She asked me this morning how I was feeling 'cause she heard moaning coming from the damned bathroom last night!"

Ano's throaty laughter echoed off the walls and he punched his pillow. "That woman, so help me... We should ask Carlie if there's a...pill for that..."

"We could go see Kate."

He sighed. "Too risky right now. It's too close to New York, too close to the coast."

"Do you think that they're safe in Philly?" her tone was worried and Jazz stroked her face.

"I think Percy'll keep her safe."

Ano didn't say anything for a few minutes.

"Ano?"

"Mmmhmm?"

"You still mad at him?"

"That man was gonna start a fistfight at our wedding!" she whispered fiercely. "In the middle of—"

"Okay, okay. He didn't though."

"Because I stopped him!"

Jazz chuckled. "He'll keep her safe. He said he was gonna telegram his uncle and if it wasn't safe to stay in Philly, they'd move somewhere safer."

"You believe him?"

"Yeah, I do. He sounded real concerned 'bout us. Makin' sure we were gonna be okay and all." He paused, knowing that mentioning it right now might not be met with the greatest reception. "He even offered to have us come stay with them. At his grandmother's house."

She was quiet for a second. "He did?"

"Mmmhmm."

"Where're they gonna go? If...if his uncle says it's not safe?"

"Don't know. Percy said they'd go somewhere and just wait it out."

"Do you think it's something that can be 'waited out'?"

Jazz had wondered the exact same thing countless times. He wanted to tell her he didn't know. Wanted to tell her it was a crapshoot, and the odds weren't exactly in the favor of the U.S. with no president and no militia. But in his head, he heard his father's voice: *'Man's job as the head of the house is to comfort his wife. Protect his family. And make sure they're secure. While I'm gone, that's your job. You're the man of this house. While I'm gone, you're in charge.'*

With that advice echoing through his head, he tightened his arms around Ano. "Everything's gonna be fine. Before you know it, soldiers'll be lining the border and you'll see U.S. flags mounted on battleships comin' into port."

He could actually feel her body relax against him. "Really? You think so?"

He swallowed hard against the lie. "Course' I do." He kissed her forehead and she settled against his chest to go to sleep. "Course' I do."

CHAPTER FORTY

Five days after my birthday, walking back to my dorm, I was tired. My backpack, weighted down with three volumes of books, sliced into my already sore shoulders and I winced with every step I took. I rounded the last corner to the housing complexes. I could be in sweats and studying on my bed within ten minutes. I tried to quicken my pace without jostling myself more than necessary. I looked at my watch. It was one in the morning.

When I passed by the front office Rob peeked his head out of the window and tried to stop me. "Hey, Kate, hang on."

Doesn't that guy ever get off duty?

I waved without responding, but his tone gave me pause. "You've got a visitor."

I stopped at the base of the stairs and looked around the lobby. It was empty. I turned back towards him with an inquisitive look.

Happy that he'd been successful in delaying me, he nodded enthusiastically. "Yeah. 'Bout an hour ago. Oh, and you got some mail."

I looked around again. "Rob...where is he?"

"Who?" he asked back, and I closed my eyes and summoned great patience to respond calmly.

"The. Visitor."

"Ooooh!" He came to the window and handed me two letters. "Said he'd be back."

A vague sense of worry crept into my mind as I considered my two possibilities for a visitor. "Rob," I asked cautiously, "was this visitor tall?"

He looked at me with his normal 'deer-in-headlights' expression. "Oh, I don't remember."

I'd be more successful in extracting information from one of the corpses I'd seen today in class.

Easy question. Think easy question.

I walked over to the window and rested my hands on the sill. "Did he have blond hair, or red?"

"Actually, it's more dark brown now than red." Percy's baritone made me turn and I smiled as he entered the lobby.

"Hi," I said, walking towards him, careful not to give Rob any more of a show than he'd received already.

"Expecting someone else?" Percy asked, his tone slightly clipped.

"No."

He nodded once. "Good."

"You wanna come up?"

"Yes. We need to discuss some things."

Percy, not normally one to deliver the 'let's talk' line, followed me upstairs and into the large suite I shared with five other girls. I unlocked the door, which opened into the main living room. Sparsely decorated, in the middle of the room sat two couches with a coffee table, and along the back wall was a small kitchenette with a sink. The lights were on. Taylor and Claudia sat silently on the couch, each studying from a different textbook. I waved as we entered and walked through to the bedroom I shared with Simone.

I turned on the light and allowed my backpack to slide to the ground at my feet. "Oh, God. Much better."

I kicked my Converse off and slunk to my bed still unmade from this morning. "You want to sit?"

Percy looked around the room I shared with Simone. "Do you think it's safe?"

I shook my head in confusion, and then really looked and *saw* what he meant. All around me was chaos. Several of my books lay open faced on my desk, a half-eaten granola bar actually saving my place where I'd left it this morning – my half assed attempt at breakfast forgotten. Jeans and t-shirts littered the floor around us, and binders with paper coming out from them made a virtual bomb field to my bed. He looked at me, sitting in the middle of my bed; pajamas and a wrinkled blanket surrounding me, and sighed.

"How do you *live* like this?"

"Quite easily, actually."

He picked his way through the mess to climb onto the edge of my bed with me.

"You can kick your shoes off, if you want to."

"Yes, but would I be able to find them when I leave?"

"Sorry. The maid has the week off."

"The week?" Percy said snidely, and kicked off his shoes. "Looks like she died." He pointed to the corner of the room that held Simone's things, which was in a greater state of disarray than mine. "She might actually be in there somewhere."

"Funny." I looked at his face. His brows were drawn up in a tense line. "What's wrong?"

"Got a reply from my uncle Thomas in Virginia."

I slid off my bed to walk to the mini refrigerator. "I'm listening." I opened the door with my foot and pulled out a soda, then offered one to Percy. "Want one?"

"Please."

I walked back to the bed and handed him one, put mine on the table, and stripped my long sleeved sweatshirt from my body. "Go on," I said, reaching for my pajamas.

Percy's hand was quicker than mine, and he pulled out the faded light blue pajamas from where I'd tossed them this morning, across my pillow. "You still have these?"

I reached for them, but he pulled them from my grasp. "They're my favorite pajamas, now hand them—"

"You still *sleep* in these?"

I stood in front of him, hand on my hip. "Yeah. And I've been in these clothes since five o'clock *yesterday* morning, so..." I held out my hand to him and motioned for him to give them to me. "Hand them over."

"Remind me to get you some better pajamas."

"I like these," I said as he placed the faded clothes in my hand. I realized I couldn't change in front of him. "Give me a sec," I said, heading for the door.

"I've seen you with a lot less on than that," he said.

My face colored. Although he was right, this was an entirely different kind of naked. This wasn't intimate, it was everyday. I hadn't even gotten comfortable changing in front of Matt, and he and I had been...

"I won't look," he said, and closed his eyes. "Much."

I laughed and walked to stand behind him, where I changed faster than I'd ever done before. "All right," I said, and kicked my worn clothes into a corner. "Done."

Picking up my soda from off the table, I sat back down next to Percy on my bed. He was shaking his head again.

"What?"

He got up and picked up the clothes where I'd kicked them, folded them and placed them on the chair. He was still shaking his head when he sat back down.

"A few things we'll have to work on."

"Your uncle?" I reminded him, and we both cracked open our sodas.

Percy pointed to the door to my bedroom. "Um, can we expect your roommate anytime soon?"

"No, she's doing a twenty-four. She'll be back at dawn."

"All right. My uncle believes that Philadelphia isn't safe."

Big shock. "All right."

"He has offered for us to come stay with him. Until everything is over."

"Over? What does that mean?"

"I don't know."

"Well then how do you know it isn't safe?"

"He can't tell me anything specific in an incredibly public telegram."

"So, when do you leave?"

His eyebrows knit closer together. "When do *we* leave."

"Yes, that's what I asked."

"No, you asked when do *I* leave."

I massaged the bridge of my nose. I was getting a headache. "When does he want you there?"

"He's expecting us no later than Monday."

"Monday. Perce, it's Thursday."

"I realize that."

Three days with him. I had three days and I'd have to say goodbye. Shit. I took a sip of my soda. "Oh. Okay."

He motioned around the room. "We can have someone help you with this. If it's easier."

"Help me with what?"

"Packing!" he said, annoyed. "Packing all your things. To take them with us."

My eyes opened wide. "Wait, I'm..." I scooted closer to him. "I'm going with you?"

"I believe that's what I've been explaining in some detail. Yes."

"I don't remember that part of the conversation."

"Perhaps you weren't paying attention," he said, eyebrows raised. "Of course you're coming with us."

"Percy, I can't."

"All right. Rationally, I accept that it will be difficult for you to leave a program that you've seemingly committed yourself to."

"Seemingly? Seemingly? I've *completely* committed myself to it!" His eyebrows knit so close together they were almost touching. "Why are you getting so upset?"

"Because I can't simply pick up and leave!"

"Why not?"

Inside, I was fuming. "Percy," I said, and set my soda down on the edge of my desk, "I made a decision to follow medicine."

"And I support that."

"Okay, so...?"

"So long as you're not in danger."

"We don't know if your uncle is right." I looked at him, pleading with my eyes. "If he's not, I will have walked away from this program and they will *not* let me back in!"

His voice was calm. Smooth. "And if they're not here, like Stanford wasn't there, then you will be forced into finding a new program regardless."

I opened my mouth to protest, but actually, I didn't have an argument to that. I shut my mouth with a click.

Sensing I would not give up that easily, Percy asked, "If someone would have come to you a month before we went down into Wind Cave and told you to leave Stanford, that it wouldn't be standing a month from then, what would you have said?"

"I'd have ignored them."

"With the amount of information you have at your fingertips, after everything that's happened, you are willing to make that judgment call *now*? Because, Kate, if you are, you're betting your life."

I looked around me, at the papers I needed to write, the tests I had to study for. "If you're wrong, then all this was for nothing, and I lose out on the accelerated program."

"You are correct." He took a breath. "But I'm not wrong."

"What if your uncle's just trying to keep you from harm's way?"

"If my uncle says it's not safe, what he really means – but cannot say – is that we are going to die if we stay."

"If he's right, and Philly does get attacked, then the need for doctors will be greater than ever."

"Yes. *Doctors.* Not med students. You'd be of little help to them, Kate. They'll need hands that know what to do, not someone who needs their instruction to do it."

His criticism stung a little, and I raised my chin slightly.

"Don't," he said, "I know that look."

"What look?"

"The look that says 'you just made my decision for me' look." He took a sip of soda. "That stubborn look you get when you're about to completely disregard what I've told you to do and go the opposite direction."

"I do not go the—"

"Sodium bi-cholorinate."

"Oh, you *had* to go there." I crossed my arms over my chest. "You *had* to?"

"You made me do it."

"You told me—"

"No, I didn't."

"You *told* me," I said, my voice getting slightly louder than his, "and I quote, 'three mL would do just fine', end quote."

"No, you're incorrectly remembering what I said."

Not to throw it in his face, but I had to point out the obvious. "I remember *everything*." I raised an eyebrow.

He sighed and massaged the bridge of his nose. "I'm not going to debate the issue with you at this point."

"Fine."

"I don't want to quarrel with you over this."

I saw his features soften, and the heat went out of my voice. "Neither do I."

He looked around and then leaned over me to set the soda on the edge of my desk next to my own. Turning around, he sat next to me, his mouth in a hard line. "You need to pack," he said, matter-of-factly. "I brought the Land Rover tonight so that if you wished you could simply come with me."

I couldn't do this. It was too soon. I had committed myself. I was in med school. "Percy," I tried again. "I just can't."

He didn't say a word for a few moments. When he raised his eyes to me, they were hard. "What are you going to do when the sirens go off and you have about ten seconds left of your life? If the sirens go off at all?"

I had no answer for that, and he knew it.

"You're being foolish."

Unfortunately, I knew he was right. And I hated the fact that he was already prepared for me to leave when I hadn't even consented to going. Hated the fact that he'd anticipated every argument I would make. And hated the fact that – despite the horrible timing – leaving was the only answer that made sense.

I nodded. "All right," I said through gritted teeth. I'll pack tonight."

I half expected to see a look of victory on his face, but there was nothing but relief. "Thank you."

"For what?"

"For saving me from carrying you down to the car like a fireman."

"You wouldn't have."

"Yes," he said quietly, "I would have."

I got up and pulled the well-worn backpack out from under my bed. "What else?"

He got up and began to gather the clothes that were strewn all over the floor. "Hmm?"

"You said we had 'things' plural to discuss. What else?"

He stood and tossed a small pile of clothes onto my bed. "Ah. Yes. Since we'll be leaving in two days, Gigi would like to celebrate your birthday. Tomorrow night. Since we didn't get to celebrate it when we returned from New Orleans."

"Isn't that kind of weird? We're leaving and...having a party?" That, and I hadn't ever had a birthday party. Ever.

"It won't be, you know, a formal one. Just you, me, Edgar, and Gigi."

"What about Phillip and Sasha? Where are they going when we leave?"

"They've been with Gigi forever; they're coming with us. My uncle's house is large enough to support more domestic help."

Of course, I thought, but only nodded.

"So," he asked, "that's a yes. Correct?"

"Percy," I began, and he rolled his eyes.

"It will be very small."

Warily, I nodded.

"Excellent." He began to push the small piles of clothes back in my pack. "Let's get you home, then."

CHAPTER FORTY-ONE

The ride back to Society Hill was a quiet one. Percy was silent driving us back to his grandmother's house, and thankfully not going to rub in the fact that I'd surrendered without a fight. I was filled with thoughts of my own, feelings that I was doing exactly what Carlie had warned me about— by selling my dreams to pay for someone else's.

I couldn't help but wonder if this was all a ploy by Percy to get me away from med school and back into science as my chosen field. Another part of me knew that Percy wouldn't move his grandmother and brother unless he truly believed there to be a threat to our wellbeing. And so, after saying a few quick goodbyes and writing a short letter to Simone warning her of what I knew – knowing she wouldn't heed my advice, regardless of what I said – I left Penn State.

Sitting beside Percy as he drove us back to his home, an odd feeling came over me. I looked over to where he sat in the driver's seat; the wind ruffling the unruly curls in his hair, a look of concentration on his face, as always. At that moment, something felt *right*. As if I was always meant to be here next to him. The large watch on his arm gleamed in the lights from the highway and I stared at his muscular forearm resting on the steering wheel. I felt... safe with Percy – in a way that I'd never felt safe before, and I was having difficulty processing that feeling.

Safety, in my limited experience, is a dangerous illusion. Once you begin to feel safe, you become sedentary, and thus are an easier target for pain when the safety dissolves. The knowledge that I was, for the moment, safe with Percy made me uneasy in its comfort.

Edgar ran out to greet us when we drove up, and Phillip came out to help with the bags. I wasn't used to seeing Percy as a big brother, but I had to admit, it humanized him; humbled him to have to play that role on an everyday basis. I knew Percy's sense of responsibility was so strong that he now saw his role to Edgar as a mentor, a guide, a role model. And, in Edgar's opinion, a playmate.

Percy was barely out of the car before Edgar was trying to punch him in the ribs. Percy deflected the blows easily, blocking but not returning them. We walked around to the rear of the car and I reached for the backpack that Phillip pulled from the back. Phillip looked first at me, then at Percy, who nodded to Phillip to carry it inside. I let my arms drop and shifted my book bag from one shoulder to the other. I'd brought my medical books with me. If I was going to leave med school, I would still keep current on everything on the remote chance I could get back into a program when everything settled down. If it ever settled down.

Edgar jumped in front of Percy, volleying a hard hit toward Percy's flat stomach. Edgar was nearly as tall as Percy, but all arms and legs; as if his body hadn't quite figured out it wasn't supposed to be that big yet. Percy caught Edgar's fist in his own hand, his face bland.

"Enough," he said calmly, and gave Edgar a gentle push backwards.

Percy led me up the steps toward the house, chatting lightly with me, as if he wasn't under simultaneous siege by Edgar. "Your room is at the top of the stairs, down the hall. Last door on your right."

Edgar's foot swiped at Percy's in an attempt to trip him, and he added in my direction, "Across the hall from Percy's."

This comment earned a sigh and a raised eyebrow from Percy who motioned for me to enter ahead of them. I entered the foyer and looked around; it was dark and I whispered to Percy, "Is Gigi asleep?"

"Yes. Her room is on the left wing of the house, so we won't disturb her by talking in normal tones." Edgar volleyed another swipe at his feet, finally capturing Percy's attention. "All right," he said, his voice taking on a stern, fatherly tone. "She's here, and it is late. Now you may go to bed and we will see you in the morning."

"I'd like to stay up and—"

"Good night, Edgar."

He glared at Percy, but there was no real malice behind it. "You promise, tomorrow?"

"Tomorrow," Percy agreed. "Now go to bed, please."

Reluctantly, Edgar turned and ascended the stairs, his curls flopping over his forehead. At the top he called down, "G'night, Percy. G'night, Kate."

With a nod Percy dismissed him, and I gave a slight wave as he disappeared at the top of the stairs.

"What's tomorrow?" I asked.

Percy reached for the book bag on my shoulder. "Hmm?"

"Edgar. You promised him something?"

"Oh. Yes. He wants me to fight him."

"Fight him?"

He smiled easily and motioned for me to follow him into the large room off the hall. "Perhaps fighting was a bit strong. Sparring. Or fencing. It's his choice tomorrow." He relaxed as we entered the large room.

A fire was lit and Percy sat down at the end of the large leather couch in the middle of the room and massaged his eyes. It reminded me of those drawing rooms you see in the movies. The fireplace was enormous and nearly overpowered the room. Mahogany bookshelves covered one entire wall, with one of those ladders on wheels rested in one corner, as if someone had just climbed up to retrieve their favorite novel. Nearly the entire wall behind us was windows, paned glass looking out over the front grounds, dark now because of the hour.

"Come. Have a seat." Percy patted the couch next to him and reached for the decanter on the table in front of us. Flipping over two small crystal glasses, he filled them each with a small bit of amber liquid and handed one to me.

"I don't really drink." I sat and accepted the glass regardless and saw a smile tug at the corner of Percy's mouth.

"Yes, I know. I figured this would help you relax, and maybe even get some sleep, so please." He motioned for me to take a sip, which I did.

Honestly, I'm not a fan of alcohol. I don't care for the taste of wine, and the very smell of beer makes me ill. Hard alcohol doesn't normally do anything but burn my mouth, so normally I stick to water or soda. But whatever Percy had put in my glass was different.

I looked up at him after I'd tasted it, and there was humor in his eyes. "What is this?" I asked. "It...it's sweet. And it almost tastes like almonds."

"It's Amaretto. A sweet liqueur and yes, it tastes a little like almonds." He took a sip out of his glass, satisfied that I liked it. He stretched out his legs and rested his arm over the back of the large couch.

"Did you spend a lot of time here? Before, I mean."

He looked around the room. "I spent a lot of summers here, with my mother and brothers. Here, or Gigi's house in London."

London. Of course. "Oh." I sipped the drink.

"When things go back to normal," he said, and touched my hair lightly, "I will take you there."

"You don't have to say that."

"I realize that. I haven't been back there in a while, so it will be nice to see it again. With you."

"Your whole family went? To London, I mean."

He nodded absently and played with a strand of my hair. "Yes, well, with the exception of my father. He stayed in New York or he flew out for a weekend occasionally while we were there. But it's been..." he ran a hand over his face, thinking, "many years since I've been there. Freshman summer just before Stanford, I think."

"Why?" I asked him. "Didn't you like going?" I couldn't help but think that if I had family who wanted me to go to London, I'd have had a hard time *returning* to school.

"I liked it very much. But I was doing the summer labs and..." he smiled at me slightly, "as you know I was occupied with the research as my concentration."

I blushed slightly. "I remember." Summer was the one time I'd been able to relax a little with Percy. The time when we'd actually talk about things other than school. Summers spent in lab with him – for me – were the most fun I'd ever had.

"What are you thinking about?" he asked, inclining his head.

I swirled the liquid around in my glass and stared at the color as it reflected in the firelight. "I was thinking how I didn't really know you then. Anything about you. Not like I do now."

Reclining slightly and turning towards me, as easy smile spread across his lips. "You knew me."

"Not the everyday things."

"You observed those down in Wind Cave."

I returned the smile. "No. Things like...what the inside of your apartment looked like, or who your friends were, where you ate your dinner at night." I shrugged. "Those things."

He took a drink from his glass. "Well, let's see. My apartment was very small and you would have hated it. It was very clean."

I narrowed my eyes and he laughed.

"I had no roommates and didn't really spend a lot of time socializing as you know, outside of class or labs. Most of the time, if I ate dinner at my apartment I would have a textbook open on the table and a plate of food next to me."

It was odd for me to hear details about his life that I had only had a glimpse of.

He pulled me closer and helped me recline a little on the couch. "What about you. I clearly earn a failing grade for skills of observation."

I shook my head in disgust. "You said a mouthful."

He poked me playfully in the ribs. "Where did you spend time when you weren't in lab?"

"When I wasn't studying, I was with Ano."

"Or?"

"Or nothing. I didn't really do anything except, you know." I blushed, and the alcohol wasn't helping.

Percy sighed and looked at me for a moment. "Except spend time in lab.

With me."

I shrugged and looked at my glass intently.

He raised an eyebrow in mock irritation. "All right, I'll ask. How long did you...." he shifted uncomfortably and looked at his glass.

"Lust and pine after you silently and ardently?"

"Something like that."

I smiled nervously. "The truth? Pretty much from our first lab."

"You know, I almost asked you out once."

"No, you did not!"

He nodded and waited to swallow a sip of his drink before responding. "I did."

"When?"

"Uh...last October, I think. We were doing the lab on complex chemical compounds and—"

"The liquid nitrogen one?"

"That's it."

I remembered it, vaguely. "Why didn't you?"

"Because you were such a good friend, and partner. We were so good together, and I didn't want to alter that and take the chance of ruining it. Of losing that." He paused and a small smile formed. "But I did notice you."

I took another sip, this time a larger one, and it dawned on me why people drink. Warmth spread through me and I felt the tension begin to fade from my limbs. I closed my eyes.

"Come here," Percy said. "I don't bite."

"Yes, you do."

"All right, but not right now." In one swift movement he had me against him. "There," he said, and reclined further against the plush leather. "Better?"

"Yes." I took another drink and then set my glass on the tray in front of us.

"I thought you liked it?" he asked.

"I like it a little *too* much," I admitted, and turned in his arms so that I was lying against him.

I could feel the rumble in his chest as he chuckled. He set his glass next to mine. "Well, in that case," he said, and slid his hands down my back, "I'll pour you one more often."

"And your grandmother will wonder why you associate with young women who drink in the afternoon."

"I will inform her that my girlfriend has every right to enjoy libation as often as she likes," he said, his eyes looking down into mine, "as long as I'm the beneficiary of her intoxicated state."

My girlfriend. He'd said it. It's one thing to tell someone you love them. It's entirely another to give them a title. A label. A place in your life. As odd as it sounded, when Matt said it, I accepted it as something he'd done before. Nothing out of the ordinary. After all, Matt Skylar had had a lot of girlfriends. I knew from speaking with Gigi that Percy hadn't. That made the title...and the sentiment...that much more important.

His mouth opened against mine and I tasted him, warm and inviting. "I'm thinking that I should show you where your bedroom is," he said.

I nodded somberly. "I'm terrible with directions. I may need a personal escort." I wound my fingers through his hair and relaxed into his arms as his kiss deepened.

The voice that came from the doorway was slightly higher pitched than his own.

"Percy?"

Had Percy's arms not been around me, I'd have fallen off the couch and onto the floor. Bolting upright from where I'd been reclining against him, I flipped around to see Edgar, his tall, lanky body standing in shorts and a t-shirt, looking uncomfortable in the doorway.

He wasn't the only one. Percy's face darkened slightly. "Edgar, I told you to go to bed."

Edgar looked uncomfortable, and didn't immediately respond. It occurred to me just by looking at him what was wrong. I knew that look. I'd worn it a hundred times, but hadn't had anyone that I could have gone to who could have made the look go away. And it now occurred to me, looking at Edgar, that I could.

I stood up a little shakily and walked slowly to him. I knew he was too old to take my hand, so I reached all the way up and ruffled his hair. "Percy was going to show me to my bedroom," I said to him. "But I think we'll make a quick stop by yours first."

He looked back at Percy, whose face still held irritation at his younger brother's interruption. "Percy?"

Sighing and running a hand over his face, Percy nodded and Edgar led the way up the stairs. His room was the first door on the right, and it was bright as day. Percy dimmed the lights and motioned for him to get back into bed.

"I'm..." Edgar hesitated, not wanting to sound like a coward in front of a virtual stranger. "Let's keep the lights on." He climbed up into the huge bed and allowed me to cover him.

"When I was your age," I said, and climbed the small footstool to sit on the edge of his bed, "I slept with the TV and all the lights on. And sometimes I left the water running in the bathroom in the hall."

"Why?" His voice cracked as he said it.

"When I didn't, I heard things. Noises. Stuff that scared me and..." I looked down at the comforter and not into his face, "it was the only way I could get to sleep."

"Why didn't you ask your mother…or your father to just…?"

I smiled up at him, unafraid of telling him the reason. "My mom…um, died, when I was four. And my dad died when I was about the same age that you are right now."

"Who did you live with? Your grandparents?"

"Didn't have any."

We sat there, across from each other, two people from completely different backgrounds, with a huge common denominator.

"Tell me," I asked him, "what you remember most. About your mom."

He slid down deeper into his bed, and I could see his eyes getting heavy. "Sometimes she would come to Avon and take me out. For no reason, just for the day."

I smiled at him, for being able to pull such a good memory so quickly. Ano would say that it was a good sign. "What would you do?"

He shrugged and yawned. "Whatever I wanted. Once we drove all the way to this carnival an hour away. We stayed there all day, until it got dark. And when we got back, she…" he yawned again and I pulled the covers up around his shoulders, "told Dean Freidrichsen that it was a family emergency."

His eyes were closing, but I didn't get off the edge of the bed. "That's a good memory," I said. His eyes closed all the way. As if on impulse, I reached up and smoothed the errant curls off his forehead. They came right back, as if on autopilot, and I smiled. I sat there next to him until his breathing became regular and then accepted Percy's hand to help me down off the bed.

We walked in silence to my room, the last door on the right; across the hall from his and two doors down from Edgar. I stepped in and turned on the light. My backpack was leaned against the dresser where Phillip had taken it and I went to retrieve my pajamas.

"I don't remember her…like that," Percy said quietly. "She was always so busy when I was at Avon. Busy with Will, or John, or…you know…" he looked up to me. "Just busy."

"Well," I said, "when you were in high school, she was. She had five boys to raise."

He reached for me, pulled me into his arms. "Thank you," he said quietly, and rested his head against my chest. This was so unlike Percy that I really didn't know what to make of it. I stood, holding him. "I haven't really talked to him…you know, about it."

"Maybe he needs you to," I said, and his head came up, his eyes finding mine. "You're the only one who shares those memories with him." I wasn't normally good at comforting, but figured it was what Ano would have said.

"I didn't know that you used to sleep with all the lights on."

"Drove Ano crazy my first year at Stanford," I said, smiling at the memory.

He nodded sadly. His face looked tired. Percy had aged far more than his twenty-four years in just a few short months.

"I want to say something," he said. "And I don't want you to think that I'm just—"

"Okay."

He looked into my eyes. "I want you to sleep with me, in my room tonight. Not for—"

"I get it."

His tone was pleading. "I just want you against me tonight." He looked down. "And I want to wake up with you tomorrow morning." Looking back up at me, he asked, "Is that...will you..."

I leaned forward and kissed him tenderly, almost painful, because I wanted to touch him so much more. However, tonight, what he needed was different. "Yes," I said. I reached up and touched his face. "Yes."

CHAPTER FORTY-TWO

Some people would describe nirvana as a large mansion, an island in the Caribbean, or piles of money. When I awoke against Percy's chest, his arm loosely around me, I was in nirvana. His face was relaxed and he looked like an older version of Edgar. So much that I smiled at the resemblance.

Percy's hair was a complete mass of dark, unruly curls and I ran my fingers through it and shivered with pleasure. The sun drifted through the thick drapes at his window, urging us to wake up and start our day. His skin was warm against my cheek and I pressed my lips against his chest in an effort to wake him. When he didn't stir, I grinned, letting my hand wander lower to see if it would rouse him. I could definitely get used to waking up like this.

He groaned and opened his eyes, a smile instantly forming on his face. He entwined his fingers with mine and pulled my hand from underneath the covers. "Good morning."

I kissed his chest. "Morning. How did you sleep?"

"Mmm." He rolled against me to kiss my neck. "Amazingly well. You?"

I inhaled the scent of his skin. "Very well." Taking advantage of his proximity, I slid my leg over his hip and arched against him slightly. My lips drifted up towards his neck and I dug my fingers into his shoulders. He growled low in his throat.

"You keep doing that," he warned, "and Gigi will have a lot of explaining to do to Edgar downstairs."

I pulled away slightly and in doing so, my hips pressed against him harder. His eyes closed and he slid a hand down to cup my behind against him. Enjoying the slight position of power I seemed to have acquired this morning, I said, "I think that at fifteen, Edgar likely knows the facts of life."

Percy wasn't paying attention. His mouth and lips were against my throat, my mouth, my ear. He was quickly convincing me that moving in with them was the best decision I'd ever made.

In order to maintain a slight advantage, I slid my hands down below his waist and pressed my lips against the spot just beneath and behind his ear. It worked. Percy groaned and slid on top of me, capturing both of my hands by the wrist and pressing them against the pillow above my head.

"You're not playing fair."

I grinned and moved forward to kiss him. "No, I'm not."

Moving his hips against mine he said, "Then I'm going to have to teach you a lesson."

A knock sounded at the door and Edgar's voice came from the other side. "Percy?"

I smothered a laugh when Percy cursed. His head hit my shoulder in frustration.

"Are you awake?"

Rolling to the side, he called out, "What is it, Edgar?"

"Kate's up, but she's not in her room and you promised that you'd—"

"Edgar!" Percy fairly yelled, and I pressed a hand against his chest to calm him down. He blew out a breath and closed his eyes. "Edgar," he said again tersely, "I'm awake. I'll be down in a few minutes."

From the other side of the door came the disgruntled reply. "All right."

I muffled my laughter in Percy's pillow as he ran a hand through his hair and rolled onto his back. "How the hell did my parents do it?"

"What?"

"Manage to have five boys and not *kill* any of us?"

"I'd say it was a miracle they *conceived* five, with even one hanging around."

He smiled towards me and lowered his lips to mine. "Sorry."

"Don't be. I need to take a shower this morning and—"

"And you and I have to go shopping today."

"Shopping?"

Percy sat up, fingering my faded pajamas and meeting my eyes. "Shopping. For your birthday." He kissed me quickly before getting out of bed. "After I go downstairs and school my younger brother in either fencing or sparring," he said, pulling a shirt over his head, "we're going into town for the afternoon."

I drew my knees up to my chest. "That's very nice, but—"

Percy stepped into a pair of pants, then paused before opening the door. "You have two hours."

For most of the afternoon we went from shop to shop, Percy knowing exactly what items he wished me to have. Arguing about the cost did no good and seemed to irritate him, so after the first few stores he simply refused to allow me to look at price tags.

Arriving back home just before dinner, we alighted from the car while Phillip removed the packages from the back of the Land Rover. "Where am I going to put all this?" I asked Percy as we entered the foyer.

"I have a trunk for you that we're taking to Virginia."

"A trunk?"

He nodded. "Gigi has her steamer trunks and we have one for Edgar. I thought you and I would share one, seeing that neither of us has that many clothes."

"I do now," I said admonishingly, and he swatted me lightly while Phillip trudged up the stairs, arms laden with bags.

"You had nothing suitable," Percy explained for the fiftieth time that day. "This might be our last chance to buy you something before...anything happens."

"There you are!" Gigi said, her arms open wide. She embraced me lightly, pausing to kiss my cheek and nod at Percy, who stood next to me. "You got her the things she needed?"

"Yes."

Now, seeing the exchange, it made complete sense to me why Percy was such a formidable force when he wanted to be. He had such a good mentor. Gigi took my arm and we walked through towards the enormous dining room. "Sasha has made us an early dinner, and after that we'll have cake and presents!" She beamed at me.

"Oh, but Percy already bought me—"

She waved off my arguments. "Don't be silly. Those were clothes. Things you needed. We can't leave Philadelphia without having your birthday."

Knowing I would eventually lose the argument, I allowed myself to be led through to the dining room.

Dinner, although simple due to the timing of our departure the next morning, was delicious. Throughout the meal we discussed the details of the trip, the train ride to get there, and Percy's Uncle Thomas.

"Percy," Gigi said, sipping her wine, "I want you to finish packing those things of your mother's in the trunk with mine. Just in case."

"Yes, Gigi."

"Now," she said, when all the plates had been cleared away, "time for cake."

As odd as this sounds, I've never had a birthday cake. I know that must mean there's something terribly wrong with me, but really, my father didn't cook, and since it was just the two of us there never seemed to really be a reason to buy a whole cake. I would always get a 'treat' on my birthday...my favorite candy, a small gift...but it just didn't seem like the big deal everyone made it out to be.

Ano had come the closest to buying me a cake at Stanford with a package of Hostess cupcakes and candles on them; I'd loved the thought at the time. It seemed a bit ridiculous at twenty-two to suddenly start having cake. Silly tradition. Unnecessary and sentimental.

However, when Sasha slid the cake in front of me, decorated with yellow and white icing, I nearly lost it. There, on top of the cake, she had written the words, 'Happy Birthday, Kate' in lovely white icing. Twenty-two candles glowed brightly and I wasn't able to speak as the five of them sang happy birthday to me, horribly off key.

I smiled and blinked hard when Sasha leaned down to me and whispered, "Make a wish!" into my ear.

I'd never, ever made a wish on birthday candles before. Silly, sentimental or not, I wanted that wish. I took a breath, closed my eyes, and blew.

"Thought we were going have to call the fire department," Phillip said, and helped Sasha move the cake out of the way so she could cut it.

I grinned at him and heard Gigi from across the table tell him, "No, that's *my* cake."

Edgar laughed. "Percy got you a gift."

"Edgar!" Gigi shook her head and I smiled as his face fell a little, unable to reveal the secret of what his brother had bought me.

Sasha put a piece of the cake in front of me. I took a bite, and Percy smiled at me from across the table.

"C'mon!" Edgar said, and motioned to Percy.

"I've got this, Ed." Percy reached into a bag behind him and produced a small, robin-egg colored box tired with a white ribbon. "Happy birthday."

I slid my cake aside and fingered the beautiful box, untying the satin bow. The name on top of the box was in black. *Tiffany & Co.* My eyes flashed up to his, and he smiled.

"Open it."

Inside was a beautiful bracelet, with three charms hanging from opposing sides of the thick braid of white gold. "Percy," I breathed, and turned it over in my hand to look at each one. The first was a charm that looked like a map.

"That's the adventurer charm," he explained and I looked to the second one.

The second charm had a small shopping bag on it and I laughed. "For our first shopping trip together."

The third charm was a heart, with a small key dangling out of the end. "And..." he said, almost embarrassed, "I'm sure you can figure out the third one."

I looked up to him with a smile on my face. "Thank you."

He knelt beside me, opened the clasp, and draped it around my wrist. It was big; I probably could have put it on without unclasping it at all. I loved it nonetheless. As inappropriate as it might have been, I leaned forward and kissed him.

Edgar, at fifteen, could always be counted on to break up any romantic activity. "All right," he said, and made a gagging noise, which Gigi hushed instantly just by glancing over at him.

"Percy," she said, and nodded towards the bag. "Kate has to open my present."

"Gigi, please, I don't need any more presents."

The thin jewelry box that Percy placed in front of me looked very old and was dark blue velvet. I didn't say anything for a long moment, just fingered the box.

"Kate," Gigi said, clearing her throat, "when Camilla had William, her oldest, Robert gave her a necklace. William's name was engraved on the back and it had a photo of William as a baby inside. Then she had John, and it became a kind of tradition. When she had Percy, Robert had another one made." She pointed to the box that sat in front of me, and suddenly I couldn't breathe. "Camilla came to stay with me often." She shrugged. "Robert was always busy in the city, and John never seemed to have time."

Gigi glanced over at Edgar, who was looking down at his plate, not speaking. "She spent time at home when Edgar came home from Avon and at the holidays when all her boys would come back."

A look of extreme remorse covered Percy's face, and my heart ached for him.

"The last time she came, she left this, and a few other pieces, by accident. She was always joking that she should just move in. She spent so much more time here than in New York." Her lips twitched in sadness and tears burned behind my eyes. "I know she would want someone to wear it who loved Percy as much as she did."

I stared at the long velvet box sitting in front of me.

"Open it," Percy said, his voice thick.

I reached forward and opened it, the small hinges creaking as I did so. Inside was a delicate chain and a smooth heart pendant made of the same white gold. I pulled it from the box and turned the heart over in my hand. On the back, in miniscule engraved cursive, was the name *Percy Robert Warner*.

I held my breath as I looked at it, and everything it represented.

"Put it on," Gigi urged, tears in her eyes.

Percy stood, the sound of his chair scraping against the wood floor, and fastened it around my neck. The last person to wear this necklace was his mother. An heirloom. I wiped my eyes with the back of my hand and my lip trembled. "Thank you," I choked out, and I felt the weight of the necklace against my chest.

Gigi smiled in satisfaction, nodding her head. "Camilla would be so pleased."

I looked down to where the charm glinted from around my neck and touched it lightly. My own heart, the one that I'd hidden away from him for so long, ached with happiness as I touched his mother's necklace, and in doing so, became a part of something bigger than myself.

CHAPTER FORTY-THREE

The true miracle wasn't getting all five of us into a car to take us to the strain station. It was the second car they'd hired to bring all the trunks with us that amazed me. Gigi had insisted on bringing her two steamer trunks along to Virginia, and along with Edgar's trunk and the one Percy and I shared, it took another hired truck to haul them all. Like an entourage, arriving at the train depot was most embarrassing.

Since it would be such a short ride down to Quantico, less than four hours, there would be no sleeping cars. We all sat together, Edgar vying for the window spot next to Gigi with Sasha and Phillip across from him, and Percy and I on the other side of the aisle.

Our morning had been slightly rushed and I was glad when we were moving along, on the way to Virginia. I'd picked out a pair of jeans and t-shirt for the ride, but had emerged from the shower to find another outfit set out for me on the bed. One we'd bought while shopping. I'd stood in my towel, looking around for the original outfit when Percy advised me it had been packed and something more suitable left in its place. Clearly, meeting Uncle Thomas was more than a 'jeans and t-shirt' event.

Percy didn't talk about his Uncle Thomas that much, and other than him doing something for the FBI labs, I knew little of the man himself. Examining myself in the full-length mirror before we left, I'll admit, the clothes looked really good. A lemon yellow pencil skirt with a very neat white sweater set. I'd chosen to wear Camilla's pendant instead of the pearls Ano gave me, and Percy had been pleased when he saw me put it on.

When the train was on its way, I stood and reached above us into my backpack for the two letters I'd received the night Percy had come to take me to Society Hill. I settled down into my chair.

Percy didn't look up from his book. "You should have stowed that with the luggage."

"I like to keep it with me. I can't keep everything in this little purse you've got me carrying."

"Perhaps that's because you don't need everything you've got in your backpack," he said, with half a smile.

I opened the first letter. I hadn't had time to read them all weekend, and now seemed like a perfectly good time.

"Who are those from?"

"Carrie and Carlie."

He nodded absently. "You write Carrie yet?"

"Sent her a telegram right before we left."

"You give her the address in Virginia?"

"Mmmhmm."

He turned a page. "You ask her to be... discreet about whom she gives it to?"

I set the letter down in my lap. "May I ask what that means?"

He didn't turn to look at me, but kept his voice low. "You know very well what that means."

I pressed my lips together and pretended to go back to my letter. "No, I did not." It hadn't occurred to me that Carrie wouldn't give it to Matt. Since I hadn't received a letter yet from Matt, it seemed silly to send a separate letter to him, saying the exact same information. Also, I didn't want to write Matt and stir all that up again. I was with Percy. I was happy. If Matt wrote me, that was fine. I wasn't going to ignore him.

Carrie's letter was full of news about the farm, about the community and some of the rebuilding that was going on. Fall River had always been a small town; two thousand people at its best. Carrie told me that with people moving away from the coast, things were changing. No fewer than five new families had moved into town and one of them a teacher. They'd had a barn raising, and were planning on a picnic at the end of summer to welcome all the new folks that had moved out their way.

As always, she commented on my last letter, where I'd told her about med school and Ano's recent marriage proposal – and, even though it was old news now, I still read each of her words with interest. In her closing, she told me I was welcome any time and asked if I could find some time to visit them. She sounded lonely. Nothing about Matt or about him showing up over three weeks ago. I sighed and folded up the letter back in its envelope.

I'd barely stowed it back into the small white purse I now carried before Percy asked, "How is Carrie?"

"Fine."

"Doesn't sound fine."

"Hmmm?"

He turned another page in his book. "That sigh doesn't sound like she's 'fine'."

"Oh. I think she's just lonely."

Percy raised an eyebrow. "With her *company* there I don't see how that's possible."

"For me. She's lonely for *me*."

He didn't comment, but continued reading, and I opened the second letter, which was from Carlie. "If she's lonely why don't you ask her to come out and stay with us in Virginia?"

"Percy, she can't leave Charlie."

"Charlie could come, too." I could see a small smile at the edge of his lips and shook my head at his juvenile behavior.

"You know they won't come," I said, and opened the letter from Carlie. Before I began to read it, I said in the most nonchalant voice I could muster, "She suggested that I go out there...for a little visit."

Really quickly, I buried my face in the letter, which I'd barely opened when Percy finally turned to me, his book in his lap. "That is *not* going to happen."

"I'm considering it," I said, and Percy gently turned my face towards him by my chin.

"Not until everything is safe to travel again."

"When will that be?"

"When my uncle tells us it's safe." He lifted his book back up. "Until then...*Carrie* will have to survive without you."

I narrowed my eyes, but didn't reply. Snapping Carlie's letter out in front of me, I began to read.

"Oh, my God."

Percy didn't look away from his book. "What?"

"Carlie..." I said, my hand going to my chest, "is staying in Seattle. They got word that Seattle is going to..."

Percy looked up. "Is going to what?"

"Seattle is going to be attacked."

He put his book down. "What? How does she know that?"

I pulled the letter between us. "Her chief, he has a nephew or cousin or something in the Navy. She says everyone is clearing out. That the bombs cleared the way for a frontal attack." I covered my mouth. "Oh, my God. They expect the attack within the month."

He reached for the envelope. "What's the postmark?"

"She's dated it September tenth."

We both stopped. Our relationships with Carlie were different, but our care for her well-being was the same.

"Percy, if it's dated September tenth, and the information she had was accurate..."

"Carlie's a fool. She should have been out of there with everyone else."

I kept reading. "She's staying with David. David's staying too."

"*Who the hell is David?*"

"The chief attending." As foolish as Percy thought it was, I would be doing the exact same thing if I had her medical training.

"What are you thinking?" he asked.

"Nothing."

"Kate, there's nothing you can do. Carlie will be—"

The deafening sound of an explosion stopped him mid-sentence and the direction of the train began to shift. The entire passenger car was shaking, and people were screaming all around us. I looked across the aisle and screamed at Edgar, who was reaching for his belt.

"No, Edgar! No! Stay there! Don't get out of your seat!"

We could hear the screeching sound of metal on metal and then a deafening crash. I gritted my teeth and braced my legs against the empty chair opposite me.

The train left the track, and we heard another explosion of one of the cars. Next to me, Sasha was screaming, and I saw Phillip with his head down between his knees.

The car began to tip towards us, and Percy leaned his body over me, as if to shield me from the impact. Above us, luggage and bags fell everywhere; glass shattered and I clutched at Percy's body as if my life depended on it. Shards of glass flew inward, slicing across my bare legs as the entire car hit the ground, landing on its side.

The train car had left the track and we were sliding on our side out of control as we felt the impact of each car striking another in succession.

The car behind us impacted us, and we slid another hundred feet before stopping. All around us we heard screaming. Edgar, still strapped in his chair, was dangling towards us and sobbing. Gigi's body hung limp, suspended by her belt. Next to me, Percy touched me, then shook me.

"Kate! Kate, are you...oh, my God!"

I looked down at my legs, which were covered in blood. "I'm...I'm okay," I managed. "I'm...okay."

The train car was still on its side, forcing people who had survived to climb out the windows above us. Percy looked at me, and then to where Edgar was struggling, sliding from his suspended position.

Percy unbuckled and stood, helped Edgar down from his chair, then turned to his grandmother. "Oh my God, Gigi!"

Percy unbuckled and accepted the weight of her body on his shoulder as our car emptied out of the remaining passengers through the shattered windows above us. The five of us were alone, Sasha and Phillip not moving in their seats. Blood was coming from a wide gash in Sasha's neck and Phillip's neck had clearly snapped when he was bent over in his seat.

Edgar started to cry again. I turned his face away with my hand. "Don't look."

Without warning, a new sound filled the air.

"Percy," I said, my voice filled with terror. "Listen!"

From outside, the sound of machine gun fire filled the air, and screams. I gasped, my hand covering my mouth.

The war was here. And we were at ground zero.

ACKNOWLEDGEMENTS

I have found that, in this long and painful process of writing a book and getting it published, there are many, many people involved behind the scenes. In the 7 years it's taken *The Cave* trilogy to see a book store shelf, there have been many hands in that pot helping it along the way.

Of course, my publisher Michael and everyone at "Team" Post Hill Press for getting behind *The Cave, The Aftermath and The Battle*. My editor Felicia, for tirelessly combing through mountains of my errors and getting me to laugh about my own neuroses. For Richard Eichenbaum, for sponsoring the first book, and assuring me I would eventually publish (even though he had the misfortune of reading the first few drafts of other books that made only the cutting room floor). And for my agent, who agreed to represent me (probably against her better judgment) but found a home for *The Cave* trilogy at Post Hill Press.

My closest friends have been with me every painful step of the way. Many of them suffered as I read them chapters or excerpts and others read it for the first time when it came out on the shelves. All of my closest friends have been there for me, and I'm grateful for their love, loyalty and support.

This short list wouldn't be complete without mentioning the three most important people in my life; my daughter Jill who read the draft of all three books at the tender age of twelve, my son Jake who kept up a steady stream of encouragement and hugs on days I needed them...and mostly my mom Nancy, without whom I would have quit after the first 200+ rejection letters. It is because of her tireless patience, unwavering faith and calming influence that I was able to make it through this arduous process of getting a manuscript published.

And finally to Kate, Ano, Carlie, Jazz, Matt and Percy for coming to me in a dream and telling me their story. It's been my honor to re-tell it to you.

ABOUT THE AUTHOR

Michela Montgomery graduated with her B.A. in Creative Writing from California State University, Long Beach. She completed the Claims Law Program with AEI and occasionally teaches classes on negotiation, litigation and investigation at her Corporate University. Although born and raised in California, Ms. Montgomery considers Boston her second home. She enjoys singing, dancing, yoga, cooking, the Red Sox, the Patriots and a good cannoli from Mike's Pastries. She lives in Northern California with her two children, a feisty Yorkie and a teacup Chihuahua named Killer. The Aftermath is her second novel.